THE WELL AT THE WORLD'S END

by the same author

★

The Well
at the World's End

by

NEIL M. GUNN

SOUVENIR PRESS

First published in 1951 by
Faber and Faber Ltd,
This edition copyright © 1985 by Dairmid Gunn and Alisdair Gunn
and published 1985 by Souvenir Press (Educational & Academic) Ltd,
43 Great Russell Street, London WC1B 3PA
and simultaneously in Canada

*The publisher acknowledges the
financial assistance of The Scottish
Arts Council in the production of
this volume*

ISBN 0 285 62648 5 casebound
ISBN 0 285 62682 5 paperback

Printed in Great Britain by
Photobooks (Bristol) Ltd

For

R. M. M.

I

Peter Munro stared into the well that was so obviously dry.

"What an extraordinary thing!" he said, and his mouth remained slightly open in a face that shed its last trace of academic life.

His wife looked past his shoulder as if she could not always trust him to see what was before his nose, remarking thoughtfully, "The old woman said there was water." The pebbles on the well's bottom were blue and brown and beautifully clean, and it seemed to her that though the well had gone dry it still retained the memory of water, as pebbles in a cave the memory of the sea. It was shadowed by great clumps of fern and the bank was mottled with flakes of summer sunlight coming through the trees.

"Look!" Side-stepping both him and the well, she quickly parted some heavy fronds and exposed a delicate growth of maidenhair fern.

His brows gathered and his mouth closed, for she had at times a genius for being irrelevant. He stared at the well again, then looked about him for water with which to fill the small tin kettle in his hand. "I can't understand it."

She gave him a sidelong glance; saw a finger of sunlight picking out the occasional silver strand in his dark-brown hair, burnishing his well-cut nose and glancing off the sweat on his near cheek-bone. The grey-green tweed suited him and she would have to get the oil smear off his jaw—but not at the moment.

"I expect it's all this tourism," he said with an irony as dry as the well. A wren let out an astonishing volume of song

7

from hazel twigs on top of the bank. In a blue flash her eyes found the small brown body, as round as a penny and not much bigger.

"It's the first time I have ever gone to a door in the Highlands for a drop of water," he said, "and been told to fetch it myself from a dry well." Then he started back along the path towards the main road.

It was his wife who had gone to the door, and she now withdrew her eyes from the maidenhair fern, from the roots of the hazel twigs where the wren was active as a mouse, and glanced up at the birch branches. Spangles of sunlight smote her eyes and the whole small glen went dappled and dizzy. Marching on in front went her athletic husband, and even he seemed to waver as the spangles flowed over his head and his shoulders and winked on the tin kettle.

But before he had gone thirty yards he stopped as though he had not yet told her what was wrong exactly and in detail. "I'm not blaming the old woman," he explained. "She doesn't keep a cow, she said, and she has no milk. She hasn't even water. No wonder. People think they can call at any remote house and be helped to everything."

"Never mind," she said, "it's a lovely day and we'll find water farther on."

"That's not the point," he said. "However," and he stalked on.

As he came by the main road and saw the top of the small cottage beyond the thorn hedge on the other side he stopped again. "I have a good mind to go and ask her what she meant."

"I wouldn't. She's a poor thing."

"But why did she send us to the well?"

"You heard her telling me we could get water there and I thought it might perhaps be a nice place to make our tea."

He looked at her.

"She would not have told us," she said, "unless she got water there herself. She's too old to keep a cow."

"But how on earth could she get water——?" He gave her up and walked to the old car with which he had been struggling for an hour. The taste of the petrol jets was still in his mouth. He had got one leg in at the driving door, when he saw the old woman's head above the hedge. "I'm afraid there's no water in your well," he called.

"Oh yes," she answered. "There's always water in the well."

"But we looked into it."

She smiled. "That well is never dry."

He drew his leg out. She had a rosy wrinkled face like some memoried moony fruit, and the white cap that fringed it had corrugations round the edge like the ghost of a mutch.

It was too much. With the odd feeling of having hunted the wrong well in another world, he turned abruptly away and went striding down the same path looking for the right well. It was a hot day, and with the back of his oily hand he now smeared his brow. You had to hand it to women when it came to the irrational. But at least he would have the satisfaction of proving to himself. . . . His feet brought him on the only path that ended, beyond doubt, at the same dry well.

It was astonishing. Before a thought more irrational than any woman's could quite touch his mind he argued it away. For a man can always see where the surface of water, however crystal, touches the sides of its container. There *is* a difference between air and water. All he had got to do was pick up a handful of dry pebbles from the bottom.

But he could not move and his eyes stared as though fascinated by some invisible spirit in the well. Then with the air of one on the brink of some extraordinary revelation he stooped and slowly put his hand down, and his hand went into water.

She saw him sitting by the well as she came with the tin kettle in her hand, and when she stood still the shaft of sunlight had time to hunt out flakes of yellow from her hair as it had hunted grey strands from his, though in age there was little between them. Her eyelids crinkled in thoughtful wonder, then she went on with watchful ease, ready beforehand for any kind of revelation.

He turned his head and glanced up her slim length to her face. There was something beyond humour in his expression, a marvelling, a critical looking at her that actually sent her eyes in a swift sweep over her clothes, as if something astonishing or ludicrous might have got exposed somewhere. After twenty years of married life this sort of incalculable moment between them could be as fresh and vivid as it had ever been.

He got up. "Come here, Fand," he said in the quiet voice that made her advance tentatively. "Dip your kettle."

"What is it?"

"Go on! Down with it."

When the kettle touched the water she cried out as if she had been stung.

How beautiful, how incredible the waves of the crystal water! She got to her knees and watched them. The smile played in her eyes like the waves in the well. That they should have been deceived! The humour of it was a sheer gift, a fairy tale that shook her into laughter.

"Extraordinary," said his voice above her. "I can't get over it."

Slowly she pushed the kettle under until it was full to the brim, then got to her feet and looked about her. "We'll make the tea here."

"Sit down. There's no hurry. Haven't we got two months?"

She sat down beside him.

"Light," he said.

"It made me dizzy for a moment when the spangles moved on you going along the path."

"At first I laughed. That there should have been water in the well when we were so certain it was dry! Water so clear we thought it wasn't there! Then—all at once—the queer feeling came over me that we were at the beginning of an adventure—setting out to find the—the something in life that we think isn't there."

"You have long been wanting to do that," she said.

"Do what?"

"Go away and find the well at the world's end."

10

At a rare moment she had a way of making an extravagant remark sound like practical sense. She was looking at a round fleck of light on her wrist. She opened her long bony hand and drew it back until the fleck lay on her palm. Slowly she began to close her fingers, then snapped them shut, but the sunbeam danced onto her knuckles.

2

It was evening before they left all highways behind and took the last hill road which, because it could not get narrower, grew ever more uneven and grass-grown until it died away into the vast primeval moor. A smell of peat smoke arrested him like a sudden hand and he stopped the car.

"Do you see the blue smoke?"

Far in on the slowly rising moor to their right she saw a low drift of smoke. "It's exactly smoke-blue," she said.

Humour soft as the colour of a dress shook him wantonly. "It's the getting back to it."

"Who made the fire?"

"This is where the crofters come to cut their peats. They would have been here to-day lifting or stacking them. There's probably someone there yet having a last cup of tea."

"They must come a long way." Her eyes were full of quiet wonder.

"Only three or four miles."

They sat in silence, then he started up the car. Half a mile farther on he suddenly saw what he took to be a small lorry coming towards them. "Hang it!" he said, "how on earth are we to pass here?" He would have to back a long way to the bay where the crofters took the peats out from the moor—if there was no spot in front.

"I don't think it's a car," she said. "I can see a wheel—more like a bicycle."

He kept going, glancing for a place where the ditch on either side might be filled in. In a few more seconds they were round the curve and there was nothing on the road in front.

"Must have been cattle," he said, thinking of two beasts coming abreast. But in the summer dusk they could see for miles. The heather was darker than at noonday and a peat hag very black, but moving life could not be missed.

Their wonder carried them past the place and then he did not stop, for, as he remarked, "At this time some night we'll come back and see what conformation of the ground produced so remarkable an illusion."

She did not say anything and was surprised to find she was not more disturbed.

Presently the tombstones of the little cemetery lifted their heads above the stone wall and against the pale blue sky. It stood on a knoll that jutted out like a small promontory over the strath through which the river ran.

"Let's pay our respects," he said. "They'll be our nearest neighbours."

She hesitated.

"You don't want to come?"

"Not yet."

He smiled as he drove on. "There's something in life?"

"It's beautiful," she said.

He saw her eyes in the driving mirror; they were staring far in front and he knew that she was thinking of her own dead.

Soon the road began to rise and a mile farther on it flattened out, rounded a last bend and then slowly dipped away from all that was behind them into a vast basin of moor that this time rose to distant mountain ridges, then, on the right, to infinitely remote glimmering horizons where sheer moor passed into sky.

But near at hand and sweeping down and away from them was grass instead of the dark heather, and set upon the green here and there were heaps of grey stones. He drove slowly now and presently swung the car off the road, bumped over tufts and sheeptracks, did an easy turn and came up against a very slight incline until he had the car sitting level with her nose towards the northern sky that ran its edge of molten silver from the vanished sun.

"This is the place," he said quietly.

13

They sat still for a few moments, then got out. She stood and looked about her, bathed in the grey light.

"It's the silence," she said at last.

They listened to the silence as to a fable, and though it was remote beyond hearing or meaning it was startlingly nearer than the quick of the heart.

Making camp did not take long, for the seats of the car had been specially hinged by a coachbuilder to flatten out into beds, but she insisted on having the sleeping bags laid out ready and all gear properly stowed before joining him over at the first pile of stones.

It was the ruin of a single homestead, still clearly defined, though grass and sorrel grew over the heap of rubble that covered the hearth. Dusk brought out the greyness in the stone, and the traceries of lichen were fine as lines on a face. Moving idly he climbed a mound beyond the up gable, and when she joined him there and looked down into a neatly built circular well of stone, still some five feet deep and nine across, she asked what it had been for.

"That's where they dried their grain."

Her eyes began to wander and she saw where the homesteads had been, away in front, down on the river flats, up the slow slope that came to a ridge against the eastern sky. Many people had lived here, families and families . . . the cries of children in the evening light, their vivid faces and flashing bare legs. . . .

"On the map this spot is marked: Picts Houses," he explained. "So the Picts were here before the Gaels. And before the Picts, the megalithic folk, as I'll show you—the people who set up the standing stones. And that's going back a long way. And it goes back beyond that. All history is here. If you sat here and lost yourself for a little you would have the illusion of the races flowing up and round you and vanishing away."

She was silent because she had never cared for school history, but now something that couldn't quite be seen, as the silence could not be heard, was flowing towards her and she had the feeling that if she steadied her thought for a moment an inner eye would see the procession coming up over the green breast—men, and women with children at their hands,

14

their eyes to the slope, their rounded heads coming on, drawing near, dividing at the grain kiln on which they stood, flowing on. . . .

"Somehow I don't feel it's sad," she said.

"No. That's the remarkable thing I found about it. I found I could live with them. I wasn't joking when I asked you to go into the little cemetery." His eyes, turning to her, caught a humoured gleam. "All the fashions are in that cemetery, too! Remember the cemetery in Paris with its fantastic stones and mausoleums?"

"I didn't like it."

"That was the old standing stone, the burial cairn, run riot—in the most civilised city in the world. That's about the distance we've got."

Not wishing to resurrect a nightmarish memory, she remained silent.

"The carved granite urns and the angels—you'll find efforts at them, too, back there in the little cemetery. Fashions from Paris! But you'll also find the flat stone slab without polish or name, the stone lid that Neolithic man put on his cist. One of my earliest memories is of a coffin being called a kist."

The talk did not disturb her much because it was of death so far away that it came alive again. Tiny grey wings glimmered in the twilight.

"What happened to the people who were here?"

"They were driven out," he answered. Then he had a thought that broke in its own smile. "Paris again. Napoleon. Have you ever heard that it's a small world?" His eyes lifted to the distance. "It never struck me until this minute that time itself is small."

Their voices were quiet and the words light as the moths in the still air.

"The Napoleonic wars affected our economy," he said, with a fine mimicry of his own voice when lecturing on history. "So sheep became more valuable than men, so our landlords drove the men away from their homes here, the men and the women and the children, knocked down their houses, and put sheep on their fields and their pastures."

15

"The Clearances?"

"Yes."

Like the stone cists, it was a story that had been told and bitterness now lay buried with it. Time stood still in its own flow like a breath in the mouth.

Her eyes came back to the mound and began travelling about the crannies in the circular stone-work, lingering upon each tiny plant, a wall fern, a miniature foxglove.

He looked at her, standing there like a woman from any age, and saw in a way more profound than he had yet experienced that she had no age. In time itself, as in the crannies between the stones, there is a livingness, an eternal essence like eternal youth.

"Come on," he said and caught her arm, and was himself caught in a happiness fine as the air.

As they went up the slope to the nearest crest, they disturbed some curlews and peewits, and the crying of these birds was so astonishingly loud that he laughed. An optimism had now come upon them, a rare freedom, like a blessing from some place they had been wandering in.

"That one has got a sore throat," she said.

She could make him laugh at nothing. "Here their throats are tough as leather."

Then a curlew ran up a series of half-notes with such increasing tempo and urgency that she felt its throat was going to burst, but it held the last note like a pipe and through it came the golden bubble of song that she thought the most entrancing sound in all nature.

Then the drums started, the drumming of the snipe.

The crest was farther away than it looked, but they reached it and found it not a crest but a tableland. They had come up into a higher dimension with a wider field for the eye. The birds were left behind, but suddenly she stood very still and, hearkening with her, he heard, far away and high in the air, the faint drumming of a last snipe.

"Once when a little girl I heard that," she said, "and I thought it was a bee on a window-pane in the sky."

"Sure it wasn't in heaven?"

16

She looked at him. "I don't think so—but—perhaps." Her voice was cool and detached and in her eyes a faint surprise. Moments like these still came upon them, as though they were strangers about to make intimate and lasting discoveries. Yet because of the discoveries they had made, the momentary experience when it came lay beyond love and the last intimacy in a place where they met in a new and strange relationship.

The north-west was very remote now, the molten silver of its horizon line like the edge of a beach, a shore, to a sea that could not be imagined. Upon it legendary craft had set out—to find the new relationship, the living essence that philosophers, lost in meditation, called the divine Ground and ordinary men, lost in dream, called eternal youth.

She saw the smile in his eyes and sat down beside him, for she felt at home now. Nothing from the world behind could come at them here. Thoughts were curlews and peewits and if a man made a story it would have the song notes behind it. At such a moment he can hardly go wrong, even left to himself.

When a man cannot go wrong, a woman has time to wander around and find small things in odd places like an unusual flower or the reflection of her face in a well.

She remembered the old woman's well and a divine humour so quietly suffused her that her eyes shone and the silver horizon ran through them. Then as the horizon held her, too, she saw it as the silver edge of a well, and she knew, with the premonition that held life itself in a faintly necromantic suspense, that he was going to say something about dipping the tin kettle in *that* well.

He was sitting with his knees drawn up, as the skeleton is found in a Stone Age cist; only in the cist the body was generally put lying on its side, perhaps from exigencies of space or perhaps because it could dream the same dream better that way.

His eyes withdrew from the silver shore, wandered over the leagues of darkling moor, and he came to himself like one who had been lost but upon whom somewhere a thought had fallen.

"Do you know what I was thinking?"

"No."

"I would like to dip your tin kettle in *that* well."

17

"I thought so," she said.

"Did you?"

"I knew you would."

"Perhaps it's not such a silly notion as all that."

"I wish you could."

"And bring the kettle back to you—full?"

She smiled, and her face in the deep twlight lost its last line and for a moment was sad with beauty.

Later as he lay in his sleeping bag, with shoulders eased up against his pillow and the car's cushioned back, he felt for the narrow window ledge and balanced his glass there. "Extraordinary how soft the burn water makes the whisky."

"There's a place for all things."

He laughed. "And a time."

A moon must have risen behind the hill they had climbed, for its radiance was spilling everywhere. The silence was now absolute, and, when she listened to it, it went from her, ballooning up and away into a remoteness that was like the remoteness of another land, of a place beyond.

"That was odd—about the water in the well," he said.

"Yes."

"What's that legend again about the well at the world's end?"

"An old Gaelic legend—with a tragic end."

"Tragic?"

"Yes. It's about a goddess that went off to find the well in the land beyond ours, the Land of Youth. When she found it, she couldn't have done the right thing—though what she should have done we don't know. The water in the well got angry and rose up and drowned her, for her body was found on a bank of the river that now flowed from the well."

He was silent for a little while. "What did she expect to find in the well?"

"Knowledge and poetry. There are hazels above the well, and they burst into blossom when you find it, and inspirations and wisdom fall into the well, and the well surges. You'll often find mention of this well in the old legends."

"You've got to hand it to them," he said. "My God," he said, reaching for his glass, "if ever there was a time when we could be doing with that well, it's now."

She was silent.

"You see what I mean? This gloom that hangs over us. Violence and death. Without end. It's not that we've forgotten how to approach the well in the right way: we've forgotten the well itself. The thing isn't even tragic: it's a bloody mess." He finished his whisky.

The silence could not be defeated. It came in about them soft as velvet beyond the touch.

"I wonder," he mused presently, "if there's any of the well left—anywhere."

"It's here now."

"That's what we have come for to seek?"

"That's what I saw in you first."

"How do you mean?"

"It was the hill air about you."

"I must have been pretty raw when I first came up as a student. You were like something from another world—the world of the city, big houses, style. Now that we have a big house ourselves and do some dodging of academic circles, it may not seem quite so wonderful. But *then*—that you and I should go out and in the same quadrangle seemed extraordinary as any legend to me. It was easier to think of flying to the moon than approaching you."

"You didn't take long to start flying," she said.

"Begod I didn't," he admitted, laughing. "You were lovely, Fand. And you're lovelier now than ever. And what a sheer blessed accident it was that there was that in us that could bring us here now. To come out on the other side of love—and find the well there."

She was silent.

"All right," he answered her. "We never come out on the other side."

"Things pass into other things but—but it's the same thing beneath."

"You think *that* will never die?"

"Never," she said.

This was the kind of talk that could take place in the car-camp. It might start in the personal but it went beyond the horizon. Its heart-beat was light, its speculation had wings.

"I wonder if this feeling of something magical is as rare as some of our misery-ridden plays and novels make out?" he said after a time. "I doubt it. But I should like to find out. I've been thinking a lot about it lately, for we've been researching into some old Greek sources. Dionysus, that god of it. And perhaps I was thinking, too, about you and me cutting all home ties and coming here together—wondering just why. That extra-ordinary moment when the invisible water moves in the well—is it as rare as all that? Do people, ordinary folk, ever stand tranced before some wonder that not only takes their breath away, but, for an instant, the human boundary itself away?"

"I know what you mean."

"Let us be quite practical. Does the hard-working shepherd, for example, whose hill ground this is, ever have his moment when he goes through the boundary? Or the man who comes and fishes the river down there. Or the man who pursues the grouse? Never mind what most of their lives may be. Does the moment come upon them? Do they know moments they would not give for all else?"

"It's their secret world."

"You think so?" His question went from him and waited beyond the windscreen. As he followed, it disappeared, leaving about him the word "world", and the word became the world and he went away through it, for that's what he wanted to do. He wanted to go away on his own, to meet people here and there by chance, to take adventure as it came and look out for the wonder. Not a conscious piece of research, not the kind of thing he had to do in his academic researches, but something quite different in the sense that it would *happen* to him. All he would have to do was to wait for it. He would have to forget himself, as he had done up there on the hill; forget his "import-ance", his notion of being "somebody".

Quite suddenly he had the actual feeling of being on such a holiday from himself, and the delightful sensation of freedom pervaded him. In this freedom he found he could not only look at people in the new expectant way, he could also look at trees and wild roses and running water. Who could tell what branch moved by what hand might not disclose the well? . . .

From this fantastic excursion he returned to the car. He could not hear Fand's breathing so he knew she wasn't asleep.

"What are you thinking of?" he asked.

"I was wondering," she said, "where a curlew puts his long beak when he goes to sleep."

3

On the third day she said she must explore the ravine because it was like a place in which life would come from the moor to shelter and in which many things must grow. It lay beyond the river and had been formed by a hill burn or tributary.

As they crossed the small river, he stopped and began to laugh at the disposition of certain stones.

"All the same, it stopped him," she said.

"You're dead right," he agreed, laughing still more.

Just above him was a pool, some six feet deep in its centre, but where he stood the water was channelled into a shallow outlet. The river had been low for a long time and the only salmon that had been left, over almost a mile, he had found in this pool yesterday. Without any tackle beyond a piece of string, he had known it would take him some time to land the fish for he would have to get it to lie where he could put a noose over its tail. But when a salmon is driven too hard it loses its head and leaves the pool, and should that happen in this case the salmon might very well tear down through the shallow water and reach safety in the dark Rock Pool where the tributary came in. So Fand had been told there and then to stand in the shallow outlet and, when she saw the salmon coming, to drop a large stone on its head. Whereupon Peter turned away from her, and, as he stripped, cast his eyes near and far and along horizons, for a gamekeeper has a way of turning up unexpectedly.

Fand said nothing, because if she said anything he would think she was stupid and order her about in a peremptory voice. "Good Lord, can't you throw a stone?" he would say, his eyebrows gathering over flashing eyes. All that Fand knew was that if a great salmon came tearing at her legs she would be terrified out of her wits and probably hug the stone to her bosom for safety. But she had learned not to argue at certain moments and as he had already forgotten her so she now in her own realm forgot him. Bare to the thighs, she went into action and because she could not walk confidently on even little slippery stones she got to her knees.

For twenty minutes he had lived in a world where minutes have no meaning; flash and colour and movement, and life itself lost in its own whirls. Then he saw his chance to land the silver fish with his bare hands, and would have succeeded if the flagstone had not shifted. There was a terrific boil under his sunken eyes and lifting his streaming face he yelled, "Look out!"

When he saw Fand standing in the middle of the outlet with empty hands and drooping shoulders he yelled again with rage and despair like a Fingalian hero in whose fists victory had all but been, for the salmon was now travelling at the rate of many knots, with a great wave going off him to either side. Clean out of the pool he went, and then before he reached Fand's white legs he hit something and shore up violently, and lashed the water, and blindly shot left and heaved himself high and dry. Overhand Peter drove and, staggering and falling, finally launched himself behind the fish before it was right turned; as its nose hit his navel he got one hand over the nape of the neck like an otter's mouth and the other round the small of the tail. Then slowly and carefully he went ashore and killed the fish, hid it in a clump of bracken, looked near and far and along the horizons, and finally looked at Fand.

When he saw the dam of loose stones she had built like a beaver, he was caught beyond laughter into the silent wonder that is pure delight. It was a revelation of another kind of thought, and he knew once again that in all the profound issues of life she could be trusted.

"I would never have thought of that," he had admitted handsomely.

"No, but I thought of it," she said.

"You are a very wonderful person," he agreed, pulling his shirt down.

"Some day you may find that's true."

His eye caught the hunter's gleam again.

"You keep your hands to yourself," she said. "And they would be the better of washing anyway."

"Go on; assume your airs and graces."

So she drew herself up and assumed them and became Fand, wife of Mananan, the god of the sea, when she cast her eyes on Cuchulain and enchanted him. "Would you like the salmon boiled, or fried in steaks with breadcrumb and egg?"

A wet leg got stuck in his trousers and he fell.

That was yesterday, but to-day he laughed at sight of the stone dam and instinctively casting his eyes towards the spot where he had nailed the fish saw a glitter of scales. When he had covered them with sand, she said for him, "What his eye won't see the gamekeeper won't grieve over."

They continued on their way to the ravine.

4

As they rounded the high bank a rabbit sat up and looked at them, for the bottom of the ravine was broader than she had expected, with a close-cropped sward softer than three carpets running this side of a small burn now little more than a series of tiny pools. Trees grew out of the sides of the ravine and a small birch out of a crack in a grey precipice.

At first sight of the rabbit she instinctively stopped and stopped him also.

Keeping his eyes on the rabbit he said in a low level voice, "He'll sit like that for a very long time once he has started to sit."

"Hsh!"

"His instincts are so caught up in astonishment that everything has gone vague round his head."

But she could not speak because of the soft brown eye and the clean perfection of the fur. In that tall strange place it became, as she stared at it, a magical creation.

"Once a little boy was playing by himself outside a shepherd's cottage," he continued in the same quiet monotone. "Suddenly there was a tall man, a stranger, standing there. He must have come round the corner of the house when the boy wasn't looking. The boy couldn't move. All the world went vague round his head. Not until the stranger spoke and took a step forward was the boy released. Then he dashed in at the front door, into the kitchen, caught his mother's skirts and said in an awed voice, 'Mummy, there's a man!'"

Her head turned and the rabbit bolted.

As she went on everything had the air of being intimately known to an order and way of life beyond man's boundary,

25

known and made use of, seen and enjoyed. The trees grew, the grass was nibbled, the birds sang. A shoulder of rock hunched sideways over ferns.

To wonder before coming to a corner what is round it induces the mood of expectancy that may go right through man's boundary before it can be stopped . . . or very nearly, Fand felt; on the boundary rather, where the known and the unknown play the first game of all, where the unfamiliar has an incredible familiarity, but evasive, for an instant only, then gone.

"I like this place," she said.

"I thought so," he answered.

But she wasn't listening to him; she went on. He stood for a moment looking after her and the tilt of her head made him smile. She was caught now all right. When a woman is caught a man can sit down in comfort.

Sitting down, he realised, was a remarkable exercise or invention. In the realm of action he took leave to doubt if man had ever achieved anything finer. It conquered the whole babble about time with a rare ease. Softness to softness and a man was sitting upon the only expanding universe that mattered. As he stretched his legs he caught a last glimpse of Fand's upright slim figure rounding the shoulder of rock.

Hunting wild flowers, familiar and rare, could become a passion with her when she got going. Once she had told him a story she had heard about a Glasgow professional man who had spent his summer holidays transforming a stretch of a remote Highland strath into a sort of vast rock-garden of native plants. He had done this with such secrecy—bachelor's secrecy—that even at the end of his days he hadn't written a book about it. He had teased her about the story but she had had her reserves.

He smiled where he sat and his eyes roved. This was the kind of ravine that might well appeal to her in a big way!

His thought slipped and turned up its own ravine. A man should get away from everything occasionally, even from his wife. He might then get a profounder view of her, if nothing else.

Mirth shook him, but his thought went on, for the idea of going away alone on foot had been growing in him; and now in a moment it got the very irk of urgency.

And he saw that there was no need to be grandiloquent; no occasion for fantasy. In simple fact it *would* be interesting to find out if among ordinary people there were those moments of penetration, the instant when they went through the boundary, the moment when they saw the crystal water in the well.

To go wandering over the hills and through the glens, taking every adventure as it came. . . .

Of windmills, at least it would be the oddest to have a crack at. A mighty *crack!* made him sit up. My God, he thought, she's found something and is shifting the rocks. But no cry for help reached him, so with relief he got back into his own ravine. A small trout jumped six inches in the air with a gleam of old gold.

She had plenty of food; half the salmon; she had the car. That's my conscience prickling me, he thought, when he felt his skin go hot. But there would be no harm in—in just seeing how she took it. At least he could make a story of it, come at it from a distance and see how she reacted. For of course if he came straight out with the notion of actually going away on his own she would agree . . . that was the devil of it.

Dammit! he thought, I would like to go! This time the cry followed the crack, and after going round the outjut of rock he came upon her. Often enough there was colour in her cheeks and a light in her look, but now she was so entranced she could not speak to him; her eyes were soft with wonder and love. She pointed.

He saw the small flowering plant and did not think much of it. "What is it?"

"I don't know."

He looked at her and realised she had made an utterance of deep mystery.

"But you have some idea from the leaves and that?"

She nodded.

"But you would rather not say?"

"Not yet," and her voice trembled.

27

"Good for you!" he said.

She stooped and caught the flower gently and showed it off against her fingers. "Wonderful, isn't it?"

"Extraordinary. Really remarkable. Superb."

She looked back at the plant and withdrew her fingers. "It is," she said, then she looked around her. "This is a wonderful place."

"Isn't it? What a fantastic rock-garden you could make of this in a couple of months, if you were left to it!" He did not bring his face back to her because he was listening now to his own astonishing words. But he felt her eyes on him.

"You can go any time," she said.

"Go where?" His eyes widened upon her.

"Away on your travels—to fill the kettle."

"Me! Nonsense! What made you think it?"

"You have talked of nothing else for nights."

"Me!"

"Yes, you." And her bright eyes mocked him but not much.

The following day at the same spot she came to a standstill. He gave a hitch-up to his simple rucksack. "Now you'll remember all I told you," he said, "about what you're to do."

"Yes," she said, "and what I'm not to do."

"I needn't go over it again."

"You couldn't," she said; "it would fill a big book."

"You have the car. The woman in the scarlatina cottage back——"

"Cotoneaster is the name. She will make me very comfortable and I can come up here every day. By the end of a week I'll be so lonely without you that I can take the car and go away and find seeds and plants in——" She stopped.

"I don't think I'll go after all," he said decisively.

"That's not what's worrying me." Her fair brows gathered. "What?"

"Who'll look after you?"

"Me! I'm the most selfish man extant."

"I know," she said, worried. "If you only even had the sense to change when you get wet. There's one complete set of underclothes and I put the silk set in as well because they take

28

up no space. . . ." She went over the items and finished, "You have your comb?"

"I always keep it in my pocket book."

"That awful hat!"

"It's pure Harris tweed."

"It may have been pure," she said. "Well, that's everything. And now you're off on your travels."

"I'm only really going for your sake."

"I know that," she said. "But try to think of yourself a little sometimes."

"I'll do my best," he promised.

The moment had come.

"I want to give you a present." She looked at him strangely. "But I have the iodine."

She turned away, and stooped, and picked the solitary specimen of the rare flower she had found, and brought it to him, and lifted her hands and put it in his buttonhole.

"Fand," he said.

"I shall wait for you till the end of time." The kiss she gave him was light and quick, and she turned away, and she waved her hand.

5

As he went on his way the ravine narrowed and the cliffs closed in upon him and soon he wondered whether he could go on or not. But as the one thing he couldn't do now was go back, he decided to risk the narrow ledge above the black still pool. As he moved sideways with his face to the rock the ledge grew narrower and at the corner seemed to disappear. Carefully he lifted his eyes and his fingers found a crack. Once he had criticised a somewhat imaginative passage in a student's thesis on an historical personage who, pursued by bloodhounds, had swum a river and "inched his way into a cave . . ." In academic history, no royal personage could be permitted to verbalise our lowly unit of measurement in that way. Now he saw that the expression should have been "half-inched his way . . ." The sweat broke cold on his brow, for if he bent a knee half an inch he would go by the back into the bottomless pool and ten to one the bands of the rucksack would slip and pin his arms. Fand would have to wait beyond the end of time.

He got his right foot round the corner, the toe no longer on a ledge but stuck into a crack that was a flaw in the strata. He straddled the corner and because he could now go neither one way nor the other he took a few deep breaths and lowered his eyes upon the bands of his pack. A fine trembling ran along his flesh and he knew that he was putting too much weight on his fingers yet dared not put less. Within a minute life would be one way or the other. That this was so, and so suddenly, was astonishing beyond measure. The urge to prayer rose strongly within him and he cried "Sweet Fand!" and because all the ultimate things he had never told her were in the cry, he felt strangely lightened and lifted up and he put his right foot forward three inches; he put his right hand forward and the rock obliged him with the use of a knob which he could actually grip; he dragged his left foot three inches and he moved his left hand. Within two minutes he was round the corner and the ledge was forming again though it wavered in his sight as if all its atoms had got restless. But they held the soles of his feet and he inched along the dizzy wall until the rock refused a hold for his right hand and the small ledge faded away. But now, looking down, he saw a little sandy backwash, a tiny bay, far enough below him to break his neck if he fell by the back. It was no time for indecision. Face round swiftly and jump. But before he had got half round, the rock hit his shoulder a malignant wallop and threw him off. He had the sensation of landing in a mixture like a pudding, his insides swamping him and even dulling the crack from his collar bone. But life remained far within, fine as air, going round and round and wanting to sleep.

Like a snake rising from its coils, he got his head up, and his feet which felt cold with frozen blood were only in the water and came out on their own. The beast on his back was the rucksack. As he struggled from its grip, scalding hot liquid trickled down his neck. Feeling he had burst the main arteries, he fumbled for the hole at the base of his skull. But there was no blood and in a little while he from his pack withdrew the vacuum flask, which proved to be the only item in his whole complex that had both cracked and leaked.

Well, he had started on his travels!

Presently he thought he would investigate the rucksack further and discovered such a disposition of his gear—Fand always did the packing—as made him conclude he owed the unfractured collar bone to the silken underwear, which was sodden only with steaming coffee. He had a vague notion or memory that tablecloths thus soiled had to be washed at once. It would be a pity if he didn't bring back underwear beyond reproach. Moreover, as he opened out the garments he was lucky enough to find that the brown stain wasn't all over but only in patches. That limited the area to be washed. However before he had right started everything got wet including several inches of the sleeves of his jacket, so he decided to make a job

of it; and this he did by spreading the brown all over the pale
silk but so faintly that it looked like a subtle dye. Then he rung
out both garments and stuffed them in the bottom of his
rucksack thus cleverly inhibiting the spread of their damp
contagion to the dry things which he bunched on top.

Women often made a lot of fuss about a simple thing like
packing. Given the bag and the things to put in it, there need
be no difficulty. He was feeling sick and this ravine was a sunless
place. His eye landed on the red flask. As he lifted it, the
broken glass inside tinkled, so he pitched it into the pool.

But it did not sink; it wobbled from side to side like a dying
clown.

He was visited by a dreadful vision: a flood came in the
night . . . carried it away . . . bobbing . . . to Fand's feet. He
saw her face.

It began to settle, slowly to fill . . . very slowly it passed
under the surface, diffusing its red like a bloody star, and sank.

Shedding his fancies, he got the rucksack on his back and
left that place. The ravine widened and grew less lofty and
when at last he emerged he was on rising ground with hill tops
in the distance.

For a while he stood with eyes lifted to the hills, for he had
to get over or through them and a long way beyond if he were
to sleep in a bed that night. What came ye here for to seek?
he asked himself as he stumbled, for the heather was long and
the holes hidden. He had had the brilliant idea of liberating
himself from all paths, though if a path came his way he would
not necessarily disdain it. But he would not be conditioned by
the human path. A man crams himself with metaphysics till
he is like the curate's egg and then thinks he's clever because
he can help himself with an ironic spoon. But he kept going.
If there was one thing he had made a vow to avoid it was
thought.

The rucksack was not so comfortable as it had been. A hard
knob had nosed through from somewhere. Its persistence was
extraordinary, wriggle how he would. But with fortitude he
thought: it's just a bloody knob.

When the second crest wasn't a crest he sat down, opened

32

the rucksack and emptied it out, then wiped his forehead with his hat. A woman may have her uses but the only one capable of dealing with all the ingredients of her mystery is herself. Where or what the bloody knob was he could not divine, and the thought that she had looked after him for twenty years did not help now. He unfolded some tissue paper and found salmon sandwiches. It was boiled salmon, yet last night he had eaten steaks.

The ball of silk underwear drew his eye. He opened the clammy things out. The sun was shining. He spread them on the heather and realised that what a man might call brown a woman would call dirty. Then something less than a gleam of humour came from somewhere. Its wintry ray touched his eyes. I'll tell her, he thought, that to celebrate my return I decided to get them dyed rose.

Call that rose? she would ask.

Well, he would explain, you know what laundries are.

He took another bite of the salmon sandwich.

But he was heartened and when at last he stood on the low watershed he said, I am on top of the world. His stomach stirred and rumbled. A puff of wind hit him playfully in the face and as he turned a ball of wind issued abruptly and loudly from his mouth and followed after. That's better, he said with relief, and solemnly tried again and was moderately successful. His guts had had a severe jolt.

It was when he was going down that the lean feeling came to him. It came to him like his boyhood after a long day's gathering of sheep from the hills. Rounding the last breast, the boy he had been saw the sheep park and beyond it his home. The sight of his home made him almost shy and a smile came upon his face and upon the face of life. "Was he any use at all?" his mother asked. And his father said, "He was the best man on the hill to-day." And his mother remarked proudly, "I don't believe a word of it." And he couldn't eat (until he started) because he was past hunger and his body was light as the warm air of the kitchen.

So he rarely found views beautiful; he only just found the hills. And to know the hills and enter among them one must feel lean. He was feeling lean enough now and there was no knob. To come to himself a man has to get away from a woman, particularly if she is a good woman. A good woman is a man's vice. She covers up all the knobs.

It was delightful leaving Fand behind. For Fand was both good and beautiful. And the truly incredible thing about her beauty was that it inhabited her. Every extra line on her face was the work of an artist who lived somewhere inside her and had hangings of gold from her hair. Good-bye Fand; I'm off! I'm away on my travels! Leaving her was delightful and rare.

He began to feel as lean as misery; and only true misery knows the last refinement of freedom. Not that he had reached that stage in misery yet, but far within swam the knowledge that, with luck, he would. A man has to go a long long way alone before he gets out at the other side of himself. He hadn't started yet so what was he talking about? He ate more sandwiches by a stream, and rested, and found he had already lost Fand's precious flower.

6

The stream grew in his company until by the afternoon it was bigger if anything than the river that ran by the Picts Houses. Sometimes a river that wasn't quite a river was called a Water, but he hadn't the energy at the moment to hunt the map from his rucksack even though he liked to see the word Water on the map. People who lived by a Water had certain qualities, the kind that mature well over a long time. But whether a river or a Water, if you followed it long enough you always reached human habitation. So he kept going, though the big toe on his right foot was now very uncomfortable, for it had clearly taken advantage of the wet sock and poked a hole through it, and when he tried to draw it back through the hole it merely pulled the hole more tightly in over it. But he left the sock alone, as he left the map, and it was not until the river began to leave him that he thought of Fand again.

For the water, tired of meandering, began to cut straight through the earth; down into a ravine, raging away as if it had wakened up in a great hurry. There was danger in the sound and he realised that Fand might sleep in the car after all, despite her promise. You always knew when Fand wouldn't do a thing by the way she said she would do it, though you could never be certain even then. She had the innocence of a river or, more precisely, a Water, that dams wouldn't stop; so strong-willed and pertinacious and irrelevant that flowers came and grew on her banks. Lord, he thought grimly, that's an apt metaphor. He should have forced her to an oath by the breath in her throat. She had a remarkable fund of pure wickedness. When a good woman was wicked she needlessly complicated life. He was getting very tired.

35

He was also getting worried about the raging river for as he came over the slope he saw that the mountain in front was the bank continued, so he would either have to go over the mountain or through the ravine, and this time he wasn't going through any ravine. Then he saw the bridge, the spidery bridge, and he thanked all the generations of deer-stalking gentry, and agreed that there were realms in which they had never got their due. Gratitude so moved in him that on a green mound he decided to relieve his big toe and he laughed when he saw how far through the sock it, like an eager trout, had managed to push itself. But now he was full of cunning and took off his other shoe and changed the socks over, and was thus able to gather the hole together and push it between the big toe and the adjoining toe, and after care and manipulation he set all his toes waggling inside the leather with satisfaction. After all, anyone could have put on a new pair of socks, he thought afterwards.

He got to his feet and in the very act of stretching himself was cramped. A man was standing a few yards behind his left shoulder. His heart gave the kind of beat that sends an alarmed, a weakening flush over the body. For the man was not like one suddenly appearing in a dream but like one mysteriously there in a nightmare. It was broad daylight. He stood straight and quite still; his face was pale and his beard thin. His alienation was evasive, a little cold, and ominous beyond the far edge of fear. The eyes lifted from Peter's face, went into distance over his head, and the arrows that fly by day were in the air.

Peter could neither break out of his stance nor speak, and when at last he did manage to turn away the other moved at the same moment, as though the conjoint action were in some mysterious way co-ordinated. Peter approached the bridge and entered upon it.

The bridge consisted of two broad planks swung from wire ropes and at once it began to sway. As he kept marching on, the planks rose to meet his feet in so disconcerting a manner that he grasped a wire rope in either hand to stop his body from being brought to its knees. By the time he reached the middle of the slender bridge its movement had become so complicated that he knew the other had entered upon it, that he was coming behind him.

Forty feet below, the water was boiling white where the rocks on either side came close together. For a man with a mania, a mania for murder, this was the spot. He had only to hit his victim from behind and pitch him over. The bridge was his trap. As the planks sank before his left foot could reach them, Peter pitched forward; his hands were torn from the wire ropes; his right foot went high and met the rising planks with so terrific an impact that his knee came up and hit him. Yet he dared not turn round and the roar of the cataract was like blood in his ears, drowning all other sounds, drowning even a premonition of the moment when he would be attacked. He went on blindly, his vulnerability terrible and impotent, like a great cry that stayed with him. His shoulders began to hunch, his steps quickened and he passed through the iron pillars that supported the wire ropes at an old man's trot.

The path steadied his feet remarkably and they went along it with sobriety, considering the looseness of his knees. His head began to turn until the tail of an eye discovered that the man had crossed the bridge and was now standing near a large boulder gazing after him. At thirty yards Peter slowed to a standstill and looked round and saw the man's head and shoulders against the sky. For a few seconds they stood like that and the man was withdrawn into his madness, wrapped round in it, remote and ominous. It was then that something beyond even the nightmare was revealed to Peter: the man was physically like himself.

When, twenty yards farther on, he looked over his shoulder, the man had vanished; but instead of taking the rest he needed, Peter quickened his pace. The path, a pony-track for deer stalkers, was cut out of the hillside above the river which it followed. Peter's legs went plunging along it, and not until he had gone a mile, with many a backward glance, did his legs take a small stagger on their own and he found himself sitting, with his breath hissing through his teeth.

Gradually he came to himself and looked slowly around. How could such a man be there? Then the thought struck him:

37

probably a fellow who had gone "queer" and become a solitary. In the same moment he remembered Queer Willie, native of a neighbouring parish in the Border country, when he was a boy. The shepherds used to talk about meeting him unexpectedly in lonely places. He was quite harmless, they said, yet none of them had ever taken a liberty with him. There was a "cold air" about him, they said. When Peter or any of his brothers hadn't time to have their hair cut, someone would be sure to say, "You'll be another Queer Willie yet."

Had something of this, an imagined picture of Queer Willie long buried in the mind, suddenly sprung upon him? Had it been enough to make him feel an actual physical resemblance? For the fellow was obviously much younger, fifteen to twenty years younger, with a thin beard. There might be much the same height and build, but no one else would see any resemblance. The thing was absurd.

Yet Peter knew there had been something in the fellow's stance, his look, that had come at him with a frightening familiarity. Heavens, for a moment it was as if some double of himself, his doppel-ganger, had looked at him with a "cold air" from another plane! There was no explaining it—unless, of course, he had had a preview of what he might expect to become if he went on like this!

His smile, however, was without humour, for he realised that here was an aspect of things, the dark underside, which he had never thought of encountering. It was quite different in kind from the "vision" of the small lorry or car coming towards them on the moor road. There had been no actual vehicle. Some conformation of the peat hags by the roadside had appeared to be moving towards them simply because they were moving towards it. He could not "prove" this, but surely this explanation, which his mind had worked out, was enough. He had not even bothered to go and investigate the incident on the spot. That kind of illusion did not matter. This fellow on the bridge was as real as the peat hags he lived among.

A deathly ravine, feet coming behind on a tossing bridge, the aspect of menace—before he had right started! If this was what his wells and tin kettles were going to bring upon him,

he had better hive off back home to Fand now. But not by
that bridge. He glanced around and, deciding he had rested
enough, went on.

His panic had left a taste in his mouth and he pursued the
path stolidly. There was nothing else to do and he had learned
how to keep on doing it as a boy. He was empty but with no
particular desire to eat. The evening was at hand, with nowhere
to sleep. There was a map in his rucksack. He left it there.

Wells and legendary shores and immortal gleams were
what troubled man when he was too well fed, too comfortable,
and felt restless.

He hadn't even faced round on the bridge and said, What
ho!

A bleakness came upon him that was beyond misery and
without its luxury.

After a long time he was still plodding away as though he
had forgotten how to sit down. The bare hillsides had a spare
look that he knew.

As the sun went down the hill-tops above would draw the
evening about them. In his youth he had watched them doing
this and had never after needed a definition of detachment,
scholastic or otherwise.

The hillsides began to stand away from him and all at
once he felt something gnawing at his foot and realised that
both the big toe and the adjoining one were now being throttled
by the hole in his sock. It was a grey sock that Fand had
knitted . . . probably on a winter's night when Beethoven was
being a bit too masterful in the wireless box. A glimmer came
into his eyes; they lifted and looked around and saw a solitary
cottage near at hand.

The hens were going in to roost, with an odd peck as they
went, missing nothing, while the great golden cock strutted
with his head so high in the air that it was a wonder he didn't
trip over himself. When he lowered his wing at a hen in a
sidling absurd motion, the hen's lack of interest was very
marked. She didn't even answer back, for there was a time
for all things and the vain fellow ought to know that this wasn't
it.

39

It was an old thatched cottage; everything about it had been lying in the same place for a long time, lying and sinking; and he knew, while he approached the upper door and the hens went in at the lower, that the sinking would continue until all things were resumed into the earth. Avoiding some droppings on the doorstep, he knocked.

There was a faint shuffling within and then an old woman came to the door, a small old woman, slightly bent, and as he looked at the dark seams in her grey face he got the feeling, and it was not an obvious but a very peculiar feeling, that this was perhaps the dirtiest face he had ever seen.

7

"I have come a long way," he said, "and I thought perhaps you might direct me to the nearest place where I could get a cup of tea and rest."

As though she weren't used to so many words at once and couldn't therefore get their meaning, her mouth came slightly adrift without exposing any teeth. She looked at him and looked far away, plainly trying to do his forgotten journey in her lost mind.

"I am feeling a bit tired——"

"Come in!" she said at the word "tired". "Come in and rest," and she preceded him into the kitchen and scooped a great tortoiseshell cat from a chair with such vigour that the cat stood on the floor and twisted her tail and blinked. She was a fat cat and though she knew the old woman very well, still she twisted her tail.

"Please to sit down." She shook the thin cushion on which the cat had been resting and a fish bone fell on the floor. "Ah, you!" she said to the cat.

He took off his rucksack and sat down on the thin cushion on the square wooden chair, saying, "Thank you very much."

These polite words released more energy in her and she turned upon the kettle which she swung in over the fire on an iron crook. As the flames from the peat on the flat hearth were coaxed round its bottom, it sighed.

"It's not long off the boil," she said. "Have you come far?"

"I have come from the Picts Houses on the other side of the mountains."

"Have you indeed?" she said. "But not on your feet?"

"Yes, all the way."

"Dear me!" she said. "Dear me! Will you take an egg?"

"Well—thank you very much, if it's not too much trouble." Off she went for the egg.

She was so old that she wasn't shy, only flustered. As he looked round the little kitchen, at the wooden boxed bed against the wall with its patchwork quilt, at the clutter about the clay floor and the traces of adventurous hens, at smoke-grimed wall-paper hanging in a torn bulge over the bed, at the table beside his right shoulder and before the window on which everything unwashed was hardly given standing room, he realised that the kitchen and the things outside were like herself and that they all lived together.

Suddenly it came to him that this was the half-way house between being on the earth and under it. For an instant the whole world went quiet in a revelation which might have become complete in some profound or final way, if a subdued cackling of hens and a high strident cackling of cock hadn't interrupted it. So she hadn't even gathered her eggs to-day. He looked through the small window and saw the afterglow from the sunset beyond very distant and dark mountains. Probably she wouldn't gather her eggs until the morning of the day when she had to meet the grocer's van. She had stopped planning.

The afterglow grew bright on his face and he realised that he liked the old lady. Here she was now with an egg in her hand and it even looked a fairly clean egg. But the egg needed a pan and she stopped, but as though there was something still more urgent in her mind, she said, "You'll be feeling very tired after your long walk?" and there was both concern and questioning upon her.

"A bit," he admitted.

"I was just thinking that from your voice you will not be living up in this wild part of the world."

"No. I live in a city."

"I thought that," she said, "for you have an educated voice. You'll just be having a holiday to yourself?"

"That's right. I'm walking the city air out of me."

"Just that. You'll always be working in the city?"

42

"Yes. I—well, I have to do with teaching. And that can be dry enough."

"Have you now?" Respect was in her voice, and a certain wonder held her for a few moments. As though she could hardly expect so high an honour upon her humble dwelling yet hoping for it too, she said tentatively, "Maybe you'll be a headmaster from a big school?"

"No. I work in a university."

"University," she repeated above a whisper.

"I'm a professor. Professor of history."

"Professor," she scarcely breathed and the egg fell from her fingers and smashed on the floor.

Well, well, if that wasn't foolish of her and handless, and she hunted around and the cat jumped up on the bed; she found something that may have been a piece of potato sacking if not of an old petticoat and she got down on her knees and scooped the mess loosely together and went away with it. The cat jumped down from the bed and approached the yellow smear with superb grace, picking her footsteps without thought. It was surely the cleanest cat he had ever seen. But suddenly there was commotion among the hens and golden cock, and this time their protestations suggested that she was dealing with them in more summary fashion. When she appeared before him she had three eggs in her hands.

Automatically she looked for the pan but still without thinking about it. "You're so young to be a professor," she said. "You must be very clever," and these last words had the objective wonder that sometimes appears when reference is made to an inexplicable visitation of the grace of God.

"Young? I'm nearly fifty," he declared.

She looked at him. "You're just a boy." Then she hunted the pan, found it outside, dunted it on a stone though the hens had left nothing in it, and hurriedly re-entered her dwelling into which the stranger had come. In the old days folk never locked their doors at night lest Christ in the guise of the stranger should come seeking refreshment and shelter. The professor was enough for this ancient tradition of her people to rise warmly within her and she so busied herself that she nearly

43

slipped on the spot where the egg had fallen. "Ah you!" she said to the cat in the wrong direction for once more the cat had jumped onto the bed out of harm's way. She swilled the teapot beyond the doorstep, put a fistful of tea into it, and was surrounded by steam as she tilted the black kettle on the iron crook.

"Well, well!" And she placed the brown teapot by the hot embers to "draw".

"It's not often I have a stranger," she said as she tackled the table. She lifted some things away and pushed others back and spoke to one or two of them as if they should have more sense and better manners than to be where they were.

She found the cup.

It was a good solid cup and the handle was on it. She looked into it and whatever she saw there she had a wipe at with her black apron. Peter's stomach was still perhaps the weakest part of him but the light was none too good and what the eye doesn't see the heart needn't grieve over. But the eye alas! will see what it has to see, and in the afterglow from the sunset which came through the window directly on her face, giving it a strange and witch-like reality, it saw the drop gathering at the nose. It was an inquisitive drop, for as her head moved here and there over the lump of butter on the cracked plate, the half of a loaf and the bannocks of oatcake, it gleamed like an opening eye in the westering light. It trembled as she looked into the milk jug. It fascinated him as no diamond had ever done, and it left him with a feeling of peace when at last she turned away to the teapot for now, as she stooped, it was bound to fall according to the eternal laws which the great Newton— blessed be his name!—had discovered and formulated.

But it did not fall. It came back with her, enlarged and globular, and he realised more than ever that all things in this half-way house between life and death had their own laws of attraction and that when the drop fell it would choose its spot. More than that: the intuitive juices of his stomach knew the spot. She was leaning over the cup and bringing the spout of the teapot towards it when the drop fell. With an exquisite precision it hit the inner edge of the cup's lip and in the same

44

instant his mouth cried, "Wait!" Leaning forward he got his thumb below the drop and scooped it up and over. "Tchach!" he said getting to his feet with the cup.

"What is it?" she asked in astonishment.

"A spider," he said; "but I nailed it." Smiling, he put his hand automatically into his breast pocket for the reserve white handkerchief which Fand always placed there.

"Tuts! You'll dirty your hankie," she cried out with concern.

"That's what it's for." Laughing with delight, he polished the cup. He was particularly pleased with his ready wit. "I have heard it said that a spider is lucky."

"I have heard that myself." She nodded, happy before his laughter.

"You'll have a good few of them round here."

"Plenty," she said. "Not that I trouble much with them when they don't trouble me, though I keep them in their place."

As he set the cup down and sat down himself, his sleeve swept the egg-spoon to the floor. "You talk about being hand-less," he declared, laughing again as he picked up the spoon and polished it too.

The tea had drawn to the rich consistency of porter and when presently—for it was scalding hot—he abandoned himself to its well-sweetened body, he knew it was the best tea he had ever consumed.

"Is it to your taste?" she asked him politely.

"It's meat and drink," he replied fondly, "as the fox said when he ran away with the bagpipes."

At that she lifted her hands from the blue-ringed bowl which held her own tea and shook her head, uttering the while a thin husky piping of laughter. "Well, well! Little did I think that the day would came when a professor of learning would repeat that old saying in this house."

"Have you been here long?"

"Eighty-seven years. I was born in that bed."

And so the great talk started, though it was not until she had pushed things back from the edge of the table, turned him to the fire, cocked the peats on edge round the central flames and swished the cat beyond, that the initial big bout of questioning

45

came upon her. At first he was inclined to hedge a little over the more personal details of his life, but soon he discarded such vanity and abandoned himself to truth as he had to her tea.

And truth thus regarded astonished himself often. His grandfather had had a small mixed farm in the Highlands and one of his sons, James, said he would neither go to sea—there was good money in herring then—nor emigrate, for what he wanted to do was herd sheep. Very well, said his father grimly, in that case you'll start at the beginning and hire yourself out as a shepherd. There was little money in sheep at that time and less in being a shepherd, but James would have his own way and a shepherd he became. He married and lived on a Highland moor and bred sheep as he played his fiddle, for he was an artist at both. A great sheepfarmer from the Borders, who always bought his Cheviot wethers at the Lairg sales, enticed him south at a good wage and he went. But James missed the Highland moors and to keep them out of his mind he turned his mind to getting on. And so he became a sheepfarmer himself, famous near and far for his sheep and for his working dogs, but no longer for his fiddle.

Of all the struggles James and his wife had—and they were many—the worst was when he owned his first hirsel of sheep, and carried his first big debt, and she carried her sixth and last child. In all she had four sons and two daughters, and the name they put on the third son was Peter. As he grew, the schoolmaster said he showed promise, for lessons came easily to him, and he could drink a Border ballad like a glass of milk. Now when his father added the second hirsel to the first one and troubles came so thick and fast that his mother could hardly lift her feet clear of them in the kitchen, it was then she made up her mind that Peter would get the best learning the land could provide and that no one would stop her while the breath of life was in her. And she thought that quietly within herself, and calmly, like a woman in a ballad.

"Yes, yes," said Peter's aged hostess and her hands rustled together like old leaves. "Yes, yes; oh yes."

And she worked with three women's hands, nor did she call halt to her husband lost in his fury of getting on, but on the

46

contrary pushed him from behind, for now and then, after a market, what had been the fiddle in him would have its airing. So she had many things to see to and their range was wide, and sometimes she would be dumb and her feet heavy, and sometimes she was a Highland burn in spate with a hand as sharp as a cry. But sometimes when her husband came back from a good market with a drop of whisky in him the kitchen would be a small place then, and with a large hand he would order food and drink for those he had brought with him, and when she found the food and drink he would boast, laughing at the full bottle, that she had never let him down before friend or foe; she would give him a sharp retort to that one, and he would put an arm round her waist and whirl her on the floor, and it's not once they danced the figure of a reel before us all, and if the young ones were embarrassed a little they were strangely uplifted too, for it was like a grown-up ballad being made there and then, and her feet went neat from one place to another like the milk squirts into a pail.

"Noble, noble. She was a noble woman."

The words suspended Peter in his own story, and beyond its movement he saw that "noble" was the word. The yellow flames flapped where the wind of logic does not disturb them and for a little while he dwelt there and the years were together like neighbours in the old farm kitchen.

It took him a long while to get to Fand, for when his listener discovered that the boy Peter and the professor were one and the same she needed time. Her brain did not work quickly, for it had stopped jumping to conclusions long ago. But when one and one came together, and she saw them together, then she could savour awe in the conjunction, and leave hurry to those who had nowhere to go and not a milestone on the road to it. She was finding a lot of milestones this night.

"Fand. It is a beautiful name, though I cannot remember it on anyone myself." She turned her face to him. In the firelight its pallor was warm with sentiment. "She will be lovely."

And she was right.

"Did she belong to your own countryside?"

47

"No," he answered. "She belonged to the city, but some-times those who belong to the city think more of the country than many who are born in the country."

"I've heard that. She would come from well-to-do people?"

So he told her of Fand's folk and their high tradition in the legal world, adding, because he knew it would please her, that she had had an uncle who had been a law lord. It pleased her so much that he saw wonder dwell in her face, and he knew once again, with a far glimpse of his mother, that the country notion of going out into the wide world and "getting on" held something of high adventure that was very old and went very deep. It was as old as the first adventurer into the unknown places of the earth who came back with strange stories that kept the aged from their beds. It was as old as the wandering scholar. In this air he saw Fand clearly and found he liked talking about her, as though she did not belong to him and was all the more herself on that account. She had always liked the country. The simplest flower that grew would catch Fand's eye.

"Fand," repeated the old lady, and as she looked at him the rifts in her face, laden with their own dark ore, ran together in a faint smile that was like a papyrus he had seen somewhere after it had been dug up. "It has a fond sound."

And "fond" was the ultimate word! The revelation so affected him that he stirred in his chair and turning his head to the window saw that it had grown dark.

The darkness evoked Fand at the Picts Houses, and in the same moment he saw the "queer" fellow against the night. He was now walking through the night towards the grey ruins. Peter saw his grey face peering through the side window of the car at Fand sleeping alone.

He got up abruptly and at once the hens and particularly the golden cock set up a cackling commotion far above anything he had yet heard. Suddenly, with thumping heart, he was translated beyond himself, where what had happened that day couldn't have happened and he was the victim of a strange illusion or dream, in which only symbols moved—and swelled as he looked at them.

She was reassuring him, telling him it was nothing, and her

voice was mournful and regretful at this disturbance of the dream.

He looked at her and saw she was old and witchlike and near the end of time. He was trapped, her realm had hold of him; there was no quick way to the far homes of the world. The cackling exploded into a winged riot as if the roosts were being disrupted and the cock already through the roof.

"Sit down," she said. "He will go when he gets the eggs."

He stared at her. "Who?"

She was looking into the fire, waiting for the unfortunate interruption to end, resigned in a peculiar way. "That cock," she said, "you would think he laid the eggs himself," and her voice was dry as an old stick.

He sat down.

The clamour subsided, the hens grew silent, and the cock proclaimed his indignation in less hurried and more confident tones.

"Yes, yes, you're the brave one now," she addressed the cock. "Crow you!"

At which rebuke the distant cock also grew silent.

"Who is he?"

"Och," she said, "bairns call him the wild man, but there's no wildness in him that ever did harm to anyone. He lives in the hills and sleeps no one knows where, and if he comes and takes an egg now and then he has got to live like the rest of us, and he knows well that I don't grudge them to him." Her eyes strayed to the bread on the table as though she was in the habit of giving him that also.

His own eyes went to the window and for a moment he thought he saw a face. The pallor of face or reflection vanished, and as his breathing eased he realised that his own rationalising of the "queer" solitary on the swinging bridge had been right.

"He interrupted your story," she said, trying to bring together again herself, the story and the warmth.

"Does he belong to the district?" he asked.

"Yes," she said, but reluctantly. "He was a gillie on the estate, but the estate here was sold and broken up; anyway, there was no job for him and he wouldn't leave the hills and in the end he went the way he is."

"Have you ever talked to him?"

"Yes, yes. He's sensible enough. But if you ask him questions, he goes away. I take him like the night itself, wet or fine, and speak away to him and then it's all right."

"Does he ever come in?"

"No, he never comes past the door." She sounded mournful and all her years were upon her. She sighed.

Listening for a footstep, he heard the night and far away what was like the sound of wind dying in a pine forest. Then, straightening himself, he said cheerfully, "Well, it's been a grand talk we have had and I don't know how to thank you for your kindness." He stood up.

"It's not going you are?"

"I must. It's probably still a long way to the nearest place where I can get a bed and high time I was on the road. If you could just give me an idea of the way, I'll soon step it out, for it has been a great rest, and a great enjoyment, being here with you, and your tea was the best I have ever tasted."

All these complimentary words brought her back to her earlier self, and she grew alarmed at the thought of his departure into the dark night. After he listened to her he realised that he might find difficulty in keeping to the neglected path and that if he tried to hold by the river it was on his hands and knees he would have to go for two miles. There was a stiffness in the shoulder that had broken the vacuum flask and a tired congestion upon his legs. But he went to the door and stared into the darkness and knew that if only he had a bale of straw in a corner he would be happy.

Back in the kitchen she addressed him: "If you care to sleep here it's an honoured woman I would be, though it's not much in the way of comfort I can offer the like of you, for I haven't had anyone sleeping with me for a long time now, but oh! you are welcome."

The cat rose and stretched herself on the bed and out of slits the green eyes regarded him in a peculiar way. It was a wide bed, if perhaps on the short side.

"I set out on this journey prepared to sleep on a bed of heather or a windling of straw," he answered lightly, feeling his way. "I would not inconvenience you for the world."

Though the kitchen flickered brightly there were dark corners, and in one of them she found a candle. "I broke the globe of the lamp the winter before last," she explained, busy now. "Come this way."

He had hardly thought from the length of the cottage, with the fowls going in at the lower end, that there could have been space for another room, but another room there was, with a brave brass-knobbed bed half-filling it and three big photographs on the wall. He smiled, hearing himself telling Fand how nearly she had come to being a betrayed woman that night. Beyond a very thin partition the golden cock made distinct comment on what had so far been an unusually disturbing night for him, poor fellow.

"Now I will air the sheets," she said with the manner of a hostess who had important affairs on hand and all the complicated ordering of them. The sheets were those that a certain good woman promised to put on her bed when she died, and she had been careful with them. Little had she thought that a living professor would warm them before then.

8

As Peter proceeded on his way next day he was in that delightful condition of mind which recognises thought as no more than the scent of the flower. He could sniff it when he liked. The stiffness in his bones and muscles was a luxury that eased in the exercise so that sometimes his shoulder indulged in a hunch on its own, searching for the vacuum flask it had broken but hardly finding it. He had nearly had trout for breakfast.

When he found himself standing on the middle of a side-road shaking with soft laughter, he had a quick look around and went on. Learned colleagues on the psychology side, with an intricate knowledge of symptoms, had a peculiar terminology; and one did one's best to dodge their arrows that fly by night.

In the tremendous press of affairs, she had forgotten the wild man, and particularly the cat.

He started laughing again even while he walked, for he had overheard as he got out of bed the whole address to the cat. The wild man had left two trout on a narrow shelf in the hen-house, fine spotted fellows, each over a pound in weight, and the cat had discovered them first. If only, as she so reasonably declared, the brute had stuck to one, but no. . . . However, there was still altogether a good pound of trout flesh left, and if her guest had a preference in the matter of frying or boiling . . . ?

She could hardly believe that he didn't like trout; for she herself loved it as did the cat. It had been a delightful morning and he would have timed his eggs if he hadn't forgotten to wind his watch.

He could do with a trout now, he thought, glancing at the sun. Then he asked: What could be cleaner than a cat's mouth? And he realised that in truth no kitchen he had ever seen had been half so clean as that cat. "You're dead right!" he replied to himself. But when he realised he had uttered the words aloud he had another look around and saw the green end of a van by the bend of a small wood.

It was a grocer's van and as he reached it and looked about for the driver a man came from behind a bush buttoning his coat and greeting him cheerfully.

After they had discussed the fine weather and the country-side, Peter asked him if a coupon was required for a bun and was introduced to the rear of the van whose double doors opened upon shelves of variegated foodstuffs. He was such an obliging and capable fellow that Peter found no difficulty in getting what he wanted even to the matter of butter.

"If a quarter-pound will do you?"

"If I'm not robbing one of your customers?"

"Ach, well, it's for old Phemie Bethune, but the Macleans, back there, churned yesterday, and didn't take their ration, so I can let Phemie have a pound if she likes. She's as fond of butter as—as——"

"Trout," said Peter.

The vanman gave him a sharp glance and laughed. "You'll have come down that way?"

"She has been acting as my hostess with an old-world grace."

The vanman gave him a sharper glance out of brighter eyes. "And she had trout?"

"Very nearly," said Peter. "But the cat——"

The vanman laughed heartily. "You had food from her?"

"I had indeed. And it occurred to me when I saw your van that if by any chance you were calling upon her, then perhaps you would help me to make up a parcel for her of all the best you have, because I felt she might have been offended if I had offered her a more tangible token."

From the spirit with which the vanman entered into the gathering of the gift it was clear to Peter not only that the

53

vanman liked the old lady but that some of his customers might be disappointed that day.

"There's them that say that old Phemie is not so clean——"

"Tuts!" said the professor. "Poof!"

When the deal was completed and the vanman had graciously accepted a carton of cigarettes from his own stock, he asked Peter if he was going far. Peter turned and looked over rolling broken country with dark mountains in the distance.

"That's the way I'm going, and the old lady told me it's a country of black superstition and ignorance. I think she even hinted at drunkenness and worse."

The vanman's laughter was merry. "Even if I don't come from that side myself, she's not far wrong!"

"Really?"

"Yes. By the old Earl, who's black, two or three of them that think they're important yonder thought they would have old Phemie sent to an institution the winter before last. She hadn't been well, and things in her house were maybe neglected a little beyond the usual. But we kept an eye on her, and I said she would see the boots off a few of them yet, and right enough if the district councillor didn't die on New Year's Day from too much drink that maybe and moreover didn't pay all the whisky duty it should. Not," added the vanman, "that I'm agreeing with the duty."

"Quite, quite," said Peter.

"And she may see the boots off more."

"I'm sure I hope so," agreed Peter.

"There's boots," said the vanman, "that walk about with so much importance you hear them coming."

Peter shook in his tracks again, for the vanman had spoken with some precision if not a little feeling. So they shook hands.

But Peter turned back and the vanman politely descended from his driving-seat.

"Tell me this. Is the wild man related to the old lady? I ask because she seemed reticent about him."

"I think," replied the vanman carefully, "that he's a forty-second cousin on her father's side. But it's not the blood in this case."

54

"Thank you. I wondered."

"She understands him," said the vanman, simply, "and she's the only one."

They stood silent for a moment, then saluted each other under the sun, and as the van drove off with the acceleration that proclaimed an invigorated foot, Peter went down through the small wood with so fine an instinct now for the most comfortable spot that he all but sat on a rabbit. The surprise so quickened his heart that a sense of the warm mystery in natural living came upon him and he realised that because he didn't know where he was going or what would happen to him when he got there he was freed at last. Ah, and warmer than that: he didn't have to argue about it. For man has got to that condition, he reflected, as he sucked a cube of cheese, that when he has no one else to argue with he argues with himself. Man is the serpent who sucks his own tail.

Even the cheese was better than that, and, by the green grass, if ever cheese was made from skim milk thrice removed this was it. Yet it no doubt contained the calories that scientists etcetera. He nodded. We are the dietetic equation. Food ministers work us out. Persons full of importance—the vanman's word—were going to put her in an institution. The hygienic, washy-wishy snoopers! His eyes steadied and hardened.

No, he couldn't forgive them for that. Alive, we are the figures in the sum, added and multiplied and put in the Budget. But death at least was an individual affair. He saw the lines in her face, he saw the earth in the lines, and her face was the picture of a grey striated rock. She was going back and the earth was coming to meet her. There was the comfort, the lostness, of that, the very very natural going away. Dear Christ, they would wash her, he thought, and the cheese fell from his fingers as the egg had fallen from hers.

His eyes came bright out of his solemnity as he realised with happy certainty that the only woman who would wash her would be the good woman, the woman who would smooth the fine sheets about her, the sheets kept for the stranger; the good woman, who deserved to be the vanman's mother . . . and probably was.

His mouth moved and his palate found something vaguely familiar in the aftermath of the cheese as if, after all, it were cream's forty-second cousin.

In the long talk after the airing of the sheets—and he had been as anxious as a forever-polishing maiden aunt to keep their ends off the floor—she had been on the defensive over the wild man. Probably the authorities would have been after him to put him in an institution or a barracks. And she couldn't trust anyone, not even the golden cock, least of all the golden cock who, like every arch bureaucrat, thought he laid the eggs himself. "Crow you!" said she to him with a finishing irony that no Parisian existentialist had yet quite achieved. "Crow you!" Peter repeated, and swayed with delight in the small wood.

He liked woods and looked between slim brown trunks and saw a gleam of light beyond. That gleam had often had a peculiar attraction for him. It was like looking through a secret window on a glade where the unexpected or unknown would happen. But then trees had always had an attraction for him. Lying on his back idly, he had more than once seen their branches writing on the sky. On one occasion he had actually tried to decipher their message as though he might thereby at least get at something atavistic . . . but he had soon given it up; as indeed he gave it up now, for his jaws were aching from chewing the tough bun food, and if it hadn't been for old Phemie's butter. . . .

Presently as he lay over on his right side a shaft of sunlight snared his relaxed hands. Sleepily his left hand moved towards a bulge under his right breast. It was his pocket-book, stuffed with bank notes, a good half of which he should have left with Fand. Funny thing, because usually she didn't trust him with a wad of notes; thought he might leave it behind in the usual way with his toothbrush. It now troubled him like a lump in a bed so his hand withdrew it and pushed it into an opening on his up side. Then he sank and floated and for a moment had a widening vision of Phemie's cat on the edge of the roof, its eyes closed in the morning sun, its whiskers at rest, and the trout inside.

When he woke up and told himself he had actually nodded off for five seconds he thought it a very marvel. But when he was walking away and something attacked him inside his trousers, he had a moment's horrible primordial panic; his hands squeezed the thing to death, then let it slide down one leg. His pocket-book appeared over his shoe. This troubled him very much and he looked about the wood and at certain blaeberry humps with suspicion. He had never really found out whether Fand believed in fairies, and had never had the heart himself to tell her that they were probably malicious little devils.

Doubtless many a man had lost his pocket-book during sleep. However, that raised issues, not to say milieus, which were far from blaeberry patches, and as Peter's eye lifted to the sun it gleamed as it recognised that the king of the heavens must have leapt a fair arc of the sky in five seconds. Between the big magic of the sun and the little magic of the fairies, it takes a good man to hang on to his pocket-book. That was one thing about Fand: she never quite gave him credit for an all-round competence, a sort of native ability; she never quite trusted him when it came to boiling an egg. No woman believes that the sand sticks in the time glass, and man needn't try to make her. She doesn't even answer. She knows. She knows.

How beautiful is a wife when you are leaving her.

With such scraps of litanies wandering in and out his refreshed mind, he went on his way towards the dark mountains which old Phemie had warned him against. Odd thing that his journey so far should have been an affair, not of crystal wells or immortal shores, but of near death and madness and old age, with superstition and drunkenness ahead. Perhaps he had begun at the wrong end and was travelling widdershins?

In the late afternoon, from a hillside above a main road, he saw two brightly coloured charabancs trundle along, laden with people from distant cities, all looking for something. But it could hardly be wells because they didn't stop. What, then, were they looking for? And why had an earlier charabanc driven him off the road? How many charabancs were there? He had an involuntary vision of a fully developed technological society where the gaily coloured charabancs whirled to its round rim like the wheel in the Monte Carlo casino. He remembered how he himself had felt with the stotting marble about to settle. . . .

Was there a connection, however esoteric, between himself and the folk in the charabanc and the ladies and gents in the casino? All were on a quest. Whatever she said to her auntie, no traveller ever found scenery enough. Many a casino hunter had shot himself. The holy grail—that's what they were after, as sure as knights. Bill Hinkley from Wigan, rolling along in the yellow and blue bus marked Private, was on the spoor of the holy grail and, not finding it, criticised the Scotch beer.

But Peter had now come among sheep—the Cheviot breed he knew so well—and decided that the lame beast over to his left was suffering from foot-rot.

This rather surprised him, for here was no heavy clayey lowland pasture. The mountains were at hand. Going towards the ewe he heard a metallic clink and saw that the right forefoot was caught in the iron jaws of a rabbit trap. His face twisted.

All his early sheep knowledge came back to him as he began to single out the ewe. When a man spreads his arms and jumps to this side and then to that, a sheep may get as astonished as a boy before his first jumping jack, but she never gets less nimble. Three times she ran round him and rejoined the main body; but the main body was so curious that it swirled in arcs rather than went anywhere. Peter began to sweat and his heart to thump for even on three legs the sheep could give him ten yards in twenty. But in the end he shed her from the flock and at once the ewe, knowing that the awful fate of separateness had come upon her, made away in front of him, baaing, and Peter kept trotting after her to stop her thinking. It was a race of many swerves and he went all the faster and his rucksack thumped him all the harder as he thought of the mounting pain the brute was suffering from the accursed trap. People ought to be shot, he yelled, for setting traps in a sheeprun. At the yells, the ewe trod on the trailing stake of the trap, all but couped, and Peter nearly had her, but no. He cursed as he thought of the extra pain that jerk had given her, but the corner of the drystone dike was drawing near and he was gathering his last reserves for the tackle. She took two seconds in the corner before deciding to swerve left and Peter launched himself. They went down together in as neat a tackle as had ever brought upon him a rugby crowd's roar—and they both lay. The sheep did not even lift her head, nor did Peter. He breathed into her wool and shut his eyes and hoped his heart wouldn't burst.

His eyes opened on a collie dog whose head was lowered. She was black with a white star on her chest and very white fangs. He knew the breed, knew the sleekness of the intelligent bitch that could drive sheep through the eye of a needle.

"Steady, Jess!"

With relief Peter lifted his eyes towards the voice and saw a head above the wall. It was an intelligent face, brown from much weather, clear cheek bones, and disconcertingly steady.

Peter eased himself up on the sheep. "People used to be hanged for sheep-stealing," he admitted.

The shepherd's expression grew doubtful before Peter's ironic concentrated regard.

"But if I had my way," Peter added, "they ought to be shot for setting rabbit-traps in sheep-runs. Come over."

The shepherd, a man of about forty, came over the wall with a deceptive ease and Peter showed him the trap.

"I've warned him more than once," said the shepherd. "He swears he sets them inside the hole. But you know the price rabbits are."

They got the trap off and felt for joints and moved the bones.

"Swollen, but all right," said Peter.

"You seem to know about sheep."

"I should. My father was a sheep farmer."

"Was he now?" said the shepherd, an unexpectedly attractive smile running over his face as the very astonished sheep, heaved to her four legs, ran away.

"Surprised at you having Cheviots here."

"Well, it's open here—and right back on to the moor behind. But right enough it's all Blackfaces on the mountains, as you'll have seen if you've come far. Perhaps it wasn't in the Highlands your father had his farm?"

And so, sitting there as the sun slid over the dark hills, they had their talk on sheep and sheepmen.

Peter had always liked shepherds and there was an inflection in this man's voice that his own father's had never lost.

"Look!" said Peter. "There's something I have never seen before."

He had been following the released ewe. She had not gone straight back to the others but had moved in a lost way a little below them. Then four or five of them had come towards her and now were actually standing rubbing their faces on her neck.

"Many an astonishing thing you see," said the shepherd, and they smiled together, the same assessing glimmer in their eyes.

They got talking about strange things with that fine appreciation which has not yet been touched by personal details, by names, by the odds and ends that bring people back on themselves. Peter's eyes travelled to the mountains; the evening light was upon all things, and the highway couldn't be seen. It was very quiet, with a quietness that was tall and far, delicate as a leaf, and soft-footed as the grass. The carpet of his boyhood unrolled before him.

"I remember once," he said. "It was the first time, I think, I ever understood sheep. I was at the far fank with my father. Just the two of us. I would be no more than ten or eleven at the time and I think it was the afternoon for I can remember still the curious sort of flat quietness that the sunlight put on everything. You know what I mean?"

"Well that," nodded the shepherd. "Many a time—but I'm interrupting you."

"There were some young sheep crowded together in a pen —gimmers, maybe—I don't remember, though I can see them still. My father had his arms on top of the wall and was looking at them. I had climbed up and was looking at them, too. And all of them got their heads round and looked at us. Their faces were white, beautifully made, and all exactly like one another in an almost uncanny way. Yet though they were alike, there was something delicate about them, very individual, something

60

aristocratic, distinguished members of the same family. Anyway, it caught me in a sort of wonder and I turned to my father. 'Do you see their faces, Father?' I whispered. And he answered me quietly, without turning his head, 'That's what I'm breeding for'."

The shepherd leaned back and jabbed his stick into the ground, his hazel eyes alight. "I doubt if you were ever nearer your father than you were then!"

Peter's smile stopped and he turned his eyes on the shepherd. "I think—perhaps—you're dead right."

"Right? I know I'm right. And it's not that their faces are the same, though they're like enough, it's the *something*, it's the *something*." He shook his head with pleasure and hit the grass with his left heel.

"You may be right," said Peter thoughtfully. "Do you know the next time I saw that look in a man's face?"

"No," said the shepherd.

"It was in Paris. They gave me some schooling, and I didn't follow sheep myself. I was long grown up by then and I was taken to a sculptor's studio. He had been working on a lump of rock with a cold chisel and you could see the man he was making coming out of the stone. While my French friend was talking to the sculptor, I had a quiet look around and I saw many human heads, one of a young girl, another of an old man, and so on. To look at, they were all quite different, yet there was a resemblance somewhere. Then I became aware that no one was speaking. I glanced at the sculptor. His arms were folded, his head slightly lowered, he was staring at the stone figure. He was quite unlike my father. He had a black beard. But the way his eyes looked from under his eyebrows at what he was creating—it was exactly my father's look at the gimmers in the pen. I followed his look—and all at once I saw the—the *something*."

"Is that so?" said the shepherd. "Oh, man! And did you tell him?"

"No."

"What a pity! He would have enjoyed hearing about the gimmers."

Peter's eyes, glimmering with light, got lost upon the mountains of superstition. Quietly he said, "You may be right again. I think—perhaps—he was big enough for that. Yet—I wonder. Not that it makes any difference. It's—it's difficult." Laughter was held far in him like the memory of a poem whose words he had forgotten. Something delicious could almost be tasted on the tongue. What a divine evening it was!

He remarked on the quality of the evening, hardly hoping that the shepherd would respond in any unusual way and hardly caring. It was dry and fine like a perfect wine. Even the midges must have fallen upon contemplation. No wonder.

"Yes, it's a beautiful evening," the shepherd answered.

In the involuntary silence that followed the way the shepherd spoke the words, Peter was aware of the pleasure in this chance meeting, of an excitement that had been created fine as the evening, less imaginary than the wine. There were odd moments when the human spirit gave off its finest bouquet, when it asked for nothing, desired nothing, and was given all. Even the coldness had gone from his face from over-taxing his heart; even his heart had settled.

"I have a vague feeling of my life coming back to me from long ago," said Peter. "I could sit here for long enough."

"That's right," said the shepherd.

"You know what I mean?"

"Well that," answered the shepherd. "I know."

The excitement gathered a faint beat.

"You have felt it?"

"I have that. And sometimes it's strange enough. It's not the kind of thing," said the shepherd, "that everyone would understand." As if under the stress of a peculiar emotion, his eyes fell to the grass and his left heel on its own enlarged the small hollow it had made in the turf.

Peter's heart got up on its elbow and gave a faint thud, also on its own. "I have had many a queer feeling myself on such an evening, when the light is going, and you wonder sometimes . . ." His eyes fell away into distance.

"It was last April," said the shepherd, "in the middle of the lambing. I was away out on the moor behind. I had had a hefty day and a few difficult births and there were one or two stubborn yeld ewes on the hunt for lambs . . . but you know how it is. I don't think I had sat down since I left home early in the morning and now the light was going and I sat down, for I was tired. To tell the truth I had forgotten to eat my piece, and I took the bread from my pocket, but somehow I wasn't even hungry. On the whole I had had a good day with not so many casualties in a crop of good lambs but that my average was keeping high. There had been a drying wind, too—not too cold. But now the wind had gone with the sun, and over the moor there was a fine light that went blue in the distance. I never before saw so—so beautiful a sight, so wide and—and beautiful. It came over me."

Peter could neither move nor speak; he felt the boundary growing thin.

"I am a married man," said the shepherd, "with three of a young family and though I say it myself I know when I'm well off. But—*I didn't want to go home*."

There was no boundary.

Peter heard the shepherd's practical voice, almost harsh in its insistence, repeating, "Sure as death, I didn't want to go home," as though the wonder of it were objective, something almost to be seen, like an unknown ewe with strange markings among his flock.

It was that—but it was more than that.

Yet it was that primarily, and easy to hold in the mind and not embarrassing.

In a way the shepherd could hardly have had less self-consciousness if he had seen a ewe with a golden fleece.

The quest of the golden fleece! With a vague feeling that he hadn't yet gone to school, Peter murmured, "That's a beauty. I have had something like it myself. I sometimes wonder if more people have had a similar sort of experience than we imagine."

"Do you think so?"

"As you said, it's not everyone you would tell it to."

"That's right," said the shepherd. "That's right certainly." And his voice was light now as if freed from the peril of self-consciousness, of being misunderstood, and freed also into that higher air where the confidence that has been told finds itself at home and able to look around on many an unexpected and wonderful sight.

Because Peter's classical lore stirred in him, he could not help telling the shepherd something about Jason and his companions who went off on the quest of the golden fleece, but he told it as he had never told it before, and as there wasn't much the shepherd didn't know about a fleece he had the more time to dwell on the wonders, and the implication of the wonders, which welled up from Peter with a humour at once homely and delightful, until the shepherd didn't notice much difference between a classical pastoral age and the age he was sitting on, and moved freely among the classical gentry without thinking once that they were fools often, because of the confidence he had given to a stranger and was pleased to be pinned by.

"So you'll have to watch yourself," Peter concluded, "or one of these fine evenings you'll be off after the golden fleece yourself."

"Do you think so?" said the shepherd, laughing and dunting the hole in the turf to twice its size.

"Talking of gold," said Peter, "how are prices?"

"Prices!" echoed the shepherd. "It's the golden fleece for the sheep-farmer all right! Do you know what cast ewes were selling at in the last sheep sales at Lairg?"

An hour later they crossed the main road and took a footpath by some small fields. "I'm pretty sure," said the shepherd, "that the visitor she had went yesterday, and if there's one thing that Mrs. Macrae cannot stand it's dirt. She's clean, I'll say that, and you should be comfortable there. But I'm sorry we haven't a spare room ourselves, for you would be welcome."

"Thank you," said Peter again.

"Her husband, Lachlan—him and me were in the desert together; he was my sergeant. Oh, a tough fellow, and if there's a practical joke going, he's in it."

Presently they came to a white-washed croft house with a slate roof and met Mrs. Macrae on the doorstep, a dark buxom tidy woman, as neat as though she were back from a party and had put on an apron to cook the supper.

64

"I have brought a gentleman with me who doesn't care for hotels and I told him he would be better with you if you could have him."

"It's not more sense you're getting," she said, "and I haven't a thing in the house." Her smile was a rosy flush but her eyes saw Peter who had lifted his tweed hat.

"Munro is my name, Peter Munro," and he smiled to her as he sometimes did to Fand without knowing it.

"If you'll excuse me," said the shepherd who now heard Peter's name for the first time, "I don't suppose you will be any relation of James Munro of Slap, the famous Border sheep man. I have heard my father tell of him."

"I am his son," said Peter.

9

It was almost dark when Lachlan Macrae and Peter Munro approached the large hotel, with its glass lounge in front, its great stuffed trout in glass cases, its fishing rights on many lochs. "We'll go round the back," said Lachlan. "We're late and Alastair will be waiting."

Alastair Maclennan was the shepherd with whom Peter had hunted the golden fleece and with whom he had made a tryst for a dram. Round the back beyond the kitchen and beside the engine-house where the electric light was generated a small board with BAR on it stuck out over a door which Lachlan pushed open. It was like going into a cave dark with big men and lit well enough to see the weathered shine on their faces and to be aware of their eyes. Through the blue warmth and the smell of beer, Lachlan began shouldering his way slowly forward to the small bar counter, nodding a greeting here, throwing a word there, until Alastair the shepherd was before them saying he thought they weren't coming.

"It's a wonder I'm able to come at all," said Peter, smiling.

"How that?" asked Alastair.

"Highland hospitality," said Peter.

"Good though!" said Alastair. "Didn't I tell you?" He glanced at Lachlan who was scratching the back of his neck. "He got you that time."

"Don't blame me," said Lachlan.

"Far from it!" said Alastair, placing the compliment fairly on Lachlan's wife.

Peter was having a few quiet words with the barman and when Lachlan got his tumbler he looked at the largeness of the whisky inside it and said with reverent astonishment, "God bless me!"

There was a laugh and Lachlan's eye shot to a burly figure of middle stature sitting against the off wall with a half-drained pint of beer on the deal table in front of him. "Lord, are you here again, Davie? Hasn't the ghost got you yet?"

"Wi' a few like that inside ye, ye'll be seein' more than ghosts," replied Davie.

Peter was immediately attracted by the voice, its lively Lowland inflection, its Border snap. Not the voice of a hillman, the voice of a tradesman rather, called in to do a job about the home steading.

As the banter proceeded, Peter became aware of something going on under the surface, of an argument that had already over nights run a considerable course; and because a point must be scored, a laugh raised, the forces underneath had to work nearer and nearer to the bone.

When the noise was harsh and merry, he got a quiet question into Alastair's ear, and, turning his back on the crowd, Alastair said that Davie and his two assistants sitting beside him were carpenters who had come from the south to do a contract job on Ardvannie estate. He was plainly disinclined to say much, but added that they found it difficult to get lodgings near their work and on being offered an empty cottage, free, as a place to doss in, they had jumped at the chance. "The cottage," concluded Alastair, very quietly and looking past Peter into the wall, "is said to be haunted."

Peter glanced at him and then at the faces in the bar.

Lachlan was plainly the arch joker on the Highland side, but against his tactic of a ghostly envelopment, Davie was ever ready with his thrust; and when he got home, the laughter burst forth.

"It's superstition that's wrong wi' ye, pure superstition— an' yer auld ministers wi' their hell an' damnation. Ye should gang oot intae the world an' see a bit o' civilisation for a change," suggested Davie.

"Some of us have seen a good bit of the world," replied Lachlan with a slow thoughtfulness. "But there's another world, and when it comes knocking on your door some night— you'll know it then. And I'll confess I wouldn't like to be there. It's no ordinary knock that comes to that door of yours."

"Is it loud?" asked Davie.

"You would think the house was coming down," said Lachlan.

"Is it wearin' trousers?" asked Davie, leading up to a rude thrust.

Old Sandy, the gillie, presently cleared the laughter and froth from his heavy brown moustache. "You're game, Davie. I'll say that for you. I wouldn't sleep in that cottage of yours not supposing you paid me a thousand pounds in my hand. But then, as you're saying, we're full of the superstition. I remember once—I was only a boy at the time, in Kinlochbervie —and that's where it happened . . ." And he proceeded to tell, with intimate vivid detail, the most gruesome ghost story that Peter had ever heard—or read in four languages. It made the air so thick that invisible things crawled in it and the barman forgot the time.

It reminded Lachlan of a young married woman and a fellow—but Davie ordered more beer loudly and Peter saw that the subtle assault was getting under his guard. And he could hardly be blamed for it. In a way Peter had quite forgotten, here was a dimension of being alive under the surface, where the characters moved like people under a spell, and the darkness was another kind of light. The compulsion under which they moved was quite fatal; and the more absurd the compulsion the more fatal. All of which Peter could have analysed and told at any time to a bunch of students: what he had forgotten was the dynamic movement in this extraordinary region, the something that sent out its ripple to shiver, to creep, upon the skin. As he looked round at the faces, too, he was aware of a manifestation of feeling, a variety of expression, so complex and subtle, and at the same time so hidden, that it was utterly beyond description, much less analysis. Lachlan, for example, seeing Davie did not wish to hear his story, went on telling it to Sandy, but in a voice politely and naturally lowered a little and though glasses moved and thumped, and voices spoke here and there and a short laugh rose, nothing was clearer than that ears were trying to catch the story and particularly the ears that for one fearful reason or another did not wish to hear it, until there was silence, when Lachlan, if anything, lowered his

68

voice to a still more confidential note. "So driven beyond himself one night with suspicion and jealousy he murdered his young wife. He kept her body all night but in the grey of the morning he carried it a mile and threw it into the Falls Pool." Lachlan described the shock that fell upon "the district", and the suspicion that fell upon the young "lover", but nothing could be proved; then one night, a fine clear night it was with a full moon, her voice was heard coming up out of the pool. Many people heard it after that and it was talked about, and then it was thought that if the husband himself came to the pool at the next full moon and listened he—and who better than he?—might know what she was trying to say. So the men of the district arranged it, the full moon came, they collected the husband and went. But naturally enough they did not stay with the husband by the edge of the Falls Pool, for this was something between a man and his wife. They kept out of sight, so that when the voice came up out of the waters——

"By Gode," interrupted Davie loudly, "it's no' oot o' water a voice like that comes, it's oot o' whisky!"

There was laughter then, and one voice cried, "You're just about right, Davie!"

Lachlan smiled, not in the least put out apparently. Sandy turned his pint in his hand thoughtfully, and as though they were still isolated from the others, asked, "What happened?"

"After allowing him a fair time with her they went back to find out." Lachlan stretched a hand for his beer and every eye in the place followed the hand. "They found him where they left him. But—he was mad."

Peter felt a broad dark hand over the room.

"Mad," breathed Sandy, looking at Lachlan with the wonder that says what comes to it, "mad—like Callum."

Peter felt the dark hand come down and grip his own heart with all the others.

But Davie pushed the table from him; its legs were harsh and one glass overturned. "Superstition, did I say? It's superstition *and* bloody ignorance. That's what's wrong wi' ye Highlanders. Now ye hev it."

The laughter was merry enough, and all the merrier to cover

69

the raw spot which Davie's thrust had at last reached. Peter could even see that Davie might have had a lot of direct support —if only he hadn't mentioned that word "ignorance".

"Perhaps we're bloody ignorant, too," said Lachlan smoothly, "only I would not advise you—in your position—to bank on it."

"Ye can leave me to ma position—I can cope wi't. When I need yer help I'll ask it."

"You'll get it," said Lachlan agreeably.

But the barman had looked at his watch and then in alarm at the inner door as if the proprietor would be upon him, not to mention the policeman waiting outside all this extra time for his own drink. As they crowded out, Peter was aware of a certain curious sympathy towards Davie. They chaffed him and his two assistants in a friendly way and when the three got on their bikes and set off on their three-mile ride, good-nights were called but not one remark about the cottage to which they were proceeding.

A three-quarter moon was in the sky among scattered cloud as Lachlan, Alastair, and Peter moved away together. Peter reassured Alastair, saying he had enjoyed the evening very much, even if he didn't usually mix beer with his whisky. But his mind, despite him, was still on that peculiar part of Lachlan's story where the men had taken the husband to listen to the wife's voice from the pool; there was something so profound about this communal action that he had not got to the bottom of it when the others stopped. Alastair bade them good-night and was moving off when Lachlan said, "By the way," and went a step or two with him. Peter stood and looked at the moon, swung his face along the sky and saw the mountain ridges high in the air beyond the hotel. The mountains of superstition. And he had mouthed the phrase for no more than the sound of it!

"We'll have to do something." Lachlan's voice had firmed a trifle and was just audible. "It wouldn't be difficult and you and me can keep our mouths shut."

"What . . . exactly?" There had been a peculiar reluctance upon the shepherd all evening and not once had he joined in the banter—though for that matter neither had Peter, who now found himself listening acutely for Lachlan's reply. And Lachlan replied:

"We'll be the ghost."

There was a distinct pause.

"How?"

"They know we're going to the sales . . . to-morrow . . . back very late . . . but we *could* be back at Davie's place before they got home from the pub . . . give them the one hell of a fright!"

Silence.

"They've asked for it and by God we'll give it to them!" added Lachlan.

"They're three hefty fellows," said Alastair at last.

"Look," said Lachlan, his voice firming still more. "You can take it from me Davie wouldn't have said yon about us being *ignorant* if he wasn't getting jumpy. You watch him when the ghost *does* knock!" His laughter was husky and rich.

Peter could feel Alastair's reluctance, his peculiar constraint. Again he muttered, almost automatically, "They are three hefty fellows."

"Once," replied Lachlan, "three hefty fellows tried to stop you in the desert and you got the Military Cross."

"That was easy." Alastair turned his head away.

After a moment, Lachlan asked, "Is it the ghost?"

"And if they saw us they would have the laugh on us. We would be the fools then."

"But they *won't* see us. That's the point. I know the place like the back of my hand. Take it from me, we'll have a grand-stand view."

Alastair's face came back from the mountains and saw Peter who now strolled away a pace or two. Within a minute Lachlan joined him and they set off along the cart road.

"You'll be thinking we are full of superstition and no mis-take," said Lachlan cheerfully.

"There was a fair amount of it in the air," Peter agreed. "Was it all a joke or is Davie really living in a haunted house?"

"He's living in one all right!" Lachlan laughed. Then his voice became confidential. "No one has lived in the place for ten years, not since Callum, the under-keeper who was last in

71

it, went crackers. But the spot has been haunted for a very long time. That's the yarn."

"Do you believe it yourself?"

"Och, you hear a yarn and you take it that same way. There's a lot in what Davie says—if only he wasn't so damn cocksure!"

Lachlan and Alastair were both rather tall men, but where Alastair had the slenderness of the shepherd, Lachlan, who worked his croft and did occasional carting and other jobs, was more heavily built, with straight powerful shoulders, and in colour ginger-brown against Alastair's rather remote darkness. He was perhaps a year or two older than the shepherd. Confidence and strength came out of him now with his warm breath.

"What form does the haunting take?" asked Peter.

"What's that?"

"What's the ghost like?"

"There's no ghost. There's just a knocking. That's the point. That's where we have them!" He was clearly delighted with his hidden scheme. "It's an old yarn—I mean the first of it; goes back to the days of the clan fights, if you believe all you hear. Heavy steps coming down the hillside behind the house—thud! thud! like a boulder—and a little afterwards you hear the knocking. When it happened the first time—back in that old days—the man who went to the door was stabbed by the fellow from the other clan. So finally they built a new house on the knoll—the one that's there now—thinking that would stop it. But no! The knocking can still come, but when you open the door there's no one there." The thing was as simple as that, no mystery about it.

"But—you mentioned Callum——"

Lachlan stopped to make matters still clearer. "You see, if you believe all that kind of stuff you get worked up. That's the whole thing. The knocking comes and you go to the door, and my God, there's nothing there. Do you see? So you go up in blue smoke. Callum was a nice chap, but a bit tender, quick in the temper. Him and Alastair were friendly enough as young fellows. That's why Alastair—well, he wasn't saying much, but I know damn fine; and you can trust him to your last breath, as well I should know. We've been in one or two tight corners

72

together and I've never seen death frighten him yet, not when he's really going."

As they went on again Peter for some mysterious reason felt thoroughly uncomfortable. To Alastair he could have spoken, but to this man, putting the night off his shoulders like a boat the sea, he could not even begin to hint that Davie should be left alone. Then he looked at the sky, at the waning moon, and smiled out of the drink he had taken, and thought he might as well go through the boundary of superstition as any other, for who knew what strange revelation might not be on the other side. At any rate, it was all source material! He saw Fand for a moment, remote and filmy thin as a piece of rainbow fading from a green hillside. In the mountains of superstition the well bubbles dark water. Lachlan staggered and said with solid satisfaction, "It was a good dram." Peter got a foot in the same wheel-rut and laughed.

IO

Mrs. Macrae was an excellent woman, lavishing upon her
house the care and attention which would hardly have been
less had she not lost her only child so far. But cheerfulness goes
with hope, thought Peter, as he wandered around Ardvannie,
with muscles stiffer than they had yet been, and when he
wondered if his right shoulder was beginning a first flirtation
with rheumatics, he remembered the burst vacuum flask, saw
it going down like a red star, and watched Fand howking in
the earth. To save Mrs. Macrae's rations, he had lunch in the
hotel, which was deserted—it was a good fishing day, overcast,
with a gentle breeze—except for two or three elderly ladies and
an old fellow, blown from much good living, with an acute
small eye and unobtrusive manners, whose life had been disrupted when he could no longer winter in the Madeiras.

Not until it was dark did he get really restless and then he
strolled as far as the hotel, saw three bikes leaning against the
engine house, listened unobserved to the voices within but felt
too shy to go in himself.

Three hours later, bursting with his exploit, full of a secretive-
ness which he impressed upon his guest—"My God, don't
say a word on your life!"—Lachlan told Peter in the stable
door, with a rich tracery of detail, what had happened at the
haunted cottage, and here in simple outline is the action as
Peter saw it.

The sporting estate of Ardvannie, with its red deer and
salmon on the lower pools, had its residence about three miles
west of the hotel. A London financier, deciding, doubtless, in
the current idiom of his circle, to use his capital while it was
still worth something, had bought it cheap over a year ago,

74

and as there were agricultural interests—hill sheep, timber, crofts, venison—had got the necessary permits to bring the productive side of the estate into reasonable repair. Hence Davie and his two men, to whom the estate agents in Edinburgh had made a tempting offer. And hence, perhaps, that easy consumption of beer on their part if only to help drown all the ghosts about. So much Peter had already gathered or interpreted from answers which his host—and hostess—had given to his questions. Thus the scene was set when Sergeant Macrae led his corporal, the shepherd, to the haunted cottage.

The cottage was on a bare knoll well up from the road, and as they stood in the fringe of birch trees looking across at it, listening, all they could hear was the sound of the river in the gorge beyond. Lachlan was taking no risks and stalked the door as he might an enemy observation post. It scraped as he pushed it open and he called, "In your bed, Davie?"

Once inside, he got the beam of his torch travelling around and laughed at the crude living arrangements of the three southern carpenters. What his wife would have said was beyond him. An open tin of salmon shook him to helplessness. "Out of a tin!" he said to Alastair, thinking of the living fish in the lower pools. They couldn't even poach!

Alastair whispered, "They should be here soon."

"Come on, then!"

They hauled themselves up into the loft or attic of the simple cottage and closed the trap-door behind them. The boards were loose and rattled under their feet, but Lachlan, stooping, knew his way about and presently had Alastair squatting beside him. "Look!" And he directed his beam through a crack into the living room below. It was certainly a grand-stand view.

"Queer smell," muttered Alastair.

"Mildew, rot. No one has lived here since Callum——"

"You'll knock here?"

"That's the idea. Remember me saying to him that he would think the house was coming down?"

"Yes."

"You see the point of it now? It came to me then. It's miraculous, fool-proof—because no one ever saw anything!"

"You think not?"

"It's what Callum didn't see that did it; that's what put him off his head. He was all strung up. The knocking came, he pulled the door open, but there was nothing there. That's what got him."

"I suppose so."

"You see, he had been expecting something awful, terrific, something he could have lammed into, for with his temper up he was headlong enough. But—there was nothing. It was the *nothing*."

"He did not look like a man who saw nothing."

"That's the point. He really *saw* nothing. Haven't you got it yet?"

"Perhaps there was something in the nothing."

"What?"

"Evil."

"You believe in the knocking?"

"Would *you* live here alone?"

"I might," answered Lachlan. Then curious to learn what had really been troubling his corporal, he asked, "You believe it's the evil left behind from—what happened long ago?"

"It may be that."

"That's really why you didn't want to come?"

"Yes."

"I see. I didn't think you——" He stiffened. "They're coming." After a while he breathed, "Did you hear anything?"

"I heard something."

But nothing came to the door—and nothing knocked.

"Davie will be having an extra pint or two—and everything his own way!" said Lachlan.

When the three carpenters at last hove within earshot their reality, their sounds, were thick with comfort. Alastair's gulping breath could be heard. Lachlan himself decided that life could provide worse things than a rough and tumble with your living fellow man, and had real difficulty in keeping himself from laughing when Davie burnt his fingers with the match that didn't light the candle. Walter, the black-haired youth of twenty-one, who had played the melodeon so well at a local soiree and dance, lit it for him. All three looked so glum and hungry that Lachlan knew they were cold from too much beer, cold and disgruntled at coming back to such a hole. Davie sliced the lump of salmon into three crumbling chunks and Jimmy hacked the loaf of bread. Hardly a word was spoken and Walter gloomed at the salmon with distaste, then turned to the ashen fireplace as if he would give a lot for hot sobering tea. Davie and Jimmy began to eat. Walter sat down reluctantly and tore the crust from his hunk of bread.

Up above Lachlan lifted the end of a loose board about an inch and let it clip back on the joist.

It was a sharp but not a loud knock. Watching them through the crack, Lachlan saw that each had heard the sound but pretended to have heard nothing. It was one of the most laughable things he had ever seen. None looked at the others. It was like an uncanny play. Davie scooped some salmon up and nearly missed his mouth. Walter's hand fell weak on the crust. Jimmy's eyes switched and gleamed against the candle.

Lachlan nudged Alastair with his elbow, then noiselessly lifted the floor-board inch by inch, up and up until it stuck; he saw a section of Alastair's face in the dim shafted light and let the board go.

It fell with so resounding a knock that it acted on the cottage like a fantastic trigger, releasing the carpenters, upsetting the chairs, sending the candle spinning, ejecting holy oaths and ugly yells and a scream that was plainly Walter's. There was congestion at the door, a final smashing pandemonium, then yells dying distantly, and silence and darkness below.

Lachlan could hardly breathe where he sat, much less laugh.

"There was something ugly in it," he said to Peter. "We left the place without saying a word." He began to laugh softly, from the stomach. "God knows what I had expected—but hardly yon. But as I said to Alastair when we got to our bikes, 'There will be less talk about our bloody ignorance now!'"

77

Mrs. Macrae's voice was heard calling him.

"Come on," whispered Lachlan, "we'll go in. Not a word, for heaven's sake—even to Alastair. He'll look in for us to-morrow night." Then lifting his voice for his wife's benefit he said, "There's no rain on that sky."

II

The following night Alastair turned up rather late, and when they got to the hotel bar, Davie and his crew were not there. Hadn't they heard the news?

"What news?" asked Lachlan.

"About Davie and the ghost," said Sandy. "The ghost attacked them last night and wrecked the place. It's like a battlefield——"

"Look, Sandy," interrupted Lachlan, "you should know me well enough not to try to pull my leg as easy as that." He turned to the barman, but Peter was before him.

"But lord, boy, it's a fact," said Sandy in so charged a voice that Lachlan cast his sceptical eye over the other faces; and the glistening constraint in these faces gave him pause.

"I have been east at the quarry all day," he began, still watching them for evidence of a leg-pull, when Sandy, realising that he had his incredible story to tell to fresh ears, grew restless where he sat.

And it was certainly a remarkable story when the bits and pieces, the questions and answers, were added together. It was not that the ghost had simply knocked on the door: the whole house had rocked under the knocking, the light was blown out, the table had risen and hit Davie in the stomach, the way to the door was turned round and the door itself was held—until Davie wrenched it from its hinges.

In the full spate of his story, Sandy, holding all eyes, went on, "Davie and Jimmy made for the road and crossed the bridge; but young Walter he took the straight way to Cameron the keeper's house, right through behind the knoll and down over the rocks into the gorge where he slipped and had to

79

swim for it. He clawed his way up the other side, wet to his
eyebrows, and might still have been all right if only he had
gone direct to the keeper's house, but when he came to the
old ruined stables he stopped. He didn't know where the others
had gone. He had lost them, and he didn't know what the hell
to do. The keeper's house was dark. Perhaps some queer thing
in him made him ashamed to go. God knows. Davie and Jimmy
had meanwhile gone round by the bridge and come up to
Cameron's house where they get their dinner every day. Davie
knocked Cameron up and told him what had happened. They
waited a long time for Walter but no sign of him. Then they
became alarmed, for the gorge is a nasty enough place even in
the daylight. They got a lantern. They went back to the road.
They shouted. And I'm telling you they were sticking together,
for the night now had sounds enough of its own. In the end,
they found him by the up side of the old stables. He couldn't
speak. His teeth were going like rattles. He was the nearest
thing to a ghost the keeper himself had ever seen. And a ghost
with something very queer in the white of his face."

"Good God!" said Lachlan.

Alastair finished his whisky in one gulp.

"He was quite biddable as they took him to the house,"
Davie continued, "and they gave him hot whisky and put him
into Cameron's own warm bed. Cameron's niece, Betsie, got
hot water bottles, for his teeth were still going. I was out early
this morning making a lead patch for the bottom of the fishing
boat on Loch Rogain, when Cameron came in on his bike to
ring up the hotel telephone for the doctor. And by God I knew
it was no ordinary illness that would bring the same man to
do that. But not a word did he say until he had put the call
through. Then he told me."

"Well, of all things," said Lachlan, convinced at last, "little
did we think! And did the doctor come?"

"Yes, but he had been out at a confinement and didn't turn
up till near eleven. I said the boat on Loch Rogain couldn't
be ready that day, for I began to think now she might need
more than lead on her bottom, and I was working on a bit of
planking when the doctor drove up and asked me if the turn

up to the keeper's house was on this side of the river or the other side; so in case he might miss his way I went with him, I didn't say a word to anyone, because it's not the kind of thing you want hotel guests putting their noses into. So off we set, and just before we came to Cameron's house, there was Davie and Jimmy hammering away on top of the new building for the electric plant. They hardly let on they saw us. I had been telling the doctor about the whole thing, for he's able when it comes to understanding anyone who's going a bit queer, as you know, and he didn't laugh. He took it quite natural, and asked me some questions, and searchers they were. Cameron was waiting for us outside and looking as if wondering what the hell had been keeping us. The doctor told him about the confinement and they went into the house. Man, I wanted then to go back and have a word with Davie, but I thought better of it. At long last the doctor came out and we drove off but he didn't say a word. Before I could ask him how Walter was he stopped, and got out, and went across and called Davie and Jimmy down. He had a long talk with them and though I could not hear what was said I could see that the doctor soon put confidence into Davie and had him talking sixteen to the dozen. My God, you could see the talk doing Davie good, loosening him up like medicine, as sure as death. Then the doctor came back and as we drove off I asked him how Walter was, and he said in that easy cool style of his, 'He's in a pretty bad way. I'd like to have a look at that cottage.' So we turned left on the main road, crossed the bridge, and drew in by the old track going up to the cottage. And that," said Sandy, "is how I can tell you what the inside of the cottage was like," and he told them over again with all the old gillie's eye for detail. But what clearly still impressed him was the care with which the doctor had examined everything; he produced the doctor's summing up with an air and obviously verbatim: " 'An elemental force has been here all right'." Then he leaned back.

"Astonishing!" said Lachlan. He wiped his mouth with the back of his hand. "And the doctor didn't say what's wrong with Walter?"

"He did, for I asked him. Walter has got it solid in both lungs, with high fever. He said it's a case of touch and go— for there's something else that's worse."

"Worse?"

"The doctor used long words like—like psychological, but I asked him if it was the ghost on Walter's mind and he said 'Exactly'."

Alastair got up and, forgetting the wooden chair behind his legs, upset it. He ordered three large whiskies. Peter glanced at him, knowing the hole it would make in a week's wages, but Lachlan paid no attention. And the barman gave him the whisky. Usually, after the first round of the rationed whisky, they had beer. But when the whisky was placed before Lachlan, he looked at it and said to Sandy, "You can see the prices were good at the sales yesterday."

There was a small smile of relief all round and Lachlan followed it up. "I'm sorry for young Walter. Right enough, I'm sorry to hear it. And I bet you Davie isn't so sure now that we're ignorant. You can't go over the score without paying for it. What do you think, Mr. Munro?"

"It's an extraordinary business," said Peter. "I have heard learned men discuss the Ghost in Shakespeare's play, Hamlet— but it's a different matter when . . . It makes you wonder if, in fact, there are more things in heaven and earth than we have dreamt of." He smiled, for this was not what he had wanted to say; the words sounded empty, literary, pompous, and he was quite taken by surprise at the effect they had on Sandy. In no time the air of exaggeration, of banter, was lost, and they were in the deeps where spirits move.

The more Peter evoked the world of learning—and it was about the only thing he could do involuntarily, without think- ing—the more Sandy enjoyed being impressed, and for much the same reason as old Phemie had dropped her egg before a living professor: the ancient tradition of the love of learning ran with their marrow and articulated their stiffest joints. From China to Peru, from Jerusalem to Ardvannie, the ghost had roamed the world of man; from the time before the written word was, down through all literatures, the ghost made its

82

appearance and troubled the soul. Whatever else it was, it was no local superstition.

It was like jotting down notes for a lecture and even while he was talking—egged on by Sandy and conscious of wanting to please Sandy—he was aware of a dreadful automatism in scholarship, an abstraction without marrow, because of the presence of Alastair and Lachlan. His words were going in at their ears, but immediately beyond the ears they were taken possession of by powers he only half understood and more than half feared; they were caught and channelled into the dark centre of each being, with its nucleus of the unpredictable act. This impression was very vivid.

Steadily pushing its way forward, demanding his attention, came the thought that by giving the ghost a position in history he was by implication giving it one in reality, and now somehow he would have to get the balance even, or confuse the issue, or in some way so treat the living situation before him that the effect upon the conduct of Lachlan and Alastair would be healthy. When complication was being piled on subtlety, and watchful eyes were hunting beneath the words, the barman called "Time!"

Outside, as happened before, Lachlan said, "By the way," and followed Alastair. In his two or three strides, such a force came alive as caught Peter's breath.

"Not a word," said Lachlan in a hissing voice. "Don't breathe one word to a living soul."

"Oh, I won't say a word," replied Alastair.

"Put it out of your mind as if it had never happened. That's the only way."

"Yes."

Peter thought he heard the gulp in Alastair's throat.

"No man can mend anything by blethering. What's done is done, and they damned well asked for it."

"They did."

"*Whatever* happens, we know nothing."

It was like a swirl below the surface of a bottomless pool.

12

The following day Peter got to know that swirl well. Lachlan found odds and ends to do about the small steading, but whether mending a bridle in the stable door or hammering a new post into a fence, his eyes would lift and search the landscape. He became very confidential with Peter. It's not that he didn't trust Alastair, he explained; far from it; and he looked about him as if he didn't even trust the shadow he couldn't see. When he spoke, his face remained expressionless, the muscles hardly moved, the bone was very firm, only the eyes lived. Confidential, friendly, thinking thoughts beyond the words, and prepared in some region of his own to move, when the time came, with a ruthless thoroughness.

Peter was glad to get away. He went all of three miles on to the moors in the hope that he would fall in with the shepherd. The meeting must appear as casual as the talk that would follow, for he had to find out first what was really worrying Alastair, and then—what then? The very question scattered his thoughts and left him staring. What was worrying Alastair was so beyond any question of courage that he could not come anywhere near it and felt weighed down by anxiety, an ominous anxiety which could not be formulated by an utmost effort of his will; for which, in a way that distressed him, there were no words.

But he saw no sign of the shepherd and by the time he reached the hotel, lunch was over. However, he was served and satisfied himself that the old boy of the Madeiras, who was going aloft for his nap, and the elderly ladies with their needles had heard nothing. And for some obscure reason this increased his anxiety.

In the late afternoon, he sat for a long time by the stone sheepfank at the foot of a slope some two miles inland from the hotel and out of sight of the last house, but the shepherd never came; then he went back to the croft and met Lachlan's face that read his own before he spoke. It was as though Lachlan had known exactly why and where he had wandered.

"The news is not too good," Lachlan remarked quietly. "According to the district nurse, Walter's condition is 'very low'."

Peter's mouth went dry in a few breaths.

What happened thereafter may be told simply enough, for at one time or another Peter got it all from Lachlan.

By devious ways Lachlan found himself that evening by the shepherd's door. Alastair's wife was feeding the hens so late that they were coming scurrying from their roosts.

"Is Alastair about?" he asked in his easy casual way.

"He went over to the fank about an hour ago. I tried to keep him in but he wouldn't." She was strained and anxious. "He's sickening for something and can't take his food."

"It'll be that chill on the stomach that's going the rounds. I said as much to him last night."

"I don't know I'm sure. When I mentioned getting the doctor he near took my head off."

"There's not much wrong with him in that case," laughed Lachlan. "Don't you worry. I was wanting to see him about the cow, for I'm blest if I know what's the matter with her."

After five minutes he got away and when he reached the fank found Alastair sitting on a stone with his two collies moving uneasily around. There were no sheep and Alastair's face looked pale in the gathering gloom.

"Fine evening," said Lachlan.

Alastair got up; his shoulders came against the wall and he looked up the hillside. There was a wildness in his expression, a strange fiery light in his eyes.

"You're not worrying, are you?" asked Lachlan quietly.

Alastair stuck his long crook in the grass, pulled it out, and glanced up the hillside again.

85

Lachlan realised that the fellow was going to bits. "It was only a joke. We can't mend it."

"I'm not blaming anyone but myself," said Alastair. "I knew."

Lachlan lost direction for a few seconds. "When young Walter will get better the whole thing will blow over. There's no need for us ever to say anything about it."

"And if he doesn't get better?" Alastair's eyes came on him for a moment; then they were off.

Lachlan weakened at the knees as if he had been hit. "Dammit, man," he said, "there's nothing we can do. If anything happened to Walter they'd have us up for manslaughter. Lord, man, think of your wife if no one else. We can't go talking now. Pull yourself together for God's sake."

"I'm not so sure we couldn't do nothing."

"What?"

Alastair moved restlessly on his feet but did not take his eyes from the hillside.

"What?" repeated Lachlan, with remorseless persistence. "Look, Alastair, we have been in some tight corners together. But if you say one bloody word about this I'll smash you up. You were never a coward, and by God I'll see you're not going to be one now." He stood out from the wall with clenched fists.

Alastair's eyes came on him again and this time his mouth was twisted. "You would let him die?"

"Die bedamned! What are you talking about?"

"You would let the ghost sit on his mind and kill him?"

Lachlan missed a breath. "Ghost! There was no ghost. There never was a ghost. There was *nothing*. You know that."

Alastair looked at him again with the same strange eyes. "I saw the nothing—that Callum saw." Then he glanced at his dogs and walked off. With their heads and tails down, they followed him.

Lachlan stood unable to move. Anger, passion, so obsessed him that when the destructive oaths came they were fierce.

The following day young Walter was still alive. With drugs the doctor had got his temperature under control, but the general condition of the patient, said the nurse, was still not only "low" but "very disturbing". Her words so impressed the postmistress who kept the small general shop that they lost nothing when retailed with the rations. Mystery deepened. The doctor's expression "elemental force" was going its secret rounds with more deadly effect than any microbe had yet achieved.

And all day Peter could see Lachlan trying to keep Alastair under observation. He could see it from wherever he was sitting. It was exactly as though a dark and ruthless fight was going on between their minds while their bodies appeared and disappeared, attending to outside tasks, slowly moving here and there over the landscape. Then at last Peter thought he could intercept Alastair, but at two hundred yards Alastair swung away as though he had not seen him, and Peter stood unable to lift a shout. The doctor's car passed, going home.

Peter made up his mind that he would tackle Lachlan. He came upon him round the corner of a dike; he was staring at the far hillside. Peter heard a muttered oath and knew that Lachlan was pinning his man where he wanted him, pinning him back against the heather, choking him to silence with a fistful of dark oaths. Lachlan was conquering. Peter kicked a stone and, when Lachlan turned, started talking about the weather.

Lachlan's mood eased and he began laughing, a low husky laughter, with an icy twinkle in the eye above. Peter felt utterly lost.

"He's thinking better of it," said Lachlan, "if I'm not mistaken."

The casual humour blotted Peter's mind out.

Just after he had fallen asleep that night Peter was awakened by a knocking on the front door. In no time Lachlan had the door open and was talking to Alastair's wife.

Alastair had got out of bed over an hour ago and had not come back. So much Peter heard with his own ears. What followed he was told by Lachlan in the very early morning, but in such stress of stark emotion that the simple record of deeds and words, as subsequently clarified in his mind, may best be set down here in consecutive order.

Lachlan, then, led Alastair's wife home and did his best to comfort her. It was the human situation he could understand and meet with a natural warmth. "The chances are he has gone to the keeper's house to see how young Walter is. The crisis, the nurse said, was expected tonight."

"But what has he got to do with—that?"

"We all have to do with it in a way." And he told her of the talk that had been going on about the haunted cottage and of how the carpenters had "asked for it". "Alastair must have taken it to heart, the foolish fellow. That's all. He had no more to do with it than me. Less, indeed, for he wouldn't make even a child uncomfortable, as well you know. Leave it to me, and I'll go after him, and don't say a word to anyone."

In a little while Lachlan was back and on his bicycle, heading for the doctor's house five miles away, for, as he argued, the only one to whom a sane man could talk would be the doctor. None but a madman would go to a patient on the point of death. But he did not overtake Alastair, and the doctor's house, which stood back from the road, was in complete darkness.

As Lachlan started back a grim anger grew in him. He would not let himself think of what might be going on at the keeper's house lest the anger thicken to wrath and choke him. He should have hit Alastair at the fank. A fight would have brought him to himself, the fool. "I'll show him more than *nothing*," muttered Lachlan, sweating as he drove his old machine up the hills under the risen moon.

After stalking the keeper's house and getting no glimpse of Alastair's dogs he stared for long minutes at the yellow light in one window. He did not want to rouse the keeper's dogs, but as he was completing the circuit of the house they started an infernal barking. Presently the district nurse came to the front door, peered around, and withdrew. Plainly there was no man on his feet inside. Old Cameron would already have been out.

Back on the main road, Lachlan stood in thought. Alastair might have gone off his head. That fiery light in his eyes as he looked up the hillside . . . Within twenty minutes he had dumped his bike behind a bush and was making for the sheep-fank. Arriving there, he stared up the hillside. Alastair had gone crazy and taken to the hills. He started to climb.

It was heavy going for the heart, but time was slipping and he had to push on, had to find the fellow, and even if he had fallen and broken his blasted neck one or other of his dogs would be there. Jess would come to meet him. . . .

But no dog greeted him and as he got up in the folds of the hills wild life scurried or crashed in a way that did not help his heart. Two burning eyes and the scream of a child being murdered turned into an owl. His wrath became a half-demented fury that wanted to shout—but didn't. He came out on the mountain ridge.

Far as his eye could travel under a half moon were the peaks and dim horizons of a sterile world. Its breath shocked his heated skin, sent shivers over it. He plunged on and down, crossed a running burn, with hand-holds got round a rocky bluff, stumbled on a boulder that went thud! thud! down the steep slope and followed it headlong.

His senses came back to him with a feeling of unearthly clarity even while he hardly knew where he was and shivered till his teeth clicked. The moon, just over the ridge, was watching him. This extraordinary feeling of a cold clarity had completely dissipated the dark congested wrath; clear as the moon it was, bright as steel, and right through him. Of all that happened to him that night this was the thing he could least explain. For in a sense there was nothing to explain. Yet the effect was much as if he had got a new cold skin on his face.

However, at the time it did anything but worry him and for the simple reason that it made everything much clearer not only outside his mind but inside it. And with the clarity came a feeling of almost miraculous competence.

.He knew his country well and in no time realised that if he kept going down, within sound of the burn, he would cross another stream which emptied into it and in due course reach the lower ground which flattened out round the haunted cottage: that was the outside of the argument; the inside part was equally assured and already unanswerably completed: it would be far better for Alastair to be dead than mad, better for everyone. He even thought of Alastair's wife and what she would be saved.

An extra knock on the head as he fell and he himself would have been dead. It was easy—and painless.

No suggestion of evil was present at all. Not a single lurking thought. Everything was crystal clear, and so certain that he knew nothing could stand against him.

Then his thought, as it were, went out beyond himself and in the instant he was quite sure that Alastair was in the haunted cottage. The certainty of this almost astonished him not by its unexpectedness but by its sheer certainty.

Only once before had this sort of clarity come to him, though in nothing like the same degree; it was on a night patrol and he had crept on the enemy and destroyed him without a sound.

He took his time, going carefully but steadily. After starting some deer out of a hollow of small birch trees, he stood still for quite a while, staring with a concentrated blankness as if trying to hear sounds beyond the tumbling water. To get away from the noise of the water, which somehow obscured the clearness in his head, he took the slope to his left. The light now had a different quality and he realised that the daylight was coming over the hilltops.

When he rounded the last crag and glanced across at the cottage on the knoll the grey dawn was about it and it looked as still as something not quite on this earth. And this too was right. A low threatening growl brought his head round and he saw one of Alastair's dogs by a near patch of bracken. It was Jess, the black collie bitch with the white star on her chest. Her head was down, her eyes on him, her fangs bare and the hair on the back of her neck upright.

Although he had played with the dog from her puppyhood he felt no surprise, nor did he attempt to placate the brute in any way. His hand went into a pocket and withdrew a black-handled knife. With the blade ready, he moved sideways, keeping below the rim of the knoll. The dog followed, trying to get behind his back, away from his eyes. In this way he more than half-circled the cottage until at last he came opposite the doorway. He made no futile lunge at the dog, and in the same slow remorseless way, stepping quietly, reached the sagging broken door. His eyes on the dog he knocked loudly on the wood; as the footsteps came his eyes switched and encountered the doctor, who stood looking at him strangely.

Lachlan's hands fell slowly to his side.

"Come in," said the doctor.

Alastair's face in the gloom was the colour of the old white-wash on the walls. It looked drained and timeless. Lachlan sat down heavily.

"This is very extraordinary," said the doctor, standing between them, a little way back, his face to the small window. His eyes were on Lachlan who now stirred sluggishly and, with a fumbling hand, put the open knife in his jacket pocket.

"You'd better shut the blade," suggested the doctor.

"The dog," muttered Lachlan. He pricked his hand getting the knife out, shut the blade, put it back in his pocket and wiped the drop of blood against his knee.

"The sight of the dog astonished myself," said the doctor, "when I came round to have another look at the cottage and found the shepherd before me." His tone was cool and light. "He has been telling me about your practical joke."

Lachlan said nothing; did not look at the doctor.

But the doctor's eyes were on him, moving over him. "You'll be glad to hear that the young carpenter, Walter, has got through the crisis and should, short of a relapse, which is now hardly likely, be all right. I've just been talking to him. His mind is quite clear again. He'll be all right, I should say."

Lachlan tried to say something but only a vague grunt came out of him.

"I can see—it's been an awkward time for you both," said the doctor, as if someone had to speak. "You touched off . . . some pretty hefty stuff."

Lachlan could feel the doctor's eyes moving over him and the cottage sagging down.

"I've been having a long talk with the shepherd," continued the doctor. "I have come across fair samples of courage in my time, but I think his notion of coming here to try to take the evil upon himself and face it out, so that the carpenter might be rid of it, is just about as good as any I have struck. And I'm the last man to say there's nothing in it. I'm even wondering if it was his concentration that drew me and not just more curiosity about something I'm very interested in."

Lachlan stirred sluggishly; sickness balled in his chest.

"I don't know about ghosts," proceeded the doctor; "I have never seen one myself. But I know their effects. And—it's just a question, an open question, whether evil does in fact exist; not only that, but whether it may even enter a material body with the devil to pay."

Lachlan was now dourly holding on, keeping the sickness back, stopping the bog from sucking him under.

The doctor said some more words, but Lachlan hardly heard them. He was like a man after a heavy bout of drinking. The congestion was in his face. It was difficult to keep his body from sagging. His head lifted and he saw Alastair sitting upright, light and disembodied looking.

"Come along," said the doctor, suddenly and clearly. "I'll give you a lift home."

Lachlan staggered once or twice and when they reached the car the doctor produced a small flask of brandy.

As Lachlan wiped away what dribbled over his chin, the doctor said, "I advise you both to keep the joke to yourselves— at any rate until the carpenters leave. Enough has been stirred up to be going on with." His eyelids flickered. "As Highlanders you ought to have the sense to let a ghost lie."

Lachlan spoke for the first time when they drew near the spot where he had left his bicycle. As he got out he thanked the doctor but without looking at him. Alastair and his collie got out also.

The doctor put his face over the window ledge. "You can trust me," he said and drove off.

13

Lachlan took a few steps off the road to the bush where he had left his bike and as he stooped to haul it out was overcome. The bout of sickness was violent.

Alastair went across and in a quiet friendly way said, "Take your time."

His head between his knees, Lachlan shuddered; then sat still.

Alastair got down beside him. "I never told you—I never told a soul—that I saw Callum come to the door. It's ten years ago exactly." His voice was drained like his face, but there was a composure upon him, a curious ease. "You'll remember Finlay, who was killed in the war. Him and me had gone out long before daybreak to poach a deer. I didn't want to go, because Callum and myself had always been friendly, and after all it was his job. However, Finlay had got the rifle and I went, for I thought that if Callum did come on him alone God knows what might happen, for they were both short in the temper. We went well west, up round the foot of Ben Bhreck, but saw nothing. We were coming back across the high slopes above Callum's, intending to cut home by the sheepfank, when we heard thudding sounds and thought it was Callum. I never felt so terrified in my life. We lost our heads and came straight down for the road. But in the fringe of trees, where you and me the other night stood looking over at the cottage, I stopped. My legs wouldn't carry me another step. I was hanging on to a tree staring across at the door when the door opened and Callum appeared in his shirt. He never saw me. He looked at something in the air. It was not a yell he let out, it was a sort of scream. He had heard the knocking. There was a minute when I didn't know where I was, then I was running like a madman."

Alastair stopped and turned his face to Lachlan.

A fresh shudder went over Lachlan and his head shook and lowered as if another lump of stuff was coming up. He retched for a little and then Alastair got a palm under his forehead and helped him to an easy seat, saying, "It's not one queer hole we've been in."

"It was the worst," muttered Lachlan.

"Never mind. We worked it out and beat it."

Lachlan saw Alastair's hand coming to him and gripped it and held on.

"I'd better be moving, boy," said Alastair presently. "My wife will be wondering what on earth has happened to me. But the good news about Walter will help. You're all right now?"

"Fine," said Lachlan. "Go you."

Alastair went across the rough grazing with Jess running quietly at his heels.

Lachlan sat on. He had never looked at Alastair.

When Alastair was out of sight, Peter got up from behind a clump of whin and strolled across to Lachlan who lifted his head and stared.

Peter smiled and sat down beside him. "I heard the car coming and ducked out of sight. I've been looking around for you. I didn't want to go back and say I hadn't seen you."

Lachlan shivered. "God, it's cold," he said.

"Let's get home," said Peter. "I squeezed a bottle of whisky out of the hotel last night. I could do with one."

It took Lachlan a while to come to himself; on the way to his house he said little. Peter got him to have a few words with his wife; and presently in his bedroom poured him the better part of a tumbler of whisky. Lachlan sat on the only chair and Peter on the bed.

By degrees, Lachlan told him the whole story of his night's doings. The way it came out of him aroused in Peter an insight that at times was almost uncomfortably clairvoyant. Occasionally he was oppressed by a sensation of bulk, of groping blindness, in the man's personality. Yet every physical thing was seen by Lachlan with acuteness, and the immediate motive in a mind

94

was so clear to him that he could deal with it at once, as he had dealt with Alastair's wife. He was not only physically strong, he was also mentally cunning. Yet when he went beyond this he was lost and his strength became a sort of childish weakness, a bulk without direction, staring blind.

"God knows what I would have done." This of course was what was worrying him.

Peter knew that he would not help matters by trying to reassure Lachlan quickly with a flow of friendly words. That would in the end send Lachlan away with the dark burden more heavily upon him than ever; and the devil alone knew what internal festering would begin to poison him then.

"Odd, that sudden clearness in the head you got almost as if —it wasn't you at all for a while. Tell me this about it. For we're all mortal and heaven knows when any one of us . . . Here, let me put a drop more in your glass."

They talked for a long time and subtly Peter tried to lift the particular into the universal, spreading the dark burden of mystery in life over all mankind. And as time went on and they drew together, the "mystery of life" became more than words. What normally would have been the merest platitudes, making Peter acutely uncomfortable, were now almost religious in their profundity. That there were "more things in heaven and earth" became a truth so literal that it had a shattering effect, actually brought the mind into a realm where it silently exploded and no more thinking could be done. Yet there *was* that realm. They could not see it, they knew nothing about it, yet they were conscious of being in it. It was like the silence he had listened to on the hilltop above the Picts Houses, a silence that was more than an absence of sound. The mind knew this; the mind found something other than the silence; yet would not have found it except in that particular silence. At the lowest, it had the suggestion of exploration, of going into a realm beyond. And as always over an actual experience, scepticism is tiresome because irrelevant. As man did not know the answers to the old eternal questions about the mystery and the meaning, there remained what had not been dreamt of in all his philosophies; it was as simple as that: a little exercise in logic; an appalling

95

platitude; a truth so profound that to become self-conscious about it for an instant was to blow its flame out.

The flame grew white and clear, and the whisky fed it.

"God knows what I would have done." It came back like a refrain. It had meaning behind meaning. It was complex beyond all analysis.

"I'll tell you what you would have done," said Peter.

Lachlan looked at him, and because he had been avoiding the direct look all night, his blue eyes had not a penetration but a sort of flat blind impact. Peter felt them physically.

"If Alastair had been in the cottage alone when you went to the door and knocked, you would have done no more to him than you did to the doctor."

Lachlan's eyes gathered penetration as the muscles in the face stiffened into an ironic expression at once weak and bitter; then the face turned aside.

"Listen," said Peter. "I know I am right. And now I'll tell you why, I'll tell you what you have forgotten. The Alastair who would have come to the door would not have been the Alastair you were expecting to meet."

The eyes came back to his face.

"In an instant you would have known that Alastair was all right. You would have seen that he was no longer troubled. You would have realised this at once. It's the kind of thing *you* see."

Peter's smile was searching, meeting the Lachlan who was now looking at him. How Lachlan reacted was a matter for himself. Here was the truth.

"More than that," said Peter. "There is a—a spiritual something in Alastair. Something of the spirit. Heaven knows what he had gone through, sitting there. But he had gone through it." He paused—and stared out the window.

"What?" muttered Lachlan.

"God knows," said Peter. "It eludes me; why exactly he did it. It's medieval. It's—I don't know." He tried again, his brows gathering, his eyes far-sighted. "It was a contest with the evil he spoke of. The doctor may be right in saying that he was trying to draw it away from Walter. There may have been something of that in it. But—that's not exactly why, in the first place. I don't know—perhaps Alastair himself didn't quite know—it's terribly difficult, but I have the sort of feeling that Alastair wanted to meet what Callum and Davie met. He felt himself to blame and he was going to take the same gruel. And if in the process he could defeat the evil thing . . ." Peter leaned back and finished his whisky. His hand trembled.

"You think so?" The words were watchful yet expressionless.

"What I do know," answered Peter, switching a piercing look at Lachlan, "is this: *you* would have felt it, you would have *seen* that Alastair had come through, and your hands would have dropped as surely as you're sitting there."

Lachlan looked into the wall of the bedroom; then he said, "Christ, it was a terrible thing."

Peter's eyes were drawn to the man's hands; they looked naked; big powerful hands with the bare wrists showing. "It was a terrible thing," he agreed.

In the silence they heard Mrs. Macrae moving around. Peter wondered vaguely if she had been listening. The broad day was on the world.

"I'm keeping you from your bed," said Lachlan in a voice thick but quiet.

"You'll go to your own bed," said Peter. "And here's a last dram to make you sleep."

When he got between the sheets Peter knew he could never sleep. The metaphysical wheels were turning in regions fine with light, thin with excitement. He assumed his normal posture for sleep. There had been a time when Lachlan might have gone maudlin. He had seen it coming; that terrible sentimental slough . . . Before his thought could touch the slough, without a single movement of his body, he fell into a deep sleep.

97

14

The following day Peter took the road, assuring his hosts that he would be back, perhaps sooner than they expected. Lachlan walked with him for nearly a mile, talking of everyday things, until Peter wouldn't let him come any farther.

"Well I can only thank you," said Lachlan, his eyes to the hills.

"The thanks are mine," said Peter, putting out his hand. "And you were right about the weather."

"Oh, it's going to keep up. You'll have a good day."

And so they parted.

Peter's heart lifted. He began to smile to himself. If Fand had been with him he would have moved her to song. Or she would have mocked him. He looked at the blue above, at the small white clouds like floating blossoms. She would be howking at the old earth this day! When he found the well at the world's end, would he be able to carry the crystal water all the way in his cupped hands? He could hardly bring it in a bottle—though a bottle had its uses.

He would have to find her something sheer out of life that would take her breath away. "I'll find it," he said, "or, like Alastair . . ."

The haunted cottage rose in his mind and when he crossed the bridge he began to look out for the side path. There it was, complete with impression of a tyre where the doctor's car had drawn up. He stopped but only for a moment. He didn't want to be discovered nosing about there now. He would come back to it.

Or should he? The idea of spending a night in the cottage had come to him when he had wakened. It had seemed not only right then but inevitable. The whole thing had to be cleaned up, and it couldn't be cleaned up in theory. That's what he was finding out. No one can go through the boundary for someone else. Afterwards he would be able to talk with Alastair, even drop in on the doctor. Not before.

It was such a lovely day that dark thoughts should be sunk in their own black hole. Birches clung to the hillside; a covey of them in a hollow let branches fall like long veils from their heads: figures caught into silence, into an immortal hour in a poetic play by a long-dead Gaelic poet. No wonder! But, Lord, what grace! He stood and looked at them. Their faces to the earth, the earth of ancient days. The veils moved in a playful eddy and sighed.

Before their beauty could trouble him too much he went on. The urge to lift his voice in song came upon him. He felt like a voyageur . . . saw the Spanish road . . . trolled a note or two and lifted his tweed hat as it were a sombrero—and looked behind him. But it was not such a good game without Fand.

As he went marching on he saw her that first time. She was all vivid life at a tea table in a student resort near the university. The yellow or pale gold into which the years had lightened her hair had then a suggestion, a warmth, of bronze. She was alive and gave out life to her companions. The warmth came into her fair skin, the fairness that is so different from milk and roses and comes to a radiant suffused glow from within. Her lips were a wet red from animation. Girls had not yet started wearing cosmetics. She was dressed in green, apple green or grass green —though to remember tints was beyond him—but green it was —as quick upon the eye as the green of young birches. It matched her. It went—and this was what withdrew her from him into impossible latitudes—with her sense of style, of distinction, so clearly her birthright that once when she spluttered and partly upset her teacup it seemed to him a confusion of enchantment.

Oh, he was badly hit!

Then he had met her on a committee that was arranging a debate, but the contact had merely seemed to make her social circle more remote from him than ever. After that, small fiends used to sit or gambol on his bed in the small hours and mock him until he sweated. As if he could ever hope to enter the charmed circle! Who was he? And what was life with all its unfairness, the equal chances it didn't give, but a wretched slough?

Came the day when he saw her animated, laughing, walking along the city's fashionable street in the company of a man more mature than herself, as splendid as herself, a lithe blond god who wore riding breeches as if he had been born to them as kings to the purple. So terrible had been that moment that even now Peter's tweed hat, which he had taken off his head, was not only involuntarily crushed, but strongly wrung out.

Dear heaven, it was no laughing matter, he assured himself, laughing. Then he remembered how, after Fand and her blond god had passed, he had by a sad mischance run blindly upon the bosom of a well-dressed elderly lady, who, like a great bark brought suddenly into stays, stood aback and cried out, probably for the police, while a lap-dog yelped up his leg. He smelt the tangle of her silken topsail still.

A bicycle bell rang behind him. A girl flew past with legs going happily up and down on their way. They were such excellent legs that he wished them luck. He started laughing for no reason and looked about him and rejoiced.

He was tired by the time he squatted among some willows that hung over a murmuring stream by the edge of a meadow. Having drunk and bathed his face, he bathed his feet and left them to dry while he turned out Mrs. Macrae's oatcakes, fresh butter and hard-boiled eggs. Chew the oatcake until it runs about the palate, until its oaten flavour, crisp from the griddle, is one with the golden-yellow butter, until together, wedded utterly, they rise in a small wave-crest off the tongue, bathe the uvula and slide far down into bliss. So many live on statistics.

Presently voices awoke him. Children were in the meadow, three girls and four boys, running around, playing some game. In a racing burst they came quite near; then a dark boy stood his ground and a veritable young Fand went up to him with a buttercup in her hand and held it under his chin to see if it would or would not reflect its golden brightness on his skin.

"You don't like butter!" she cried.

"I do so like butter!"

"You don't! You don't!" she cried and ran away.

"I do so!" he yelled with remarkable rage and ran after her.

Another boy tripped him up.

She watched the resultant battle in tranced fascination. But nothing could withstand the dark boy's rage and he chased the other from the field and young Fand looked over the buttercup in her hand and smiled secretively while the sun shone on her yellow hair and on her bare legs. She was perhaps eleven.

Late that afternoon the colour note came back to him; the sheer sun yellow of the meadow. He had decided to return and sleep in the haunted cottage, but not by the road. He would swerve inland, over the hills and through the glens, and come down on the cottage from behind—as Lachlan had. If a man is going to do something it is well that he should do it thoroughly. That any native would be so curious as to visit the cottage in the night was so unlikely that the mere thought of it was fraught with an unearthly excitement, particularly for the native. The clever doctor had sounded like one who might even bring the affair before the Psychical Research Society—were it only to demonstrate the extraordinary psychical results from a knocking which had been elaborately consummated by a living hand in jest. That was a nice point of the doctor's about evil existing so to speak in its own right. And after all I must have an unusual bed somewhere, thought Peter. Otherwise he might as well go from hotel to hotel, looking at the scenery like the girl in the charabanc, or catching trout, or having a nap to drown the impertinence of a regulation which would not permit the spending of a bountiful capital in the Madeiras.

But do or think what he would, the colour note from the meadow, the sun yellow, persisted in haunting him, as though at any moment some further essence of it would be revealed; what Alastair the shepherd had called the *something*. And wasn't that what he had set out to find? Even biologists, after analysing the human brain, were coming to the conclusion that man evolved by *seeing* things in a new way. Artists who mattered had never believed anything else. . . . Thought, words—let him give them a rest for heaven's sake and enjoy the moment as it came. Hang theories! Didn't he spend his life among them? How could one who had never left the highway presume to lecture on Pythagoras?

If the sheer habit of thought often attacked him like this, he now impatiently swept it aside.

As he followed the slanting path the bushes came together into a low sheltering wood that had looked from a distance like a coverlet on the hillside. Stunted birch trees and hazels full of small singing or chirping birds: chaffinches, tits, green linnets, a scolding blackbird, a resounding robin; a flash, a flight, a scurry; with bounteous green-leaved space for one and all. Looking upon this ardent coloured world he forgot himself and thought of nothing, so his eye had time for an extra clarity of vision, an unusual capacity to perceive and to distinguish. It was delightful, forever shading off into the subtle and the rare, delight behind delight in an objectivity external as the bird-notes and almost as clear; beyond him, like the fragrant air he breathed.

After listening to the gurgling prattle of a tiny rivulet that leapt down its stoney course, and after looking up for its entrance and down for its exit, he stepped over it and found himself beside a bush of wild roses. It was a strong healthy bush, so full of ardent life that it vied in height with birch tree and hazel. Its thrusting vivid green freshness was truly remarkable. Its flowers, of which there were many, had even more of this astonishing freshness, from the red nipple of the bud to the pale pink of the wide-open flower. It was an apparition of a bush, to be there, like that.

Peter looked at it, and kept on looking at it, until his eyes were held by the topmost blossom of all. It was a particularly large bloom, flat open, flat out, but snared to the bush. Peter could not just stand and stare; he found for comfort's sake that he had to do something and the only thing to do was to make it move. Its face was so wide-open, so still, in that place, that he had to bring it to itself by giving it a shake. That would ease tension all round. As it was far beyond his reach, his eye picked out a stem, and thrusting a cunning hand in between many stems he got pricked before he tugged. Buds and flowers swung above him in a startled flight, but the topmost beauty barely shivered and certainly didn't take off. He must have tugged the wrong stem. As he sucked the blood-drop from the back of his hand, he stared at the rose and now its stillness was more ardent than ever but with a strained anxiety added, almost tragic.

Peter walked on and up sucking his hand.

But after a time he stopped. He would like to make that rose move. Back he went. It astonished him more than ever. And now, there *was* something ardent in its face. If ever nymph, caught in the instant of taking off from her bush . . .

Red nipple and wide-open face . . .

The satyr's hand thrusting below . . .

Peter blinked, and blinked twice.

He gave a slanting look down the path he had ascended, then proceeded up and on his way. But after a time he stopped. He sucked his hand thoughtfully, without thinking.

There had been *something*.

The alertness in his face was the thrush on a lawn.

He hearkened for an unimaginable glimpse. The hairs in his eyebrows sharpened; his brown eyes glistened ready to pounce; his face was firmly lean; yet his stance was deceptively easy as if it might thereby lure forth the unknown.

Yet all the time—or nearly all the time—his practical sense was never deceived for a moment. There had been nothing there but just an unusually ardent rose bush.

All the same, within that topmost rose and beyond it, beyond his utmost reach, had there been *something*—or not?

The appeal to thought scattered most of the fanciful nonsense, but now even thought produced its own wonder, for it urged him not to be defeated but to go and pull that rose down, pluck a petal from its crown, and send it to Fand as a reminder of what he had come for to seek.

It seemed one of the brightest, gayest thoughts he had ever had, for it covered over the nonsense—without doing away with it. He actually took seven paces down the path before he stopped once more.

Terrible! The tragic at last! For he knew that though he could pull the rose down he could not pluck the petal now and destroy the flower. He could not. By heavens, his hand wouldn't do it.

Not only that, but if Fand were with him and had seen it as he had seen it she wouldn't let him.

He sagged, and turned, and plodded on and up.

It's not easy plodding on and up, dragging the body with you, so that it might keep its vigil, like some knight of science, during long dark hours in a haunted cottage, waiting for what wouldn't come—and wouldn't much matter if it did. The world was full of black knives and stabbing; crammed to the topmost locker. And knockings, and poltergeists, and the devil himself knew what all.

Trumpery, hellish trumpery.

He slipped and recovered his hat, for even the path had faded away.

But all the time the *something* was far in him, like the deposit receipt the starving miser keeps locked in his kist.

As he came out on the crest he saw that the view was magnificent, though that was nothing new. Mountain ranges, glens, trees, remote horizons suave and still as the perfect indifference of God. Vaguely he fixed on the location of the haunted cottage and probably came within a couple of glens of it.

Quite suddenly he decided to have a real look at that deposit receipt and sat down.

For he had had one disturbing glimpse of Fand and himself, walking away with bowed heads from the rose bush like Adam and Eve from the Garden of Eden. Only Adam and Eve walked away from the Garden because they *had* plucked the apple; Fand and himself were walking away because they could *not* pluck the rose petal.

There was a nice reversal; there was a beautiful conundrum.

Ah, to blazes, I'm tired of it, he said, and lay over on his right side which was the side he slept on.

15

It was heavy going, the dusk was deepening, and he was pretty certain he was lost. The heat had drawn thick tablecloths over the tops, and from the last ridge he had not seen the houses of Ardvannie though he had expected to see them; yet he had found a burn and followed it, fancying he was following in Lachlan's footsteps. He had even set a boulder thudding down the hillside and had thought, not without a qualm, that it might initiate the big magic. Mist has a way of making monstrous shapes loom and then wiping one's face with its deathly clout. It is very grey and, squatting belly-flat on a peak, can weave its tentacles slowly. When he got below the last tentacle he looked back and saw it writhing up upon itself, ghostly thin. Ghostly was the very word for its grey soundless movement. He could just see through its tail.

However, having started following the burn he kept following it. He might be lost, but the burn would hit the main road somewhere, and once on the road he would find the bridge and so the cottage, though it might mean an extra mile or two. All at once he was assailed by the usually paralysing notion: I am going the wrong way.

Aimlessly to pursue the wrong way was a thing he had never done in his life. Yet here he was doing it. An extraordinary business. Has any man ever gone the wrong way against all his interests, licit, illicit and ghostly? He took leave to doubt it. He kept at it.

It was grimly exciting. For what would it mean? It would mean that when it grew dark it would be pitch dark, thanks to the mist, and so cold that he wouldn't be able to sit for long, much less lie, but would have to jig up and down on the one spot until the day broke—unless of course he went boldly on and broke either his legs or his neck.

Everything was set fair for as fine a night's misery as he could have wished.

What was wrong with Fand—he was fairly finding out a few things about her—was that she made a fellow too much at home. She could turn the inside of a car into a floating double bedroom with everything but h. and c. Yet of this, his Greek colleague had said, with a smile, "Roughing it?" His physics confrère, who should have known better, "Primitive a bit, what?" Holy Hydrogen, if they saw him now!

And he had produced a treatise on history's meaning for man; he had attended international conferences; he could tell a ewe from a tup.

When it grew too dark for his feet, he discerned a bend ahead and decided that if, when he got round it, he could see no sign of human habitation, no glimmer of a distant light from some lost shepherd's or stalker's cottage, he would find a sheltered spot and made a dog's bed.

There was no glimmer, only a noise from the burn farther on as if it went through a ravine; whereupon the very earth seemed to rise in bastions and gloom upon him fearfully. But he found a cavity of sorts and cut a heap of old heather; chewed the last oatcake and decided that he would put on everything in the rucksack including the silk underwear.

This made him think of Fand again, and a great hankering for tea came upon him. With tea he could have got nearer the heart of the night; the mountains would have come closer in communion. He fell upon reverie and saw Fand's hands the first time she had given him tea.

"What about some tea?" he had said to her on the street with youth's casual smile of desperation. The meeting had been accidental; at least he had seen her walking alone and had overtaken her.

"That would be very nice," she answered as if he were a genius to think of so brilliant an idea. But she had also smiled to him; she had in some mysterious way smiled to himself. Either the pavement or his feet had gone rubbery, and he couldn't think of a tea-shop within miles. She hesitated before a door. Why, of course, there it was. Of course. He saw her full back view as he followed her in. There were other back views, lumps of shapeless matter that nearly got in the way. Her shoulders. He followed her in. Her head. Her head turned and she smiled. He went ahead. He found a small table in a corner.

"How nice!" she said.

The previous Saturday he had scored the winning try for his university and had thought he had felt airborne.

"Yes, isn't it?" he said.

"I rather like this place," she said. "Don't you?"

"Yes, very nice," he said. It was an hotel lounge. He had never been in it before. There was a waiter in black and white to whom he signalled as from a raft. But the waiter, true to his kind, did not see him.

"You were rather devastating in the debate last Tuesday," she said.

"Debate? Oh, that! Yes."

"I can't say I agreed with you."

"Neither did I," he said.

She laughed as at a consummate witticism and that helped him enormously for a long sentence might as yet gulp in the middle. He looked abroad for the waiter who brushed past him from behind.

"I should like to tackle him," he said, smiling desperately, "in his own twenty-five."

"Do!" she said, and shook with delicious laughter.

"Would you—uh—mind if I did?"

Then he saw her eyes for the first time. They were looking into his and wondering, terribly tempted; they were a deep violet blue and spilt light. "You wouldn't?" she said.

"Wouldn't I?" he said. "Why not?" Her eyes blotted all sense out of him.

"Yes, sir?" said another waiter.

"Oh," said Peter. He looked at Fand. "What would you like?"

"Tea," said Fand.

"Yes, sir," said the waiter and off he went.

It was the kind of place he couldn't afford and this had a

wonderfully uplifting effect upon him. Many a desperate run he had taken for no more than a lump of leather.

Then the tea came. She put sugar in his cup, she put milk in it, she poured tea into it, then she lifted it and handed it to him. Nothing so incredible had ever happened to him. Enter drama, high and tragic, into the lounge of that hotel in the person of the blond god, this time in a dark-grey suit and in the company of an elderly man who by his austere air was at least a Writer to the Signet if not a K.C. Peter stared and Fand turned her head. As the god, pulling up his trousers, negligently subsided in the distance, he saw them.

"Oh, excuse me," said Fand, "I *must* speak to him." Up she got and off she went, moving quickly, with animation. Both men got up. She sat on a chair-arm and they sat down.

Peter removed his eyes.

Virtue oozed out of him like wind out of a punctured ball.

As a mere matter of style, apart from money, from the pennies he counted for his mother's sake, this was beyond him.

The flatter the oozing brought him the more his eyebrows sharpened.

Well, so be it! But this was his tea, and, blast them, she was having it with him. She mightn't—she needn't just have *shown* . . . but all right. He was a fool. All right—but.

She was coming back. He didn't turn his head. He drained his cup. "Ah!" he said and got up and sat down.

She was flushed with animation. "He said you played a stunning game last Saturday."

"Who?"

"My brother. We are supposed to be like each other. Wouldn't you know?"

"No," he said. "Yes."

"He used to play for 'varsity. He's in law."

"Oh," he said. "In law."

Then she looked at him, and she asked him if he would have some more tea, and she smiled, and she hadn't a buttercup either.

Peter snuggled into his dog's bed like the ancient of days. Already it was getting distinctly chilly and he was beginning to think it mightn't be a bad idea if he skinned his silken underwear over his person, when he heard certain far sounds that had a resemblance to human voices. His head lifted and his ears searched for the sounds within the distant rumble of tumbling water. But now they were gone . . . *There again!* He sat upright, listening so acutely that his mouth went dry. It was dark, but not pitch. His eyes lifted and saw stars. What was left of the moon would not be up for a long time. Then, beyond doubt, he heard something like a smothered voice, but he strove to be sensible about it. A loosened boulder going down a short cataract? A stag on the move? . . .

A feeling that the place was peopled came so strongly upon him that he tied up his rucksack with the utmost quietness. He would steal back the way he had come. But once on his feet he decided to go forward—nearer the fatal area—to make sure. A man just can't let himself be beaten by silly notions; not, anyway, one who was to have kept vigil in a haunted cottage. If he could feel as shaky as this over nothing . . .

Once by the bank of the burn he followed a narrow sheep or deer track. It was treacherous going but soon his feet had recaptured boyhood's trick of feeling for the step and instantly shifting a stress from one to the other. Now he could plainly see the greyness of water . . . the blackness of near masses . . . a suggestion of opening distance . . . and quite suddenly he got a smell which had a remarkable effect upon him inasmuch as it evoked the Palace of Holyrood, seen from the lower end of the Canongate in Edinburgh; his youth swept him in a fabulous way and he paused to wet his mouth; then he sniffed again, remembering that remote night of revelry, and now couldn't be sure whether it was a smell or a bewitchment. The only thing he could hear was his heart. But he went on.

Across the burn the black mass fell back and his wandering eyes were arrested by a slim shining rod, like a rod of gold some four feet high. . . . It must be light, coming through a crack or slit in the mountainside.

He stood and stared so long that he had to blink, but he could hear nothing beyond the noisy tumbling of water into a pool below.

No tinkers or gypsies would ever come so far from human habitation; as for poachers, all the deer were on the high tops; shepherds and stalkers were in their beds. It was, in its underground way, damned uncanny. He retreated until the light was hidden.

Yes, he remembered all about the fairy hill and the shaft of light that issued at midnight from its inner halls of revelry. Smile away, said Peter to himself, solemnly chittering. One thing was certain: human or otherwise, the thing was dangerous.

At the word "dangerous" his eyebrows sharpened and within a few minutes he was across the burn and advancing very carefully indeed. Again he got a whiff of that soft yet pungent scent and somehow it did have to do with revelry. In an instant it was gone like a passing breath. Holding himself at the ready he looked round upon the air. Nothing touched him. He went on—until all at once the narrow shaft of light was there, on his left, not ten yards away. Something showed grey and seemed to move beyond his feet; he took a step forward, was tripped neatly by a rod, and yelped as he pitched on his face.

He got on hands and knees smartly, saw the thing that looked like a grey face, waited for it. It vanished. He turned his head. The light was gone. He got to his feet.

Nothing happened. Then—then there was a scarcely visible movement where the light had been, followed by one or two soft footfalls; and silence once more. Peter knew he was being looked at.

"Who's there?" he challenged in a surprisingly authoritative voice.

No answer.

He didn't like it, and because he didn't like it his anger grew. "I see you," he was beginning with some force, when a solid shadow detached itself. In an instant it was coming upon him and though Peter yelled challengingly he also ducked. His rucksack caught a punch that bowled him over, but right nimbly he got to his feet, and, crouching slightly, threw a punch of his own that stopped a very solid body and made it gasp. It sounded like a human gasp even if the thing had a black face or no face at all. This absence of the ordinary grey human face roused the destroying fighting spirit that comes out on top of fear. If it's a fight the thing wanted it was going to get it.

It was altogether an extraordinary sort of whirlwind, with more drunken staggerings and punches thrown upon the vacant air than could readily be imagined. Peter had always been good at a tackle but quite expert at avoiding it, and he had to avoid it now. Twice the uneven ground saved him by sending his opponent lurching sideways with outflung arms like a fantastic ballet dancer; and twice he butted with his head the man's lower regions, producing on each occasion an abrupt grunt which to his ears was a not unmusical sound. I'll make him speak yet! thought Peter, for the black man had never spoken, and if there was something relentless and horrible in this silence, there was also something that insulted Peter very deeply. Wind! breath!—with more wind he would have wiped the glen with the devil. But with what wind was left whistling through his teeth, Peter managed, when his duck and side-step were too slow, to shed his rucksack into the grasping hands, and in the instant when the hands didn't know what to do with it, Peter hit out at where the face should be and scored so solid a crack that his knuckles tingled with the pain that was so sweet a pleasure.

"Get up!" he cried exultantly, for alas! he was old-fashioned enough to feel that a man can't be knocked down again until he gets up. It was his utter undoing. As he leaned forward, hands on knees, wheezing like an internal combustion engine on one leaky cylinder, he was hit out of the night on the head and fell forward softly into a deep dark abyss.

16

His eyes opened, then his mouth. In their sockets his eyes slowly revolved—and settled on two figures on their knees, their faces and hands in a downward beam of light, black as the faces and hands of childhood's devils. His eyes lifted and roved. A dark dungeon, thick with acrid smoke, with a dry brimstone heat that got him in the throat and made his mouth gape.

Was this—Hell? Was he in it?

For quite a few seconds all his acquired knowledge, gleaned so thoroughly over long years, over patient studious nights, from volumes numberless, was as if it hadn't been. Yet he had hardly expected to awake here.

One of the figures made vocal sounds; if it was a language, he knew it not, but his eyes switched and saw a pair of hands and something in the hands—something familiar in the hands. . . . It was his fat pocket-book!

Like a talisman it brought the far earth back.

A hand took out the bunch of banknotes and the other older devil laughed, a windy squeaky laugh, but rollicking of its kind. There was comment. Then the notes were stuffed back into their long pocket and the fingers were slipping into the half-pockets. A card was held in the light from the hanging electric torch and the voice read out the name and address of a French colleague in an excellent accent.

"Froggie!" said the squeaky voice and held up some garment at full stretch. His silken underwear. The fellow was ransacking his rucksack.

The other was glancing at one or two more visiting cards, but swiftly turned as a piece of hanging canvas rustled and a third man came in.

"Not a sound anywhere," said this third black fellow in English. "Must have been alone. Found anything?"

"Looks like some learned sort of johnnie. May have got lost."

"That's right," said Peter, weakly.

They were round on him in a moment; the light from the near torch was searing his eyes and his head suddenly throbbed. He shut his eyes and turned his face away.

"Anyone with you?" asked the commanding one who had read the visiting card.

"No."

"Who are you?"

"Munro—Peter Munro."

"What are you doing here?"

"Looking," said Peter, tremulous with weakness and nausea, "looking for the well at the world's end."

The squeaky rollicking fellow leaned back on his old heels. "Holy God!" said he solemnly.

"Fetch him a drop, Jock."

Off Jock the squeaky one went in the torch's beam and came back with a cup.

The cold dribble once it was over Peter's throat burned its way down like liquid fire. He coughed until the tears poured from his eyes, but a little afterwards he felt much better; sweating, but easier.

"Strong stuff," he said.

Jock laughed. "Strong stuff for strong men." But he brought Peter a cup of water. Then he joined the other two already whispering in a corner.

Peter wasn't greatly concerned. Whatever might happen to him, his life, he felt, was perhaps safe enough—if he could hang on to it, for a lethargy was coming over him, an exhaustion. A man gets out of training. But it had been a good fight. He turned over on his right side with no more thought for his pocket-book than if it had been a toothbrush. To gain time he would pretend to be asleep . . . his mouth slowly opened and heavy gusts of breath began to issue naturally from it.

He came to the surface with a feeling of strong reluctance,

113

and he might have let go again if he hadn't become aware that the cavern was lit. A paraffin lamp stood in a niche; a glow came from a fire; above the fire was a pot, a large pot, bulbous below but narrowing to a neck that turned sharply away like a chemist's retort. Beyond it, to the right, was a barrel, set up on end off the floor; and beyond that, on the floor, a wooden tub.

"The boxie, Alick," said Jock, whereupon he himself held a jug under a pipe that trickled into the tub. Alick, the commanding one, fetched a brown wooden box that might have held dominoes, opened the lid, and picked out a glass bulb the size of a small marble with a stem like an elongated drop of water.

Jock set his jug on a stone shelf; Alick put the glass bulb into it. All three heads leaned over the jug. The test must have been satisfactory, for at once they got busy, Jock calling on Hamish, the youngest of the three, to give him a hand with the tub while Alick turned to the fire.

The scene now for Peter was one of decided interest, for he realised at last that he had landed in a smuggler's bothy at that time of all times when the whisky was in full flow. Moreover he was still in life. Not only that but he was feeling much better. Hell wouldn't have been such a miracle. The smell he had got outside was the smell of Edinburgh's breweries.

As they were far from remembering him, and as Gaelic slipped out anyway, he had time to observe them and their doings. The real smuggler was plainly Jock; around sixty and in his element, slapdash, strong at a sheer lift, burly, and as full of fun as the tub of liquor. Whereas Jock had his foundations in crofting, Hamish was more probably a stalker or gillie not out of his twenties. Alick had the cool intelligence that would have directed the over-all strategy, dark (the only one with his cap off), lean, rising forty, and educated to the pitch of having read the Frenchman's visiting card with ease. From the way he paused once to rub his jaw thoughtfully, Peter decided that that was the jaw he had hit—and Jock the man who had grassed him with a mallet.

Suddenly there was a fierce sizzling hiss, and ashes and smoke belched up and out in a cloud. Jock's language sounded anything but Christian; Hamish defended himself with earnest vigour; Alick leapt towards the pot and snatched off Jock's cap, thereby exposing a head unexpectedly bald and astonishingly white.

While he observed the three struggling figures dim in their choking inferno, Peter realised that when they had first heard him outside they had instantly blackened their faces and hands with soot and put the lamp out. Naturally they had thought that Revenue officials were upon them: a terrific moment! At the worst they would have fought their way out; but until the worst was established they were not running away.

They must have accepted him—so far; though they would have carried him into the cave because they dared not have risked flashing a light on him outside.

Alick spread a piece of sacking over the tub; the cloud subsided and a dry ashen air reached Peter's throat; but they were all barking so hard that his own subdued raspings were lost.

As the culprit who had probably spilt some of the pot's spent contents on the fire, Hamish was still muttering his righteous defence, with Jock's squeaky voice rising to a whistling pitch of sarcasm, when Alick quietened them and went outside to hearken to the night.

Presently he returned and stood with his back to the entrance, surveying the scene, before his eyes came to rest on Peter; then he moved towards him in a casual relentless way.

Peter thrust at the floor until he was sitting with his back against the rock.

"Feeling better, are you?"

"Yes," answered Peter.

"What are we going to do with you?"

"Best way for me would be to trust me."

"You think so?"

"You could—with safety."

Peter felt the man's eyes going over his face, his clothes, his hands—quite a second or two on his hands—his out-thrust shoes.

"You think so?"

Peter shrugged. The other two were now standing still, listening.

"Where did you stop last night?"

"In Ardvannie."

"The hotel?"

"No. With Mr. and Mrs. Lachlan Macrae."

"You knew them?"

"No. I was directed there—by the shepherd, Alastair, whom I met on the hill."

"What do you do?"

"Teach."

"Where?"

Peter told him.

"A lecturer?"

"No. Professor of Ancient History."

"Holy God!" said Jock with awe.

Peter's mouth opened and his tongue clacked drily.

Alick turned away but Jock got in front of him.

"No, no," said Jock. "We'll give him the best." Plainly he wasn't going to let his skill be brought in question by so learned a palate. Tapping sharply with a wooden mallet, he started the bung from a small cask; into the bung-hole he inserted a piece of thin rubber tubing, pinched its end, smartly drew out most of it, and thus began syphoning the liquor into the white porcelain jug. He syphoned for quite a time.

"How do you like it?" called Alick.

"Half and half, thank you," Peter replied.

But when Jock saw Alick fetching the water in a cup, he objected, he objected strongly. "Ah t'hell," he said in his best English, "why spoil it? Let him try it naked first whatever." Plainly he had taken a fancy to his learned guest.

"But——"

"No, damn me, no." He snatched the cup from Alick, dashed the water on the floor and after pouring a generous measure from the jug, approached Peter. "Try that, sir," he said.

"Thank you," said Peter, and he raised the cup to Jock. "My compliments, sir."

"All the nations!" replied Jock very respectfully.

Peter took a small sip, sent it round his mouth meditatively, gauged its strength from its effect on his gums, diluted it with saliva and let it go; then breathed out strongly, harshly, but without undue facial contortion. "Clean," he adjudged huskily, "unusually clean . . . and sweet . . . nutty," he decided. He chewed the memory of it thoughtfully and exhaled. "I perceive how astonishingly right is your use of the word 'naked'."

"It takes yourself," said Jock. "That fellows now, you wouldn't think they knew what naked was."

Peter took another sip, for he was genuinely astonished at the cleanness of the whisky. He had thought it would be harsh and crude.

"Remarkable," he said, "—and searching." It was terribly strong.

Jock nodded, taking his bouquet like a prima donna, but more primly, with an air that started Hamish laughing internally, for with his clean bald head, sooty face and, now, piebald moustache, Jock was something that no footlights had ever shone upon. He said to Peter, "They have no manners," but he put his hand on his head, conscious at last of a nakedness there, the suspicion of a draught. "Where the hell?" He stared around.

Hamish laughed outright.

"You!" said Jock to him. "You couldn't even hold your water," and he began casting around for his cap like an agitated sea lion. From the search Alick unobtrusively brought Peter a cupful of water.

Jock pounced, lifted his cap, dusted ashes from it, smelt it. "Ah t'hell," he said, "my best bonnet." It was singed, but not holed. "Yes, yes, laugh away: that's about all you're good for." He was very angry with them.

"But why did you throw it in the fire?" Alick asked.

As he put his cap on Jock looked at him suspiciously, then at Hamish. Suddenly he let out a high hee-hee of mirth. "Two Santa Clauses! Lord, if you could see yourselves!" He rollicked consumedly. "You're like something hell threw up from a bad stomach." He found a cup, a mug, and Alick set down a cup. "If I was you," said Jock to him, "I would wash my face." Then he distributed his finest distillate from the white jug, went to Peter and politely but firmly insisted on adding a dash to his cup, said "All the nations!" tossed his mugful off, observed "Ha-a-a!" appreciatively, and concluded, as he went into action, "Come on, you chaps, it's not younger the night's getting."

Peter was now aware of having recovered in a remarkable manner. Even the ache in his head had dissolved, as in a burning quicksilver, and left in its place a wonderful clarity, a delightful lightness. He looked into the cup and couldn't see the liquor . . . as once upon a time he hadn't been able to see the water in an old wife's well.

His eyes glimmered and he helped himself carefully to another good sup.

He had always thought of whisky as a drink that somehow contrived to be born coloured, like sherry. But, of course, being a distillate, it would be born crystal clear. The naked spirit. How right Jock had been! Colouring, like a mood, was something that would be added afterwards. As colouring to a medicine bottle. Quite. But the naked . . . An old saying came back to him: "There are two things the Gael likes naked and one of them is whisky." He nodded. One lives and learns, for hitherto he had thought that when a certain old shepherd— who now appeared before his inner eye—had first uttered the saying in his hearing the reference was to the adding of water to the whisky, the dilution of its strength. Even Jock had meant something of this. Which showed how an old saying itself could become diluted, how even the concept "naked" could lose its pristine meaning. Not but that . . .

Having emptied the pot they were now obviously going to charge it again from a tub which Alick and Hamish carried from a bay in this remarkable cavern. For cavern or cave it was, with solid juts of rock from the roof. Hundreds of thousands of years man had lived in caves, Peter remembered. In fact it was only now being realised by scholars on the anthropological side how deeply the concept "cave" interpenetrated our notions of civilisation, and if only, thought Peter, in a flash, if only Freud, obsessed with the concept "womb", had instead given more thought to the profound significance of a cave in the race memory . . .

"Ah t'hell," said Jock to Hamish, "use your own dam bonnet," for plainly the pot was hot.

When they got it charged to his satisfaction Jock went upon his knees, the better to coax red embers and dark peat into flame beneath the pot's broad and slightly concave bottom.

"And now we'll have a dram," he said, once more on his feet.

At first Peter refused but, on being pressed, accepted "a very small one".

After that the three smugglers went outside to their ablutions.

Peter sat on. Odd thing that the needles and pins which had threatened him a little while ago should now have completed their knitting into a reasonably soft rug beneath, so that he found it just a trifle difficult to determine where he himself ended and the rug began. However, to get back to the fascinating vista which the cave concept—but even before one permitted oneself to enter upon that burgeoning illumination, even at the beginning where it was a simple—but how necessary!—precaution on the part of the research worker to have first acquainted himself with a real cave—that is, a cave which, though it might not be permanently inhabited, was yet a cave that man, moved by a deep instinct, perhaps ineradicable, or eradicable only over a period of time comparable with the domestic occupation of the cave in man's history . . .

Before Peter's preliminary sentence, austere in its exactitude, had swung to its farthest point, with attendant clauses in their own roundabouts, Jock came stamping back, blowing, with reddened cheek bones shining. "Foof! It's cold. But did you ever find water any way else? How are you feeling yourself, sir?"

"I think—and I am talking with some precision—I think I could hardly feel better."

"God bless you!" said Jock laughing right pleasantly. "But come in nearer the fire now. We'll have a long while to wait until the pot boils and boils off. It's a thing you can't force. In the making of whisky the boiling of the pot is an art in itself."

"Indeed?" said Peter, from his rug.

"Indeed yes. For the pot is like a woman in many ways and I'm not thinking just of her shape."

Peter also considered her nether amplitude. "Pray, what then were you thinking about?"

"Her temper," said Jock. "Force her and you'll get some wicked stuff, oh coorse."

"Really? And how do you force her?"

"By boiling her too hard. Coax and nurse her with just the right heat under her bottom and she'll give you of her best. She'll hum."

"Hum?"

"But even then she's tricky, you've got to watch her!" His manner was mysterious and he glanced towards the entrance. "Last year when we were making our drop for the New Year, she sang. It was the most beautiful song I ever heard. She's solid copper, and her copper was shining where I had rubbed her just to see the shine come up. I was sitting as easy as yourself admiring the shine, when she began singing quietly. Oh, beautiful it was. I clean forgot everything. Do you see?"

"Not—perhaps——"

"Don't you see? She sang me to sleep!"

"Ah!"

"You've got to watch her, the same lady." He caressed her flank. "She's hardly warm yet," he said with fond understanding.

"What happened, may I ask, after she sang you to sleep?"

"She went with me . . . but what's the good of talking?" He moved towards Peter, however.

"I think this is good and excellent talk. It reminds me of the classical stories, about the ancient Greeks. It's high learning. What was she like?"

"She was tall and she had long golden hair. She was like a picture in a book of olden times I once saw."

Peter nodded. "I have seen many such books. There was a woman named Helen of Troy——"

"That wasn't the name on her. And the book wasn't about the ancient Greeks. It was just about the ould Fenian heroes. And well set-up men they were; well put-on, too. Exceptional. I'll say that for them. And there was this woman. Tall she was and beautiful and bending towards a dark man on a grassy slope, bending like a willow wand—by God, that's the name—Wand! . . . Or—or is it? I thought I had it there!"

"I think I know the name."

"What?"

"Fand."

As Jock's right fist exploded in his left palm, the canvas curtain, which had once been the sail of a boat, rustled and Alick and Hamish came in.

"Fand!" said Jock to the cave's roof. "Fand! How often I have tried to mind on that name!"

"Good Lord!" said Hamish. "Drunk already!"

"Will you look at them?" said Jock. "Trash!"

There were a few cross-currents before the incomers gleaned that Jock had been relating his mythological experience. But supported as he now felt himself to be by professional authority whose depth was as the Atlantic Ocean, he handled the cross-currents with more than skill. In the process, Peter gathered that Jock had been left to watch the pot on this particular occasion while Alick and Hamish had climbed to high ridges in order to command the approaches during the onset of night. When they returned they found Jock fast asleep on the floor, the fire out, and "a last dribble coming from the worm that wouldn't fill an eggcup in ten minutes".

"That's all they know!" declared Jock to Peter with a wink of esoteric and mutual knowledge. "And Hamish, there—you wouldn't think he was getting married next week. Yes, he's getting married on as sweet a girl as ever swung from your arm in a reel. Isn't that why I'm making this drop?"

"You could hardly make it for a better occasion," Peter agreed.

"And I'm running some of it through the pot again to make it doubly strong. Do you know for why?"

"No," said Peter.

"Because he'll need it," said Jock.

Hamish, whose fair face was ruddy, grew ruddier.

"Not any more, thank you," said Peter to Alick. "Even as it is——"

"Foof!" interrupted Jock. "Take up your dram, sir. I'll need your help before the long night is over if it's any civilising we're going to do on that fellows."

"One minute," said Peter. He got to his feet—and was able to stand on them. "I thought for a little while that—that sleep was going to overtake me but—but it seems, I must admit, to be receding."

"Beautiful!" said Jock, who had a deep appreciation of what he called "language". "Come over to the fire, now. We'll make ourselves comfortable there, for we're here whatever, and it's only Himself knows why the wandering footsteps of a stranger should be brought to our door." And he looked challengingly at Alick.

Alick said nothing.

Peter began to walk towards the fire with that higher sobriety which side-stepped only twice.

"I'm thinking it's food you need," said Jock critically. "When did you eat last?"

"I had my breakfast," said Peter, "and Mrs. Macrae very kindly gave me some oatcakes——"

"Is that all? I was just going to put the kettle on when we heard you outside; and on I'll put it this minute. No wonder you're feeling light."

Which was exactly how Peter was feeling, but delightfully so, almost choicely. He knew he had to deal finally with Alick, but somehow he liked his reserve that was never self-conscious; there was strong bone in his face, rather a thin sensitive mouth that yet was anything but weak; in a fight he would be tough and utterly relentless but not vindictive. He knew deserts of the intellect unknown to his companions from the same homeland.

"I have often wondered," said Peter to him, "how whisky was made."

It was a quiet challenge and for a moment or two Alick looked at him, then, as if he had been asked by his professor in distant student days to demonstrate an experiment, Alick replied, "It's very simple."

Jock swivelled on his knees, for he had been building the

fire and thrusting the kettle into its outer rim. "Simple!" He groaned. He had his speechless moments.

But Peter was relieved. A relationship had been established. At least he was on the way to being accepted by Alick.

As Alick explained the process of distilling it seemed simple enough. His voice was cool, his descriptions precise. What was at the moment taking place was the second part of the whole process of turning barley into whisky. The first and complicated part—the malting and fermenting of the grain—had to be completed before distilling began. How or where this was done Alick did not mention, and Peter realised that the organisation and secrecy involved would be considerable and not of a kind to be disclosed lightly. But the pot was a straightforward copper still in which the fermented barley brew was first boiled in order to draw off the alcohol from the ferment or wash.

"But how can you draw it off?" asked the professor.

"Because," answered the student, "the boiling point of alcohol comes before the boiling point of water. So the spirit rises first—in vapour of course. Now, look!" And then Peter's eyes followed the pot up to a neck that bent over and narrowed gradually to a pipe no thicker than the spout of a crofter's kettle. But the pipe had no opening: it continued as a pipe and entered the upended barrel, round the inside of which it spiralled widely in many turns until its end came through the barrel; underneath this open end of the pipe sat an empty tub. "The spirit comes out there and into the tub. But, as I said, it rises into the head first as vapour and that vapour has to be condensed into liquid. You know how, when you hold a cold plate to the steam from a kettle, some of the steam condenses into water and trickles down the plate? The trickle is, of course, distilled water."

"I see," said Peter. "So your problem is how to condense *all* the spirit vapour?"

"Yes. You need a long cooling surface. That's provided by the copper pipe winding round the inside of the barrel here; it's called 'the worm'. Now the barrel is full of water, as you see, but that water has to be kept cold to do the condensing, that's why we have this small pipe at the bottom of the barrel bringing water into it from a well higher up, outside, and here, at the top, a bigger pipe carrying it away outside because if you didn't carry it outside the water would overflow the barrel and put Jock's fire out; and if that happened," he concluded in the same informative voice, "he would start singing, so we are very careful to keep all pipes clear."

After Jock got the first word or two out, the rest came in a rush. His eloquence cleared the floor for action and got Peter a comfortable seat upon a heap of folded grain bags with a support for his back if he wanted it, which he did. He might have expected oatcakes and flour scones and butter and even eggs that hadn't been hard boiled, but hardly a solid round of cold pot-roasted venison. If salmon or trout had now appeared he would not have been surprised. As an afterthought Hamish slapped down on the boards that served as table a bowl of crowdie and a pot of honey.

It was a noble spread and Peter's head hung in a kind of divine meditation upon it. The fruits of the earth, of the barren, cold, hungry, neglected, superstitious Highlands.

He became aware that they were all sitting down and that a certain restraint was upon them.

"They're heathens," Jock explained to him. "They had the upbringing but they've lost it."

"Indeed," said Peter.

"But I have always done it," said Jock. "I think the least an honest man can do is to return thanks for His mercies. And return them I will while the breath is in me."

"Nobly said," said Peter.

"It takes yourself," said Jock, so stirred that he gave himself a sort of complicated hitch. "Perhaps," he added, greatly expectant, "you would offer up the word yourself?"

"Well——" Peter paused. "I once remember reading," he proceeded thoughtfully, "of a church elder in Kiltarlity— it was in the old smuggling days—a kirk elder who, before making his drop of whisky, always got to his knees and prayed that the Almighty would see fit to misguide the footsteps of the gaugers."

"Beautiful!" said Jock. "And I will confess to you now, sir—and it's not the whisky that's talking for we haven't had any—or none to notice," he corrected himself, for this was a serious moment, "I will confess that often I felt moved to offer up a word myself before coming away with the heathens, but—but——"

"But he's not a kirk elder—yet," explained Hamish.

"Time enough for you to speak when you're holding your first-born at the christening," retorted Jock. Then he took off his cap and bowed his head.

"O Lord," said Peter reverently, "we thank thee for these Thy mercies. And if it should so happen that the despoilers of Thy bounty should pass by us and see us not, as the Pharisees of old passed by, then indeed should we know, sinful though we be and without any merit, that we were yet not without favour in Thy sight. Amen."

Jock opened his eyes but sat quite still, his face beaming in beatitude.

17

Peter lost the sensation of time. If he had, perhaps, out of compliment, overpraised the naked spirit, for its youthfulness had a sharp ardour that was as yet, and naturally, unacquainted with the mellow reaches of time, he was not so sure how exactly to phrase his appreciation of that same spirit with hot water and honey added in Jock's proportions. Happily this was unnecessary for other and more complicated matters came pressing upon his attention.

Jock had brought his pot through the first boil—brought her in, as he said—after tapping her head with his mallet, finding it "hard" and removing the congestion by "drawing" the fire; otherwise, apparently, she might have boiled over in one wild tantrum, flooding everything before her, including the worm, and sent her contents gushing into the tub in the same condition as they had left her bounteous body.

Now she was humming gently, purring, and the steady trickle falling into the tub was as crystal. That she had the right heat under her concavity could hardly be disputed, and every now and then Jock did not forget to stack a peat or two around the central glow.

"I got lost," Peter answered Alick, "looking for the haunted cottage."

There was a distinct pause wherein Alick's eyes observed him with a certain detachment. "I thought you said you were looking for the well at the world's end."

"I am. But *then* I was looking for the haunted cottage, for it struck me that it might be on the road that leads to the well at the world's end. Before you reach that well you must find the way to it."

"That's only sense," said Jock. "But this haunted cottage —where?"

"In Ardvannie."

All three of them regarded him concentratedly.

"But isn't the haunted cottage near the main road?" asked Alick.

"It is," Peter replied. "But I conceived the notion of coming down on the cottage from behind, down from the mountains, for that is the way the first man came, according to report, before he knocked on the door of the cottage and stabbed the man who came to it with his black knife. But, as you must know, mist descended on the tops in the early evening—and I lost my way."

"Is it true that the young carpenter died?" Jock suddenly asked.

"No. It was touch and go for a good while, but the doctor says he should pull through all right now."

"I'm very glad to hear that." Jock was plainly relieved. "It went round our place that he had died."

"No. Is Ardvannie far from here?"

"Not so very."

"Depends on how you go," said Alick.

Peter looked at him.

"The haunted ground," said Alick, "lies between this place and Ardvannie, so the more ghosts the better as far as we are concerned."

Jock moved uncomfortably.

Peter smiled. "I see. Perhaps someone was relieved when his wooden mallet hit a real head outside?"

"I'll always thank God it was only the flat of my hand I gave you," said Jock, and any kind of smile was far from his face.

Peter laughed. "It's been a generous hand to me."

"You have a hand yourself," said Jock, and he cocked an eye at Alick.

"It was the darkness saved me then," said Peter.

Alick smiled. "Talking of ghosts——"

"What kind of talk is that?" interrupted Jock uneasily.

"—what did you think of the business?" concluded Alick.

"It had some curious features. I happen to know quite a lot about it but—I cannot say much. However, when all the ghosts have been shooed away there does remain—something."

"What?"

"Very difficult to say. That's what I was going to try to find out by stopping a night in the cottage."

"All by yourself?" Jock gaped at him.

"That was the idea."

"You must have some idea of what you were expecting?" said Alick.

Peter was aware of a remote satire. "Actually I rather think I was moved by the notion that evil may exist—like many another force."

"In its own right?"

"It is, I grant, a difficult speculation; so here, I thought, might be a case for first-hand investigation."

"Did you expect to *see* it?" asked Alick.

Peter did not like the satire now that it showed in his smile. "I don't think that an empirical investigation is helped by an attitude of mind which may be—prejudiced—either way."

Alick lifted his cup, looked at it drily, and took a mouthful. "You think you could have found something without deluding yourself?"

"I don't know." And Peter drank.

"I think ghosts and evil spirits should be left alone," said Jock. "Have they ever done anything but turn even the drink cold?" He reached back and brought the kettle to the board. "Stop thinking of next week, Hamish, and hand me that jug."

But something cold had entered the cave.

Jock compounded his drink and as the steam rose Peter let himself rise with it, and all at once his mind was again in an ampler air where reserve and its egoistic likings or dislikings faded like the steam. He had nearly got caught by a mood of satire, by scepticism's eternal grin!

"This is my holiday," said Jock. "This is the only bloody holiday I get."

"You!" said Hamish. "This is the only honest bit of work you have done in six months!"

128

Jock laughed richly and lifted his mug. "All the nations!"

"All the nations!" repeated Peter, and took a good draught, coughed, and wiped his eyes. He turned to Jock. "That's a remarkable toast."

Jock thrust a hand at Alick. "Ask him!" And he laughed as at the joke of the night. "Him saying he doesn't *see* things!"

Alick was not in the least embarrassed and glimmered with that inner mirth which seemed to have an ultimate core of good nature. But Peter saw there was a far arid region in the man.

"It was a story he told here one night of what happened to him in Spain. There's some naked Spanish girls in the story, but that's not the main point!" Jock grew warmly congested, delighted with everything once more. "Come on! Tell him the story. We'll make a night of it and have yarns all round. Wait till I see herself." He got up—and turned from the pot to Peter. "What was her name again?"

Peter smiled. "You said you went walking with her."

"I did. She was beautiful. She had long golden hair and the flowers grew about her feet where she was walking."

"What were you looking at her feet for?" asked Hamish.

"You would never know," said Jock. "If only you hadn't come in then so that I would have seen the far country we were going to." He paused. "I'll never forget it. The flowers were that real I could have picked them and handed them to her."

"But you didn't?" Alick was looking at him.

"No, man," said Jock. "You did not give me the chance."

"And you had no idea where you were going?"

"That's the odd thing of it," said Jock. "Ever since the professor said he was looking for the well at the world's end it's as if—that's where we were going."

Something of wonder touched the cave.

Jock turned to the tub—then he slowly faced round again. "Holy God," he said to them on a lowered voice of wonder and reverence. "I have found it. I—I have found it."

They waited.

Jock pointed to the tub of crystal spirit. "The well at the world's end."

Even Hamish did not laugh.

And laughter did not touch Jock. He seated himself and turned to Peter.

"It's very profound that," said Peter. "I hardly know where I am."

"You see what I mean?" Jock looked through his window of marvel.

Peter was silent in his own house. "It's *one* of the wells," he said.

"It's the only one a poor ould bugger like me will ever see," said Jock, on a sudden strangely regretful tone.

Hamish laughed so abruptly he spilt his drink.

Jock looked at him, but distantly.

"I wouldn't say that," said Peter. "You're as near seeing the other well as any of us—perhaps nearer . . . much."

"What?" said Jock. "Where?" But they were not strong questions, as though there was another kind of question, for which there were no words.

"I don't know," said Peter. "That's what I should like to find out. But you have taught me there what will keep me thinking for many a day."

"It's the only real well," said Alick of the tub.

"No," said Peter. "It's the *false* well."

Soft expulsions of ironic breath came from Alick's nostrils.

"I now see that very clearly," said Peter. "It's the well that creates the illusion of the other well."

"Illusion is right."

"Illusion itself is false. But we like an illusion that puts us on the way. That may be—why we consume—alcohol."

"The alcohol is the only reality in all that."

"We don't drink alcohol for its reality; we drink it for the effect it creates, the illusions it engenders."

"Illusions. Agreed once more."

"Illusions of what?" Peter kept his eyes on Alick.

"Any mad illusion you like—like Jock picking flowers for a golden-haired goddess."

Peter withdrew his eyes and smiled. "It's easy to describe our illusions: not why we have them."

"May I ask," inquired Alick on a curious note, "if you are *really* hunting for the well at the world's end?"

"You haven't been *quite* sure if it was a joke?"

"No."

"Perhaps—neither have I." Peter smiled with a frankness that acknowledged Alick's scepticism and suggested that, perhaps, it didn't matter. "I only know that I should like to pick up all the illusions I can and see if, by plotting them carefully, I can find the way to the well at the world's end."

"And what do you expect to find in the well?"

"That which we have the illusion about."

"You're not serious?"

"Quite serious."

"You mean you expect to find a . . ." But Alick stopped.

"Real well?" Peter was now smiling at Alick's hidden judgment, but pleasantly. He turned to Jock. "Have you any idea of what the well at the world's end is like?"

"If it's not a real well, it's beyond me." Jock's smile was strained and troubled, and Peter saw that the arid words were destroying the well in him, and he saw it so clearly that he sat quite still, saying nothing.

"Have you found many illusions?" Alick asked him.

"A few, but I haven't been long on the road yet."

"And as a stranger you will have difficulty in finding specimens?"

"Oh no. You always find them by not looking for them. You find the finest—when you are lost."

"If anyone is lost it's me," said Jock.

Peter smiled. "Not you." He glanced at Alick. "What's so extraordinary about it?"

"Well, what?"

"You can dig up prehistoric kitchen middens, you can study the vagaries in the love habits of the tomtit, and have honours heaped upon you."

Humour assailed Alick. It came through his nostrils softly.

"Pray, consider the matter," proceeded Peter. "Take a simple instance. Some evenings ago, I fell in with a shepherd. I had shed one of his ewes and ultimately run her into a corner where I managed to get a rabbit trap off her leg. It was a beautiful evening; we got talking about sheep, about breeding." As he recounted the talk with the shepherd, Jock sat up, began to smile. In the Paris studio, Jock was enthralled. As Peter described the occasion when the shepherd didn't want to go home, Jock nodded, his eyes far-glimmering. "Words are difficult; but if I say that for a moment the shepherd went through the human boundary, well—can you suggest simpler or better words? Anyway, isn't it worth thinking about? Isn't an attempt to given an appreciation of that situation, as we used to say in the army, at least as worth while as an attempt to appreciate how a tomtit slides down a piece of string to a monkey-nut?"

"Monkey-nut!" Jock's voice hit a new ceiling in squeakiness as he rocked with laughter. This talk was more like the thing! "Who else did you meet?" he asked.

"I met the wild man," said Peter smiling upon him.

"The who?" asked Jock, with arrested brows.

Peter told of the meeting at the swinging bridge.

"I knew him," said Hamish.

"Did you?" said Peter, looking at Hamish who was full-fleshed, fair, naturally reticent in strange company, plainly a decent lad with perhaps nothing very unusual in him, finding his outlet in pulling Jock's leg because he knew Jock as he knew a difficult and fruitful corrie.

"Yes," answered Hamish, "I haven't seen him for some years . . . he was terribly good on the hill."

"Was he? What happened?"

"I don't rightly know," said Hamish. "It's not . . . he would tackle anything. That time he went down the rock to rescue old Phemie's ewe—it nearly made me sick."

"I wouldn't believe it myself," Jock agreed, "when I saw the place."

Peter felt the presence of some taboo that inhibited speech, that could not be penetrated by questions, even if he himself had felt like asking them. How had the wild man actually managed to evade military service, what extraordinary complex, communal as well as personal, was here?

"Were you asked about him?" The question in this vague form came from Peter with a peculiar sensation of rightness.

"I was," said Hamish. "I said—he was a bit queer. I suddenly felt mad. I told them to leave him alone." He smiled in an awkward, satiric way. "I knew damn fine they wouldn't catch him whatever."

"I'm afraid it's a case," said Alick, "of a fellow going through the boundary, and not being able to find his way back."

And that, thought Peter, deliberately shuts off the personal questions. "You may be right," he said.

"But you're not sure?"

"How can I be? In the first place, he may not want to find his way back. In fact it looks pretty like it."

"What kind of well would you say he's found?"

Peter regarded him. "That's exactly what I should like to know." Then he looked at the liquor in his cup. He realised that he would have to meet the wild man. In some way it was as if he would have to make this journey over again, or go back on it. He would have to reach that place where the wild man was. He would have to go there. This seemed extraordinarily clear.

"And how would you find out? Do you think he would tell you?" Alick asked him, too polite to stress the final *you* except by implication.

"I don't know. I cannot therefore speculate about it. To find out I should have to go to him. By going—I should be on the way."

"Let us be logical about this," said Alick.

"Certainly," said Peter.

"I gather that to reach a point on the way to the well you have to go through the human boundary. All the points lie beyond that boundary. Therefore the well lies beyond it, and by the time you get there you yourself must be totally beyond the boundary?"

"It's not a very good syllogism. For example (a) one may be able to go in and out the boundary as, in childhood's song, one went in and out the window, and (b) one may discover once one has gone through the boundary that the boundary, like the window, is transparent—or even isn't there. To one

133

who has gone through the boundary, the boundary may be an illusion."

"By that time he is in the land of illusion."

"From the point of view of the one left behind. But presumably not from his. So finally, in your logical process, we arrive at a choice between two illusions, or, more exactly, a choice between two conceptions of illusion."

Alick smiled. "We generally treat the man who has gone through the boundary as mad. There are institutions for him."

"That's better!" Peter smiled also. "In this realm syllogisms are queer things like spiders. The most beautiful webs. But no fly is *fated* to go into the web. Or what do you think?"

"Things are getting a bit fine spun."

"It's the whisky." Peter laughed with pleasure and turned to Jock. "You're a magician."

"I feel spiders crawling on me," said Jock, "right enough. But don't let me come in on you if you're going anywhere."

There was something at once so solemn and so droll in the way Jock spoke that laughter welled up in Peter and over-whelmed him.

"Once," said Jock, "I lost my wife in the dark. We had been to a wedding and it was a good wedding. On the way home I was making fair weather of it, but stopped for a little relief on the way. Then I tried to make up on her, but whether the footpath got lost or my wife I couldn't say, and there I went barging about looking for her until I lost my voice thinking she had fallen into a burn; and the more I looked for her the angrier I got, for I was frightened. At last I reached home and put my head round the door. 'What on earth kept you?' said she, quite short."

Alick listed a little from his mirth.

"It's a fact," said Jock. "She was quite short with me." His eyes were beginning to gleam again. The talk might have its ups and downs but plainly, over all, life was beautiful. Exceptional. "And you can stop laughing, Hamish my fine fellow my lad: wait until your one is short with you."

Life is truly good, thought Peter, pulling himself as best he could together and wiping his eyes. But a fellow must stop laughing. He must. At the thought of it he let go again and laughed on. He shook his laughing head. Once more he did his best and slowly surfaced.

"The great thing about whisky," said Jock, "is to take it not too often. If you never abuse it, it won't abuse you. That's what I have always said. A little at a time." He looked into Peter's cup.

Peter put his hand over it. "Give me breath," he prayed. "Your hospitality is too great. Yet he wonders about a window!"

"Who, that fellow, is it?" Jock waved a dismissive hand towards Alick as he got up, then singing "Out and in the window" in a prim voice, nodding the while politely to the vacant air, he danced, with both arms extended, a *pas seul*, based on the simple polka, and only the unevenness of the floor set him sitting by the humming pot a trifle earlier, perhaps, than he had intended. But he was not at all put out. "Will you hearken to her?" he said. "There's talk for you now!" He caught a peat in either hand and pressed the core of the fire in upon itself and left them leaning there. "You have a small song to yourself, too," he said to the kettle and gave it a friendly push farther into the ashes. Then he got up and, scooping a drop from the spout over the tub, tasted it. He pondered. "Where's the boxie?" In this box, Peter now observed, were several small glass bulbs with numbers painted on them, and discovered that they were used to find, at any particular moment, the specific gravity— the strength—of the running spirit. The one with the W on it told when all the spirit was gone and only water left in the pot.

Jock's pursuit of a correct reading of his instruments was accompanied by a thoughtful whistling of the melody to which he had danced; his manner was solemn and precise and the whistling gave it a remarkable air of optimism; he was like an alchemist who knew what he was about, a scientist for whom measurement was the last drollery. "Ha!" he said to an elusive little bulb, "you would, would you?"

Peter now supposed that he himself was experiencing that higher sobriety whose mark is a capacity for subtle distinctions, for exquisite discrimination. The all too obvious parallel was the old German achievement in the higher criticism. But how

135

little it needed, whether measured by a glass or by a dialectic, to make either bedrunken! How little! and how imperceptibly that little crept upon its little task! He would definitely have no more to drink and thus maintain the highest on its height. Who knew what might not be vouchsafed him yet?

And how deeply ran his gratitude; how beyond measurement this hospitality; how ineffable that movement of the spirit which lay beneath it all; both spirits, he added, the false and the true, for mirth had not left him, nor joy departed, as though joy itself dwelt in the ultimate well that was creation's very fount. "What's that?" he said.

Jock was sitting beside him again, hospitably suggesting food.

"I have eaten well," Peter assured him. "Its goodness swims within me like a trout."

"Are you fond of trout?"

"Trout? Well . . . The truth is," he said confidentially, "on this journey I was once already offered trout and I refused, saying I did not like trout, but that may not have been strictly true, yet the old lady had been so hospitable to me, giving me of her best, giving me her bed, that I was unable to partake of her trout."

"Why weren't you?" asked Jock, "if it is not a rude question?"

"Well, you see, the wild man had brought the two trout for the old lady and had placed them on a shelf in an outhouse——"

"The wild man?" Jock's face opened slowly.

"Yes. Are you surprised that he should be able to catch trout on the other side of the boundary?"

"No," said Jock. "Yon fellow would lure trout out of the streams of paradise." But there was no mirth in his face.

"That's a point," said Peter, nodding; "an interesting one. Yes. Well, as I say, he had brought two trout in the night—we heard him—two trout which he placed on a shelf outside. Now when the cock crew for the twentieth time and morning was well come, the old lady opened the door of her dwelling and let her cat out, a large, fat, beautiful tortoiseshell cat. But her mind was doubtless so preoccupied with the exercise of her great hospitality to a stranger, that it was yet a little while before she herself adventured forth, and came by the shelf,

136

and found what the cat had left, and the remnants thereof together would have made one trout. After she had spoken to the cat, and right well she spoke and strongly, she came to me, saying, 'Do you like trout fried or boiled?' "

But Jock, for whose benefit Peter had worded his story as he did, was not moved to laughter.

"Who," Jock asked, "who—was—the old lady?"

"Old Phemie."

"Holy——" And there Jock stopped, like one suddenly stricken with uncertainty regarding him who, after all, had come to them in the guise of a stranger.

18

If time is no more than a sensation, there are times when the sensation is no more: a proposition which would have presented little difficulty to Peter as the small numbers grew on night's dial had he paused upon its adolescent simplicities. Much indeed of such book philosophy as he had imbibed—and at imbibing he had not been without merit—would now have appeared to him as artless—or artful—in a delightfully precise way, like the way Kant had of swinging his legs out of bed. Quite beautiful and forever to be applauded. But not complicated. The eye could follow the arabesque of thought, twist as it would. The eye could even stand away and see that all the arabesques came back on one another like more or less friendly serpents; serpents that slid and writhed and reared a head that did not bite; serpents that moved in the way they did because they were moved to move in that way categorically; serpents whose outer outline could be seen in an enclosed system which could be apprehended.

But when Jock, assured at last of his guest's simple humanity, and moved profoundly by his recital of his happy sojourn with old Phemie, arose to his full length and breadth and lifted Peter's half-drunken cup and threw its remnant in the fire for no other reason than that it was cold, and when the fire instantly responded with a blue flame that shot up and vanished with the devil's own speed, then Peter knew less than ever where he was or in what philosophic system, though yet he was miraculously there.

"If ever," said Jock, turning upon him a countenance of contained glee, "if ever you want to give the devil a fright throw your whisky in the fire." He sent a laugh aloft after the flame. "It's that unexpected," he explained. Whereupon he proceeded to compound new, hot, and honeyed drinks, with something added of the flour of oatmeal, so that the steaming whole might be, in his own words, "meat and drink". "It will sustain you," he added on a note of sound sense.

And sustaining, Peter realised, was what he needed. Jock's concoction might indeed prove no more than the final honeyed deception, but when hospitality has a sweet mouth far be it from any academic gentleman to examine its teeth. Yet realising that not many words might be left him now, and anxious to give what might be a final one some point, for the academic habit is strong, he lifted his cup and looking around upon his companions said, "Gen'lemen, I give you the toast of the evening: All the nations!" The articulation was well nigh faultless, and after he had drunk with the whole-heartedness so noble a toast demanded, he leaned back carefully upon a state of divine rest.

Jock was so deeply impressed that he responded to the last drop. More he couldn't do, so he looked at Alick. "We have you by the short hairs now," said he.

Peter looked at Alick and instantly had the intuition that somewhere in his story Alick would go through the boundary. This was at once utterly astonishing and exciting and yet in the same moment explained the division in the man, the impersonal friendliness and the final scepticism, the near warmth of the boiling pot and the far arid moor where the roots of belief wilt or wither. A Highland product he was, like the smuggled whisky; as modern as a Paris studio, as old as a peat. My God, here was the modern spirit's dichotomy in a choice setting.

"There's nothing in it," Alick began, "but at least it may illustrate your kind of illusion. There were three of us and we had set off for Spain in a car. I don't suppose we were actually looking for anything, but we were young enough to talk of colour and wine and sun—all the things for which the northern barbarian is supposed to hanker. It was many years ago, in the inter-war period, when young men had bright ideas of a new world—the brotherhood of man, an internationalism of all the nations. You know the sort of thing?" And he looked at the professor with a slight smile.

In the early part of his journey he often thus paused to draw comment, as though the story should hold something from them all, become part of the cave itself where the traditional story had always been told in the detail that created, touch by touch, its own time and place. In this way it was lifted beyond the personal. A new world of experience was created by a voice.

Peter had not heard this long and often intricate way of telling a story since he was a boy, and now he so revelled in its creation that he would pull Alick up in order to get a more precise description of the stained glass windows of a small Oxford college, to appreciate the comparison with those of Chartres Cathedral, to sample a particular wine in the Loire valley, until by the time the car with its three adventurers had crossed the Spanish frontier, hesitated in San Sebastian, and finally come to rest before Henry's café in the small town of Zarauz, Alick had at last become the pure story-teller, at home with his listeners. And the more Peter saw the man himself unconsciously emerge, the more he liked him.

"Henry was a remarkable fellow," Alick went on after a mouthful of liquor. "I forget his full name—though he did give us his card—but Henry was how we decided to pronounce his first name; and I do remember that he was a German by birth who had served on a submarine in the first World War and, after that, had taken on Spanish nationality. He spoke to us intimately of Seville and of how he had prepared splendid feasts for Spanish royalty and we believed him absolutely because of his wonderful knowledge of wines, but particularly of sherries. On the shelves behind the counter were whole rows of bottles, bottles of all shapes and colours, and between the bottles were stuck little flags of every nation you could think of. Talk of a display of internationalism! Here it was. He spoke quite good English, though he stuck now and then for a word. We didn't seriously ask Henry there and then if he was a political internationalist because—well—to have all the little flags up meant presumably good business for his café. Yet we were delighted with it and made funny jokes when

Henry wasn't there; because after all even if it was only commercialism, it was, if I may use a phrase of yours," and Alick gave Peter a quiet smile, "on the way."

Peter acknowledged with a slight bow.

"Zarauz was, I think, a sort of aristocratic watering-place; or, at least, had been. I have often been going to check up what Henry told us about it when the Spanish nobility used to go there, but, somehow, I never have. If this reluctance seems strange you can put it down to what happened—or didn't—in the Spanish garden. However, there were certainly some fine houses about, for we stayed in one of them. Henry's café was on the front and handy, for during all the days we stopped in Zarauz we did nothing but sun-bathe and sea-bathe and drink Henry's wines with discretion." He paused. "I remember the look on Henry's face when John—one of the other two—said the miraculous Tio Pepe was too dry for him. You know how a small air of wind comes on a pool? Henry's face withered like that. But he was a man of great tolerance and produced—what do you call it?—that exquisite blend of sherries?—and what a perfect wine it was!—and he said, 'It is more—*sweet*.'" Alick's eyes glimmered and Peter floated in his hammock.

"So we had been taking it easy and absorbing a little too much sun. We had been warned about the sun, of course, and had been trying to take it in small doses, but when you see a couple of Spanish beauties, with a bare minimum on, taking the sun as if time didn't exist, it's not so easy to sit near them and huddle under towels and shirts like barbarians. But there was always the sea, and it was a magnificent beach of sand. The combers came curling in as they do on the west side of the Hebrides, only this beach shelved very slowly and you could wade out to meet them and dive through them. It was good sport." Alick hesitated for a moment as if calculating something. "That forenoon we had been in the sea three times. The Spanish beauties had turned over on their faces. The younger one had already swept John with her dark eyes, a look—for I happened to see it—of such aristocratic intolerance that he kept his eyes to himself for a little while as if he was getting on fine. It was about time to think of calling in on Henry on our way to lunch at our grandee's house when I thought I would have another dip. I was feeling drowsy and sticky and there was a sort of faint roar of the sea in my blood. But the others wouldn't budge. So off I set. I waded out a bit, headed through a comber, and while still within my depth turned to swim along the shore. It was good! In a way as good as Henry's wine, as perfect. So I kept going, lazily, until I really felt tired, then turned toward the shore, swam a few yards, and let down my feet—and my feet found no bottom. This was so unexpected that my head went right under, but I swallowed nothing. I am not a long-distance swimmer, but I can watch out for myself in water. I decided, of course, that I could not have been swimming as parallel to the shore as I had thought so I struck out in earnest. It was then I found how slow my muscles were, how tired and sort of languid. A little late we had bought tubes of cream to rub on sunburn and that very morning I had massaged my right shoulder with the stuff, for in near the bone was a dull awkward drag like rheumatics. You know the Spanish proverb that only an Englishman and a dog keep to the sunny side of the street. We had joked about it saying that at least we were not English, which had rather narrowed the issue. No doubt the sun had rotted my right shoulder a bit, for I began to feel it now and cautiously tried for bottom again, but did not find it. At that moment the keeping to the sunny side of the street wasn't such a good joke, but I was still a little way from panic. An overhand reach with the right arm comes naturally, so I did my best, keeping my head well down in the plough through. After a time I got on my breast for a look at the shore. My friends were far away and the number of waves between me and them seemed very many. . . . It was then the thought dawned on me that I was not only making no headway but was being slowly carried away to sea. I needed a rest badly, but to turn on my back if I was in fact being carried away . . . I could hardly risk it, and for a time I swam a breast stroke with little pith to it. It was a difficult position in several ways. I hated the idea of shouting for help while there was still a kick left, and having been in a few rough spots I had learned how the will can blindly keep the body going; yet I didn't want to disappear without giving the lads some inkling of what was happening; and, anyway, short of magic one just couldn't be carried to sea on such an open beach. Hang it, we and others—and doubtless the whole Spanish nobility—had been swimming around. . . . But the time came when I shouted. The third shout had all I could give it. No one heard me; and I heard only the thundering crash of the waves."

Alick paused to light a cigarette. His face, it seemed to Peter, had gathered a perceptible pallor or greyness, yet it was so alive in its contained way that—yes, it was not pallor so much as a touch of the liquor's whiteness. A transparency, a suggestion of clairvoyance, came into the cave. Something oddly remorseless about the story had now the quality of "second sight".

"When it seemed that drowning couldn't be avoided, my whole past life did not flash before me, but I did have the very distinct thought: how strange that I should have come all this way to die. When I could hardly push my arms forward, it was the length of the trip that came before me. That I should have deliberately planned to travel so far in order to end here seemed strange, mysterious. I cannot explain this—I cannot now quite get it myself—but at the time I did have the feeling absolutely clear, not that I understood the thing, but that I was in that place where cause and effect . . ." He took a pull at his cigarette.

"The fact is that at such a moment a man grows cunning and cool . . . he slips back into earthly time, of which he still has a little. I had been keeping an eye on the waves, for I knew that if a bubble of froth went the wrong way and caught my breath I would simply suffocate and sink. As it was, I was losing my buoyancy a little, settling down. But now I consciously observed that around me the waves heaved but were not near breaking point, whereas some way to my right they were already peaking up for the curl over. Was the water shallower over there? . . . perhaps I had got into a deep sea-going current . . . I altered course from a direct bearing on the beach to an angle of perhaps 45°, to an angle, anyway, that brought Henry's café head on. Then I got down to it. I knew it was my last effort and I left it to the blind will."

Alick thoughtfully considered his cigarette as he tapped ash off it.

"One point here I perhaps should mention for it remains extraordinarily clear. It was a remarkable illusion. For some seconds I suppose I must have lost ordinary consciousness. Yet—no, for I knew where I was. However that may be, how many states of consciousness we can keep going like a juggler I'm sure I don't know, but what I suddenly saw was myself going down through the sea, standing quite upright, slanting away down through it, slowly, through still water that was green and luminous. Perhaps it's the way nature has of preparing us. Perhaps it's the kind of acceptance . . ." But he stopped and smiled.

"The next thing I knew was that the water gave me a small slap in the face. I lifted my chin and was aware of a curious agitation on the surface, a sort of cross-welter. I stared at the beach and saw human beings, houses—very still in the sunlight like oversize toys, but I felt, with a sudden gulp that weakened me, that I had won nearer. My legs sank; the big toe of my right foot touched something that gave as a great swirl swept me away back. In an instant panic had me and my mouth ripped out a terrific yell. Yet somehow I managed to right myself. And then I saw John, I saw that he had heard me. I saw him sit up, and then stand up. He was stark naked. Nor did he wait upon the order of his going. He charged. He came down that beach, arms and legs flying, as only God made him, and not only did the panic fly from me but the Spanish ladies flew from him—or so, at least, I was told afterwards. The naked and unashamed barbarian had emerged. It was a gallant sight! I had heard that in the old clan days the Highlanders, when going into battle, were known to take off their shirts. Now I knew it was true. You cannot get past blood!" Alick paused to laugh, having with these last words come clean out of himself. "The sea frothed from him. He came for me like a great retriever dog. I no doubt looked as all-in as I was. Anyway, not a word did he say. He just grabbed my right wrist, swung over and hit out for the shore as if I was a shot pheasant. It probably hadn't occurred to him to take me in his mouth."

Jock so enjoyed the last touch that he cried, "Hold your horses! The night is young!" He laughed to the fire, as he attended to it; he addressed the pot on Spanish ladies; he brought the steaming kettle to the board; he sent the devil in blue flames four times through the roof; and after he had completed his hospitable and steaming rites, he said, "You can go on now."

"I could see John had no notion of life-saving, but after a time I managed to get words through to him. By putting my open right hand on his shoulder, I freed all his limbs for action and could even give a kick astern myself. But John's bayonet charge must have been observed by more than the Spanish ladies, for the next thing I saw was a Basque, a tough small age-less man, with wide brow and pointed chin, coming running in, high-stepping like a trotting horse. When the great swirl of water swept across his thighs, he stopped. He stopped dead and began to take off his shirt. A wonder came on me, for though I was completely exhausted my head was extraordinarily clear. You know how, when you have had a few over the score and you may not trust your legs, your brain remains as clear——"

"I know," said Peter with some precision.

They all laughed with an air of delighted surprise.

"Holding his shirt by a wrist-band, the Basque cast it towards John, like a primitive man casting a net to catch fish. I was greatly taken with the grace of the action even if the shirt fell short. John reared a bit but I blocked the water in my mouth. At the third throw John got the tail of the Basque's shirt in his fist, and that small dark man waded to land hauling his heavy catch behind him. I had a longing to lie where I grounded, but I know I was on my feet when I saw the Basque's face talking, for I fancied it was speaking of sea-serpents and other monsters in the weird sounds that only a child would have understood. When we got to Henry's café, Henry explained the whole mystery. The waves that rush up on that beach at Zarauz tend, on the east side, to swirl round and ebb out in a deep stream. At certain states of the tide, say a spring tide, that ebb will be fairly strong. Henry told us that in actual fact two visitors had been drowned there the previous year. He looked very grave and disturbed. He said the signals should have been up. Then he

145

looked at me, and that German, who was a naturalised Spaniard, turned to his shelves and took down a bottle of French brandy. I had really come to believe that no drink could have the perfection of his sherry. It was revealed to me then that Henry's internationalism might be real. I had been the worst doubter. When it had come to a matter of a bet on it and we had to be sort of definite, I had plumped for commercialism pure and simple, business for the café. The other two had varied between a general sort of vague sentiment for international peace and a clever disguise for espionage. Now, as I looked at Henry's shelves, how quietly the different bottles sat there side by side. Full of colour. Here was France—actually, I thought this— here was France putting warmth into me, warmth down to my hands, and my hands warmed the goblet back, and brought out of it France's finest bouquet, her fragrance. I didn't feel I was being poetic, for wasn't it actually happening before my nose? The brotherhood mood seemed pretty pure then."

Peter refused a cigarette, he refused everything, he was waiting now.

"I don't remember a great deal about the rest of that day. As the evening drew on I was haunted by the notion that I hadn't thanked the Basque properly—if I had thanked him at all. Speech had somehow receded. It was an odd sort of gabble, it seemed to me, at the best. I have, since then, looked up an encyclopedia about the Basque language. You will doubtless know about it, sir," said Alick to the professor, "about its being holophrastic, which means apparently that a sentence is a single verbal unit. That's certainly how it had sounded to me in the water. So I hardly needed to be told that it was pre-Aryan or came direct from the Old Stone Age. Real life seemed much older that evening than the Old Stone Age. I remember standing in a side street, in the darkness, looking into a low room where dark men sat at tables drinking wine out of fat glass bottles with spouts. Their faces turned as I stood in the doorway and I had the illusion that the face of the Basque I was looking for was multiplied many times. In the moment when no one moved the whole picture was queerly arresting. After that there was some open space or square, where dancing was going on. And here the faces of the señoritas were anything but intolerant or superior. Indeed John gave it as his considered opinion of the trip as a whole, taking the ups with the downs, that whereas men of different tribes may sniff at one another like straight-legged dogs, a woman has a mode of communication that is pre-Basque and is understood even by a barbarian. However, that night, as I got to my bed, I remembered that I had not found my Basque."

Alick paused, tapped his cigarette slowly, took a small sip of his liquor.

"When I awoke the dawn was in the window. It was a tall window. Immediately I was wide awake, with a pleasant feeling of lightness. I listened and knew no one else was awake. I could not lie still. I got up and went to the window, and found myself looking out on an old Spanish garden. The dawn was quite clear but there was as yet no sign of the sun, only the freshness of the morning. The garden was very still. Stone walls, architectural lines, the shoulder of a building . . . the whole was somehow arranged to hold this stillness, as—as a case holds jewels. Only the jewels were flowers, coloured bushes. And this suggestion of arrangement, of formal pattern, gave it an extraordinary beauty. I don't much care for formal things, but . . . I don't know . . . for though it was formal, yet it was so with that sort of aristocratic air, that assured, perfect manner . . . and yet what particularly drew my attention were some small trees with a feathery green foliage of wonderful delicacy and completeness. My eye kept coming back to them with a feeling of wonder that no slightest feather moved. Then I saw that the stillness went out beyond the garden; and I held my breath in an effort to catch the suggestion of an utmost sound. But there was no sound. It was now that the odd feeling came over me that the stillness itself was holding something, much as the walls held the garden; and in a moment I realised that what it was holding was time. Time was stopped, not by any kind of magic or enchantment, but actually. Have you ever listened to a clock that has, quite unexpectedly, just stopped? But though it was like that, I was also aware that that's not really what it was. In our world you cannot hold up time. But it's very difficult to analyse, to be precise, here, for whenever you analyse you break down, and what I experienced was the very opposite sensation. Quite simply, then, I knew with an absolute conviction as I stood at that window gazing out on the old Spanish garden that there exists an order of things outside our conception of time. . . . There was nothing at all in the ordinary sense 'religious' about this experience; but what is astonishing, I think, is that there was nothing personal. The moment—however long it lasted— was one of absolute impersonality; and at least, where everything may seem vague, I can prove this humorously enough. I must have moved, I suppose, and so felt the stiff drag of that right shoulder, but I was also still under the spell of the window in some degree, so that my hand on its own went groping vaguely for the tube of sunburn cream. I was aware of this movement as of something slow and yet ethereal, luxurious . . . then suddenly there was the bite of pain, a harsh dragging real pain, from a gluey cream that my fingers could not spread. I turned my eyes from the window and saw that the tube which my hand had picked up was a tube of toothpaste! Now the pain was really gritty and harsh, as if the skin had been torn, not at all the thing to laugh at—unless it has happened to someone else. But as I sat down on my bed, looking away towards the garden, I was overcome by a divine, a delicious sense of humour."

Alick paused and smiled at the recollection with a suggestion of detached critical pleasure. "The trouble with explanations and all that is somehow that it's boring, just words. I have tried, so I know. John appeared at breakfast full of a plan. I rather think his wild bayonet charge had stirred him up. Moreover someone had given him a leaflet the night before. He had thought it was a religious tract . . . Are you saved? . . . but emptying his pockets before undressing he had had the curiosity to look at it and found it to be an advertisement for a bull fight in Pamplona. He had already found out that we could make Pamplona that day and asked us if we were game. We were. But first of all I had to see Henry, for the thought had come to me that Henry would be the very man to arrange my little affair with the Basque. So off I set. Before turning in to Henry's I looked away along the beach to where I had had my swimming adventure and saw two slim poles, each with a red flag, stuck in the sand some distance apart, and I could not help wondering if the Spanish authorities were the least bit put out by having to fix these poles before fate had shown that it was absolutely necessary. But they are a courteous people and I supposed they had decided that fate had been given every reasonable chance even with a barbarian. I turned in to Henry's. The café was empty for it was not a drinking hour. I told Henry that I wished to give the Basque something. He was touched and assured me that the matter could be arranged by him and that the Basque would be pleased. He was sorry to hear we were going and offered to write down addresses in Pamplona for the place would be very crowded. When it came to good-bye I wanted to stand him one. My eyes ran along the bottles and stopped at a label which, somehow, they must have missed before. It was a label of a well known brand of old Scotch whisky, a flat bottle with five small stars on it, but with no little flag of the old Scots nation above it, yet there it was. I must have stared at it, for when my eyes turned from it they found Henry's eyes also turning from it. For a little while I looked at him; then I said, 'All the nations'. A smile came into Henry's face, but not the polite smile which acknowledged a man's right to drink the wrong wine—for the wrong reason. And now I had my last and perhaps clearest illusion, for it seemed to me as I stood looking at Henry that something came up out of the green sea water and in from the old Spanish garden and was there in the silence between us. Something of that absolute stillness, and within it I knew, beyond all doubt or argument, that Henry's internationalism *was* real. Quietly, as if pushing across a glass of invisible wine, knowing that we knew each other now, he murmured, 'All the nations'."

19

Peter put a hand on his breast and stopped; he searched all his pockets: he hadn't got his pocket-book. He didn't like to go back; his impulse was to ignore the thing, yet without conscious reasoning he turned and waded through the burn again, came round the high bluff and saw Jock returning to the bothy entrance and Hamish already some way up the slope above.

"I've dropped my pocket-book somewhere," he said to Jock.

"Your pocket-book?" Jock thoughtfully scratched his growing beard. As he was turning towards the bothy he stopped. "Sure it's not in your kitbag?"

Automatically Peter slipped his rucksack off and on opening the main flap found the wallet on top. "Yes, here it is." He looked at it, opened it, withdrew a five-pound note. "Tell you what I would like to do: give Hamish a wedding present. Do you think you could slip him this some time and say it's a present from me with my best wishes?" He pushed the note into Jock's hand.

"Look——"

"Hsh! Make your speech to Hamish." As he moved off again he remembered the little scene in the cave when his effects were being examined. Alick must have dropped the wallet into the rucksack. The kind of thing that would naturally happen there. It was a grey morning and when the cold water came about his feet again he felt chilled to the bone; but not until he tackled the mountain-side did the real throb come into his head. He was in a bad way, his breath in very short supply, and once or twice a weakening flush, coupled with nausea, stopped him. But he was dogged, and behind the aches and follies of the body—and he didn't need to be told just then that his body wasn't getting any

150

younger—the far fount of life sent up its tiny spout, its wriggle of an evident and perhaps immortal worm. But even the humour that watches can grow grey, leaving only the hillside, the next step, and the grip on a tough heather runt. But at last he came out on the high ridge, and it was a ridge, for he could see into the glen beyond it. Presently he turned and picked up Hamish's diminished figure on an opposing ridge, made the agreed signal, got the agreed response, and lay down. Jock and Alick could now continue their dismantlings and removals.

The *false* well beyond all mortal doubt. He felt he was going to die for good.

Man is a very silly animal, his folly perhaps the most remarkable feature about him. He does things for which he pays a price beyond computation, and then does them again. There would need to be a god behind all that. If folly were all it wouldn't be folly. There could be no measurement.

"Be empty," Peter admonished himself in the austere phrase of an ancient Chinese sage, and succeeded fairly well.

When at last he went on and down, leaving that nocturnal cave behind him, he was feeling both better and more bodiless, an almost attractive, if unsteady, combination. That Spanish garden . . . It was the last thing he remembered—until Jock roused him to a cup of tea and an air of completed operations in grey daylight. Good fellows; grand chaps; even if Alick had been bitten slightly by the agenbite of inwit and could not quite trust his Spanish garden. The bitter bite of man's own distrustful snake. We all knew it, and the sensitive knew it well. Hold hard! said Peter to himself as he slipped.

He went down . . . he went along . . . he was going up when the sun came out and looked upon the earth with brilliant astonishment and hit him. It was a delightful knock and he curled up. The warmth on his face and on his hands grew murmurous with divine sleep, but sleep didn't quite wander in, but it wandered about. A wandering bumble-bee circled his face, although, unwashed and unshaven, it could hardly be mistaken for a clump of flowers. He blew at it; it sideslipped drunkenly in the stream of his cave breath and made off. He saw some tall grasses laughing their heads off. He really did not think a great deal of their primitive humour and sat up, and got up, and went on.

Sheer weariness was overtaking him and a need for real sleep which wouldn't come because his brain was poisoned or excited. When the brain gets the illusion that it can go on working at high speed without a materialistic basis it can be very tiresome. A bed—an impersonal bed—in an impersonal hotel—after a hot bath—that's what he needed. To frolic with the folk a man needs to be offensively fit.

He went up . . . he went down . . . he went along. The sun climbed . . . and reached its zenith before he struck a road. By this time he wasn't fit even to encounter an hotel, so he went in off the road, hid himself, curled up and fell into a very deep sleep.

He was awakened by a dog, a liver-and-white spaniel. The brute's sniffing nose withdrew. Beyond the moment's panic and beyond the dog stood a man. He knew him instantly. It was Cocklebuster. Amid a haze of sleep and whisky Cockle-buster had the clarity of an apparition, of something that couldn't be there, yet was. Peter pushed himself onto his seat; his eyes stared and roved. Cocklebuster carried a shot gun under his arm at the proper sporting angle; he wore a plusfour suiting of discreet checks and unpronounced bagginess and was capped by a deerstalker of the same tweed with unobtrusive peaks fore and aft. He stood as a cool sportsman stands for his photograph in the *Tatler*.

"Didn't expect to find you here," said Cocklebuster. It was the very voice, the high ha-ha "county" voice, that had made some of them seriously wonder if the man could in fact whisper.

Peter now felt more lost than ever and looked it.

"Glad you have your trousers on," said Cocklebuster.

Perhaps it was the absence of mirth that shot the hot feeling through Peter, like that feeling of dreadful guilt which in a nightmare paralyses a man who knows he is naked and shouldn't be. He looked at his trousers; his right hand even came in among the front buttons, but found them tied.

"Why," he said, "wh-what did you expect?"

"Shorts," said Cocklebuster.

152

A great breath came out of Peter and he sagged. "It's you all right," he said, and began to laugh weakly, and Cocklebuster's seriousness helped him to laugh on. For of course Cocklebuster's logic was always water-tight in its way. Here was Professor Peter Munro (whom Cocklebuster had last met in a back room in Whitehall, London) going about at his time of life like a hiker, with sweaty unshaven face, and bearing—of all things—a rucksack like some peculiar Continental. Amid all this, that Peter should have hung on to his trousers exhibited at least a remnant of decency. Shorts would have been a final blow.

It really wasn't a laughing matter. It was quite logical. Merely Cocklebuster's mode of statement. Peter remembered the extraordinary yarn about Cocklebuster and the American security officer. Although Cocklebuster was considered utterly impeccable by his own M.I.5 side, the G-man just could not believe that a fellow like Cocklebuster could be trusted with matters of even child-high security. In short, Cocklebuster was a trifle too good to be true, too much of an immaculate creation not to be hiding something. So it was arranged at the highest level in the interest of international friendship and mutual aid that the G-man should be given an opportunity of leading Cocklebuster up the crazy paving to confession. But after only four hours, Cocklebuster's mode of utterance—as in the simple instance of Peter's trousers—so worked upon the G-man that the said G-man found difficulty in distinguishing his own trousers from his own wet handkerchief (wet from sweat) and requested, as a last glimmer of reason died within him, to be conveyed to a psychiatric clinic.

Of course no one really believed this story; certainly not altogether; any more than anyone believed a score of stories about Cocklebuster. But the reality of him did Peter good now. Indeed of all men he could readily think of in the world at that moment none could have come so near the core of his desire, if not of his affection, as Cocklebuster. There were neither Spanish gardens nor gardens of Allah about him, nor wells at his world's end, nor gleams, nor anything that went through boundaries. For Cocklebuster was as sane as a cliché. His face

153

which was not large, had the fresh bloom of true cleanliness and his ginger moustaches had the definite suggestion of wings, as his athletic slimness of height.

"What on earth are you doing here, at this time of year, with a gun?" asked Peter, making way for him.

"Fishing," said Cocklebuster, sitting down.

"Ah," said Peter. "I wondered. Hardly thought you would have been poaching out of season."

"Good God," said Cocklebuster.

"Good sport?"

"Plenty of them, but small."

"Loch?"

"Yes. Have you eaten?" Cocklebuster swung his cartridge bag forward.

"No. The hotel far—or are you stopping at one?"

"Yes. A few miles." He withdrew tissue-wrapped bundles and opened them with some curiosity. "Hm. Boiled mutton again. Ever ate boiled mutton?"

"Many times."

"Have you?" said Cocklebuster, turning a genuine curiosity upon Peter. "Don't you find it dry?"

"A bit, perhaps."

"I find them demn dry." He unrolled some biscuits and cheese. "What do you think of the cheese?"

"Dry," said Peter.

"Demn dry," said Cocklebuster, spreading the total repast, including a slice of cake, within easy mutual reach. He foraged again and produced a small silver flask. "Have a snifter?"

"No, thanks. I'm teetotal."

"You are?" His eyebrows lifted.

"You don't think I look it? Perhaps you're right."

"Easing off, eh?" Cocklebuster poured a reasonable gush into the heel of the flask and tossed it off. "Taken before and after, it wets the stuff. Help yourself."

Peter was hungry and the conversation all that could be desired—or at least expected, for perhaps he would die still wondering why Cocklebuster went about his fishing with a shot gun and spaniel while the twelfth was still distant. The deep sleep, however, had done him good, and the boiled mutton on buttered bread when chewed far enough developed a wonderful flavour, brought back his remote boyhood. The more ravenous he got, the more Cocklebuster nibbled and eased off.

"If you can eat the stuff, do," Cocklebuster encouraged him, and extracted for inspection a sliver of cheese. He nibbled a tiny portion, then swallowed it like an insult without batting an eye. "What I can never understand," he said on a burst of confidence, "is why when they are making the stuff they demn well don't make it. Do you?"

"No," said Peter. "I don't."

"It's like making a fire of camel dung when there's coal about—or even peat. Demned if I can understand it. It's beyond me."

"Been out East since we foregathered?"

"Yes."

"More trees and twigs about?"

"Much. In fact that—round about—oddly enough, is how I'm here."

"Here!" exclaimed Peter. "You don't mean that—good God, not here?"

Cocklebuster laughed like a forest bird, high and hard.

"I merely wondered at your disguise," said Peter, excusing himself.

"Disguise?" repeated Cocklebuster, looking very pointedly at Peter. "How disguise?"

Cornered, Peter said, "You know you were always a bit of a mystery bird. It was even rumoured, I don't mind telling you now, that you occupied a high niche in M.I.5."

"Aw," said Cocklebuster. "Really. So you think I'm snooping around?"

"You look as if you had never carried anything but a shot gun all your life," said Peter.

"I have carried it a good deal," said Cocklebuster coolly.

"But not usually," said Peter, with a touch of desperation, "when you're fishing."

"I rather think you have got tangled a bit," said Cocklebuster.

155

"I sure have," said Peter, with a light-hearted effort at American.

The effort worked, for Cocklebuster was reminded of an "American security wallah. Very nice chap. Spent an afternoon with me. Wanted to get the hang of things, he said, among fellows like us, you know. Thought the best way would be to dig into my past, so that he could get what he called a 'living picture'. I could see his point—fair enough—'living picture'— quite all right. But, this family business and all that, not too easy. I mean a fellow has an aunt or a school or whatever it may be, and that's that. He didn't seem to get the hang of things, and at last thought he would, as he said, begin over again by pinpointing my grandfather." Cocklebuster paused, though obviously interested in the memory.

Peter encouraged him to go on.

"Remarkable man, my grandfather. I have never met such— well, manners. Old school—but with a real Chinese gloss. Right to the end . . . he bowed to them as he withdrew, died. He had gone to the Far East on some diplomatic mission, had stopped on, and then years after found he couldn't see eye to eye with our Foreign Office on a certain affair, and, well, there it was. He wouldn't budge. Had a tremendous respect for the Chinese. Then, of all things, he went into trade—got in in a big way—trading right through to the Russians—and so forth. When he retired, he impressed me no end. Always, you know——" Cocklebuster actually bowed, winging the air with not uncourtly hands. "Remarkable. But what impressed me, and by God it did, was the solitary piece of advice for life he gave me. Never forgotten it. We were walking past a covert. I had a popgun. He had his hands in his sleeves. A pheasant showed, an old cock. The bird stood. We stood. 'Granville, my boy,' he said to me, 'I always want you to remember this: Confucius never shot at a sitter.' Terrific, what?"

"Terrific is the word."

"Never forgot it. Never shall."

Never had Peter seen him so moved. "That would be— around 500 B.C."

"Yes. You'll find it recorded in the *Analects*. Right down for nearly two thousand five hundred years. Different peoples. Different civilisations. All the way. Never at a sitter."

"Almost incredible."

"Gives you a knock."

"Flattening. You would think that it was in the scheme of things; the civilised scheme anyway. Extraordinary."

"Absolutely."

Lost in wonder, they both forgot about the American. Peter had, in fact, quite involuntarily a sudden remarkable intuition of the principle of conservatism in human affairs, not as something that merely holds on but as in itself a perfected achievement in creation; and from that he got a penetrating insight into Cocklebuster's essential nature, and particularly into his quite miraculous capacity to decipher the signs and symbols which primitive peoples left around, in desert and jungle, bits of trees, trees themselves, strokes and spirals . . . and from that to civilised men finding themselves in primitive surroundings, and so on. That Confucius never shot at a sitter was like handing Cocklebuster his own higher criticism.

"My first memory of Confucius," said Peter, "is his saying, 'The treatment you would not have for yourself, do not hand out to others'."

"It's got a familiar ring, what?" Cocklebuster was almost jocular.

And then Peter remembered the American.

Cocklebuster gathered himself.

"You were pinpointing your grandfather, I think."

"Oh. So I told him about my grandfather—diplomatic mission—trading right through Manchuria—been often in Petrograd—and so forth. The fellow cottoned on to Petrograd like a leech until I felt he was losing his way, so to bring matters to a head and let him right in on the kind of man my grandfather really was, I thought I couldn't do better than simply tell him that, like Confucius, he never shot at a sitter. But with that he seemed to get a bit muddled. In fact, to be quite candid, I rather gathered that he thought a sitter was a Russian. So I had to explain that a sitter was a sitting bird. Then he seemed to mix up Confucius and my grandfather, and altogether the matter became involved, particularly when we went back to 500 B.C. and he asked me how the heck Confucius could have shot a bird anyhow, sitting or flying, seeing guns hadn't been invented then and therefore he couldn't have had a gun. I said he had a bow and arrow. It was then something rather mistrustful came into his eye. I rather think he thought I was having him on, for from then on things began to get complicated. A very nice fellow. Very earnest—but *too* intelligent. That's their trouble. Sorry to have to say it, but there it is. The simple truth—like Confucius not shooting at a sitter: unless you can *get* that, I mean to say, where are you?"

"Nowhere," agreed Peter. "Not a blessed place. What happened then?"

"I asked him in the end to stop for dinner, but by that time I could hardly get his drift. Looked depressed to me. And he wouldn't stop. Just toddled off."

"I think you put your finger on it: too intelligent."

"Absolutely."

"Pure intelligence, fine; but where is the place you walk on without thinking?"

"Exactly. How do you know how? I mean, you need a certain amount of intelligence. Naturally." He unscrewed the cap of his flask. "Haven't changed your mind?"

"I have," said Peter.

Cocklebuster poured half the contents into the silver heel and handed it to Peter. "Cheers!" he said and put the neck to his mouth.

"Cheers!" said Peter, and they finished in a dead heat.

"Going anywhere?" asked Cocklebuster.

"No, nowhere in particular."

"Fact is, I was going to have a look round a peculiar kind of shoot. Oddish business, I think, but shoots these days are not what they were. There are syndicates and things." Cocklebuster made a *moue* which lifted his moustaches. "A forestry chappie in London, nice fellow—Forestry Commission, you know—he said it might be worth having a look round, so I thought I would. The plantations are over the top, sweeps of them, with some cultivated ground about. He gave me a line to the head forester, an awfully nice Scotchman. I don't think there's much, mark you; but an odd pheasant has been seen, and even capercailzie, and woodcock come in definitely. The Forestry Commission lets it—for such an old song that I fancy it may be an overcharge. But they net against rabbits, and, for getting your eye in, the old bunny takes some beating. Then there's a small loch somewhere for duck, mallard. Roe deer, too; head forester says he heard them barking. Interesting, I thought; possibilities. And trees."

"So you were on the way to inspect?"

"Before signing on the dotted line; that's the idea. Feel like a stroll?"

"You're going back to the hotel after?"

"The car dropped me here and will be back in about three hours to collect. It's five miles to the hotel."

"Then it's providence. If we're returning this way I could dump my kit here."

"Jolly good idea," agreed Cocklebuster, animated by the thought of the thing being dumped anywhere.

20

Of all that happened to Peter in his prospectings along the byways and highways of this beautiful land, the hours with Granville Cocklebuster amid the dark green trees of the Forestry Commission had an intermixing of fantasy and fact which in retrospect achieved a realm of its own, a realm neither on the earth nor off it. To have it happen with Cocklebuster might be like living in a paradox, but then twice in a hushed forest aisle Peter had the distinct glimmering of a notion that that was how or where we actually lived. And there were moments when it went beyond that.

It started with Sally, the liver-and-white spaniel. They had lifted her over the close-mesh fencing designed to keep out rodents like rabbits when trees are young, and moved along their first ride, which was broad as a carriage drive with the young pines shooting up twenty feet or so on either hand. The going was heavy, charged with great clumps of ancient heather and full of pits, for the ground had been trenched for the planting. Some of these pits were concealed by the heather. Sally had been broken in by a real gamekeeper, but though biddable she was young and keen. In fact, Cocklebuster had found it easier to take her on the lead the last part of the way than further overtax his throat, and she had consistently strained at the lead and even panted. Yet immediately they got over the fence and he put the lead in his pocket, Sally came to heel and stuck there. Now Cocklebuster's idea, like all his ideas, was simple and direct; in fact he was merely following the practice of any good keeper who, well before "the day", takes a long walk round to see what birds are on the ground. To flush even one family of pheasants might well draw a signature out of Cocklebuster; and his arithmetical imaginings had far transcended one. Quite naturally he anticipated surprises. Capercailzies fed on pine tops, there were millions of pine tops, and capers are big as turkeys and very like them. A flight of flying turkeys might be something to look at. The woodcock would not be in until October, but there is always the odd native about. Not to mention rocketing pigeons by the dozen, or even gross, at any time. Roe deer. Duck.

In short, he was keen and could not understand Sally. He was fond and secretly very proud of her, and now here she was skulking behind as if the place were full of devils. As he swept his right arm forward and urged her on in clear not to say ringing tones, she obeyed and entered the edge of the tree belt but in no time was back at heel again. It got the better of Cocklebuster. It was not so much anger as shame, Peter felt, shame that she should behave so and let him down, for on the way he had confided to Peter, who had expressed admiration of her action and appearance, that she was "awfully nice", and he had said it in a way that had touched Peter's heart and increased his liking for the man. For she was in truth an awfully nice bitch, groomed to a shining sheen by her master's fond and capable hands.

"Come on!" yelled Cocklebuster, with the enraged and splendid élan of a fellow taking his men over the top, headed straight for the trees, stepped on nothing and went by the right ear into his first trench.

As Cocklebuster emerged, the effect on Sally was almost neurotic. She whined, visibly dwindled, and if her ears could have fallen off they would.

"Come on!" said Cocklebuster, with no less assurance if less sound, and headed for the trees with, this time, an eye for the terrain. Sally followed; indeed she would have followed him into the last ditch. In matters of density and height tree growth was not always uniform and Peter could get Cocklebuster in snatches. He was distinctly earnest, lean and nimble, and, above all, he encouraged Sally to range. But Sally would not range. The undergrowth grew spotty and now Peter lost sight of them. There was a crash, a shout, and silence. They must have flushed a roe, even if presumably a deaf one; but Peter, trying for a viewpoint, saw them both emerge from the same pit.

"Can't understand it!" said Cocklebuster, back on the ride, angry or heart-broken or both.

"Certainly mysterious," Peter agreed.

Cocklebuster now did not look at Sally and Sally tried to look as if she wasn't there.

"It can't be——" Peter stopped.

"What?" said Cocklebuster sharply.

"She couldn't—I mean, you would almost think she had lost her scent."

"Good God!" said Cocklebuster, really stricken. "Absurd!" But he was able to look at Sally again.

"Let me try her on this side," said Peter.

And it was some measure of the depth of Cocklebuster's sportsmanship that he not only did not pooh-pooh the idea but actually made sounds which might be construed as almost encouraging Sally to go with him. Certainly he left it to her. And she went, lingeringly perhaps, dutifully even, but she followed. Peter was now not concerned about flushing game so much as finding out what was wrong with Sally. So he was keeping the tail of an eye on her as she crept behind him and accordingly went into his first pit stern first in a complicated manner. For a thumping second or two he thought he had startled the father of all capercailzies into craking hoots of unimaginable astonishment, but it was no more than Cocklebuster, head up on the middle of the ride, laughing. And by Jove, he laughed. As he presently explained, it was "demned funny".

The score more or less even, they went on, with nothing broken but, so to speak, the ice. The ground rose and the trees thinned, stunted, leaving comparatively unencumbered spaces where birds of the most active kind might well have loved to rustle their feathers and sleep in security. Tacitly now they paid no attention to Sally and put their hearts and feet into such active even turbulent ranging that anything with fur or feather must, if there at all, have lain unbelievably close.

Exhaustion began to creep upon Peter in a light-headed way. The cave, the spirit and the honey, he thought, not to mention the Spanish garden, for the sensation was not unpleasant. When at last he sat down with a thump, Cocklebuster came and sat by him, and Sally flattened by Cocklebuster. Her tongue went out and back over her teeth at a speed Peter had rarely if ever seen in a dog. And when she gulped it was noisily.

"You would think," said Peter lightly, "she had flushed all the game for ten miles round."

"Perhaps she has," said Cocklebuster grimly, not looking at her, taking out a map which he unfolded. It was a large official working chart of the whole plantation area. The many-angled outline was broadly red, broad as red tape. The rides were black dotted lines. After a time Cocklebuster said, "We're here," and put his nail on a spot. Then he said, "There's the duck loch. We'll have a look at it. Then we clear out there." He folded the map.

"Of course," said Peter, who needed a rest, "the trees are young, but I don't get the feeling of pines, pine forests."

"I don't get the feeling of anything."

"You would think life had deserted the place."

"Gutted."

"There's no scent: that's what's worrying Sally. Nothing else."

"You think so?"

"Absolutely. Ever heard a symphony by Sibelius?"

"Pine forests grow on that fellow," said Cocklebuster.

It had been a long shot on Peter's part and now he shook with silent laughter, though on trees and twigs and primitive reactions thereto Cocklebuster was uncanny, as he might have remembered.

"Trolls wander through them," pursued Cocklebuster. "The fellow has it rummaged." He sounded relieved as if, after all, Sally might be all right, was hardly to blame.

"You don't think it's trolls—in her case?"

"No," said Cocklebuster definitely.

"I got an uncomfortable feeling coming up there that the place was psychoanalysed," said Peter.

163

"Who by?"

"Forestry Commission."

Cocklebuster weighed the matter. "I should doubt it," he said. "Odd thing is I can't put a name to it. It's like nothing."

And Peter cried, "You've got it! It's *nothing*!"

Cocklebuster looked at him and looked thoughtfully away. "You have something there. Hm. That composer chappie, he has passages of nothing off and on, but they're full up, high potential. This—it's the emptiness—demned if I can get it."

"But Sally's got it!"

"What?" Cocklebuster stared at him. "By Jove!" he said.

"Not only no scent of game, but no scent of other dog, scentless—dogless—utterly void—*nothing*."

"Absolutely," said Cocklebuster. "Millions of lamp-posts and not a—not a demned sniff." It was terrific. He apprehended Sally's scentless void in the profound way which so often made a judgment of his on such elusive matters almost uncanny. He bent to her; took a fistful of her right ear. "Good old girl!" Her eyes melted like brown balls of sugar candy and she gave herself utterly through them. She lost her head and kissed him wildly. He was rather more than moved and got up. "Let's go," he said; and added, "duck pond".

But when they got to where the loch of the wild duck should have been it wasn't there. Cocklebuster had a second careful scrutiny of his map, and decided they should have gone on a bit, farther back, and taken the ride which branched off the next one to the one they had been on.

But after doing all this the loch was still not in its place.

Cocklebuster now scrutinised the edges of the chart for those signs and symbols which would assure him that the whole was not a piece of hanky panky. But—unless some very curious game was being played—it seemed official enough. After eliminating every possibility of error, he arrived at a definitive conclusion, adding, "I'll find that demn pond or drop."

"I'll drop," said Peter. "Give me a shout when you find it."

"Hello?"

"No sleep. Got lost on the mountains last night." He smiled.

"Aw. So that's what it was!" Cocklebuster was a bit upset. "Righto! I'll just nip along and—you'll hear from me. Sorry and all that." Off he went at speed.

Peter stretched himself on the heather and relaxed. At first he sank through himself like water through hot sand, but stopped short of full sleep in that curious in-between region where, it seemed to him, he was conscious of his dreams. His eyes were shut and his breath heavy. The forest he was now in had full-grown pines, girthy reddish fellows, with tough crinkled bark. Columnar pines, for he was among them. Lost in such a forest a man makes a fire and, as the long night creeps on, every now and then—he looks over his shoulder. As Peter looked over his shoulder he got the primeval impact of the forest. It was terrible and authentic and older than his marrow. As he listened acutely he became aware of a distant music and knew that it was the music which Sibelius had caught in this place and, with the austere enigmatic face of the master, written down. Yet when he listened still more acutely he found he actually could not hear the music. He had the kind of sensation which a man experiences when looking through sound-proof glass at an orchestra playing a symphony. Then one theme leapt at his heart and, in glancing over his shoulder, he saw a troll's face peering at him round a pine's column. His scalp stirred, he got slowly to his feet, slid away, then ran full tilt.

He was stopped by a sea-inlet, a fiord, with spout-tops of green on dark blue water, for it was in commotion, not long waves, but a real sea-jabble, with light on it but not open sunlight. The headland beyond was immense and solid and capable of brooding, but not brooding now. . . .

He deserted Sibelius and his land and fled back to his youth, and found himself in a wood of old birches and of old hazels with root crops of young spotted withies; and he was afraid because he was poaching. Now this was an actual wood of his boyhood and the poaching an actual experience. As he listened, holding his breath, he beheld the branches again, saw them turn

165

and twist without moving, shaping their queer frightening serpentine characters on the air. He hearkened to the silence beyond all sound, before sound was, before music was even a dream. And his eyes came down, slowly, and between the trunks and beyond them, he saw the far gleam on the edge of the wood.

It was a very strange gleam, like a gleam at the end of the world, and suddenly he knew that through it, towards the wood where he was hiding, would come the old man with the beard, the man of authority with the power of courts, the man who could put terrible shame on him, the old gamekeeper.

Lying here now in this new pine forest, Peter actually began listening for the gamekeeper as acutely as he had listened when a boy. A voice called; he stirred and his eyes opened in a scared way.

The voice called again. It was Cocklebuster in the wrong turning.

They met at a sharp corner.

"Sorry," said Peter, "if I dropped off."

"*Either*," said Cocklebuster, "we have been given the wrong map *or* if we have been given the right map we are in the wrong forest."

"That, I think," said Peter, "clinches it."

"So no demn good wasting more time. Agreed?"

"Agreed."

"Now," said Cocklebuster, rather righteously stirred, "what we have got to find out is where are we."

"Fine."

"I figure it like this. The road we left—where I met you—runs roughly west perhaps 10 degrees north. We left that road at an angle of roughly 30 odd degrees, also going north of west. It's now 4.12 p.m. so the sun is 18 degrees west of sou'west. There's the sun, here we are. Now if our main traverse here according to these calculations was north-west, as it more or less certainly was, then if we move back on a sou'easterly bearing we should at least fetch up somewhere on the original road." Having thus very simply defined their position, all Cocklebuster had to do, with the help of one or two imaginary ground lines drawn in relation to the sun's position, was to find a south-easterly bearing, which he did. "So that's the way," he concluded, thrusting an arm at an army corps of healthy young pines in exceptionally close formation.

"Clear as glass," said Peter. "But need we——?"

"No," said Cocklebuster. "We can go up this ride and take the next to left to compensate error."

"So long as we roughly keep the sun on our right——"

"Absolutely."

As they went on, Cocklebuster said, "It's not often I make such a bloody mess."

It was actually the first time Peter had ever heard him commend himself, and he knew, from past experience, how true were his words. There were places where Cocklebuster might not get the hang of things, as with the G-man's probings, but not in forests, not on the old earth. Of course Peter knew that the root of the trouble was Sally. She had put him all wrong. There was something truly touching about this.

They reached the first opening to the left in silence; but it was not the entrance to a ride for they couldn't see along it. It was more like a natural bay, with arboreal stragglers, positively unplanned bushes, here and there and together, which they pushed through with amaze until they stood on a peak of astonishment—gazing upon the loch of the wild ducks.

It was a small loch, a lochan, an oval mirror, a long bright shield, a poet's enchanted place. Floppy old-fashioned trees gathered midway on the right side like a nosegay at the lochan's waist, a posy at her girdle. Even Sally stopped shivering and quivering, even her tongue stopped, and far-sighted she stared at this enchantment; and, following her example, far-sighted Peter stared also at this tapestry of times long past and beheld a troubling of its surface at the distant end and lo! out two wild duck swam, darkening the silver. Deep in her throat the lost Sally uttered the whine of disbelief and in that instant Peter heard a rustle of chart paper. But just as Confucius would not shoot at a sitting bird so Peter now did not turn round to look at Cocklebuster. There are times when a man does not look at his fellow, or there were times.

Peter moved slowly on and Sally followed him and the two wild duck were released by the lochan. So fast did their wings beat and so loud did the drake quack that they may have had their own notions on the nature and appearance of trolls, far beyond gun-shot as they were. Peter wandered on, refreshed, for the rest in the ride had done him good and Sibelius had done him no harm. Indeed he would have to listen to that sound interpreter of the Northland with a more attentive ear sometime. Remarkable that Cocklebuster should have penetrated so deeply into the music . . . almost out of character . . . though why? If Cocklebuster had, as he had, certain primitive apprehensions, uprisings from the unconscious, that conservative stronghold . . . then why not? What was art but—but Peter caught thought by the tail. My God, like the serpent in the garden, thought was ever ready to leave its rightful region and wriggle in. Thought, that thief of beauty, thought Peter with thoughtless pleasure as he wandered on. Cocklebuster was coming behind now on very definite feet. They would be going places in a moment. Sally could not find her lost scent but instead of whimpering was inclined to stand and stare. A lochan and a mallard's quack-quack. There were moments when her tail stub stood still.

A delicious and futile laughter assailed Peter, but he dared not show it lest Cocklebuster misunderstand, so he kept going, past the clump of alders, the willow and the three salley bushes, and came to the far end where reeds grew, among which the duck must have been feeding. Peter had the notion that the drake had been warning the family to hide because the most dangerous and bloody of all trolls were approaching. He moved towards the reeds, went in over the shoe-tops in deceptive marsh, heard Cocklebuster's "Ha! ha! ha!"—no more—and backed out.

"This way," said Cocklebuster with such high decision that Peter, as he followed, wondered if he had laughed. In no time they were at a fence. Using his deerstalker cap as cover for the barbs on top, Cocklebuster got one leg over, stuck, was released in time, and stood on the other side. Peter handed him his gun and then Sally, whereupon he took his jacket off and covered such a stretch of spikes that he got over without sticking.

"That's that," said Cocklebuster, lifting his gun.

"You mean you're not taking it?"

"Absolutely."

21

There remained the enigma of Sally and her scent. Had she actually lost her scent or hadn't she? Peter could see in the first few yards that it was more than a moot point to Cocklebuster.

And Sally seemed really at a loss. True, she did leave her master's heels, but yet could not be said to go either here or there with even subconscious purpose. They were coming down upon an old ramshackle croft house inhabited by an old woman. As they passed it they saw her widowed head look out from the low doorway like one left behind from a tide long ebbed. Some fowls were pecking about the door and a hidden cock crew a triumph that sounded barren. Over now on the left was a small soured field which had grown clumps of rushes on its back like hairy warts. Sally was in front when suddenly her nose jerked half round as if it had been invisibly hooked. She followed the hook. She was running.

"By God!" yelled Cocklebuster, whipping his gun from under his arm. He was terribly moved.

Sally was running, not fast, on her nose, beautiful action, reached the wart that had hooked her and out popped a rabbit.

Then Sally lost her head. After all, she had been through a lot. The yelping as of an excited mongrel could have been forgiven her; but she not only yelped she ran, and she ran as she never ran before. She tore after that rabbit at such muzzle velocity that her master, though he slipped the safety catch and swung his weapon, dared not shoot lest he hit both. In no time they were out of range and then Cocklebuster began to roar to Sally to come back. That his throat stood up to its own

170

sounds as it did spoke well for its general condition. But it had no effect on Sally. Nothing short of the end of the world was going to stop Sally, and then she would go over it. About a quarter of a mile away she disappeared into an old wood.

Peter stood up for her at once in a forthright way. But Cocklebuster wouldn't have it. Not only are there in general things which are not done: there are in particular things which no good dog ever does.

"I think if I may say so," said Peter, "that you are carrying your Confucian precepts too far."

"You sound confused to me," said Cocklebuster.

"It's you who are confused," said Peter. "That wasn't the only mode of thought in old China——"

"Confushed! Ha! ha! ha! Demn funny!" For, secretly, Cocklebuster was rather touched by the support for Sally.

"She was following, for her, the Tao, the Way. Her dynamic charge was *joie de vivre*," explained Peter.

"I'll admit she shows a turn of speed—for a spaniel, I mean."

"She proceeded," said Peter, "like a guided missile."

"She certainly ran," agreed Cocklebuster, increasing his pace still more and thus defeating Peter's intention to slow him up. As they neared the wood of old deciduous trees a yelp pulled him into a trot.

They found Sally well within the wood, on top of a warren, in an open space fringed with dappled shadows. A fine friable soil obscured the sheen of her breast, her face, her ears, and slid from her jaws and tongue in a sort of cook's batter.

"Good God," said Cocklebuster, "what a mess!"

Sally decided to wag her stump.

"Did you expect to dig him out of his burrow or what?" demanded Cocklebuster.

Sally bowed and twisted and made eyes at him.

"Here!" Cocklebuster sat down beside her and, while he cleaned her eyes with her ears, spoke to her so severely that she made a pass at him and got the point of his nose with her tongue and left some of the good earth there.

Peter lay flat on his back. Clearly there were times when Sally could overlook her master's being a bit of a fuss-pot.

Presently Peter began to hear something. And then, as if suddenly waking up (he had let go) in paradise, he became aware of bird song. His opened eyes roamed among leafy branches, oak and ash and elm and even a beech, a beech with drooping foliaged branches gracious and widespread, like the skirts of the woodland mother, the ancient matriarch, the first and only goddess. Small birds flitted and twittered, and here and there from the green depths bits of song aspired or tumbled down. Suddenly he remembered the old woman peeping out from the low door. She had been left behind. And he knew that he would never forget that glimpse of her, that sensation of a whole way of life left behind, peeping from its last door. He was stirred profoundly and knew also that this wood had been left behind, that somewhere nearby there would be a big house with no one peeping from its door, silent, lintel stones askew. And in this curious light in which he saw all these things with a clear certainty, he wondered: are we chasing the birdsong from the face of the earth?

He sat up. Cocklebuster had just finished Sally's toilet. "Hearing anything?" Peter asked.

"What's that?" Cocklebuster looked at him, at the hearkening expression on his face. "Birds!" he said at last. "By God," he exclaimed, "there were no birds!"

"Nothing."

"Absolutely," said Cocklebuster, gripped, listening to the birds, trying to spot them, following the sounds with eyes that suddenly were themselves gripped.

Peter twisted round to follow Cocklebuster's gaze and saw to the right of the spreading beech, across a hollow with a trickle of water, the trunks of trees, bare trunks, and between the trunks and beyond them, he saw the gleam on the far side of the wood like a golden light in a lattice window. Whether from the angle at which the afternoon sun hit distant grass or leaves or what not, the light was golden . . . paradisal . . . warm.

"Oddish light, don't you think?" said Cocklebuster.

"Very," said Peter, not turning round.

"Gives me an uncanny feeling of sin."

After a heart-beat, Peter brought his eyes back to Cockle-buster with a questioning effort.

"I mentioned the old grandfather and what Confucius said—you know, about not shooting at a sitter. The demned thing was," explained Cocklebuster, with a distinct heightening of colour, "that a few weeks before then, I—I had shot at one."

"You had?" said Peter.

"Not only that but I—aw—shot it dead."

"With your air-gun?"

Cocklebuster nodded. "A slug—thirty yards—right through the ear. Never really expected to—but—well, there it was. Odd thing about it was that I actually aimed at the ear."

"The ear?"

"Yes. And but for a spot of blood there wouldn't have been a trace."

"Oddish, certainly," agreed Peter thoughtfully.

"When a boy is out with a popgun in good country on his belly and a gorgeous old cock pheasant is looking about—well, there it is."

"After all, that's why he's there," Peter agreed.

"Strictly speaking, no," said the Confucian. "He's there for rooks. But a rook is a wary bird."

"When you have carried a slug in a popgun for an hour or two there is a temptation to let it off. War among nations. No good pretending otherwise."

"I'm not," said Cocklebuster. "But"—his colour deepened—"it was out of season."

"Ah," said Peter. There was silence. To lighten the dark moment, he added, "War hadn't been declared. You were modern for a nipper."

Cocklebuster eyed him.

"In war you look for sitters in or out of season," said Peter in a thoughtless way. "What happened?"

"I carried the bird well into the wood. I was terrified Hobbs, who looked after my grandfather's place, would find out. Stinking with fright. Mostly beeches and absolutely no undergrowth. I was scraping a hole with my hands and feet to bury

173

the bird when I thought I heard something. Then I saw on the far edge—that light." Peter, turning his head, saw once again the golden unworldly gleam. "Don't know why," proceeded Cocklebuster, "but it gave me an awful uncomfortable feeling. Then I saw legs—man's legs—Hobbs. They stopped. He called in a loud voice. I was stiff. Then the legs went away." Cocklebuster breathed heavily.

"Like God," said Peter.

"Absolutely," said Cocklebuster at once. "Following Sunday the aged vicar, awfully decent man, was holding forth on Creation, quotations from Genesis and so forth. I hunted out a copy of the Book from the library and stole to a remote corner and there conned the words in secrecy. Remarkable bit of writing—but I expect you know it?"

"Somewhat."

"Awfully good on trees."

"Really?"

"Demn good. I had never—not until then—sort of thought of Adam under the trees; hiding, I mean."

Peter had involuntarily thought of the tree of the knowledge of good and evil which, as a boy, he had imagined as an immense apple tree with red-cheeked apples glistening. For the first fruit tree he had ever seen had been an apple tree. Theft then was a sin which he had not committed, certainly not outside the home boundaries, and within these boundaries all might be considered tinged with community, so that the secret purloining of a brotherly knife for a spell partook of the tribal concept of goods held in common. But this first apple tree grew in the garden of a gentleman farmer, a pocket laird, and by no stretch of sinful imagination could it be considered—then—as being held in common. As, posted at the corner of the garden which commanded the wooded path from the pocket laird's house, a very small Peter kept watch, he was beset by a notion of the awfulness of theft, of sin. A long and fearful vigil it had been before he had been whistled away and in a remote place had sunk his teeth in the stolen fruit.

But as this obviously wasn't the tree that was worrying

Cocklebuster, Peter egged him on, and Cocklebuster surprised him with a word-perfect citation.

"*And they heard the voice of the Lord God walking in the garden in the cool of the day,*" quoted Cocklebuster, "*and Adam and his wife hid themselves from the presence of the Lord God amidst the trees of the garden. And the Lord God called unto Adam, and said unto him, Where art thou?*"

"By gum!" said Peter thoughtfully. "Amidst the trees!"

"Absolutely."

Peter looked over his shoulder and saw the gleam. The garden of Eden. That Cocklebuster, of all men, should have given the gleam a name and a habitation! Life was so mysterious that he thought of Fand. "I had forgotten Adam's wife," he said.

Cocklebuster merely cleared his throat.

"Before the voice," said Peter, "they would have seen the legs."

"Presumably," said Cocklebuster.

"Demned interesting," said Peter, feeling upon him the mysterious urge to speak as Cocklebuster spoke. Perhaps that's why Cocklebuster spoke as he did. To mystery there was no end. "Only, in Adam's case, the Lord God found him," he said, back in his own voice if still with Cocklebuster's cast of thought.

"He did."

"And Adam?"

"Adam said he was afraid and felt—aw—naked."

"Naked?"

"According to the Book of Words. *I heard thy voice in the garden, and I was afraid because I was naked; and I hid myself.*"

"Naked," repeated Peter. "That's a psychiatric nut."

"Bit of a maze."

"Labyrinth?"

Cocklebuster made a *moue*. "That's jumping a bit."

"I doubt it," said Peter. "I thought Adam blamed Eve?"

"He did—with the second barrel."

Peter pondered. "Do you know, I can't remember whom Eve blamed."

175

"The serpent," said Cocklebuster.

"Of course!" said Peter, nodding in profound wonder. There came upon him another inconsequent glimpse of Fand. "Do you think that during this first conference about the tree of life also in the midst of the garden, and the tree of knowledge of good and evil, do you think there was a moment when the woman, unperceived, looked Adam up and down, and looked the Lord God up and down, and realised that they were all she had to go places with?"

"Um!" said Cocklebuster, smelling a doubtful theory, for they were now experts on familiar ground and a subtle man always jockeyed for position before the starting tape. Cocklebuster wasn't giving anything away before they were off.

"As a," said Peter, "as a myth—though I rather dislike a too free use of the word——"

"I certainly do," agreed Cocklebuster without hesitation.

"Well—whatever we call it, it does show, it is a striking instance of the *volte-face* from the immensely ancient concept of woman as the—the——"

"The only god," said Cocklebuster.

"Admitted. Over immense aeons of time the only god was a goddess——"

"The Savage Goddess," said Cocklebuster.

"That's right," said Peter, whose eyes were on the beech tree, "though doubtless she would have had her gracious moments, her poetic—uh——"

"Personal conjecture of so-called civilised man."

"But is conjecture impermissible? By the way, you haven't got married?"

"No," said Cocklebuster, who knew an impermissible conjecture when he heard it. He shifted restlessly on his seat like one jockeying good and hard. Sally, watching him, now permitted herself to sniff the exciting if forbidden air.

"Anyway, the poets also knew her as the White Goddess, and if she destroyed them, still until they had fallen for her absolutely they were not—and they knew they were not— real poets."

"*La Belle Dame sans merci*," riposted Cocklebuster, with

such contained irony that he tilted the right wing of his moustaches with the knuckle of his left forefinger. "My dear fellow, you simply cannot help infiltrating from your civilised periods."

"I wasn't thinking of Keats exactly."

"Possibly, for I remember, if I may say so, how you tended to bog down with your Miletus johnnies—Thales, Anaximander, *et cie*."

Peter laughed. "Good times!"

"Demn good," Cocklebuster agreed but watchfully, for the professor was a wily bird.

They wrangled for a bit, wandered down mazes and came upon each other unexpectedly at corners as they had done in the Forestry Commission's new forest, for the period under discussion, with its emergence of the individual questing mind from the communal mind, of the philosopher Thales from the blood-bound tribe, excited them both. What was over half a millennium B.C. was just far enough away to permit that precision of thought, that certainty of judgment, which the too near so often obfuscates. Each not only knew where he was but also where the other wasn't. And when neither was there but only the hurdle, Cocklebuster could suddenly appear in the guise of Dionysus, the dynamic one, sweep the Olympic Peter to one side, and go for the hurdle bald-headed. Though in point of fact Cocklebuster was anything but bald-headed, for once, giving a tug to his twin-snouted cap, he tugged it right off and so disarranged his thick reddish-brown well-brushed hair that it looked alarmed and waited till he landed, then lay down at once under his hand. Not that Peter either was or meant to be Olympic man, nor for that matter Cocklebuster Dionysus (before the god took to wine and went effeminate), but there are moments in the press of affairs when a man can no longer wait upon the order of his going: he jumps first and argues afterwards, and at least on such an occasion he never argues less. But somehow they got back to the Garden of Eden and at once were completely almost fatally in accord.

For what a change from the Savage Goddess to Eve!

"From the Savage Goddess to God," said Cocklebuster, slackening the bit.

"Matriarchy to patriarchy."

"The patriarchal Jew."

"The man who put woman in her place."

"At least," said the Confucian, who was a stickler for exactitude, "the man who put a fig leaf in its place."

As Peter laughed Cocklebuster blew through his moustaches. And so they completed the circle and were back among ordinary trees. In fairness, Peter told his own poaching adventure in boyhood and how to him it had seemed that the leafless branches wrote upon the air. For time—or its absence—was now doing tricks with him as he reclined upon an evanescence of spirit and honey, and that trees should in fact write upon the air need not be more surprising than that the Garden of Eden should glimmer between their trunks.

"They did," said Cocklebuster.

"Did what?"

"Write upon the air."

"Ah," said Peter.

"A certain Welsh scholar has observed that in all Celtic languages *trees* means *letters*. Twigs of various sorts come into the Druidic mysteries. Then again the oldest Irish alphabet has the name Beth—Luis—Nion, which means Birch—Rowan —Ash, and the initial letters of these three trees were the first three letters of a series, each of which is the initial of a tree."

"Holy——" Peter's response from Jock's far cave paused upon its own awe.

"You haven't researched there?"

"I should say no—but . . . it's very queer. At this moment it has an extraordinary familiarity, as if you'd slid back a veil."

"Never heard of the Battle of the Trees? 'Great is the gorse in battle.' 'Cruel the gloomy ash.' 'The birch, though very magnanimous, was late in arraying himself.' According to Celtic tradition, the Druids could transform trees into warriors and send them into battle."

"I suppose so," said Peter.

Cocklebuster gave him a look.

"I don't suppose that you and I," said Peter dreamily, "are lumps of enchantment."

Silence.

"I mean transformed into," Peter explained, his eyes held by the latticed gleam from Eden.

In a voice of anger and agony Cocklebuster suddenly cried to his Maker.

Peter's right hand came across his heart.

But it was Sally; at least, Sally wasn't anywhere to be seen.

22

Peter enjoyed bowling along the very narrow road beside the driver while Sally was putting the finishing touches to a somewhat drawn-out reconciliation in the rear. As they rounded a blind corner at high speed he floated up against the driver and then floated back until the door stopped him. Apparently another "party" should have been picked up an hour ago somewhere else, and the driver was not too happy at having been kept waiting so long. It was remarkable what one small spaniel bitch could do when she got going. But luck was with them, for here in no time was the hotel with its great white face.

Peter got out and pulled his rucksack after him and was wondering if he could assist with ready cash or whatever was the custom when the car shot off in a way that would have surprised him had not an attractive woman smiled in so charming a manner that his hand, reaching for his tweed hat, didn't find it because he had left it in the car. But in a moment he saw that the lady wasn't smiling to him but to Cocklebuster, and Cocklebuster swept his deerstalker from his head handsomely, smiling and ha-haing in so boldly shy a fashion that Peter recognised he was, in his by no means undistinguished way, a demned handsome fellow. Glimpsing his own rumpled trousers, and feeling as unwashed and unshaven as he was, he thought he might be doing Cocklebuster a good turn if he pretended he didn't belong, so slipping the rucksack negligently over one shoulder he proceeded towards the main entrance.

There was some glass frontage through which he was inspected, and in the hallway sportsmen were clustered around a brown trout of such outsize dimensions that it was described as a big-headed cannibal by all except the angler who had caught it. Their jokes were so vociferous that they neither saw nor heard Peter, but he got through the press to the office desk, where a young lady met his request for a bed by simply asking him if he had booked. It was deadly.

"Any kind of room would do," Peter persisted foolishly.

"Sorry. Full up."

"Absolutely nothing at all?"

"Nothing."

Still Peter stood for he was very tired. As a doubtful cross between a tramp and a hiker he hesitated to ask for a hay loft. "I suppose I may have dinner?"

"Seven-thirty."

"Thank you." He turned away, found a chair just inside the lounge, and dropped his rucksack on his clay-grey shoes. Perhaps Cocklebuster would let him shave and brush-up somewhere. Through a glass panel he caught a glimpse of Cocklebuster's charming lady obviously telling Sally that she didn't believe for a moment that she, Sally, had been naughty.

Cocklebuster himself could be heard drawing nigh, and presently here he was. "Fixed up?"

"No room."

"Aw!" His brows gathered somewhat imperiously.

"If I could wash up, then I could eat and thereafter move on."

Cocklebuster deftly led him to his own bedroom, and, before Peter was right out of his clothes, had his red silk dressing-gown ready for Peter's arms; then he conducted his guest to the bathroom, and as the door was closing said, "Let them demn well rattle at the knob!"

As the bath filled, Peter shaved. In the bath he wallowed languidly for a time then reclined. At the first rattle of a very loose knob he sighed so deeply that bubbles ran from his mouth, but from that moment he began to think of getting out, for he had never been able to rid himself of his communal conscience, despite Cocklebuster's Olympic jibes.

Back before the bedroom he was beset by a slight misgiving, put his head cautiously round the door, said "Beg pardon" before he had seen too much and retreated. Must have taken the wrong turning. As he rounded a bend a feminine voice exclaimed, and when he turned his head there was the charming lady, who, however, at once exhibited some confusion, presumably at the unusual face above the dressing-gown. Peter gave her his foreign smile as he bowed. "I'm afraid," he said, "that I have got lost looking for Mr. Cocklebuster's bedroom. Don't even know the number."

This effort at persiflage lasted long enough for a man to come round the corner and fetch up alongside the lady with a distinctly odd expression on his face.

"I think," she said—and in the same instant her face blew pink as a wild rose—"I think," she concluded for she was game, "that it is thirteen."

Bowing once more like a foreigner who knew no better, he murmured his thanks in French, swept on and in time found 13. No one in. He quietly shut the door.

Cocklebuster, eh? For the man who had caught up on the lady was undoubtedly the lady's husband. There it was, by God. A triangle. The triangle. Bisected by the husband's indubitable look. And for ineptitude, sheer and all too effable, he, Peter, had surpassed his dimmest hopes.

He sat on the bed; his drooping head kept shaking at the bed until they met sideways; then they all shook silently in a huddle.

Cocklebuster! The bachelor who regarded women as existing, and savagely at that, only B.C., in the dim time before Europe produced in Asia Minor her first philosopher.

Cocklebuster briskly entered the room.

Peter sat up and wiped his eyes. "In sheer gratitude," he explained, "for that divine bath, I weep."

Cocklebuster gave him rather a look, but manifestly the professor was trying to be amusing.

"To tell the simple truth," confessed Peter, "I'm so tired I'm light-headed. However, that bath——"

"I've fixed you an awful hole," said Cocklebuster. "No need to take it——"

"It's taken," declared Peter. "And while I'm in this light-headed condition let me inform you that you've been damn decent."

Even a far less direct statement of the kind always knocked Cocklebuster for six. He now made one or two extraordinary noises very deep in the throat, then began undressing rapidly to a shrewd commentary on stalking a solitary bath in a longish corridor that zigzagged.

Whilst Cocklebuster removed his clothes as one inspired for a point-to-point race ahead, Peter got stuck in his shirt, putting an arm where a head should be, and finally gave up on the bed again, consumed by Cocklebuster's all too earnest wit and covered in a sort of deep abasement by his shirt, from which came rumblings of prayer for deliverance.

Cocklebuster looked at the rucksack whence Peter had extracted his shirt. Oddish fellow the professor. Cocklebuster had taken to him long ago at the first glance, for at the first glance he had seen not only that the professor's clothes were right but also that he wore them as if he didn't know it. Yet there now was this sack. Demn him, if, unrolling itself like a tired lump of engineer's waste, there wasn't an undervest—and a knot of pants—of silk. And the trousers on the floor, as nearly resembling an expired drunken concertina as didn't matter, were yet in texture of tweed and in blending of green and grey absolutely right in a way that was difficult to lay a finger on. And the rummaged shirt that now covered the head, even though it was green—of all bilious colourings, green!—and before a man went down to eat his dinner, too—there it was, with that *something* of green that one would never find in any of one's own shops. And the socks, grey crofter's socks, whose rumples had never known a suspender. Greenish shirt, grey-green suiting, grey socks, and all so absolutely quiet that the very rumples were necessary to give the quietness that higher negligent something which is unconsciously worn as a distinction by the bearer. Rummaged but right. Had the professor been wearing shorts, Cocklebuster would indeed have had a shock to his system. Had the professor even been wearing cheap grey flannel bags . . . but he wasn't. That's where the whole thing came in again. He wasn't.

183

On the swirl of air from the departing Cocklebuster, Peter struggled up and into his shirt. If he noticed anything in the green it was no more than its freshness, for in such matters Fand could be trusted. If ever he felt uncomfortable it was when she decided that a perfectly good suit was done and, by way of extra measure, that she was sick of the sight of it. Then he was taken in hand and sometimes by the hand. It was awkward a bit and always inconvenient in point of time, but once he got among the bales and swatches he was deeply interested and full of preferences which were as near as possible in colour to the discarded suit, with Fand luring him on, then being quite blunt, then luring him again, the shop fellow and herself now seeing eye to eye, until, well, there it was, and he was measured for something quite different. The oddish thing, as Cocklebuster might well have said, was that Fand made Peter accompany her when she had decided on a suit for herself. She simply wouldn't go without him, so when he went he was full of immense knowledge, and stood aback, and half-closed his lids and said "Um" doubtfully as the tailor draped her shoulder and so on, thoroughly enjoying his own very good taste, until it came, as it always did, to a final choice of two. At this point Fand seemed to depend upon him in a positively helpless way and stood frail and beautiful like a lonely flower whose petals gleamed, and Peter, feeling the full surge of that manhood which alone is capable of making final decisions, would come as near a Cocklebusterian *moue* as the important moment warranted before saying definitely, "That one." Whereupon Fand would finger the cloth of his choice with a sort of loving kindness and murmur her admiration while Peter looked around for his hat. "You're sure," she would say, "it's not this one?" And there she was with the other cloth draped over her shoulder and down her arm, smiling to him. And in an instant, by St. Andrew, there was—there was something. It had it. The ineffable was there. At such a moment, to his credit be it said, he not only recanted but also was handsome. The whole thing was settled, with lingering reluctance in her shining eyes, and once outside Fand took his arm for just a little way but far enough to make him feel that if only he gave his mind to this sort of thing he would revolutionise an industry.

Cocklebuster pranced in like a restive colt. "Balked," he said.

"Ah!" said Peter.

"Seventeen lochs at a higher level," said Cocklebuster, "and only one flaking tub."

"But surely," said Peter, "there's another corridor with——"

"There is," said Cocklebuster in a tone that was far from playful and said no more.

Peter struggled into his trousers.

A door slammed distantly and Cocklebuster was off like a shot.

The last squeezings of his laughter left Peter rather weak. He had been laughing too much. An insidious sort of thing that could grow on one, leaving one with the peculiar feeling of becoming something other, if not indeed of being somewhere else. Ever since he had started out with an irresponsible feeling, looking forward to taking things as they came, as though freedom existed where debate left off, he had been, he could now see, the victim of a concealed attack by those underground forces which can so easily disrupt that conception of dignity so firmly held by the best people, among whom he might, not unreasonably, number himself. He was combing his hair very carefully when Cocklebuster returned, blowing a little.

"Bit worried about my shoes," said Peter.

Cocklebuster looked at them. "Good God, you can't," he said.

In a moment they were in earnest colloquy, and when Cocklebuster had unrolled two brushes and a small glass jar of polish, Peter brushed the clay up the chimney so that the dust would not rest upon his host's effects. Then he departed to wait in the front lounge.

Here were comings and goings and voices given over to fishing sagas. "Seen the cannibal?" introduced a levity which stretched legs and tilted back heads thick-haired, grey-haired and hairless. Old boys were young boys and soda gargled the whisky. Among five round one table Peter saw the husband of the charming lady with a smile on his professional face that made him a boon companion. Forty-three or so against her, say, early thirties, though it was difficult to tell with women, even if he hadn't already observed that a woman of thirty seemed to grow younger in direct ratio to the lengthening of his own perspective. A modest little man with thin hair and soft hands stuck to his story that the cannibal had taken a grouse-and-claret on his 3x cast, and that Erchie had rowed the boat after the trout all over the loch and ultimately netted it at the exact spot where it had taken the fly. "Trust Erchie!" said the husband, whereat the table laughed with renewed vigour. An obscure reference to Erchie's "beastie", which Peter knew from of old was an "otter", did not help the modest man, particularly when he asked in obvious innocence, "What is a beastie?" "Come off it, Joe!"

The cannibal was a godsend which, as Peter could see, made the goodness of the day crawl about relaxed joints. Women drew near and drew off, for the men were hunters who plainly hadn't much time for them. Hunters can be very touchy at such a moment, and a wife who deliberately obtrudes may darken her husband's brow, for no man likes to be deemed hen-pecked when sitting in council among his hunting peers. At any other time life has to be borne; but the hunt is a man's business; man has to fill the pot; fundamentally man remains the pot-hunter, obscure it as things may, and it only needed Joe's cannibal in such a setting to bring the matter even nearer to them than whisky in a glass, and some of the whisky was by this time much nearer them than that. All of which Peter apprehended with pleasure. Then the charming lady came in, simply and attractively clad, saw her husband and approached the table of the five blooded warriors.

"I expect you're telling fishing stories," she said with her delightful smile.

Smoke in one closed eye, her husband crushed out his cigarette with a silent: Well, my God!

But Joe was gallant; he actually made an effort to get to his feet, which with excellent consideration she defeated by putting her hand on his shoulder. "Do you know, Mrs. Douglas," said Joe, "I think they're a mean crowd. I have not only had to stand drinks, but they are insinuating that I didn't catch the trout."

"Jealous," she said. "They're just jealous."

Joe now got to his feet and bowed. "Thank you. Allow me." He went to the wall-bell and pushed it. "You must drink," said Joe, "to the biggest trout they have ever seen."

Now they all got up.

"Please," she said. "You mustn't let me interrupt."

"On the contrary," said Joe, who after all had genuinely landed the monster on a 3x cast. He got a chair for her and, well, what could she do, so she sat down. After all, she could hardly refuse to toast Joe's success. They all sat down. And there they were.

With the clairvoyance, or illusion of clairvoyance, which had taken an increasing fancy to Peter since he had started on his irresponsible travels, he divined that Douglas and his wife had been married for ten or twelve years and that in the mysterious interactions of things she, at this particular pass in their wedded bliss, couldn't do anything right in his sight. There was no known cure for this condition while it lasted, which might be quite a long time. Worst of it was that the more the woman tried to do the right thing the more wrong it was. She had obviously meant to be pleasant, even to her husband, and yet—look what she had done! Not that she looked at her husband now. She merely spoke too much—and knew it. They might as well have been in the Savoy or any other civilised place awaiting their grouse and claret from a menu.

Peter's vision was interrupted by the waitress in the lounge door and at once he got a peculiar and intimate kind of shock. His breathing came to a dead stop. She was pale and dark, her white linen very white, her eyes dark brown; straight figure, perfectly shaped, beautiful; advancing now from the lounge door like a figure he had once dreamed about or known in a past life. Her reality made all other figures in the lounge shadowy. Then his throat swallowed and over him went a melting flush which he had also known in times past.

As she took Joe's order she smiled, and the smile, so utterly unexpected, the gleam of light in the eyes, stirred his turmoil still more deeply. As she walked away he looked at her legs, her shoulders, her head. And she walked, not with slow grace, not with aught breathing of the warm south: she walked in the northland with life.

She went out through the lounge door and was gone.

His breath went from him heavily as he turned his face to the window lest those whom he had forgotten might have been watching him. His eye ran along the skyline of the mountains. Calm stood the mountains and nothing moved upon their great flanks. But hidden within that outward calm Jock had distilled his illicit spirit. You couldn't go by appearances. The arrow that flew by day—or night—could hit you in the mountains—or out of the blue. And apparently you couldn't get past the time when it could hit you. It was astonishing.

Then a very odd thought indeed struck Peter. Could it be that in this curious adventuring of his he had been actually going backwards or widdershins? And had he now arrived within himself at the age of nineteen or twenty? Certainly he realised that he had quite forgotten what it felt like to be bowled over completely by a new face, to feel the quiver of the arrow in the quick.

But more astonishing still, perhaps, was the next thought that came to him, namely, that the experience was bewilderingly delightful. More: it was a pure gift. Far from feeling qualms, he stirred in his chair, and sat up, and his shoulders squared themselves. Optimism and mirth intermixed divinely within him.

Cocklebuster appeared and advanced steadily, nodding in upright greeting as he passed the table of five men and one woman, and sat down.

"Sherry?" asked Peter.

"Yes," replied Cocklebuster absently.

Peter set his eyes on the door and there she came with a golden wine glass on a tray. Mrs. Douglas's gracious acceptance of the glass set the table in commotion and Joe was voted some of his own medicine though they had already gone over the score, but it was not every day they brought home a cannibal for the tribal pot.

Peter's eyes dwelt upon her until her eyes paused upon him. And she came.

"Two sherries, please," said Peter.

"Dry," said Cocklebuster automatically.

"Dry," said Peter.

She inclined her head and went away through the northland and out through the door.

Now Cocklebuster, the whole lounge, was going to say something about her. Peter waited and Cocklebuster began, "I'll have something to say to the Forestry fellow." He went on about it.

She came back.

On a salver before her she bore, finally, the two glasses, golden tulip-heads on silver.

"How much?" asked Peter, smiling to her eyes, and, when she told him, he found silver for the salver and said, "That's all right."

"Thank you, sir," she replied formally but also with a servitor's subtle benison so that the moment was created.

Cocklebuster drank and remembered too late.

Peter drank in remembrance only.

"Sweetish Colonial grape juice," said Cocklebuster.

"Tio pepe," said Peter.

"Ha! ha! ha!"

The astonishing sounds produced a disturbance at the door, and here was Sally hunting the sounds and finding Mrs. Douglas en route. The lady got to her feet and stooped and held friendly converse with Sally while here and there throughout the lounge thoughts were indulged and glances momentarily held.

"Looking for master?" concluded Mrs. Douglas, and helped Sally to find him by throwing a smiling glance at Cocklebuster who at once got to his feet, whereupon Sally saw him and came.

"Where have you been?" demanded her stern master.

Sally wagged her stump playfully. Mrs. Douglas thanked Joe and graciously withdrew as the gong went. It had been everybody's round and they trooped into dinner.

Cocklebuster had found one drinkable wine, he said, and had

ordered a bottle, claret, for something was needed to balance the blank day.

"And salute the occasion."

"Aw," said Cocklebuster, not displeased.

But Peggy—for so a loud-voiced angler had called her—was not serving their table, did not bring the wine.

Cocklebuster wiped the nozzle with his napkin, poured a few drops into his own glass and filled Peter's. Peter observed the familiar motions with pleasure. When Cocklebuster had charged his own, Peter raised his glass, smiled over its rim and perceptibly bowed.

Cocklebuster acknowledged.

"Tolerable?"

"More," murmured Peter; "and, by the grace of God, the right temperature."

"You flatter me," said Cocklebuster.

So Peter knew that Cocklebuster had arranged the little affair with the perfect tact, the concealed generosity, of primitive man. He was really an exceptionally nice fellow, true at heart and sound at bottom. The meal was good, too. The wine got even better. Peggy wandered among the meadows like a tall flower, like a dark tulip—but no, not a tulip.

And not a rose.

"Someone should tell them about coffee," said Cocklebuster. They were in the lounge again.

"Ah," said Peter. "Perhaps a trifle more bite?"

"You think so?" Cocklebuster was surprised.

"To balance that wine which—uh—rather grows on one."

Cocklebuster cast him a glance.

Peter smiled. "More body and smoothness, you think?"

"More body, certainly," agreed Cocklebuster.

"More beans."

"Roasted in modern times."

"Ah."

"The things that matter, so demned simple."

"Makes you wonder why."

"Absolutely."

They were smoking cigarettes and looking out upon the

mountains. The inconsequent talk took many odd turns and fell like leaves which they pulled from their hair or like blossoms which Peter blew.

As the evening came upon the mountains Peter saw one of the sky-lines move, a slow sinuous movement that stopped when he had blinked. "If you don't mind, I think I'll turn in. Fact is, I haven't had much sleep lately."

"Aw." Then as Peter did not volunteer any information, Cocklebuster merely asked, "Staying—or pushing on to-morrow?"

"Staying. Could do with a lie up."

"If you feel like fishing, I have a spare rod."

"Thanks very much. Very good of you. But perhaps—later? To-morrow I'll take it easy."

Cocklebuster got going, made contacts, collected the rucksack, and they came before a squeezed cubicle which Cocklebuster was deploring when Peggy appeared with an armful of her belongings from within.

"I'm not turning you out?" Peter stood dead still.

"It's all right, sir," said Peggy. Her pallor caught a hint of the dawn. Her eyes—her eyes—"It's all ready."

"Very nice of you," rumbled Cocklebuster.

She simply went away.

"Good God," said Cocklebuster, stooping. With his fist he tried unsuccessfully to depress the mattress on the iron bed. "You can't—I'll tell you what——"

But Peter wasn't having Cocklebuster's or any other room and asserted he could sleep on rock. Presently he was alone, looking out of a glazed loophole at a line of garage doors. The chug-chug of an engine beneath abruptly stopped and a voice that had been talking through the explosions sounded loud and clear.

"No, ma'm, it's as true as I'm telling you. And if you don't believe me you can ask the minister—Mr. Cameron, not the other one, ma'm, no, not the other one. For Mr. Cameron has names for the weeds itself. And he'll give you the right name of the plant, the saving plant. And the woman I'm telling you about found it in the mist on the west side of Loch a' Cheo, for it's a loch for mist, and what you find there you won't find again. But she found it, and she ate it, and she got her virtue back, and believe me, ma'm——"

"Erchie," said Mrs. Douglas. "Really!"

"It's fact as death, ma'm. I myself have seen it tried on a cow——"

But at that moment a distant peremptory voice called "Erchie", and he excused himself and went.

Peter could not see anyone and was rather inclined not to believe what he had heard. After the smuggling cave, Cocklebuster; after Cocklebuster, the Garden of Eden; after the Garden of Eden, Peggy. Saving Mrs. Douglas's virtue could well be the straw that would topple the day into unreality.

He sat on the bed—Peggy's bed—and took off his shoes.

Life at its most wonderful, its fullness of wonder, was a waking dream. Silence was in its wandering and in the silence the sounds heard by the musician before he has yet writ down less than their pale echoes and given them a dying fall where there is no dying and no fall.

He draped his jacket with his trousers and his trousers with his shirt in the one mound for there was no chair but only the floor and little room on the floor. He tied the cord of his pyjamas and two silken tassels blue as periwinkles fell an unequal distance. His legs went out of sight; his hands pulled the bed clothes up under his chin. Staring at the loophole, he perceived the nature of—no, not of freedom but of human release. For there was a severing, a severing of the cords and the bindings. And no one called, Where art thou? for there was no gamekeeper. As his eyelids fell, the severing made no sound for the binding never was, except where it had been put, even as an old croft wife ties a hen by the leg lest she go into a far place. *Or ever the silver cord be loosed, or the golden bowl be broken, or the pitcher be broken at the fountain.* . . . Even as Cocklebuster had broken the golden tulip by drinking and had thought demn little of the sweetish juice, for there was beyond the window a Spanish garden, and in that garden the sherry of Spain that cupped its living tulip . . . but no, not a tulip . . .

The lost paradise was in her eyes. That was it. Windows to the garden. The light that lit the way to the lost well at the world's end. She was the Tao's acolyte. She was what he sought but she did not know it yet, and he did not know it yet, for when he tried to know it he stopped and everything stopped . . . and where was he in all this boundless beautiful space, with a host of tulips blowing about his feet and clouds wandering as if they were smiling in sweet sad understanding of the soaring lark he was up to.

He had burst his bonds. But what then? Whither now? And where was the one to take him by the hand? Why was the tulip dark?

Why? he asked, and there answered him a mighty roar of engines going off, an infernal racket, hell's shivering sounds, and the light was hotter in the loophole and—there was a knocking.

"Come in."

The door was pushed open and Peggy entered with his breakfast.

23

A bearded greyness of spiders' webs, a cool freshness, a morning of honey dew, though indeed the morning was now well on its way according to Peter's watch as he stepped forth from the hotel. But the hills must have slept even better than he for they were still under heavy blankets. Fresh, invigorating, cool,—and here was Jehu in his car with the brakes that proclaimed themselves.

Over his shoulder Peter heard the driver address Erchie who replied, "I'm in an aaful hurry." Peter went back and handed the driver something for having retrieved his hat. As he went on again he glanced over his shoulder and saw the driver and Erchie disappearing with the windfall round the back of the hotel in the direction of the bar. There were so many things to be seen off the road that Peter loitered, but in half-an-hour or an hour Erchie came pushing a creaking bicycle and jumped off when Peter gave him good-morning, for the road just here inclined upwards if anything.

"Good morning, Professor, sir," replied Erchie.

"Forgotten something?"

"Indeed yes. Didn't Mr. Hinkson take the only two grouse-and-clarets he has out to have a look at them last night to make sure they were all right, and then he put them into the wee case to be handy, and then didn't he come away without it."

"And of course for really big trout you need a grouse-and-claret."

Erchie was a medium-sized comfortable man of a good but active age, with a round red face that for all its simple cast now turned a slotted eye on the professor. "It's a good fly whatever."

"An all-round fly," Peter agreed. "And if you are trolling it forty yards behind you even on a calm day an astonishing accident can happen."

"Do you think so now?"

"Wouldn't you say so yourself?"

"Well, now," said Erchie, "I wouldn't say I haven't. Many a queer thing can happen on occasion. Not that I'm saying anything."

"Quite," said Peter. "What's the best fly here just now?"

"I will reply to that question, sir, as old Donald who's dead and gone replied to the salmon-fisher. 'What's the best fly, Donald?' asked this gentleman who was forever sitting down and changing his flies, and Donald answered, 'The fly that's in the water.' "

Erchie so enjoyed Peter's mirth that he hardly noticed that the road was now going down, and indeed the conversation grew so interesting that the road was left to go up and down as it pleased.

"You have a keen eye and a thoughtful way of looking at things," Peter politely complimented him, "so perhaps you can answer me this question which I have often pondered: What is a woman's virtue?"

Erchie glanced at him out of his eye-corners again but the professor looked very solemn.

"I doubt," said Erchie with preliminary caution, "if I have a grouse-and-claret for that one."

"Difficult fishing now?"

"A lot of broken water about, sir."

"See that cow, with her head through the fence, reaching for the bite she shouldn't have——"

"That's the minister's cow," said Erchie as a man and woman came into view round the bend. "If you'll excuse me, sir, I'll be going now for I'm in an aaful hurry."

The man and woman stood by a garden wall below a house with a church beyond. The woman looked very like Mrs. Douglas and the man was plainly the minister. Sixty though he was, Erchie pedalled past with such speed that he had hardly time to return the minister's salute.

Peter raised his hat and Mrs. Douglas bowed; but before he had gone many yards she called to him.

"Mr. Cameron would like to meet you," she said. "Professor Munro."

"An honour, indeed," said Mr. Cameron.

"The honour is mine," said Peter. "Expecting a swarm?"

"No, then, because we had it yesterday, but this kind lady found it," and he glanced at the small bellows in his hand, "by the roadside where I dropped the skep as I now remember. Sometimes I am a little forgetful."

His smile held the kindness and humour which, thought Peter, no bee ever stings. Rumour had it that the old church had lost men of this kind. From bees to flowers, from flowers to particular plants, from vegetable dyes to medicinal virtues, was a sequence in thought and in culture both natural and pleasant. Peter said he had a wife who was very interested in plants and who had heard that there was one wild flower in particular which, according to old Gaelic lore, had the power of restoring virtue——

"Well, now, if that isn't a remarkable coincidence," said the guileless old man, "for in the course of our talk before you came we had arrived at just that very flower. As I was saying, in the Gaelic it is called *mothan*. It is a flower which, if we may believe those who lived here before us, had the power of restoring virtue to that which had lost it whether in the case of man or of beast."

"While I should not wish on so fine a morning," said Peter, "either to interrupt you or to touch upon matters of philosophic difficulty, perhaps you could indicate lightly how the word virtue is to be construed in this particular context?"

"Very good," said the minister, nodding with pleasure. "Very good indeed; and here, as in other matters, I find our forefathers always had the meaning definite. Let me illustrate. Sometimes it would appear that from one cause or another, and especially from the exercise of the evil eye, the cow's milk would lose its *toradh*, its substance, and then the *mothan* would be hunted for the cow so that the milk would get back its substance, its goodness."

196

"Substance, goodness," murmured Peter appreciatively.

The light in the minister's eye met the light in Peter's.

"Well, now! . . . However, let us pursue our subject. Sometimes the *mothan* would be placed above the door, so that when the fairy host was about no one would be spirited away from the household. But if I make mention of yet a third use it is because this is the use to which, I fear me, it has been put in this district, according to tradition. In short, ma'm," said the minister, not without an innocent twinkle, "it was used for what some of our greatest poets have called a love-philtre."

"Really?" said Mrs. Douglas with a surprised smile.

"Yes," said the minister. "From such accounts as have come my way it would appear that if a maiden took a piece of the *mothan* into her mouth before she kissed her sweetheart the effect was potent upon him, rendering him her slave from then on. Even if her lips had been no more than anointed, shall we say, by the *mothan*, that in itself exercised a compelling attraction upon the beloved; whereas if she took water from a still place and made an infusion in silence and drank thereof, then was she armed indeed!"

"And has not this plant an English name?" Mrs. Douglas asked out of her courteous amusement.

"Now we are in difficulties, for the matter is in dispute, but so far as this district is concerned, I am in no doubt. It is a pearlwort—an uncommon variety of the pearlwort peculiar to a few of our Scottish mountains, and with us is to be found, and found only, on the west slope above Loch a' Cheo."

"How interesting!" declared Mrs. Douglas.

"And at least, ma'm, botanically verified. Indeed if you would care to walk up to my humble dwelling I should be able to show you a pressed specimen."

By the time they left the manse they had to step out briskly if they were going to get any lunch.

"Isn't he a dear old thing?" said Mrs. Douglas.

"He's something we have forgotten how to make."

"And not one of the hotel guests—including myself, I must say—went to his church last Sunday."

"I would have thought Mr. Cocklebuster would have turned out."

"He did—but not to Mr. Cameron's church."

"Ah."

"There is another church. Terribly narrow sect. Mr. Cocklebuster says it's a primitive miracle and wouldn't miss it. The singing is quite incredible. He got an awful thrill. The minister is against concerts and dancing and even football matches."

Mrs. Douglas was so animated that when they entered the dining-room rather flushed with haste three ladies regarded her even more curiously than if she had been a daughter. Their interest increased when Peter, ignoring Cocklebuster's table which at common law was now his, followed on and sat down in Mr. Douglas's chair.

"I'm afraid the mist is not going to lift to-day," said Peter.

As there was no apparent reason for Mrs. Douglas's laughter it sounded almost wanton. From the spoon of one of the maiden ladies a piece of stewed peach slipped with a plashy plop that sent juicy sparks up and on to an elderly corsage. But Peter saw none of this: he was waiting. The service door swung and Peggy appeared. She was straight as a lily and her eyes recognised him.

"I'm afraid we are very late, Peggy," said Mrs. Douglas.

"It's all right, ma'm."

Peter said nothing. Peggy toiled and, doubtless, span, but in her white linen she was the white lilie on the banks o' Italie. In coming she filled the room with its virtue and in going took its virtue with her. Not even a minister of the Auld Kirk could have found a more perfect illustration of substance. Amusing Mrs. Douglas was so agreeable that he excelled himself.

After lunch he withdrew, and presently with discretion consulted the six-inch wall map of the hotel's fishing area. Loch a' Cheo—yes, there it was, small and very high up—three to four miles away. He traced the stream that issued from it very carefully until it at last passed under the highway less than half a mile from the hotel. Easy, mist or no mist. And that there should be mist was, according to Erchie, dead right.

As he struck the stream and began to climb he thought

of the flower called love-in-a-mist. Remarkable, the names ordinary folk had given to flowers! Some very odd speculations kept him company before he reached the beginning of the mist and sat down to rest. A tiny trout jumped six inches in the air out of a tiny pool. He remembered the jumping trout in the ravine where he had left Fand. She seemed to have been receding lately, and the hillside against which he now saw her as a piece of rainbow was far away. She was stooping and her face was hidden. For an uncanny instant he thought her faceless.

Once again the notion came to him that perhaps he had been travelling backwards. The first ravine so nearly the ravine—of death. The wild man on the tossing bridge—half-way between life and death. The old woman—still in life but only just. The mountains of superstition, where man was lusty. Jock's false well, with its crystal glimmer of the immortal spirit, its garden in Spain. Cocklebuster in his prime, with sin in the Garden of Eden and a married woman in the hotel. Then Peggy—say, twenty-one. Love—or, at least so far, love in a mist. If this went on, he might very easily, by the time he got back to Fand, if back to her he ever did get, be a child in arms at the beginning of the world. It was a remarkable and serious notion.

Then something remarkable actually happened. His back was propped against a small knoll and when a ghostly sound touched his ear he screwed round and through the rank heather on the knoll's top saw a phantom woman in the mist twenty yards above him. She was slanting up the slope, going steadily and noiselessly. She paused and looked far into the mist ahead. She went on and got lost in it. It was Mrs. Douglas.

The astonishment on Peter's face grew troll-like. Heavens, she couldn't be . . . not for poor old Cocklebuster. The thing wasn't right. Not charms . . . not, not love-philtres. And yet Peter saw, with a feeling of profound penetration, that it could very well be that, as Cocklebuster had so lightly pointed out, patriarchy, the worship of the Old Man of the Tribe, was in truth but an affair of yesterday compared with the aeons-old worship of the Savage Goddess, whom every true poet sang until she destroyed him. Let Douglas and Cocklebuster play their male games, but let woman get the pearlwort in her teeth, her immemorial virtue back, and by the Goddess she might astonish them!

It's no laughing matter, he said. Then he began to feel anxious, for what if she got lost in the mist altogether? Was she walking blind? He scrambled up the slope and saw what could hardly be called a path or even a sheep track. He followed it until it forked. He stood and listened and could but hope that the Goddess was with her now. His own mere male caution made him go back to the guiding burn.

When he reached its outlet from the loch he was glad of occasional eddies of wind, even if they thickened the mist in an eerie way. On the left the ground lifted rather abruptly but to the right it had a slow rise with looming boulders fallen from the peaks. He advanced upon the first boulder with some care, for this was the west side of Loch a' Cheo on which the *mothan* grew and at any instant, if Mrs. Douglas had won so far, she might loom upon him.

As he leaned against the boulder, which was not half so big as it had looked from a little distance, he found himself listening to the silence and realised it was something new in silence, a spectral silence. Wind came across his face like a cold breath. The floor of the loch opened out in a wide arc and smoked. Quite possibly the mist had not been here all day, for he had often looked down from the mountain-top on a belt of it that rose as the sun's strength declined. It was eerie and damn dangerous. Let her turn round twice and she was lost. The wind died and the mist crept back over the water.

Should he shout—or would a shout frighten her? He went to the next boulder, stood, and went on. The wind came more strongly against his face, thickening the mist to a smoke that quickly thinned out and trailed up the slope. He could suddenly see some distance; and along by the loch's edge, fifty yards away, there was someone, upright, quite still—then there was no one. The vision was upsetting because it had the nature of an apparition, and his certainty that it wasn't Mrs. Douglas was quite absolute. Nor was it any use trying to make himself believe that it had been an old fencing post or tree stump. It hadn't stood in that way. As visibility lessened again he went forward very carefully, keeping above the loch. If the wind was actually beginning to rise the whole place might clear. By the next lump of rock he squatted and waited, his eye ready to pick up what it could on the loch's edge below him.

Then something was coming down . . . softly . . . swish-swishing . . . coming . . . and before his crouching face, at four yards, a woman's legs passed, her skirt . . . he lifted his eyes without moving his head . . . Mrs. Douglas, looking about the ground, searching . . . he saw her face and the eyes that were now going to see him . . . but they switched before they reached him and she went on, slowly, not directly towards the loch, at a slant, her head moving slowly from side to side, searching for the saving plant.

Something in this fantastic quest made his skin cold. It exposed the human condition. It was neither pitiful nor childish, it was stark.

And here came the mountain's cold breath to find out what she was about, round the boulder and past his ears, not lifting the grey mist but thinning it, changing the grey to a diaphanous green with the hill grass as under-skirt. As she loomed upon him, taller than life, there came a thin unearthly screaming from the winding of some ghostly trout reel . . . and down by the water's edge the figure which he had seen before, moved.

When they saw each other, the figure and the woman stood like characters in a supernatural play on a sloping stage. Without sign, she began searching about her feet. The figure came up from the loch on a slow swirl of mist. It was her husband.

"What on earth are you doing here?" he demanded.

Growing taller she slowly looked over her shoulder at him. "What's that to you?" Her voice was colder than the mist.

"Christ!" he said.

And through Peter's mind shot the memory of the wise old minister in his study telling them that the *mothan* was a "blessed plant" because it was the first plant on which Christ's foot fell. At the sacred name the woman turned her face from her husband and looked about the ground—and paused—and took one step —and stooped. Peter felt the wonder of her movement in him and as she came erect, looking at what she held in her hand, he knew that she had found the *mothan*.

Slowly her hand went towards her nostrils and she sniffed the blessed plant, then she looked at it again, and then she brought it to her mouth and took the taste of it and ate.

"Who the hell brought you here?" Her husband was now standing in front of her with the trout rod in his hand. Peter wondered if the man had seen him.

She looked at her husband. "What the hell's that to you?"

If her husband was taken strongly aback, so was Peter.

"It's got a damned lot to do with me."

"Really?"

"Yes. It has." His feet got restless.

"Since when?" she inquired.

"You have been carrying on like a fool. Hell, you make me tired."

"No need to shout," she said.

"Who's shouting?" he shouted. "Frightened Lord Haw-haw will hear me, eh?"

Even Peter did not like this undoubted reference to Cockle-buster.

"Lord who?" she asked.

"You know damn fine Lord who," he answered and the point of the rod shook upon the air.

"You're getting excited," she said coldly. "Please control yourself."

So at once he lost control of himself and shouted, "Where is he?"

"I am quite alone."

Her control, her power, frightened Peter a little.

"Alone? You're a liar!"

"You're a baby," she said. "You are so taken up with yourself that you have forgotten how to behave."

"Me, behave?"

"Yes, you," she said. "Everything must be right for you, everything I do must be according to you, every movement I make must be O.K. by you." Her voice was rising.

"Right by me? When have you been right by me?"

"Not for a long time," she said. "And I am growing tired of it, very—very—tired of it."

"Really?" he cried.

"Yes!" she cried. "Sick of it."

"Ha! ha! ha!"

"Shut up!"

It was the first whip-lash. It steadied him. He took a step nearer to her. "What did you say?"

"Shut up!"

"I have a damn good mind to shut you up." He threw the rod away.

"You wouldn't dare."

"Wouldn't I?" He was breathing fast.

"You haven't the guts."

Then he slapped her.

But before he had time to see the effect he received a slap in return that staggered him. By heavens, it made him goggle.

"You!" she said, like a savage goddess looking upon something that wriggled.

It took yet a moment for the primitive man to come through, but through he came, bone-hard, and Peter gathered himself.

But she saw the savage coming and then did an extraordinary thing for instead of screaming or turning away she launched herself upon him and grappled. She was certainly all of ten stone odd and the impact staggered him. He tried to throw her, but her clinch was too firm, and as she lost her footing her sheer weight got him off his balance and they fell with a thud and rolled over, over the trout rod, whose greenheart snapped like a fine brittle bone. It was he who shouted, not she. She was silent though panting wildly. As they came to rest with him on top, he tried to break himself away, thrusting himself from the ground with his hands. "Let go!" he yelled savagely. But all he did was raise her head toward his. Then as he gathered himself, she swiftly transferred her right arm to his neck, round his neck, congesting the blood in his face as he heaved. Peter saw her teeth, they were coming up, they fastened on his mouth, mouth to mouth. And then—and then—Peter saw the strength go out of the man, the substance. He slumped and slid over. They lay side by side in their embrace. Then she drew

203

away and turned over on her face and Peter backed round the boulder.

Not perhaps according to that wise Auld Kirk minister's ideas of administering a love potion, but manifestly it had served after its fashion its wonder to perform.

Not wishing to peep, yet anxious to make sure that all was well, he poked his head round. Douglas was on suppliant knees, murmuring to her ear, for her face was in the grass, "Marjorie, my—my love." There was a thread of blood from his mouth.

So Peter got back to the upside of the boulder and lay there, his grey-green tweeds an excellent camouflage, while the wind and mist whirled in spectral dance. He would gather a specimen of this interesting flower when they had gone.

24

That evening Mrs. Douglas did not flaunt her triumph. She did not need to do anything because she could do nothing wrong. When she gave her husband a secretive push with her elbow towards his brother hunters at the saga hour, the fellow clearly thought it a marvel of understanding on her part. Only when their eyes met in a fleeting gleam of profound collusion did he actually turn away. Plainly the Savage Goddess believed in a second honeymoon; probably in honeymoons all the time.

Douglas soon had his table in two doubts over the monster which had broken his rod on Loch a' Cheo as the mist came up upon what had been a fine fishing day, for there was no boat on the loch, therefore no gillie, therefore only his own word, and he certainly looked like one who had had a memorable experience and, dash it, a fellow does not break his trusty rod for the fun of it. Moreover, Joe's monster had given a decided jolt to the sceptics, and as it was his turn for Loch a' Cheo next he was very interested and didn't mind telling the table that he had wired for some outsize grouse-and-clarets. "Your mistake, if you don't mind my saying so," said Joe, "is that you hadn't a split cane with steel centre." And Douglas admitted handsomely, "I am rather coming round to that point of view." It was all very exciting, full of immense possibilities in those deep waters of mind and loch which monsters inhabit, and if Douglas ordered an extra round of drinks the general sympathy was all for it.

Nor was Cocklebuster neglected. He had had a blank day with the loch like a pond and the mist belt unable to make up its tenuous mind, but Mrs. Douglas had so greeted Sally, and

Sally Mrs. Douglas, that in a way it was almost like coming home. If Peter now realised that Mrs. Douglas had in a certain involved fashion been making use of Cocklebuster, via Sally, who was he to question the ways of the terrible goddess? And at least let it be said that she did not now turn away from Cockle-buster, but on the contrary couldn't have been more charming to him. Laughing, he carried his deerstalker in his hand. He even went so far as to say to Peter, who admittedly had led up to the subject: "Demned nice woman. Knows a dog when she sees one."

But somehow the savour had gone out of it all for Peter. He was irked by unusual feelings and felt restless. The only sane thing to do was pack up and go. When Cocklebuster decided to write the Forestry fellow about the so-called shoot, Peter wandered up to his cubicle with the actual notion of gathering his belongings and packing what he wouldn't need before he left in the morning.

As he rounded the last corner of the back corridor he saw a lady in semi-evening dress come from the door of his room. She had a pair of strong shoes in her hand. When he realised it was Peggy, he just stopped and she could not pass.

"What's wrong?"

"Nothing, sir. I—I couldn't find my shoes. They were under your bed."

"What's wrong?"

"Nothing." But she was holding herself with difficulty, looked past him to right and left. He saw she had been weeping.

"You tell me what's the matter," he said so firmly and yet so gently that her top lip came down over her teeth, pressing her emotion back strongly. She made to get past. He caught her hand. "Where are you going?"

"To a dance," she said. "Ina and me—but—the car has broken down."

"The hotel car?"

"No, sir. The one that was going to give us a lift."

He pressed her hand and then shook it before regretfully parting with it. It was like an introduction, and her hand had neither been afraid nor unfriendly. "I'll order the hotel car for you."

At that moment in the shadowy corridor, her eyes, as they looked at him, were two dark wells.

"Surely I owe you something for giving me your bed. When do you want to go. Now?"

"Yes, sir. But—it's—at Badenscro."

"Is that far?"

"Fifteen miles."

He smiled and glanced at the shoes. "Were you going to walk it?"

"Ina thinks she can get a bicycle but I—I——"

"Just the two of you?"

"Yes, sir."

"You don't belong here?"

"No, we are just for the season. We belong to Portessan."

"That's a long way. Well, you get hold of Ina and I'll see you right."

But now she did not pass. "It's too much, and—and——"

"And what?"

"It's too much."

"Are you shy of having the hotel car ordered? If that's all, I'll go with you myself. But if so, I'll claim a reward."

She glanced at him and glanced away, but before she could think of anything, he added, "One eightsome reel; just one."

Something of shyness, of wonder, of relief, of unbelief, the turn of her head, the light in her eyes . . . and in a moment what had been troubling and obscure in his love for this young girl was made clear to him.

"Off you go!" he said cheerfully before emotion could have its way. As he stood in the door of his room he heard her feet going down the back stairs like a rattle of sticks on a drum.

So it was Fand the whole time. He sat down on the bed.

Fand had been difficult at nineteen, gay, elusive, scenting a solemn mood in his undergrowth like a wild creature scenting danger. And he had tried to bring the mood to a test too

207

soon. They had struggled and she had repulsed him. How this had worked upon him! for if she had really cared for him, as he for her, she could not possibly have thrust him away, not in the wild irrational way she had done, as if her life depended on it. In the small hours, when logic murders sleep, he saw this very clearly. Nor did logic stop there. It went on to apply its finding to what his Greek lecturer called the inexorable nature of tragedy as exemplified in the classic Greek drama. She could not help herself any more than he. The situation was given, the end inevitable.

So why should he, of all mortals, go on reading Greek plays? Or studying the ways of tyrants? Or the plenishings of tombs? What a mockery of his mortal condition! If, from habit, he still appeared to listen to lectures, he left his books shut. He avoided Fand. He passed her distant house only at dead of night. He went to places where he could see her without seeing her. He circled like a planet that had lost its true orbit but had not yet, because of a terrible hankering, got lost in outer space. This went on for a vast period of time, nearly three weeks. Then one night, very late, in her own quiet street, he saw her coming in the company of a gay young man whose chatter was so bright that it might have been witty. That the street could have opened and swallowed him then! And she recognised him though he was four paces past and going strong before he raised his hat. The old pride of the hills made him grovel before himself, for what could she think, finding him at this hour so near her door? His legs carried him almost to the end of the street before he put his hand against a lamp-post and wondered, as the quivering took him, whether he would have to sit down and let the kerb take his full weight. His breathing had gone wrong. There were sounds in his head. There were footsteps. Coming along the street. A woman—running, not so much fast as terribly earnestly.

She stopped, with the light of the lamp on her face, her eyes, her fear, her terrible silent questioning, her beautiful, her tragic face . . . Fand.

So clearly did Peter see and experience once again these moments of wild, intoxicating reconciliation, that it was as if

Fand had come into the cubicle where he sat, bringing the lamp post with her.

When he got off the bed he knew what was wrong with Peggy.

Combing his hair in her little looking-glass, he fancied, as he contemplated his well-worn features, that he knew what was wrong with himself. "Conditioned reflex," he murmured, "like one of Pavlov's dogs."

In her private life Peggy was in love; and his spirit, quickened by his wanderings, had apprehended the condition. The old turmoil had been set going! And why not? Wasn't Peggy as beautiful an armful in her dark right—as Fand in her fair? Thank God there was always a kick left in the old horse! And age was very far from him at the moment! Love is so very wonderful an affair that even to be in its company is surely a pleasure, and to be of service a detached delight. Detached more or less.

There was no difficulty about the car and soon Jehu was bowling along, with Peter beside him and Peggy and Ina, who was dark and thirty, behind. The scenery was so lovely in the late evening light that Peter cunningly got the driver to lessen speed by asking him questions. The dance was being held, he was told, in order to swell a fund for renovating the harbour, for Badenscro was on the coast and had known better days.

"Fair going to ruin," said Jehu Donald with the full weight of middle age, "and what's left of the young fellows know more about the dole than catching lobsters—or flukes."

"As bad as that?"

"Worse," said Donald. "Nowadays if a fellow can get something for doing nothing not a hand's turn will you get out of him. Not that you would mind that, if he didn't look down on you for doing what you could. Some of them are that cocky." Down went his foot on the throttle.

Peter rather thought that Donald was probably suffering from the rivalry or jealousy that sometimes assailed neighbouring districts.

"But if they're gathering money by their own efforts——"

"Hah!" said Donald. "They won't get the government grant

unless they put up so much themselves!" And round the corner he went triumphantly. "Not," he added, slackening off, "that there aren't decent men in Badenscro. Some of the old men there—you couldn't meet better. The old school."

"But surely the young fellows find the dole——"

"They don't find it enough to buy cigarettes. And some of them are not that young neither."

Peter could see he had touched on a sore subject.

Suddenly Donald took his eyes off the road and looked at Peter. "When I think, sir, of how gentlemen like yourself will be coming up here and spending money, a lot of good money, on catching small brown trout—hah!" And he swerved in time.

Peter remained silent for now there was a sheer unguarded drop on the left.

"But perhaps you will not be understanding what I'm at?" said Donald giving him a peculiar glance.

"Not quite, perhaps."

"No," said Donald, going flat out for a short steep hill. As they roared to its crest, Peter thought: what if another car . . . And before his thought could finish, he saw the top, the nose, of a lorry. The lorry swung into a "passing place" with squealing brakes and Donald called "Ay! ay!" as he swept past its swinging tail with half-an-inch to spare. "That's Jimmy," he said over his shoulder to the girls behind. "He won't be pleased at being late for the dance!"

"Do you all drive fast up here?" Peter could not help asking when he recovered his breath.

"Oh no, sir," said Donald. "There's only one man you have got to watch for on this road and that's the doctor. He is a holy terror. He once took a mudguard off me and then if he didn't tell me all about my own people for three generations. But he's a good doctor. When my horn is working I give it a hoot now and then if I think he's about."

"It's not working just now?"

"Ach," replied Donald, "you don't need it at this time of night whatever."

Peter's stomach shook with quiet laughter.

"But that's not what we were talking about," said Donald, waiting for encouragement to proceed.

"About brown trout?"

"That same. It's not brown trout that fellows in Badenscro would look at for nothing. Hah! Brown trout!" He gave her extra throttle. "Nothing but salmon for them. Box loads of them."

"They'll pay a steep rent for that?"

Donald took his hands off the wheel and clapped it as he swayed. "Rent, is it? That's a good one! They're getting that bold now they poach on top of the day, and I know enough to know that they should be paying more in income tax than I get in years. And when it's not salmon it's deer, and by getting the deer when they come down at night they haven't to climb for them, for it would be a great pity if they had to exert themselves a little."

"A thriving community."

"Yes," said Donald. "All out to get a grant for the harbour for—for flukes. It's a hard life when you're living on the dole."

"But surely that's exceptional in the Highlands?"

"That may be. And in Badenscro it's only a few of them with one or two bad devils among them—as I have good cause to know. But it's sad to see the fine old spirit going when a man never got a salmon or a deer but he shared it."

"I see. It's not exactly the poaching?"

"Poaching a fish or a deer for the pot is in nature, and many's the good night I have had at it. No, sir, it's every Highlander's birthright, for time was when it was the clan's land . . ."

It was pleasant listening to Donald with the car at a crawl, and when at a knotty historical point she stalled, Peter got out his cigarette case and offered it to the girls so naturally that they hardly hesitated and Donald puffed and unravelled his knot as if he were stopped for the night. There was a touch of something Spanish, Peter decided, in Peggy, and the Spanish Armada sailed diaphanously across Donald's analysis of the Crofters' Act of 1886. She had smiled her thanks and looked down. If not the Spanish Armada, then the ancient Iberian, but something, some grace carried over. He had met it in the Outer Isles. There were those who would say that her eyes could have fallen more slowly, with just a suggestion of sophistication, but he preferred the natural. . . .

"And got their Act, their security of tenure, because they founded their case on the very fact that the clan was a clan of men occupying ground which was the clan ground and which they defended."

"Quite right," said Peter. "And I think it was a tragedy that that whole system wasn't allowed to develop in its own way. I don't mean merely in the matter of game rights, but in the wider realm of language, culture, and our attitude to time."

"Ay, ay," said Donald with such admiration that he couldn't find another word, so he pushed his door open, picked up the starting handle, paused as if to say something, then went wordless before the bonnet and with one jig of the handle set the engine in a roar. They flew past a loch with water lilies, debouched from a pass, and through the darkening air saw the grey floor of the sea. Donald pulled up before a house in a long street. As Peter was about to get out Donald said, "Wait, sir."

Peggy and Ina smiled their shy thanks, then Peggy turned the knob of the house door. As Donald drove slowly off, eyeing a knot of three or four young men at a corner, Peter heard a voice say, "Donald-the-Politician!"

"But look," said Peter, "can't I pay these girls into the dance?"

"No, sir, you'd better leave them. That's Peggy's aunt's house, and that's where the two lads from Portessan will be meeting them."

"Ah."

"I was thinking it would be safer to park the car at the hotel."

As Peter got out in the bay at the back of the hotel, the bar door swung open and he invited Donald for a drink. Donald muttered something about the lounge but Peter wasn't interested in lounges. The bar was crowded, noisy with the life that could

pay for its drinks and did. There were sallies of greeting, cheerfully ironic, for Donald, who was all at once smooth and pleasant,
pleased to see them, giving as good as he got but in the friendliest
way. You would think Badenscro was a place he specially liked
to visit.

"No whisky," said the barman to Peter. "Rum—or gin."

"They took good care to drink all the whisky before we
came," Donald explained to him in a jocular voice, "but the
rum is always good."

Peter smiled, ordered rum for Donald and gin for himself.
And this memorable night for Peter started with a discussion,
which lasted for half-an-hour, on how the Highlands couldn't
buy its own whisky freely because of a southern government that
ordered it to be exported. As it grew hot, Donald grew smoother,
and when the cross currents of politics were swirling about him
he still kept his head up, smiling. Peter was beginning to think
that Donald was a bit of a weak trimmer when someone called
him "all mouth" and he just laughed; then he glimpsed his
greeny-blue eye and saw that it was hardening. But as they
left, Donald was still cheerful and friendly, and then they were
out in the dark.

"That's some of them," said Donald with such arid dis-
pleasure that Peter laughed.

He had an extraordinary impression of strong swirling
currents under the surface where an unfortunate history had
thrust them. But they were potent—and liable to erupt. Clearly
the Badenscro lads knew that Donald had been "shooting his
neck" about their poaching. Equally clearly they thought he
was "just jealous", and though Peter believed that this might
be an over-statement, still, human nature was complicated.
They had better get to the dance.

The hall was brightly lit and the dancers merry, a world of
gaiety, of young confident people with their own manners. It
lifted his heart up and when he saw an elderly fisherman stepping it out like a youngster he decided to enjoy himself. Visitors,
too, and one happy-looking man with a bald spot, in shorts.
Shades of Cocklebuster! He was curious, too, to see Peggy and
her partner, but when the dance was over and the girls went to

the long side seats he still could not find her. A polka was announced and the memory of Jock the smuggler rose within him. He was late in the rush, but a buxom motherly woman in black with her hands on her lap drew his attention.

"Och no, thank you," she said declining his bow.

"Go on, mother," called a girl's voice from the floor.

"Madam," said Peter, this time presenting an inexorable arm, and hardly knowing in her excitement what she was doing she just gripped it the better to tell him that she hadn't danced for twenty years. So he helped her up, and she said "No! no!" and the small band played "Out and in the window." "Dear me!" she said, and then she was dancing.

"You saying you couldn't dance!"

"Be quiet!" she said, dancing with a solid lightness. "I just came for a whilie to see them."

"With your heart as young as the music."

"Indeed it's not much older it feels."

"Ay, and you refused me!" said a young man as he galloped past.

"Dear me!" she said, confused by all her suitors.

But Peter gallantly persisted in his court and when she sat down and he hoped she had enjoyed her dance she turned her eyes upon him and they were shining.

"I just loved it!" she said.

In the hallway where the men crowded to get cool a voice whispered in his ear, "They're not here."

At the moment Peter wasn't interested in the complications that were Donald's political birthright. They gave the world's weary stomach indigestion. The homely motherly face that "loved it" had touched the emotion of love in himself and he felt like a knight who would gladly joust in her honour and do her great service. The light in her eyes he would never forget. Romance—but how wonderful!

"Something's gone wrong," whispered Donald from one side of the fist that wiped his mouth.

The gleam on the knightly armour began to fade.

"Give them time," murmured Peter. For weren't they in love and why should they hurry to the public place? Wasn't there the dark forest and hadn't she wept for her Tristram? He permitted himself to be pushed aside from Donald and now it was "Strip the Willow". He tried to remember its steps and evolutions but the willow wands were too many and he hesitated. Besides, his lady in black was being hauled to the youthful ring with that reluctance which many a good man has exhibited on being hauled to a ruling Chair. And she knew the ancient rules right well so that even exuberance curbed itself somewhat in her honour and the dance took shape and the leaves were stripped in both workmanlike and magical fashion.

"They must have broken down," whispered the dark voice without aid of fist for the hallway was empty.

"Ah," said Peter, knowing he would have to take his eyes from the whirling rings, the brightness, and look upon the forest's dark tempter.

Donald gave him a secretive nod and Peter followed into the night.

"They may have had an accident," came Donald's thick conspiratorial tones. "I'm just frightened of it."

"Who?"

"Angus Keith and Willie Duncan. It's Willie's motorbike and it's all bits. They should have been here two hours ago."

"What can we do?"

"The girls will be anxious. Or perhaps word has come through from somewhere. You never know."

"You think we should find out?"

"That's what I was thinking. I would like to help them if I could."

"You mean, take the car? Certainly." Peter realised that while he had been in the courts of romance this practical man had been thinking realistically. "Do you wish me to come with you?"

"If it's all the same to you. It would be a pity if the girls missed the dance and everything."

"Absolutely."

It was dark but Donald knew his way, and after a time Peter began to see dimly, for the wind was blowing and the sky clear.

As they rounded a corner a scurry of excited voices smote their ears.

Donald gripped his arm. "That's him."

"Who?"

"The damn devil that won't leave Peggy alone. One of the young Badenscro poachers."

Peggy screamed. They ran forward.

"Leave me go!" screamed Peggy. Ina's voice rose even higher. It was a dim whirling knot of bodies and voices.

"What the hell's all this?" shouted Donald.

As Peggy wrenched herself free, she fell heavily. Peter stepped forward and got a blow in the mouth that blinded him. Presumably it had been meant for Donald for a vindictive voice said, "That'll sort you, you bloody politician."

But Peter wasn't a politician and far from being sorted, for his voice said "You damned rat!" and forward he went and promptly measured his length beside Peggy. But the world was now lit up in so glaring a way that he saw Peggy's long legs as she got up. It was the headlight of a motorbike whose engine abruptly stopped. Two or three dark local figures scattered and ran.

"Angus!" yelled Willie Duncan. "For God's sake, stop Angus!" he cried, as he heaved his motorcycle back on its stand. Peter realised that Angus Keith and Willie Duncan had just arrived from Portessan and that Angus, having seen what happened to Peggy, was on the war-path. The moment was thick with district rivalries and bad blood. As Peter got to his feet and blinked, Peggy cried out at sight of him. He wiped his chin and his hand dripped blood. Some of his teeth felt rootless.

"Watch this!" cried Willie to Donald as he left the motorcycle. "They'll kill him." And off he went after Angus in his overalls, a small man, by no means young, running.

The sight was just what Peter needed and off he set after Willie in good style and with more real fight in him than any international war had as yet aroused. Immediately he got out of the beam of light the dark would have blinded him were it not for window lights here and there, but soon he had lost these lights, lured by running feet, and was suddenly pelting down an unexpected declivity and might well have gone head first into the harbour had not a pile of old fish boxes intervened in so kindly a fashion that they not only gave way but also toppled over on those who may have been waiting in ambush, for from the general clatter uprose oaths of no uncertain kind. Though winded thus unexpectedly, Peter had the wit to keep sitting on one box while another lay like a coffin in his lap. Now they were trying to find him, for the manner in which they addressed him and the places to which they were about to consign his teeth roused in him a desire to retain what teeth he might still have. As a match was struck he swallowed his blood and gripped the fishbox. But swiftly as the wind blew out the match, its flare, like a fiery cross, was enough for the men of Portessan, for here came feet pelting down the brae, and if Peter hadn't yelled "Look out!" Angus the young warrior might have been tripped in full career by an empty fishbox, and if that hadn't finished him there were plainly those who would mak siccar. Above the sound of splintered wood, another advancing voice yelled and an eye of light shot down the lane, picking out Angus swaying on his feet. As Willie trotted down giving tongue, his swinging torch picked out a figure rising with a box which he began to lift above his head with the obvious intention of smashing Angus. But Peter, not waiting to lift his box overhead, simply thrust it forward with all his might and it caught the enemy in the tender middle region so shrewdly that he grunted, doubled up, and was tumbled upon by his own box. Angus leapt forward and there was so resounding a smack that Willie in his urgent desire to have both hands free for the fray dropped the torch. It was at this critical moment that Peter yelled in tones that Cocklebuster could not have bettered:

"Company, charge!"

The sheer unexpectedness of the command in such a place completely demoralised the enemy who fled. Again there were running feet and again Peter found himself alone.

He needed breath. His tongue investigated an inner fraying of the upper lip. Fingers tried his front teeth and found them fairly stiff if tender at the roots. He was probably smeared with blood, for it was still coming, but now he could spit in good

217

heart. If only these damned young fools stopped short of murder.

As he went up the brae, under the notion that he could both retrace his steps and command the main approaches, he heard a distant cry. Something of horror, of death, in the cry sickened him and he went ahead so fast that he ran into a wall. He backed away and tripped and got entangled in a hanging net. A salmon net. He found the wall again and was groping round it when voices stopped him. "In here!" "Why not into the harbour?" "Drop it!" A heavy body slumped. "Let's knock the guts——" "Get out! We can come back." In a moment they were gone.

Peter approached on hands and knees, feeling for the body, but his hands landed on metal, pipes, handlebars . . . a motor-bike! He realised at once that the enemy had captured the Portessan transport service. He was so relieved that he felt faint and, having nothing to swallow but his own blood, did so.

A feeling of evil beset him as he sat there. Dark streets and hanging yards. Evil was a horrible power that ran along a street and ran along a young arm to the fist. Evil was the black knife that struck. Young bodies full of love and strife and the desire for a damn good fight; young bodies lusty with life but meaning no death. In an instant they were used by evil and the black knife struck. The amazement, the horror, that the knife should have struck. Murder.

Peter got up and decided to skulk back as best he could.

When he found the street with the subdued window lights he paused. They would return and knock the guts out of it, would they? If he could push it into some other fish-yard, they would be deceived and deceived mysteriously. He retraced his steps, spitting quietly, and fell over the edge of a tub that smelt most evilly of old fish guts. The whole place must be a warren of ancient stores and curing stations "fair going to ruin". Up against a stone wall, he moved cautiously along it until he hit an empty drum that boomed. Must be the wrong yard. He waved his arms for nets but there were no nets. The smell became more human and more objectionable, but he followed the wall, from one angle to another, went in and out of openings, and followed the wall and went in and out, until he was beset by quite a new notion of the ancient Cretan labyrinth and took it upon himself to doubt, as his mouth dried even of blood, if Cocklebuster had a full knowledge of the subject. A vision of the Cocklebusterian *moue* cheered him and when a metal arm hit him in the stomach he grappled with it, discovered it was a handlebar, and realised he had been going widdershins. So he turned the motorbike and went forward confidently, pushing hard over a mound, knowing that the front wheel would hit first, but the wheel hit nothing and soon he found himself not in another yard but on the street of the dim lights. Furthermore, the motorbike now required no pushing, so he stopped in order to wipe sweat from one eye, and to do this properly he put a leg over the saddle and sat on it. At once a knightly confidence was his and when he had wiped, he waddled off. Soon his feet were up and he was sailing through the dark deserted street. Danger added its spice to exhilaration until, deciding that a touch of the brake would do no harm, he pulled and waggled levers on the handlebars without, however, producing any effect on the revolving wheels. Trying to brake by grounding his feet he swerved so wildly that one hand shot up and came down fiercely on something that yielded and produced a klaxon roar that would have wakened the dead. Now there was a moving light ahead and dark figures, and as he approached ever more rapidly he decided that something desperate had to be done so he hit out with his feet at all possible brake levers. As gear was engaged the motorcycle bucked violently and threw its rider.

As sense dribbled back into Peter he realised that a constable was charging him for riding without a light. He had nothing to say and when the light came full on his face others for a few moments were also silent, for rarely could a human countenance in time of peace have exhibited so complete a picture of blood and sweat.

But Donald of the ready word was there. Willie recognised his own machine. For a while there was such confusion that the constable didn't even make a note. Presently they were all inside a house, including the motorbike, and Peter saw Peggy's face behold his own. Her horror was wild and pale and beautiful, for it came from below her heart.

Peggy's aunt was a quick-footed woman who divined that the only drink on earth Peter desired was hot tea.

"Where's Angus?" Peter asked her.

"He's here." She lifted her voice: "Angus, the professor wants you."

Peter looked at the athletic young man, whose attractive features bore traces of combat. He smiled to him and turned to the aunt. "You should lock him in."

"I'll do that," she said, but in no time here she was with a basin of hot water and a sponge and Peter, submitting to having his face washed, had a far memory of himself as a child.

Meanwhile a rumble of talk came from the next room where Donald and the constable were heavily engaged, for though Donald knew the constable, the constable also knew Donald, and when two are playing three moves ahead with mixed motives, complications can ensue.

The constable loomed in the doorway and addressed Peter, who was now thoroughly enjoying his strong tea.

"Could *you* recognise any of them, sir?"

Peter looked at him and at Donald, who shook his head while appearing only to scratch his neck as he entered the room.

"Do you mean, constable, any of the local men?"

"That's what I mean."

"No," said Peter, "for the simple reason that I never saw any one of them."

"How did you find the motorcycle?"

Peter explained how he had got lost in what appeared to him to be old fish-curing yards, how men had come with the motorcycle and dumped it there, and how from certain remarks which they had let fall he deduced that the said cycle had been stolen. "Unfortunately I did not know how to put on the lights or I should have done so. I am sorry about that. But you see my dilemma? In difficult circumstances I merely tried my best to defeat theft and support the law."

"Thank you, sir. If others cared as much for the law there would be less trouble."

"But that's what I'm telling you——" began Donald.

The constable interrupted him. "I'm not at all satisfied that none of you knew any of them. I wasn't born yesterday."

"You know best when you were born yourself," began Donald, when Peter interrupted him.

"On the whole, officer, it's such a dark night that I doubt if, in fact, anyone could lay a charge which could be confidently supported against learned counsel who knew his job."

"If you say so, sir, I may let it go at that."

"That's very good of you."

The constable departed.

"Why were you worrying him?" Peter inquired.

"Well," said Donald, "he knows that we know who they are, and we know that he knows. It's not so easy as all that." He looked just a little bit offended over the facile success of the professor's very unorthodox methods.

Then Peter realised that neither side in so personal a feud could demean itself by showing its own weakness in asking the law's help. Laughter might have got the better of him if he hadn't seen Peggy lift the teapot awkwardly with her left hand.

"What's this?"

"Nothing, sir."

"You just stand still." As he poked the swollen right wrist she winced. "This is nasty. It'll have to be X-rayed."

Amid the concern, Peter saw all hope for the dance fade from her eyes.

Things grew more complicated. Peggy at last admitted pain and Peter sent Donald for the car. Willie accompanied Donald, but Peter saw that Angus stayed inside. To his surprise the car arrived in almost reasonable time and he packed Peggy off to the doctor, with Angus as escort.

Willie was a thin wiry man of thirty-five to forty on the look-out for a bit of fun. Things happened, and what would life be unless? Nobody living was dead yet. He had been having glances at the professor, for he associated great learning with ministerial dignity, and here was one who carried his learning more modestly than a bridegroom his flower at a wedding. So far for Willie the night's remarkable happenings, preceded by a burst front tube and a somersault over a bank en route for Badenscro, achieved a climax in a bloody but learned face as it rose from the dead and was accused by Constable Kenneth McAlpine of driving without a light. The very thought of the saga now giving birth to itself warmed the inmost cockles of his heart, for he was a good story teller in the right company. With more luck it would be a memorable night.

Willie grew so entertaining in the description of his breakdown and the number of somersaults Angus had made through the air that the car was back before they had right missed it. Peggy's wrist was bandaged, the doctor said it must be X-rayed, she would have to leave for the hospital in Portessan by bus in the morning, and her aunt put the kettle on.

"So it's Ina and me for the dance for the honour of Portessan," declared Willie.

"What would you like to do, sir?" Donald asked.

"I had been promised an eightsome reel," replied Peter, "but as that honour is now alas! denied me, the only question is how or when Ina is to get back to the hotel."

"I have a motorbike that has never failed to get there yet," said Willie.

"One way or another," agreed Peter courteously.

Willie hugged himself.

"I am sorry to say it," said Peggy's aunt, "but—but your mouth is a little swollen, Professor, and I think you should go home at once before the cold gets into it. I am going to fry some fish and that will help you on the road."

An hour later Peter departed, dropped Ina and Willie at the dance hall, and then rode on beside Donald, who had come through the whole action without a blot on his face or a stain on his hand.

As he relaxed, Peter realised that perhaps action had been too much with him. Let him be quite honest and admit that when he had heaved the fishbox at the enemy with notable success he had known a moment's keen delight. Action of that nature, like successful oratory, induced a very agreeable sense of achievement and power. For how differently he might have felt had his fishbox arrived half-a-moment late! Still that was

222

not quite the kind of action he had foreseen when he had started on his travels. Stretching his legs, he realised that Donald was driving like the hammers of hell with a gale whistling through the car's many crannies.

"Aren't you driving a bit fast?" he asked rather definitely.

"Oh no, sir. You can always make up time at night, because you know there's nothing on the road."

"How can you know?"

"Because you can see the headlights coming. At night you're safe even from the doctor."

"Have you never heard of anyone driving without lights?"

"Wasn't yon the joke!" declared Donald. He swayed back and forward as if urging on his iron steed. "But it's just what you would expect from 'the king'—for that's Kenneth McAlpine's byname. He is that important he can't sit down. Hah! I put more than one crick in his back." The car responded gallantly. "But he very nearly went too far once, and he knew that he went, and he knew that I knew it. For, you see, the last thing that he wanted was a case against the Badenscro rascals, and because he didn't want that, he had to appear to want it, just to show that he was impartial, don't you see? But I didn't let him off with thinking that I didn't know that. Not that I said anything that he could put a finger on, but a nod's as good as a blink when there's a blind salmon on the back doorstep, as I told him, meaning nothing one way or the other, unless he cared to find a meaning in it, but he didn't care, for he knew well that if he had asked me what I meant, then I would have asked him what he meant by asking me, and that would have made him come out with it first, and maybe he didn't want to come out with it first."

"I'm not sure that I quite follow," said Peter, hoping the perceptible decrease in speed would continue.

"It's not so easy maybe," remarked Donald rather drily.

"But you can hardly blame me for not knowing what I couldn't know."

"Indeed, sir, I could see you didn't know much. But how could you be blamed for that? No, no. What was troubling the king was how much I knew. For they say that the taste of a

223

bit of salmon is not unknown to him nor the sight of a haunch of venison in the season—or out of the season. Not that you would hold that against any decent man, no not though you were the poacher yourself and he had brought a case against you, for a man has to do his duty, especially when things have happened in such a way that he can't do anything else."

"Look," said Peter. "Do you mean that the policeman is in collusion with the poachers, that those who attacked the Portessan people were the poachers, and that accordingly the policeman did not really wish to proceed against the poachers, though proceed he would had the matter been brought to that point where—where—he would have had to proceed?"

"That's not even the beginning of it," said Donald. "Baden-scro has been getting a bit of a bad name for reasons which I can go into, but Portessan is a fine place with folk in it—like Angus's father, a great seaman—folk you would be glad to meet. You should go there some time. Well, now," continued Donald, getting down to those intricate considerations which are shocked by the brutality of a word like "collusion", while the car ambled on so agreeably that rabbits could double three times and dodge it. . . . For five minutes Peter tried to hang on to the winding thread which Donald span, but when the thread itself began to divide, and labyrinth spawned labyrinth, his mind unwound itself and he came up to breathe where Hamlet was reasonably simple and the Ghost the whole play. Which somehow made him think of Cocklebuster.

Donald was now luxuriating in that very intricacy of thought which, he, Peter, had denied himself. Why shouldn't he let his mind rip in a bout of its own? Upon a basis of two large gins and something like a small concussion, the excellent image of Cocklebuster now inspired him. For the simple fact was that he had long been troubled over the nature of the background out of which the first Western philosopher, Thales, had appeared. Historical materialists might talk of a sudden or revolutionary qualitative change, and for a time he himself had been deluded by this beautifully simple notion, but to think that at one moment there was primitive unphilosophic man and at the next there was Thales was too utterly childish.

Had Donald been living at that time—some six centuries B.C.—the notion would have more than astonished him, might have made even him, Donald, despair of beginning to explain. And then a rather odd thought struck Peter: perhaps Donald *was* living then. Hearkening to him once more, he had the thought: only some such background as Donald's could qualify a modern man to be a truly penetrative Professor of Ancient Philosophy. The implications here so inspired him that his mind launched itself completely, charged with such profound and ever more exciting thoughts that it swept Cocklebuster's paleolithic caves, zoomed through labyrinths, had a look at the Savage Goddess among her trees, looped over Egypt and Babylon, landed at Miletus, and very nearly got that movement of Thales' mind when it surprised the fundamental notion that everything was made of water. . . . What made Thales think of water? Nay, what did Thales mean by water? And at once he was back at the haunting question: out of what did Thales' water come? Unless one understood the background where was one?

It was all very well to say that Thales looked upon water as the primal substance. What exactly did we mean by primal substance—and what Thales? For example, when old Jock the smuggler filled his tub with the crystal liquid he called it in his own tongue *uisgebeatha*, which being translated means "the water of life". The *water* of life! His modern brother in Paris, like his older brother in Rome, called it exactly the same thing, namely *eau de vie* and *aqua vitae* respectively. Peter's own Highland parents had always referred to "a glass of spirits". Spirits! A modern chemist's word, too. What kind of change (if any) is here? In trying to pronounce the word *uisgebeatha* the Sasunnach made the sound "whisky", not having, as it happened, a "water of life" of his own. But though the friendly Sasunnach might call it whisky (from *uisge*, water), his bureaucratic overlords would never demean themselves to so low a colloquial level, as was clear from the bluebooks issued by His Majesty's Commissioners of Customs and Excise wherein Jock's "water of life" is never called "whisky" but invariably "Plain British Spirit." My God, thought Peter, riding his seat a little, even as Donald was now doing, it takes the bureaucrat to call the great mystery "plain"! As the car swept on without need of a blast from the siren that wasn't working, Peter, outspeeding it in space and time, was with Thales again, for he had caught a glimpse, an exciting apprehension, of water as the primal substance, of water that was both water and spirit, primal matter and primal mind, at one and the same time. Lord, that was it! Though there again— there again—did Thales look upon water in one aspect of his thought as the material presence which was also the *sign* of the spirit, and was this the background, the primitive background, which conditioned the very direction of his emerging, individual, questioning curiosity which we called the scientific spirit? Scientific *spirit!* Then for an instant Peter had a blinding intuition of Thales' total concept, of both actuality and sign, of substance and essence in the well at the world's end, but only for a moment, and in his desperate desire to get hold of it again, he called upon his thought to wait . . . wait a minute! . . . stop! And with a squealing of brakes, as if Peter had indeed surprised the primal in its ultimate lair, the car stopped.

"So maybe now you see why?" said Donald.

Strangely disinclined to move as the excitement ebbed, Peter said quietly, "I see."

"Things are not always that simple."

"Far from it."

"I had to size up the king, and he knew it and knew I knew it."

"In ancient Egypt they sized up the king also. Your exposition has been masterly."

Donald turned his head but couldn't see the professor's face, but his strange words sounded as if he had been impressed. "Everyone is in bed," he said.

"Bed I suppose it is," Peter vaguely agreed.

Donald got out and opened the professor's door. "I hope you're feeling none the worse, sir?"

"Fine," said Peter, straightening himself.

"I'll get you in."

Donald opened the front door and switched on a light.

"Lock the door on the inside, then you can turn off the light at the landing."

Donald waited. For a little while lights popped on and off, then there was total darkness.

"I hope he finds his own bed," muttered Donald with some anxiety, for this most unusual and learned gentleman had maybe had enough trouble for one night, game though he was.

25

When the anglers were gone in the morning, Peter left the hotel with the rucksack on his back, his hat on his head, and a smile on his face for the lifting hills. A strong wind was blowing and the white clouds bellied amply. Trees showed their pale green undersides as they shook and tossed and threw their flames. A dancing tree came much nearer to his conception of a Maenad than an abandoned woman in the modern idiom. An outermost birch caught in the wind's teeth frolicked so furiously that Peter laughed and suddenly remembered one of the rules of the Pythagorean order: *Not to walk on highways.* So he left the road.

Extraordinary fellow Pythagoras; one of the few really great men in the world's story. The square on the hypotenuse of a right-angled triangle is equal to the sum of the squares on the other sides. What lyric perfection, what ecstasy for the pure in mathematics! Peter glanced over a shoulder but he was all alone, except for the dancing trees—and such Maenads as might be about. And tough girls they were, if the playwright Euripides was anyone to go by. Over the hills and through the glens they swept on flashing feet, heading off the goat, falling upon it, tearing it limb from limb, and eating the raw flesh, eating their god, Cocklebuster's Dionysus. Savage, eh? But many a woman who ate her own heart in a suburban villa mightn't think it so savage if her truth were known. My God, she mightn't. Flinging her high heels into the kitchen sink and hitting out for the dancing hills would be a change to say the least. For there was more than the beast and the sacrifice. When the wild rapture was over and hands leaned on the old wash tub:

Will they ever come to me, ever again
  The long, long dances,
On through the dark till the dim stars wane?
Shall I feel the dew on my throat, and the stream
Of wind in my hair? Shall our white feet gleam
  In the dim expanses?
O feet of the fawn to the greenwood fled,
  Alone in the grass and the loveliness . . .

Not a passing technique, not a short-lived mode of poetic utterance! Professor Gilbert Murray had there been translating something not far short of 2,400 years old. A fair life for verse. And Euripides was reputed to have been a bit of a misogynist at that!

As Thales said: all things are full of gods.

"Enthusiasm" was the old word of the Bacchic ritual, and the word meant having the god inside, so that the worshipper became one with the god.

He might be one with worse! For enthusiasm had not been lost, it had merely shifted its locus and focus. But what a shift was there! What a face-about from the hills and the glens and the swift feet chasing the stars into the morning—to the prison cell and the slow analysis and death in the underground corridor. Patriarchal man was at long last getting his cerebral machine into top gear. Having slain the Savage Goddess and gone peddling in fig leaves for a longish time, he was now on the rampage with an enthusiasm so grey that gods withered in its passage and the poor old sheep were blown into what was no longer eternity.

And he thought it not only wonderful but also good for the sheep.

Marvellous fellow, this new kind of grey totalitarian super goat.

At a spring on a hillside Peter drank and turned on his back for the nook was sheltered, then let himself ebb upon the air, for enthusiasm was heady. Alone in the grass and the loveliness. That's what it came back to. The body's full cup, emptying and never emptied, cleansed and made quick.

But when he got up and went on, the goat which he had evoked stalked his thought. For it lived on grey matter. Not on birdsong at morning or starshine at night, not on honey dew or manna wild, not on wonder or swift delight that passed on white feet or feet of the fawn. Just on grey matter. And it could suck a skull as 'twere an orange.

Then an odd thing happened: he saw the goat quite clearly in the field of his mind, its long grey face, its slit eyes, its derisive expression.

As he wandered on he knew it was waiting for him. Its self-assurance was complete. It could deal with Peter's brainpan at any time. His highest argument would wither in its derision.

Peter was not deceived by this involuntary creation. After all, it was the kind of image that poets deliberately created in the exercise of their trade. Take the poem that Cocklebuster had evoked in the forest: Keats's *La Belle Dame Sans Merci*. Keats had never seen his "wretched wight" in the flesh; yet how clearly he had described him from the first blush of life and love when he had set the fatal dame on his "pacing steed" and "nothing else saw all day long" until he woke up, via a dream of pale kings and warriors with starved lips horrid and gaping, and found himself on the cold hillside:

> *And this is why I sojourn here*
> *Alone and palely loitering,*
> *Though the sedge is withered from the lake*
> *And no birds sing.*

It was the kind of myth poets used to make. La Belle Dame was no doubt one of the incarnations of the Savage Goddess.

Peter wandered on, preoccupied with his thought, loitering here and there, but aware that the goat was waiting.

Suddenly this irritated him, because he just wasn't going to have any argument with any grey, totalitarian, bloody goat. There had been far too many arguments about the hellish compulsions of totalitarianism already.

The mere memory of them turned him bleak. He felt the bleakness of his face like a pallor.

Then he had his moment of illumination and its effect was at once startling and warming. For he suddenly saw that no poet of to-day would ever dream of writing a poem like Keats's one. The *femme fatale* was as dead as the dodo; or, more precisely, as dead as the Savage Goddess. As Cocklebuster had contended, patriarchy had supplanted matriarchy, the Old Man of the tribe had done the Goddess in, and the "wretched wight" had become the billy goat triumphant.

The cerebral he-goat hath the world in thrall.

But though Peter wandered on and up and down more happily, he knew he hadn't got rid of the goat. And at last by the grasses of a lochan in a fold of the hills, he came to a standstill and eyed the goat, and proceeded in a manner severely dialectical to analyse and comb out into their miserable shreds of destruction the goat's unspoken arguments.

And then—and for the first time—the goat smiled.

It was a smile that might well have withered the sedge from the lochan.

Peter looked at the sedge, at the green grass about his feet, at the golden kingcups. Nothing, of course, was withered, but he realised that something incomparably more subtle had happened: they had lost their substance, their virtue. Not things of beauty and a joy for ever; just things.

He cursed the goat by the Auld Kirk minister.

"I am getting under your skin," replied the goat.

Peter felt a certain crinkling of the skin on his scalp.

"You can't keep your grey matter from me," said the goat with the total self-satisfaction of a demonstrated ego.

Peter scratched that part of his cranium where a tingling boring sensation had already begun.

But he couldn't make a sign; he had lost the traditional power to make a sign. And he couldn't say: Get thee behind me, goat; because that's where the goat was.

There were no horns on this dilemma. And then he perceived that in fact this totalitarian goat had one horn only, rising from the middle of its forehead, one boring tool, one suction pipe. And he realised how ghastly could be its persistence in its own one-way traffic.

All at once he was angry with himself. A whole day, a beautiful flying day, destroyed by an argument with a goat. No wonder we were going under, no wonder the primal substance was being sucked out of our grandmothers' eggs.

Peter stalked on. What you didn't want to be bothered with you could ignore. He tackled a last hillside in good style. Nothing like devastating physical exercise for dissipating the ideological vapours. But unfortunately as he paused on the ridge to wipe his brow, he wondered if the goat was still there.

Naturally it was there. Hadn't he wondered about it?

His mouth closed grimly. And as grimness spread bleakly over him, he realised at last that the only thing with which it could be met was its equal and opposite, laughter. But, by Bacchus, the tragedy of it: he couldn't laugh. He, who had so often in his present journey been invaded by laughter to the point of shame, couldn't even raise a hollow echo of Cocklebuster. And the more he couldn't laugh, the more he knew that laughter, deep laughter from beneath the belt, was the only specific for the goat, the sole charm against its evil eye, its whole spectrum, its spectral tee-totum. But he couldn't laugh. His diaphragm had gone away on him.

But wait! Charm? A charm!

He took out his pocket-book and from one of its compartments extracted no less than two specimens of the *mothan*, the pearlwort of the mountains.

As he looked at them he saw that alas! they were almost withered. Had the virtue been taken out of them, too? As he stared and wondered a very odd thing happened: between his eyes and the pearlworts came the grey goat's face, and its way of smiling broadly was to smile narrowly.

Resorting to charms, eh? To withered charms? To feudalistic love-philtres! And then if the goat in its grey enthusiasm didn't murmur ironically:

> *The sedge is wither'd from the lake,*
> *And no birds sing.*

It was the touch that was too much, the certainty that over-reached itself, the one confession too many. With the obstinacy that knows neither diaphragm nor dialectic Peter lifted one of the wild flowers to his mouth, drew it between his lips, caught at a petal with his teeth and nibbled.

A piquant flavour, love's slight sting!

Suddenly the poet's words, as quoted by the goat, evoked the opposite of all withering, namely La Belle Dame sans merci herself. And La Belle Dame sans merci promptly faded in Cocklebuster and faded him out before the Savage Goddess.

Then Peter looked at the grey goat and the grey goat was looking at him, but backing away slightly.

"The Savage Goddess," said Peter.

The goat backed farther.

"La Belle Dame sans merci," said Peter, "has been given a billy goat's total whiskers."

Very thin grew the goat now.

Peter's diaphragm moved abruptly and breath was expelled from the nostrils in his solemn face. Five times in quick succession his diaphragm heaved, then laughter rolled him in the heather.

As he lay happily exhausted, the first thing he became aware of was the tang of the heath in his nostrils, the smell of the earth, and he soberly knew that though poets and mythmakers might talk of the Savage Goddess she had another name for the folk and that name was the Earth Mother. The enduring one. The first and the last. And she had a good smell, a friendly, a healthy smell, with that slight tang in it, love's sweet sting.

My God, what goats and strange beasts man evolved out of himself!

Rising to his feet, he went down the hill, his eyes now and then on the far sea, stumbling a little occasionally for both the day and himself were far spent, but reaching a road and standing there to let pass a small van which was being driven furiously.

The van zoomed to a stop. "Hop in!"

Peter hopped in.

"I'm late for the ferry," said the dark and merry driver, "but it's a gamble anyway, for at what hour they stop crossing God alone knows and the tide is always wrong. You won't know?"

"No," said Peter.

"Going far?"

Peter hesitated, for whereas Donald at least knew his roads this man obviously did not. He braked heavily on hairpin bends, which Donald never did; but whether it was better to brake on the corners you didn't know or fly round those you did was a new problem for Peter.

"As far as the next place," he said hopefully.

"Here for the first time, what? Hell of a country."

"It's considered rather beautiful."

"What? Bloody miles of rocks and heather. I like something a bit more civilised myself. I prefer to be gone with the wind."

"That's about your speed," said Peter.

Whereupon the merry fellow laughed again. "Got to get some kick out of it, and boy! amn't I hitting out!"

"You sure are."

"A refreshment, you are! I was feeling lonely."

"On business?"

"Yep. Travelling in aspirins."

"Aspirins?"

"Didn't you know the whole Highlands is a headache?"

Peter suspected a joke. "Economically speaking?"

"Got me!" He chuckled. "Do you know, I said that to an old buffer back at what's-its-name and he thought I was serious. He asked me if I was the new doctor." The car rocked.

"What are you really travelling for?"

"Men's underwear. I have a show pair of pants—drawers—so stout that they stand up on their own legs. Never fails to do the trick. It's the weather."

Peter knew he had met a commercial gentleman who was a practical joker and when the second snappy story was hitting the blue spots they all but hit a cow and if Peter hadn't been pressing hard against imaginary brakes he might well have gone through the windscreen. From the middle of the road the cow stood and looked at them. A furious blast on the siren made her swing her head slowly and turn stern on.

"This is where I get out," said Peter. "Thank you very much." He drove the cow off the road.

234

"Cows and ferries, what a country! Talk of stupid! Cheerie-bye!"

As the van disappeared, Peter drew one or two deep breaths. It took all sorts, thank God. The world was large. It was suddenly full of peace and hope. A merry cove! Peter began to laugh. He sat down and after foraging in his rucksack found a small-scale map. It was as he had feared. Going the wrong way. A mighty long stretch of country lay between him and the Picts Houses now and if he continued south he would have to return left-handed. Widdershins. He had started off on the wrong foot somehow right enough. The Picts Houses where Fand was turning the ravine into a hanging garden. Decorating the old Earth Mother.

A deep and distant longing for Fand came upon him. So he went and had a look at her. Not a bit of rainbow now but tough flesh and bone, digging and tearing away and asking no help. Even had she been ugly she would have been beautiful. But she wasn't ugly. Faith, no. Far from it! His smile grew fond and his eyelids quivered critically as if he might have to defend himself from her attack at any moment. But she didn't even look at him. She was too busy.

He liked watching her at such work. How often he had done it! And she really didn't mind. One might honestly swear that the less he did the better she liked it. The kind of lovely consideration that could only come from a lovely person. Absolutely. He hadn't even sent her a postcard.

But his humour was too fond to be satisfactory, so with a sigh he looked at his map again and saw Portessan. He needn't go so far north before turning from the coast and taking the moors and hills to the Picts Houses and Fand on the shortest cross-country route. At last he would be going with the sun, *deisil*, so perhaps on that final lap, in some far inland spot, he would find the well. In any case, he would find something unimaginable and rare for Fand, or die in the attempt. He made it a vow, took off his hat and murmured, So help me, God. Looking up, he saw an old man with a grey beard coming for the cow, and he saw the old man reading to him that night from the Book.

And the old man did.

235

26

Peter could not get ahead for the sea. From a sheltered nook, he sat and watched it. On came each wave and smashed on the skerry, then in came the rest of it, lifting, curling over, and smashed on the sand. Sea-froth and seething swirls, lace and white feathers. The rumbling and pounding, the streaming away of the sound, taking his senses with it, until his eyes watched for the curl-over only, the green crest, the shining instant of pure green crystal in the perfect curve that held until it could not hold and crashed in an ecstasy of froth.

What a game, what a wanton excess of power that did not know what to do with itself and did it so splendidly, with such spectacle, in Technicolor. When the roar came inside him and he felt he was roaring with it in sheer wantonness, the green brightened and the spindrift swept on and far, far to other beaches . . . to other shores . . . and the word "eternal" was apprehended in space, for time was now.

He was an inland man. This was the sea.

The last of the oatcake was dry in his mouth as he started chewing again and brought his spittle back and with it the last slipping flavour of the old crofter's wife's butter. Then he got up, returned to the road, and stuck to the road for the glimpses it gave him of the sea. A game of hide-and-seek, up and down, peat bog and water-lilied lochan, and—the sea.

Passenger ships and troopships he had known, but this— this came to one's feet. One was not on it but of it. The creator's own emotion, the creator who couldn't be drowned.

Identification with the creator brought a smile to his eyes. And if it did, well, why not! At least one was part of the creation —and he jumped as the piercing note of the siren skewered him from behind. But the new glittering car swept smoothly and slowly on, after sweeping him off the road. And that's part of creation, too, he supposed. May it not fall over a cliff and scratch its paint, he hoped. Cheered, he turned his attention to the fringes of the ocean and, seeing a likely spot, left the road, stripped and went in.

An hour later, he took to the road again, cleansed and lightened, feeling the sea roll through him now.

Sometime in the late afternoon he entered a long village street, got a whiff of fish guts, was touched by a nightmarish feeling, and remembered the dance at Badenscro. Down a side lane he saw a policeman standing by a pile of fish boxes on which some dark-jerseyed men were sitting. As he looked down, their faces looked up. He kept going. He didn't even glance back, and soon he was through and beyond it—on the road to Portessan.

The sea. His last night before he turned for home and Fand he would spend by the sea. But it must be a place from which real seamen fished. That would somehow give his wanderings balance, swing him between the one element and the other, earth and water. There was a lot of water in the sea. Some well! And for a little while he was shaken rather badly, indeed disconcerted considerably, for it came upon him that all the races of men who had reached the end of the world had found beyond it—the sea.

If the sea was the well at the world's end, he might as well go home now for all he would make of it. Yet the opening out of the land with its real and legendary little wells, its springs and fountains, into this thundering ocean, this vast well in space, had something exciting about it. Nothing could be ignored . . . not even that the ocean itself was a very tiny well in the sun's system; and when one went on to the universe that included the sun as one of its dots, and from this universe to the next island universe, and so on, each of them shaped like a bun . . . Perhaps there was an animal that ate a universe every morning.

Thoughtfully he plodded on, realising that his quest for the well at the world's end had been light-hearted and poetic rather than stern and realistic. The coastline was growing bare and rugged, trees had gone and the wind roared in his ears; his head was down at last, for he was dogged, and with his head he would have rammed the lorry if it hadn't stopped.

The driver opened the door, dropped out and went into a small quarry. There was something familiar about his face. In the quarry he found a motorcycle and looked it over, then looked around as though estimating how best to get it into the lorry. He wheeled it to the roadside. As he was backing the lorry into the quarry Peter examined the motorcycle, gave a neat punch with his fist to a black button and produced a klaxon roar.

The driver hopped out again. Peter went forward and asked, "Is this Willie's motorbike?"

"It is."

"Had he another accident?"

"No. He thinks the big end is gone. She's old."

"You are Willie's brother?"

"I am."

"Perhaps I can give you a hand."

"You know Willie?"

"Slightly, yes. He was good enough to give me a run on his bike."

In build he was slight, like Willie, but quieter, more earnest, with an air of almost gentle sincerity. He slowly rubbed his palms, as if wiping them of grease, then took two planks from the lorry and with Peter's help soon had the motorcycle safely stowed on board. When he asked Peter if he wanted a lift, Peter thanked him and they set off.

His driving aroused the pleasant feeling of complete confidence, yet Peter knew he was making good time, and soon gathered that he ran a "small place" with petrol pumps and repair shop in Portessan. Willie gave him a hand often, but his heart was in the sea. David did not speak readily but Peter drew him out and soon had the picture of Willie, Angus, and other two fellows clubbing their war gratuities and other resources towards the purchase of a large double-purpose boat, seine-net or herring, now complete and fitting out in a boat-building yard on the Buchan coast. There was a Government scheme for loans and assistance and David himself was financially interested. Peter was glad to learn of such enterprise and asked who was to be skipper of the new vessel. David told him that that wasn't settled yet, for Angus's father, Malcolm, though a great seaman, was an independent old man, who disliked loans and debts and assistance of any kind. The idea at the moment was to get the old man to skipper her for a couple of seasons, for what he didn't know of the sea from Yarmouth to Lerwick and round to Barra wasn't worth learning. It would give them a flying start, and the book-keeping could be done on shore.

"You think he'll come round?"

"Oh, I think so. It's maybe the book-keeping that's bothering him. There's not much Willie doesn't know about engines, and as for the sea it's what they were brought up on."

"Did your father follow the sea?"

"Yes," answered David quietly.

"You don't care for the sea yourself?"

"The sea doesn't care for me," said David.

Peter looked at a smoking spit as they rounded a corner and something more intimate than had yet touched him came from the tumbling waste that lifted slowly to the horizon. "Stormy to-day."

"Ay, it's been bad with us for the better part of a week, but the wind is taking off. They'll be glad to get to sea again."

"What are they doing?"

"Just hanging on, working lobsters and white fish in old Malcolm's sailing boat. Been doing fairly well, too, for the old man not only knows the grounds but smells the fish when they're on them."

For some reason Peter found the easy talk extraordinarily interesting. It had to do with the lives of men in a way the land could never know. It was beyond the edge of the land, beyond the world's end. In the first dim smother of evening under a grey sky he had a vision of lives toiling in this primordial element, this primal substance whose spirit was something beyond courage but of that kind. He could not follow his thought and was queerly moved.

In time they topped a rise and he saw Portessan in the distance. When the lorry drew up before the garage, he got out and here was Willie in dungarees.

"Well, if it isn't the professor!" His respectfully astonished face ran into laughing wrinkles, his eyes shone, and he began cleaning his hands on his haunches.

"I thought," said Peter, "that you had a motorbike that always got there."

"It got everywhere I wanted but home."

"What happened to it—a broken heart?"

Willie laughed as if he had never heard a better joke. "If you felt your ears burning last night it's no wonder."

"How's Peggy?"

"You were right. There was a wee bone out of place, but it's back now and she's doing fine. She'll be glad to see you. You'll be stopping for a long while?"

"Just for to-night. I'm looking for a bed."

"The best hotel is round——"

"Can't you think of something simpler?"

Willie hesitated, uncertain.

"There is a temperance place."

"Admirable places, I'm sure," said Peter. "But somehow I have never taken to them."

In the end Willie permitted himself to realise that this learned gentleman, who ordered hotel cars for dances, would rather sleep in an ordinary quiet house. This so astonished him that he began talking of his aunt and in a short time he was introducing Peter to her. She was thin, earnest and anxious, seventy-two years old and nimble. The appointments of the solid five-roomed house may have been old-fashioned and even congested but they had the polish of a luxury yacht. He had once spent a holiday in a small town on the Moray Firth where the houses were painted both inside and outside and the women weren't happy until they could comb their hair in the polished surface of the kitchen grate.

"Well, sir, I hope we'll be seeing you?" said Willie.

"I hope so indeed." Peter glanced at his watch. "I had no idea it was so late—or we could have arranged dinner somewhere. I should like to have seen Peggy—and Angus."

"Och, it's not that late. We may be seeing you yet." And off he went.

Whereupon Mrs. MacIver became very earnest and anxious indeed. "I have nothing in the house, and that nephew of mine he has no more sense than the man in the moon. It's not often I take anyone in. There's no fresh fish itself."

He soothed her and said that a cup of tea was all he needed.

But when he was putting on his shirt after a good scrub down he felt such severe pangs of hunger that he pressed a hand to his stomach and found it flat, whereas it had been tending to a distinct fullness. More of this, he thought, looking at his bronzed reflection, and I'll be the primitive hunter—the kind of one who might even shoot at a sitter. He should have gone to the best hotel, though there again, because of a Catering Wages Act or whatever it was called, they would have scowled at him and he would have known that the left-over food, cold as it was, would have been served at a dead loss to the landlord and at no great profit to himself. Wonderful what civilisation continued to do to the Highlands. Better a hot cup of strong sweet tea from the hand of kindness. And, anyway, for a budding philosopher to be concerned with his belly . . . A rattling of the front door interrupted his meditation. He thought he heard Willie's voice. Then the door rattled shut. He resumed his dressing and presently at the foot of the stairs got a strangely exciting odour and was suddenly confronted by Mrs. MacIver, who asked:

"Can you take bacon and eggs?"

"Bacon and eggs!"

"It's all I can manage to-night——"

"Madam," said Peter, getting his wind back and bowing courteously, "had you searched the menus of all the hotels from Inverness to Paris you could not have hit more exactly the core of my desire."

"Isn't that beautiful," she said, acknowledging his courtesy with a nod made queenly by her smile and right nimbly she retired.

Three eggs, soft in the yolk, may look a lot when displayed triangularly upon a dish of bacon. But the first egg is little more than a snowflake where the river is strong. Between the first and the second, one observes the toast, one crunches a mouthful, one recognises the floral pattern of forget-me-nots on a tea-cosy. Beautiful, indeed. Folk art.

The second egg begins to be food. There is no real need for haste. No prowling beast can enter the cave and snatch the dish away. And the bacon had just that smoky flavour, that admirably elusive remembrance of a tradition that probably went back to the first cave where smoke would not be unknown. The last of the second egg vanished softly.

He lifted the forget-me-nots. Her best silver tea-pot.

"Demned nice woman," said Cocklebuster's shade.

"Absolutely," agreed Peter.

No wishy-washy discoloured water, but rich dark amber. He put two heaped teaspoonfuls of sugar in his cup and stirred. Succulent as the dish was, he spread upon his toast a fine skin of butter, negligently, forgetfully. He took a mouthful of tea. Ah-h, excellent, perfect. He added, however, a half-spoonful of sugar.

He trimmed the third egg by cutting away the white adhesions and consuming them with the bacon until nothing was left on his plate but the yolk, bulbous, whole, and yellow. A deep yellow with a suggestion of bronze. He drank his tea. He took hold of his knife only. With all of boyhood's skill in illicit matters he inserted the blade under the yolk, got the point of balance and lifted slowly. It wobbled but only slightly, so steady was his hunter's hand. Once—a solitary occasion—he had missed his mouth when Fand had cried out in horror. But he didn't miss it now. The knife came away and his cheeks bulged like a boy's when he is blowing bubbles. Then he settled down to enjoy his tea.

When Mrs. MacIver appeared to clear away he got to his feet, and his compliments were at once so fitting and well turned that she lost her nervous anxiety and beamed with pleasure. The plates also spoke for themselves. So pleased was she, indeed, that she was disposed to linger. Her husband had not been a fisherman, he learned, but a sailor, and while serving as mate on a cargo steamer had been lost off the China coast.

As always in the Highlands, the far world came into the room. They talked for a long time and he found that behind the nervous concern was a bright intelligence. Cape Town and Vancouver might have been down the next street; the rug before the fire came from Rangoon and the ship in the bottle all the way from the South Seas. The parrot had died and maybe it was just as well, for that nephew of hers, Willie, had taken to talking to it and it was never much sense he had at the best of times.

Recollecting herself, she grew busy, cleared the dishes away and left him a newspaper.

But he could not get rid of the wide world all at once. For well he knew how every village in the Highlands, every crofting area to the farthest Western Isle—especially there—had kin in the ends of the earth, and long before world wars were the fashion. Cleared out by landlords or adventuring on their own. In the silence he heard a faint distant boom. The sea.

He picked up the newspaper. The cold war was getting colder. Berlin . . . Moscow . . . New York. . . .

"Goats!" he muttered with an arid and irresponsible humour. He laid the newspaper aside, for he wanted no more internal arguments.

The outside door rattled and soon Mrs. MacIver appeared, saying that that nephew of hers, Willie, was wondering if Professor Munro would care to pay a visit. What an idea!

It turned out a good night. Against her own background Peggy had a natural ease; whether she moved slowly or dived— for Willie was unpredictible—her body couldn't do wrong. She had that quality which Peter had occasionally found in a Highland girl from the poorest home, namely, grace. When she sang everyone listened as though a favour beyond the singing were being conferred on them. Her bandaged wrist at her breast, she sang without effort, rather with the air of remembering what the song was about but not being moved by it, translating it for others so that they also would know what it was about, and leaving it with them.

Listening to her, Peter remembered his own mother. His own mother, who was dead. Fand. This girl, Peggy. The whole process went on. For each man there were the moments when the flower bloomed. The flower—over all the earth—that never died. Youth or age, it made little difference to the cleansed eye.

And this cleansing Peter recognised in himself. Indeed it was what he used to put them all at ease, and brought Willie onto the floor of the room with a bottle, singing as he poured:

> *"My bonny is over the ocean,*
> *My bonny is over the sea . . .*

Come on, Barbara, up with it!"

And Barbara, a shy girl, blushed furiously, for her sweet-heart was in fact beyond the seas.

Angus had some intolerant quality of the sea in him that would not let him bend easily, but when it came to a round dance his movements had a remarkable surety and balance.

David was quiet and appreciative and thoroughly enjoyed Peter's story—for Peter was called upon in due course to make his contribution—a fantastic improvisation of a man and a motorbike who set out to conquer a place called Badenscum. His simplest remark like, "Now Badenscum was ruled by the king," produced gusts of laughter that rose higher before his apparent astonishment. How the doughty champion on his trusty steed sent the fish-boxes flying into the harbour, how he was unhorsed and wandered for a spell through the dark and evil labyrinths that smelt of fishguts which ancestors had left there to mature, shook them strongly; but it was his delineation of the king, in Donald's intricate terms, that brought wonder into their mirth. Peter was sorry that truth compelled him to give his story a tragic end. But man is weak and the doughty champion's weakness lay in his eye. It was a roving eye, and the motorbike was deserted during a night of dancing and revelry, and pined, and finally gave up the ghost on the way back to its old home in Portessan and died in a quarry.

But Willie, who had been hugging his chest with his arms, had his own saga ready, which he related in matter-of-fact terms, describing phenomena like blood and sweat with exactitude, and Peter was astonished how much he had noticed or learned. Slowly he built up the situation of the fish-boxes, the utter hopelessness of that situation with death at hand, and then—and then—the voice that rose from the boxes and gave its mighty cry: Company, charge! . . .

That night Peter fell asleep as his head hit the pillow.

27

He was wakened by a loud knocking on the door and at once knew something was wrong. "Come in!"

Mrs. MacIver entered. "Oh, sir, it's a terrible storm. They're on the sea."

"Who?"

"Willie." Her eyes, which could gather concern quickly enough, were now tragic. "He's with old Malcolm and his son Angus. The three of them. I'm just back from the harbour again. They're going to launch the lifeboat." Suddenly she was overcome and went out.

Peter dressed quickly. Tea and a couple of boiled eggs were waiting for him.

"Can you manage yourself? There's no good me going, but I can't—can't stay——" She was broken-voiced.

"Surely," said Peter. "I'll drink a cup of tea and come with you. When did they go to sea?"

"In the early morning. Willie was never in his bed. Nor Angus. Old Malcolm thought the weather had taken off for good. There was a little sea running, they say, when they went out but hardly any wind. It came up of a sudden. It's terrible now."

When they reached the harbour Peter saw the lifeboat standing out. Sometimes he lost sight of her. The tide was on the turn and smashing along the shallow bar. The churned water blew its froth into his face. The wind whistled. Knots of men and women, girls, running boys; some figures towards a headland away to the left. It was one of Willie's sagas come terribly to life, as he later learned in detail.

Again Rock Island boomed, but this time a scurry of spume swept their three faces. Old Malcolm lifted his head and stared at the sheer cliff-edge on the weather side. Slowly, automatically, his right hand hitched the deep-sea fishing line to one of the wooden rowlock pins.

His son, Angus, swiftly drew his line in over the gunnel and landed a thrashing cod on the footboards. Willie looked at the old man's face and then at the whirl of spindrift which this time eddied right round the open eighteen-foot boat. There could be no doubt about it: the wind was veering, and when it went a few more points to the west they could not live where they were!

The rock-face was no longer a shelter; it was a death-trap. Malcolm's high cheek-bones glistened from the salt spray as he surveyed the seas which, here and there, out in the open, crashed and smoked.

When death reared and reached from the sea, the men of their breed grew cool, gathered themselves, and when they spoke their voices were calmer than by their own firesides. Sometimes, indeed, a gentleness came upon the face of a great seaman, and Malcolm was the greatest on that coast.

"What's the time?" he asked.

Willie got his watch out from under his yellow oilskin and answered, "I make it twenty-past ten."

Malcolm thought for a little while.

"We'll give it half-an-hour," he decided.

"It should be on the turn then," Willie agreed, thinking of the tide. When the tide turned it would not only be going with the wind, which would make the seas longer and more predictable, but also would be increasing the depth over the treacherous harbour bar. And their only hope of life now lay in crossing that bar.

Once Malcolm had ridden out a gale in this shelter; the others knew it had been in his mind when he had decided on his fishing ground in the grey of the morning. No other boat had left the harbour.

"Your line," Angus said.

The old man began hauling in his line, at first as swiftly as Angus had done, hand over hand, but then more slowly until he was checked altogether.

247

There was a long fight until Angus got the gaff into the biggest turbot he had ever seen and straightened the iron as he heaved the great flat fish over the gunnel. His eyes gleamed like a schoolboy's.

"That's the king of them!" declared Willie. "We're doing fine!" And he winked to Angus. The surge against death was rising in him.

As the skipper began baiting his two hooks again, Willie laughed and, turning away, was pitched head first over the lug sail. The wind screamed where the cliff-edge knifed it.

They could see the far low coast of the mainland beyond the waves that raced like converging herds of monstrous beasts. Willie glanced over his shoulder at the island which was little more than a huge rock in the sea. In calm weather he had landed on it to climb its face and collect gulls' eggs or birds like puffins. Now the water rose and fell twelve to fifteen feet and streamed white off the landing ledge. Nothing afloat could risk going within yards of its boiling turmoil. And the boil was growing fiercer as the wind veered. Apart from this straight face of cliff that sheltered them, there was nothing but curving precipice right round the weather side. The motion of the boat was steadily growing more tumultuous. When eddying swirls began to swing her on her anchor towards the rock, they stopped fishing.

Presently Willie said, "The tide has turned."

"Yes," said the old man, his eyes narrowing on the seas. He had to make his decision. "The wind is still rising."

"It is," said Willie. "I don't like the look of it to the west'ard."

"There's a nasty lump of weather there," the skipper agreed, "with a root to it by all appearances."

Their chance of survival in the open was now very slim and fast growing hopeless.

"We could do with more water on the bar yet," said the skipper.

"Perhaps you're right," said Willie.

Both stared towards the mainland.

At last the old man stirred. "Well, boys," he began—when his son interrupted him with a cry.

They were all long-sighted and though she was hidden often they soon knew that a craft of some kind was making for them. It was Willie who said, "It's the lifeboat."

Neither father nor son spoke but they could see it was the lifeboat. As she drew nearer she showed the tremendous seas that were running and when a green one broke clean over her bows Willie stole a look at Malcolm and saw the change in the old man's expression, saw a face hard as stone, with a concentrated glint in the eyes. With discomfort Willie looked at the bottom boards, at the well of dead fish, for he was suddenly sorry for the old man.

It was not that Norman, skipper of the lifeboat, and Malcolm were political opponents, with Norman all for the new way of life, complete with Government assistance, and Malcolm for the old individualism; that kind of political warfare enlivened many an evening and no harm done; it was that the old man should be caught out in his sea lore, that he should be wounded so deeply in his sea pride, that he should be saved by Norman of all people. And to make matters worse Norman had said last night that more dirty weather was coming because he had heard it on the wireless; there was a depression off Iceland. . . . "If we were going to wait until there wasn't a depression off Iceland," Malcolm had remarked, "it's living on winkles we would be. I prefer to smell the weather myself."

The climb down was not going to be easy.

Eager and buoyant under her engines, her sensitive helm, the lifeboat now smashed the foaming crests to either side and left them to lick in over her. Norman's sou'wester was steady and purposeful as a cowl of black iron. Up she came and hove to, engines idling.

"Ahoy, there!" roared Norman.

Malcolm, who had stooped to put things shipshape, looked up and across at the lifeboat and its crew of local men with apparent astonishment. Then he stood up and roared back at Norman, "What are you wanting?" The viking blood in him was rising.

Every face took on a strange smile and Willie felt a shiver of wild mirth go over him.

"We've come for you," roared Norman.

There was always something authoritative in Norman's voice beyond perhaps what he intended.

"Who sent you?" shouted Malcolm.

"Common sense," shouted Norman.

"Thought you had parted with it to the Government long ago," called Malcolm.

There was a laugh, for the conversation was shaping well. A few more jokes of the sort and Malcolm and his crew might climb aboard the lifeboat with reasonable grace, giving nearly as good as they got.

But Norman had to show his hand.

"The National Lifeboat is going to save you in spite of yourself. I always told you it would come to something like that." The laugh could now be seen on his face. "Stand in to come aboard!" he ordered.

Malcolm made no move, his features hardened.

Willie cursed Norman in his soul. In his self-importance the man could not understand how the little too much in a joke could turn it rank, how the direct order could not be obeyed. Malcolm was still in his own boat.

Then Willie saw Malcolm turn away and look over the swinging seas and he knew, with an awe seeping cold to his roots, that now the decision was being taken.

"Hurry up, man!" cried Norman, giving his engines a kick astern for the back eddy was drawing him to the rock. "Get a move on!"

Malcolm did not answer; he looked about his boat, then at his son's face, and pointed to the anchor-rope. A curious sharpening in the old man's expression sent Willie's glance to Angus's face and he saw a twist of the features, uncertain, like a weak silent laugh.

But the lad was already hauling on the rope, hand over hand, with the swift deft action that characterised him. Willie left him to it, for it was a light fishing anchor, and in a few moments Angus swung it clean in over.

With a glance at the skipper, Willie made to handle the oars, but the skipper's open hand stopped him. "Her head's falling off," said Malcolm; "she'll do."

"Look out for the rope!" cried Norman, as one of his crew stood up with the coils of a heaving line in his hand.

Malcolm, with his boat swinging under him, stood to his full height and pushed his open hand against them. "We'll manage," he cried; "thank you all the same." Then he turned his back on the lifeboat, stooped, picked up the tiller, and getting to his knees fixed it fast on top of the rudder.

And every man saw at last that Malcolm was going home under his own sail in his own boat.

The rock boomed; from its weather edge a swirl of spindrift lashed their faces, but no eye blinked in that involuntary human silence.

Suddenly Norman's voice boomed: "Good God, are you mad? Don't you see the sea that's running?"

But Malcolm turned to the brown sail wrapped round its yard-arm. "To the last reef," he said.

Willie got going but Angus did not move as though a lethargy had struck his body. The uncertain look was back in his face, the queer smile that twisted his mouth.

"If you cannot think of yourself," yelled Norman, "think of your crew!" Norman was a good seaman, and genuine fear lifted his voice to anger. For he would never have come if he had thought an open boat could live in these seas.

Something of that genuineness seemed to touch Malcolm for he now looked at his crew, looked at his son's face. And it was then Willie saw that the old man thought his son was afraid. It was a terrible moment. It obliterated all thought inside Willie's head. It would destroy the old man.

Malcolm's face gathered an awful impersonal calm. "Do you want to go aboard?" he asked his son.

And Angus could not meet his father's eyes. He glanced here and there with a congested petulance while the drawn skin whitened round his mouth. "I think we should," he said and gulped, and his blue eyes suddenly flashed in a sort of dumb wrath.

The old man drew his eyes away. They rested on Willie. And Willie could not speak.

"Very well," said Malcolm, "I'll put you both on board."

Out of Willie came in a flash: "If you're not coming yourself you won't put me!"

At that moment the heaving line shot across their open boat like a whip-lash. And Willie saw it act on Malcolm's face exactly like a whip-lash. O God, he groaned, as if never in all eternity would Norman learn what moved men at the core in a desperate moment.

"Take hold of the line," said Malcolm to his son, "and I'll put you on board."

Angus looked at it and looked away; did not touch it.

A bleak deadly smile came to the old man's face. "There are times maybe when it's better to drown." Picking up the heaving line, he methodically coiled it as far as he could and pitched it into the sea.

Back on the coast, on the cliff-heads beyond the harbour, excitement was mounting. As word went round that Malcolm was at sea, more and more folk gathered.

Peter drifted from one point to another, and when he spoke to a seaman he found him quiet and courteous, like one who makes a lull about him, suspends all tension, so that he may answer the stranger simply. He met David and David had little to say. For what was to be said? Peter was moved by the abiding sincerity in the man, the gentle smile, the seaman's far look, for the sea that would not have him could not take its endurance from his eyes.

But what was suspended had its under currents and as Peter listened here or there he became privy to them. From the younger men, who had to find an outlet somehow, came sudden arguments and spouts of queer delight, as though by this very means they would hold disaster at bay, make it unthinkable.

That it was Malcolm who was caught and that it was Norman who had gone to rescue him—if rescue there might be— was clearly the sort of awesome joke that assailed their lives occasionally. If the joke came off, Malcolm might have less to say about Norman's committees and his letters to the Board!

But the older men said very little, their weathered faces still, their eyes steady.

Peter climbed the slope from the harbour towards the short bluff headland. A few daring young spirits were out on its point, rising to lean against the wind or down on all fours. From the skerries below them clouds of spume rose and large bubbles soft as feathers burst on their faces. Excitement was already grouping them round a crouching figure with a telescope.

In a very short time everyone knew that Norman was standing in to Rock Island—so Malcolm must be there! He could not have run for anywhere else. And if he was there—what about his boat? Youthful voices lifted their shrill arguments against the roar of the sea. No open boat could live in that sea. She would fill long before they were half way. They would have to cut her adrift.

The boat, the member of the family, the bread winner. Malcolm wouldn't like losing the *Rose of Sharon*. An eager voice crying that Malcolm could sail her into the eye of the wind with a sail tight as a board was smothered in irony, for the very young could not yet believe in tragedy, could not entertain the thought that Malcolm might not come back, nor Angus, their star footballer, nor Willie who would pour a laugh out of a dry bottle.

When a knot of schoolboys heard some old women, with black shawls drawn tight round their heads, cry to one another in mournful voices, they ran off.

Five young women hung together, well away from the cliffs but with their eyes on the white horses of the sea. The wind moulded their bodies and pushed them back but they clung together as to some desperate thought or hope. Peggy was one of them, and her pale face looked cold as the flying foam and her eyes dark as tragedy, a darkness that deepened as she sometimes smiled a queer drawn smile and glanced neither here nor there like Angus in the boat.

Peter turned away from them.

Then the moment came when the harbour master's son, who had the spyglass, said something and the others on the headland clustered round him crying, "What's that?"

"They're sailing her! Malcolm is sailing her!"

"Here, give me that glass!"

They wrangled for a little, their voices sharp as the cries of seabirds. Suddenly the harbour master's son handed the glass over to the oldest man there. "You can see the peak of the sail—clear of the island!" His voice quivered.

Then the youngest ran with the wind, crying to those he passed, "Malcolm is coming!" The five young women heard him, and four of them ran after him, leaving Peggy alone, as if the virtue of motion had been drained from her like the blood from her face.

"What?" An old greybeard looked after the boy as though language was an invention whose meaning he had forgotten.

Peter hesitated, looked back, but Peggy had turned blindly away.

The news was now among the crowd by the harbour.

No! no! there was a limit to what even Malcolm would dare! But the news scattered them, some to climb to the headland, others to press towards the outermost point of the quay-wall. And in the faces of the old was fear that comes from the high foreshadowing of calamity and in the faces of active men a quickening like laughter that dare not break. Eyes glistened and shot their glances at what was only half-seen inside the mind.

At last the naked eye caught that peak of sail that looked no bigger than a shark's fin, could see it for an instant before it disappeared.

But it came again.

Now it was lost completely, it was gone! . . . but no, by the ancient ones of the ocean, there it was! Malcolm was sailing her! If ever a boat had a hand on her tiller, she had it now!

Men became restless. They stamped the earth. Their eyes shone and the cold got behind their skins as if it was the cold of the white foam.

Now the lifeboat could be seen wallowing and disappearing in

254

the high seas. She was following the *Rose of Sharon*, standing by her. Whatever had happened in the lee of Rock Island, Norman was at his post. And what might have happened, grown men, knowing the ways of thought between Malcolm and Norman, did not allow themselves to think—yet.

Not that Norman could do anything now. He had enough on hand, lifeboat though she was. But he was there; and what Norman could do, he would do with every last inch of him. Let that be said.

But the *Rose of Sharon*, she was coming first, she was coming on her own, small and open and terribly vulnerable, and oh she was coming gallantly. They could now see her dark hull, could see her bow cocked up, before it slid back as if sucked under.

Then the schoolboy, who had raced down the slope with the news and who felt himself important accordingly, cried suddenly, for Angus was his hero: "Won't Angus and Willie be bailing now!"

And some grown men laughed to relieve the tension and an old woman suddenly wept.

For many a boat had fought out stormy seas to be pitched and smothered on the bar. The end of the fight—the end . . . and it was coming upon them.

Practised eyes gauged the depth on the bar by the way the great waves curled over and crashed. Too well they knew that, with sea room about him and depth beneath, a man can put up his fight with courage and design; but over the shallows of treachery the finest hand is useless. Yet even to this utmost pass Malcolm had not come blindly, not without knowledge of the end, for he had let the tide rise until now across the deepest part of the channel, some two fathoms wide, the sea swung solidly on, leaving its extended arms to churn to froth on the bar.

Malcolm was coming straight for that swing of unbroken water, committed at last to the clean run through, making dead for the heart of it. They could see him clearly, his right forearm along the tiller, bending forward a little in an easy posture. But they could also see now, by the motion of the boat, the wildness of the storm, the awful heave and thrust and rush of the ravening tumultuous waters.

255

The crash of the ocean deafened them, and they cried against it silently from braced bodies, sending their spirits like indrawing saving hands to the three men sitting quiet and motionless in the boat.

All at once the *Rose of Sharon* was coming at speed, racing like a yacht, her trim forefoot cutting and cleaving . . . and then they saw the monstrous wave heaving up behind her. My God! cried silent voices in agony. The wave caught her like a piece of flotsam and flung her forward with great velocity, then swept right from under her.

Malcolm had missed it! had lost that ultimate thrust of chance on which the greatest have to rely; he was broaching to . . . the next one would roll her keel up and over like an empty box.

Malcolm lay back a bit in some queer steadying motion of his own, as if talking to his boat, and the watchers saw that she hadn't lost way, that she was slowly answering Malcolm's hand, coming round, facing on, moving, getting ready, lifting her head.

And a voice, that did not know it spoke, roared, "Look out, Malcolm!"

But Malcolm did not even turn his head. For he could no longer avoid a drowning sea—all that was left to him now was to take advantage of it.

The great bank of water hit him, and lifted him, and the nose of the *Rose of Sharon* went down, but she had her own way on her and her own clean lines; Malcolm held her to the wave, to the onrushing water, and the water took her in a great heave over the deepest part of the channel, across the bar, and as the wave slowly moved from under her she began to lift her head, and lifted it high; as the wave outraced her and swept on, her head came down, dipping deep into the sea in final salute, then lifted once more to the normal level in the safety of the harbour basin, and still with her own way on her she moved towards the harbour wall with a grace so simple and noble that many eyes grew blurred looking at her.

A high sound like a drawn-out sigh rose from those strung along the edge of the quay; here and there a woman's voice broke; and Peter saw that there were no words for the wonder that had come upon them, for the relief and joy, for the gallantry of this old man of their blood who had fought death and conquered.

As the *Rose of Sharon* moved into the high wall Willie glanced up and his eyes were caught by Peggy's face. Perhaps its pallor, its strangeness, held him for there was no movement in the features though they were wet with tears. She was staring at Angus, but Angus was looking straight into the wall, and when he caught an iron rung of the ladder that went up the wall, the *Rose of Sharon* swung quietly to his mooring hand.

Someone had to say something now, and the harbour master's pointed beard was weaving restlessly under the surge of his feelings. The boat lay directly below him, and looking down he called, "Ay, Malcolm, I see you have a good fishing!"

It was the native stroke, and relief ran along the wall as if a trigger had been pulled.

Malcolm straightened his back and glanced up. "Fairly good," he admitted with a faint smile.

"We thought there was a bit of a sea running," called the harbour master, heaving from foot to foot.

As Malcolm turned seawards a wave from the rising tide smashed clean over the quay-point. "There's a bit of a lift in it," he agreed, using the local idiom for a quiet swell. Then he turned to unship the rudder.

It was the kind of humour they loved. It was the way their legends were born.

But there was still the lifeboat and as the crowd began to move from the wall, Willie handed Angus the stern rope. "Take this with you and make it fast; then hurry and give them a hand with the lifeboat. We'll be on your heels."

But Malcolm, the skipper, said no word, nor did he look at his son.

The lifeboat station lay between the quay and the headland in a narrow hollow with a slipway of its own direct into deep water. Thither now men were pressing, for manoeuvring and hauling the lifeboat to safety would be a difficult business in the present state of the tide.

Ever since he had seen Peggy's face Willie had been in an extraordinary condition of repressed excitement, and now as he fixed the sail, he said, "I have a confession to make to you, Skipper. It's about Angus."

Malcolm turned his head and looked at Willie; his face was hard and his eyes the colour of the sea water.

"It never struck me," said Willie, "I clean forgot!"

Malcolm waited, and Willie grinned, taking his time, as though held back by the very devil of mirth.

"After all," said Willie, putting a fist in the small of his back, "I might have thought of it; I should have, for who knew better?" Then because he also knew he dared not hesitate longer, he glanced at Malcolm. "Didn't you know?"

Malcolm neither shifted his eyes nor spoke.

"It was Norman. Angus did not want to annoy Norman. That's why he said he wanted to go on the lifeboat. Have you never heard that Norman has a daughter called Peggy?"

Willie saw Malcolm's lips come slowly adrift.

"Angus and Peggy; they're walking—and dancing when there's a dance going. I confess I could not understand the lad out yonder for he has your own blood in him. Lord Almighty, he would sail us both under and not notice it! Didn't you know?"

Malcolm stood still for a little; then he sat down as if his legs had weakened; and Willie for the first time in his life saw the forearm that had held the tiller shake.

Willie bunched the fish, so that watching eyes might be misled as to their talk, then he added quietly, "You'll go and thank Norman."

"Yes."

"I could dish out the fish as a present to the lifeboat men, if you like."

"Yes."

"I could give Norman the turbot," said Willie, his wild humour mounting dangerously in him.

"Yes, do that," said Malcolm, all with the solemn wonder and simplicity of a child; and it was only then that Willie realised how deeply this man loved his youngest son, the only one of his three boys who had followed him in the ways of the sea.

As they crossed over the ridge and down to the slipway, the lifeboat, hauled by a mass of hands on the winch, was being drawn into her shed. Men talked to Malcolm and tried to take a rise out of him, for humour now wanted to fly with the foam, and Malcolm replied but with no edge to his words as though the great struggle with the sea still dazed him.

Willie had got Peggy and Angus together but was standing between them, for he knew they were too shy yet to face the public alone. Peter stood a little way from them. "Watch your father now—and you'll see a bit of *real* courage." Willie laughed and turned to Peggy. "His father couldn't understand why this brave son of his wanted to come back on the lifeboat to please its skipper!" He shook. "I had to tell him!" His mirth reached for an outlet.

"What a night we're going to have!"

Suddenly colour flamed into Peggy's face and she tried to look everywhere at once and succeeded in looking wildly beautiful.

And now there was her father, Norman, coming away from the housing and fair in his path stood Malcolm. Norman had to stop.

Simply and sincerely, in a clear voice heard by all, Malcolm said, "I have to thank you, Norman, for standing by us." Then he put out his hand.

Norman looked at him and looked away, as though not seeing the hand.

All those who had lived through the desperate hours stood utterly still in that hollow of shelter behind the headland, watching Malcolm holding out his hand, and suddenly Peter knew, because of the greatness of the sea that was in the man, that he would neither withdraw his hand nor drop it until Norman decided on his course.

And with an austere sense of justice, some of the older men, aware at last of what had happened under the lee of Rock Island, knew that Norman was entitled to his moment—if to no more. It was in their eyes.

Norman's face came back to Malcolm's, and something of the grave peace in that face, with its friendly smile, must have touched him, for his hand came out straight, and there and then their two hands gripped openly and strongly.

Instead of a cheer a deeper silence ran through those who were watching, before they turned their heads away, their eyes shining, as though they had been witnesses to an ancient rite.

28

He waved goodbye to David in his lorry and turned inland,
the swinging sea behind him and in front the leaving leagues of
moor and mountain. The two wings that supported man on his
most mysterious journey. Mystery? He was going home to
Fand and the hanging gardens of the Picts!

It was so beautiful a morning that all around innocence
smiled—or slept—after its tempestuous orgy. But ah! there was
nothing gorged about its lightness. He skipped across some
stepping stones, and as the last stone rocked picked himself up
so neatly that he danced onto the firm ground beyond the shallow
swamp, thumped by his rucksack from its weight of food. He
would have some stories to tell Fand, with the climax in that
great story of the sea!

Its wash surged about him and he was uplifted by it and by
the actions of men, and was glad to have been there and among
them. He had been privileged. Luck had been with him.

For a little while he walked, remembering.

The earth was solid under his feet and as he became aware
of the earth, he was pervaded by its security, its comfort, and
a sheer love of it, its variety, its beauty, swept him like a fine
and heady air. No slightest premonition touched him of what
lay ahead, of the decisions he would have to make, even as
Malcolm had made his decision, and of death drawing nearer
and nearer, until, as the invisible companion, it lay with him
and smoothed his mind out on the edge of the abyss; the last
abyss.

But on this the first morning of the first day of the final
terrible journey when his hand so often fell from the tiller and
the dark seas surged over, Peter could see the full course as a

crow's twenty-five miles across country and was merely smilingly embarrassed when he thought of Fand, for where was his wonderful gift, his present, and where his famous well?

But there is at least a whole day yet, he thought, and many strange things could happen in a day as he had reason to know! Over quite a distance he explained to Fand at great length how it had so happened that he hadn't had time to send her a post-card. In their duologue he gave Fand the last word and the last look, then laughed, and overcame her with the delicious trick that never failed. If a man of his years didn't know where his woman was vulnerable he hadn't learned much!

He opened out a strath with croft houses dotted here and there and liked the place, so hidden away from the sea. Here was the immemorial pattern. It kept him company as he crossed above it, bearing left, and before it sank away he sat down to rest and have a last look at it. For its quiet world stirred long thoughts in him.

Landlords could not burn them out now, but other dis-integrating forces were at work, as he well knew, and heaps of ruins were not difficult to see where the houses and byres stood so snugly. He himself had started out from ruins. But man would come back. And the greater the devastation of this fruitful earth, the more remorseless and farflung the bloody hunt, the more certain that he would come back *here*. The little fields, coloured with crops, the grazing cattle, a woman walking inside a wooden hoop carrying two buckets of water from a well, a man mending a roof, a boy rushing after a puppy dog, a trundling cart. Then he did a thing which he could never have conceived of his doing before: he blessed that little community.

As the day wore on the vistas of inland moor and hill opened out, and in some mysterious way the blessing which he had given to the community came back upon himself. He walked with it as with the sun, the grouse rocked over the nearest ridge, and the breath of the earth, sharp with heather, was in his nostrils.

His watch was going, the sun visible in the sky, so he had no difficulty with his main bearing. Indeed he settled it for good by fixing on a conic hilltop against the horizon and deciding that if he kept just to the left of it he should come out not very far from the swinging bridge where he had met the wild man.

As he ate his lunch in a place that had the silence of the back of beyond he began to think that a night spent in the company of the wild man might well prove the strangest night of all. The more he thought about this the more he knew that he would have no great difficulty in gaining the confidence of the wild man. In a few moments he could see the meeting taking place. He knew how to behave. He had, as it were, the trick of it.

And a very simple trick it was. All he had to do was to forget himself. Immediately the ego with its demands was forgotten, everything was alive naturally in its own place, everything was given its own place, nothing intruded any more than the wind upon the heath. Yet the wind came upon the heath.

He smiled, for the trick was a cunning and delightful one. As he had proved, once you pushed through the boundaries of personal importance things opened out; a wider range of freedom, an ampler air; the sky was the limit. As bargains went it was jam for no money. Mrs. MacIver had even remembered a paper screw of salt for the hard-boiled eggs. It had been a good night, last night. The laughter had had the lift of the sea in it.

There was a meal left over when Peter packed up the remnants, drank from the hill stream, and cast an eye on his peak. He wasn't going to die of hunger anyway!

He followed the stream for some way, watching its turns and leaps, its sounds, its life, a wagtail, a plaintive cry, a golden plover; then left it, struck across a slope, saw some deer go over a near horizon, and came on a small loch. The way was not always easy, but he won through tiredness to the endurance which just goes on with the far from unhappy illusion that it is coming nearer to the core, the abiding essence, of that which it traverses.

He stretched himself flat out by the loch. Why should he hurry? The only real appointment man had was with death. That would come soon enough. No need of rushing towards it, or thinking about it. Then he began to think about it. . . . Something consciously suspired from him like a breath, mingled

263

with the air, lifted and went far in a far mingling and he travelled with it care-free and infinitely relieved. . . . He blinked and saw the loch and the waiting hills. He must have nodded off!

The refreshment was all wine and for a time he felt light on his feet and part of everything. But once the habit of argument has become chronic it is very difficult to overcome, though fortunately this time it was with the wild man and not with a grey goat, metaphysical or otherwise. For his trained academic mind had not missed the small lacunae in a short earlier argument. When all the fancy trimmings were removed, he was out after the wild man in order to pump him, to get from him something—for nothing. Surely a blatant enough case of the demanding ego?

So it was! He suddenly shook with delight in what to a logician is unreason. But it is not unreason; only a higher reason, my dear fellow, he explained to the logician. For in this trading account it is equally blessed to give and to receive. Giving and receiving are aspects of the same thing; as time and space are aspects of the one time-space continuum, according to the latest mode of scientific deliverance.

By blessing the community you bless yourself.

Conversely, by destroying the community you destroy yourself.

Results may take a little time to come in, but they come in, one way or the other. This trading account never fails to balance.

It was an invigorating argument. Peter rose to shrewd heights. For as he said—and history was his demesne—where the wise man sits in his cave, thither the footpath leads. Through all the ages. Why the urge to follow the footpath? Ah! you're asking now! Why the perennial flower of wisdom itself? And how comes it that it contrives to bloom in this corner or that of all places in all times whatever the state religion, the ownership of the means of production or even, most important of all, the weather? From what water doth the perennial flower of wisdom—*Sophia perennis*—draw its substance? What well feeds its roots?

If your syllogisms are in deep water now, my dear sir, take my advice and let them swim for it.

The cockle of the heart is not busted.

264

Laughter assailed him as one of the stories about Cocklebuster swept away his argument. For it was alleged that Cocklebuster had changed his surname, having been christened, in paternal orthodoxy, Granville Musselbuster. But he had lived through life at a famous public school, and, when he came of age on the death of his father, decided to get rid of the moist, the damp, even the oysterish implications and jests; and as nothing in sound could be harder, firmer, or whiter than a cockle, he had opted by deed poll for Cocklebuster. But why (asked an obvious fellow) hadn't he when he was at it, and seeing he was such an aristocratic sort of bloke anyhow, changed over to something like Vere de Vere? Which, of course, was to miss the whole point of Cocklebuster. For if Cocklebuster belonged to the shellfish, with the shellfish he would remain. That was implicit in the profound nature of his conservatism.

A remarkable yarn, and Peter wondered who had made it up, for it was, as he knew, completely fictional. My God, thought Peter, who *did* make up these yarns that were like myths? Out of what wisdom were they drawn? Oddish, indeed. Would one call it a precipitate, after the chemist, or a distillate, after Jock the smuggler? Peter opted for Jock and thus happily continued on his way.

Twice he tried deviations from the main bearing and merely lengthened distance five fold. After that he more or less climbed up and then climbed down. But it took time and a great deal of energy, and he was trudging very wearily when at last he viewed the base of the mountain whose cone had been his guide.

Observing a slice of cliff on his direct bearing, he bore left over hag-ridden ground and scrambled slowly up the heathery slope to a crest beyond which the ground dipped before it rose again as the mountain's northern shoulder. He sat on the crest and surveyed the hinterlands of silence whence he had come, then lay flat on his back and looked at the sky. The temptation to wander about the sky was so strong that he sat up again. He could hardly hope to get within view of the Picts Houses before the night came down now, but it would be as well for him to push on. More than once he had consulted his map, as new landscapes appeared, and, as he listened again to a bleating sheep, he felt fairly confident that with any luck he should get a glimpse from the northern shoulder above if not of the swinging bridge at least of the Water that ran under it. Then he would truly know where he was, and could do with the darkness what he would. And while he rested, he might as well eat. For he could hardly expect Fand to be at the Picts Houses after dark. Hadn't he warned and instructed her? He had. But well he knew that in such matters he might as well talk to a fence-post. There were times when that woman had about as much sense as an ass, and a thrawn ass at that. Some day he would begin at the beginning and tell her. He laid out the sandwiches, two pieces of shortbread, two boiled eggs. He had not liked to hurt Mrs. MacIver's feelings by refusing to carry the original load of food. She had seemed about as senseless and persistent as Fand. In his present state of appetite, however, he admitted that the remnant of her consideration, now all before him, was not unduly large. What kept that sheep bleating? He looked along the crest but couldn't see it; then because he fancied something was wrong with the brute and wished to eat his meal in comfort, he got up.

As he came to where the cliff began he saw the sheep, a heavily fleeced Blackface ewe, farther along, and at once guessed the trouble: she had lost her lamb. The anxious sound of her baa, the thrust of her head, the quick circling movement, all proclaimed the eternal mother in distress. Her lamb had obviously fallen over the cliff and the stupid brute couldn't think of doing anything but haunting the fatal point of departure. Yet the distress was just a shade too concentrated, too vivid. He had a poor head for heights so he made no bones about crawling very carefully to the edge. Then he saw the lamb and the lamb bleated up at him. Damn it, he thought with a sinking feeling, I can do nothing. He closed his eyes for a few moments and rested, then he looked down again.

The cliff face was broken up into cracks, funnels, thin ledges and sheer drops. There were some tufts of wild flowers, and rooted in the rock, just below the grassy ledge on which the lamb stood, was a solitary small rowan tree whose topmost leaves had probably attracted the lamb. Indeed as he looked

266

the lamb nibbled a leaf, stretching its neck out, before turning to bleat again. It would! The sight angered him and he backed away before sitting up. He could do nothing. With lowered head, cocked ears, and glistering eyes, the ewe baaed at him. "Ah, ye stupid fool," said Peter, "what the devil made you take your lamb here?" He felt very angry now. The famous mother instinct! If there could be anything more blindly stupid he had yet to find it.

However, the shepherd on his rounds would pick them up. He gazed far as his sight would carry and in all that expanse nothing moved . . . then it came upon him: there were no other sheep. My God, could it be that this ewe had been missed at a gathering? Had she, with her precious lamb, jinked the dogs by hiding in some old hag? He stared at her and right enough she had a farouche appearance, a sort of savage-goddess look, not lessened by the curl back of her horns. Blackfaces, he remembered, lambed later than lowland Cheviots. And now between mother and lamb there would be a special communion. Large as the lamb was, he could see that the mother's udder was bulging. Still making milk for the hefty young devil! No wonder it had leapt down cliffs! Well, it could leap up them again. Peter rubbed his palms clean and started back; but hadn't gone five paces when he stopped. He now felt very angry indeed, his features congested and stormy. For he knew quite well that the lamb could never get up. It would be found dead at the foot of the cliff.

He crawled to the edge again and saw how the lamb had got down, jump by jump. It was barely fifteen feet below him, and some seventy feet below that a scree sloped steeply from the base of the rock. Not a nice place to drop on. What annoyed him particularly was that he saw he might, with luck and every hand-grip holding, reach the lamb. But what then? He would never be able to bring the kicking brute up, wouldn't be able to bring himself up. The thing was quite impossible. He pushed back, got to his feet, and stood.

Then an extraordinary thing happened to him: he suddenly had a spectral glimpse of the long ironic face of the grey goat, and silently it said: So you are not going to save *the lamb*?

Peter was not deceived, for there was, of course, no question of the existence of even a hallucinatory goat, nor yet of any kind of psychologist's neat "projection". He could be ironic enough about that. The vision was conjured up in his own head, much as Freud conjured up visions of censors like policemen. An old human habit, and man had become adept at it, man the story-teller, the poet, the artist who created beautiful or hellish things from inside his own noddle.

Yet that slight emphasis on *the lamb*, the tincture of blasphemy in the irony, was just a bit too much, wherever it came from. He could have drawn the goat's face, though in its mixture of goat and satyr and human it was elusive as the movement of ripples on a small narrow pool. But its expression, its intention, was not elusive.

Peter's anger grew cold and slightly deadly. He sclaffed his palms to rid them of the sharp feel of the heather.

Washing your hands, eh?

Childish, but devilish annoying. Peter paid no attention, and with an air of competence looked up the mountain slopes, dismissing all goatish imaginings and such nonsense. Thought of the wild man came to him, for this must be the outer edge of his territory, and in the same moment he remembered Jock the smuggler's story of how the wild man had rescued one of old Phemie's ewes. If the wild man appeared now, how naturally, how perfectly, the lamb would introduce them! How naturally their communion, based on saving the lamb, would develop! It was too good to be true.

But he started walking along the crest above the cliff, for the wild man would, of course, never come over the peak of the mountain, he would come round a shoulder, and if Peter got a fair view of the southern shoulder then at least he would have done what he could.

At last he pulled up. No point in deceiving himself. What was too good to be true never happened, not at a moment like this, not at the fatal moment, when the impersonal forces had gathered for their queer work. The wild man was not in this. No one was in this—except himself.

And the lamb.

268

He strode back and, to keep his mind away from what he might do, began forestalling the goat. Naturally, he said, I was expecting the wild man to risk his life, for that would save me risking mine. You should always get the other fellow to save the lamb. You do the talking, lead the other fellow to the brink, and then stand back. If it's tragedy—what a story you're left with! What wonderful symbols put straight into your hands! You thought the idea of Pilate washing his hands was pretty neat, didn't you?

The thought of symbols gave a turn to Peter's stomach. He so hated the things at that moment that he deliberately glanced at the goat. Don't think I am deceived, he explained to the goat. You may pretend to an interest in the lamb, in human salvation and all the rest of it, but I know that what you really want is the death of the lamb and me. That's when you'll lick your whiskers.

All this turning and twisting, this indecision, was draining his substance. Even his use of the goat was but a way of dodging the direct look at the terrible act.

The ewe wheeled away from him as though about to race in fury over the mountain tops of the world, then wheeled back, baaing without knowing she was baaing, her wild eyes in her lowered head watching him.

He stood and looked over the long stretch of moorland across which he had come to this spot. It had been a pleasant journey; even the weariness of the flesh had induced a detachment in which the spirit had found neither tie nor tether.

Seeping in upon him came a sensation of profound desolation, deeper than ever symbol sounded or goatish creation knew.

That the occasion should be so haphazard, so trivial, made it unavoidable and mysteriously anonymous. He became aware of the weak trembling in his flesh, and by perceiving it commanded it without exercise of the will, and it slowly ebbed away. Then he got down on all fours and crawled to the edge.

Even now at this last minute, if he could honestly show himself that neither he nor the wild man could hope to rescue the lamb, he would back out.

He studied the pattern of the descent and saw that where the lamb had got down he might get down. It was not impossible. Assuming he reached the lamb, he could then heave it up to the next foothold. If he could reach that foothold, he could thrust it in front of him on to the next. A further effort or two and the thing might be done. Everything would depend on grip and purchase. Two precautions were perfectly clear: he need not look down the cliff and he could move slowly, with precise care. In a moment of calm he made his decision and having made it his head cleared. He would use the last ounce of fight and cunning in him.

He took off his jacket, saw that his clothes were properly tucked in, got on his stomach, and lowered himself away to the first stance, reached it, tried to bend his knees in order to crouch down and couldn't. With a little sideways manoeuvring he got to his knees, then off his knees, with the legs going over, his stomach taking the edge, slipping slowly over, his elbows, his arms, taking the strain of his weight, his feet searching, finding nothing, not even a toe-hold on smooth rock, slipping, his hands giving, his feet touching and taking his full weight. By the side now, very slowly, one slow step down . . . another . . . a step back . . . one down . . . one more and he rested against the wall. Carefully he looked over his shoulder. The lamb was below him. He could almost jump for it.

The look down the cliff had sickened him slightly, but the lamb soon dispelled the head's weakness by its restless, anxious behaviour. It was bleating continuously, turning this way and that, in its wild desire to escape. His muscles were quivering. He began speaking to the lamb: "It's all right. I'm coming for you. Don't get excited." The lamb must gain confidence from his voice, get used to it. His knees, his whole body, was trembling finely. Slowly he got to his knees, and, still talking to the lamb, lowered himself, face to the rock, until his feet at full stretch touched the platform on which the lamb stood. Up above, the wild ewe now let out a terrific baaing. Something in the lamb responded and as Peter turned he saw it was going to leap from the ledge. He lunged for it, caught it, but the sudden thrust of his own body and the fierce heave outward of the heavy lamb contrived to take him just off balance. There was a long moment before balance was quite lost, then with the lamb in his arms he went over the cliff.

This is it! he thought upon the air of space and before the branches of the small rowan tree swept his back and tilted him feet down. Directly beneath shot a narrow rock funnel. The first impact was not painful so much as dull and flattening, the second against the other side of the funnel was softer still. He had time to think of what was happening with a peculiar surprise, surprise that it should happen thus, not only without real pain or agony but without fear. This was it, the falling into the mystery. His arms tightened on the lamb as they struck and slithered and began to fall again . . . again . . . then a squashing impact and no more feeling of any kind.

29

Peter was first aware of himself as a vague thought in heavy darkness, an incipient wonder. His eyes opened, and in a few moments he knew that his eyes were open. But it was still dark. He waited . . . listening . . . Within the darkness, he remembered, but not strongly. His head stirred and pain gripped the body in its claw, lower down . . . the right hip . . . beyond which there was no feeling of a leg. The darkness was the darkness of night. He heard the night wind sifting the rock, and heard the height of the rock and the wind passing away like a cold sigh. He was alive. His left hand knew the feel of stone. He must be alive on the scree.

Slowly he began to touch himself; his hands moved to his breast; moved through the pains of movement, and now his hands were on something soft and yielding and slimy. His thought got a shock, had to gather itself again, before it came to the knowledge that the lamb had broken the final impact, had acted as a cushion, had . . . saved his life. He made to sit up and fainted.

In the first grey of the dawn, lying over on his left side, he pushed himself away from the squashed body of the lamb, slowly. The stones began to move under him and on the noisy stream of stones he floated down for a little way, outthrust hands trying to shield his head. He was hit but not heavily and came to rest on his back, with pains in the lower region of his right side. He lay for a time and wondered, quite clearly, like a gambler who would know his fate in a few moments, whether the right thigh was smashed and the useless leg really useless. He stared at the sky, at the high thin veils of the morning, and had a moment's strange and lucid peace, an interval of being that he would have liked to prolong. He turned upon his shoulder and saw the body of the lamb beside him. He looked at it for a long time, then pushed away, and came to the first of the grass, negotiated the upper end of a boulder, and on a small terrace of flat ground just beyond it came to rest.

In a dim effort at exploration he found no bones protruding, from the right thigh to the foot.

As he lay back he experienced a peculiar bodily intuition. It was exactly as though his mind had searched about the bones internally and come back to his head and said, No, there's no bones broken; whatever else may have got squashed and bruised, the skeleton is whole enough.

His teeth suddenly chittered. He was devilish cold. A sensation of sickness flowed into his chest, as though his insides had at last begun to sort themselves out and crawl back to the places they had been shaken from.

The sickness, the weakness, grew and he let go. His mouth fell open and his breath came away in thick gusts. His mind wandered and would not go to sleep, yet when next he opened his eyes the sky was swept of its hazy veils and the warm sunlight was on his face and on his hands. He moved, and stopped moving, and lay.

The sick brute curls into itself, comes to rest secure in the centre of itself. It is cunning, it knows what is waiting to pounce on it. But within the circle it can lie secure, and the sun lies with it.

Croaking sounds struck upon his ears from the ground above. Ravens. They were feeding on the lamb.

He did not stir. He tried to go to sleep.

A flap of wings went over him but he heeded not. A near sound opened his eyes and looking back behind his head he saw a grey crow on the boulder just above him. The bird flew off.

An hour later he remembered his rucksack and the food laid out on the heather. He might need that food yet, though already it would be too late to save it. But the thought persisted, pierced his reluctance to move, his lethargy, and at last he began to stir. His persistence got him onto his left knee but no higher. He had no control over his right leg. Two ravens took the air; beyond them circled a hoodie crow.

On his left knee and both hands, he began moving off, dragging his right leg. He was in no hurry, and learned when to stop. The body has a lot of private knowledge. Nor was his reason forgotten. To expend himself utterly in order to reach the rucksack, where the food was by this time bound to have been gobbled—was it worth it? Presently pausing to look up, he saw two crows flapping and hopping at a spot along the ridge where his rucksack must be. Hunting the last crumbs from the heather. So that was that. He was relieved and, lying flat, let his breath come out in the gusts that helped him to sink away.

Later, he was sitting up, probing his hip, his knee, feeling for reactions, coming to conclusions. The main nerve of the leg must have got a hefty wallop, a real shock. The lamb would have cushioned the upper region but the right thigh must have whipped down on the stone. His mouth yawed in a futile nausea. His left leg was functioning, therefore not the spine.

He lifted his head and looked abroad. Someone might come walking. He turned his head to see how far the cliff still extended. Barely twenty yards; and now it was tapering away, with the hill grass growing up to its base, where a dark hole gaped. The entrance to a cave. A blackened fruit tin, a piece of brown paper, just below it. He stared and gulped. He cried. He shouted again. Nothing moved. But he thought of the wild man and knew, with a feeling of absolute certainty, that this was his sleeping place. There might be a strange enough communion yet! Time . . . take it easy. . . .

Reaching the cave mouth he lay panting, then crept slowly in. It was not a big cave and he could see its walls clearly enough. Here, in a short bay, a scoop, to the right of the entrance, was a bed of heather and hanging from the rock above it a grey-dark blanket. Ashes, an old-fashioned iron pot with an arched handle that swivelled, a tin with a rough wire handle, a brown teapot with a broken spout, an armful of peats . . . No trace of food, unless there was some high ledge or hole . . . Peter crept to the heather bed and lay.

The journey had taken a lot out of him. He felt himself fading out through pains that dulled; then he was gone.

It was the afternoon before he came fully to himself with a dry mouth and a craving for water. The chill in his body brought him wide awake. Before he knew what he was doing he had moved his right leg and the sharp pain made him yelp. A thousand needles and pins attacked his foot, his toes. So it was coming back to life, was it? He was feeling very weak. If only that wild fellow would come! But he wouldn't come until the night. The only plan was to lie low, not to move, give whatever swelling or contusion was interfering with the nerves a chance to die down. If that's what it was.

An hour later he was at the cave mouth with the wire of the small tin over his wrist. The whole world was bathed in light. Because its beauty was in some way heedless, remote, austere, it affected him. Its absolute lack of concern for him was final. It did not interfere. It left him to do as he would. It had the tolerance that let a man die in his own way and on his own. It was his world. He set off on his own, with the notion that the path would lead to water. One might approach a cave from many angles, but the footpath would lead to the well. Let it not be too far so that the body, which had its limit in pains, wouldn't black-out. He had slept so much that his head was clear. Then he saw the spring, the fountain, coming out of the rock, bubbling up and over into the basin scooped for its reception. He rolled the first cold mouthful around his hot tongue and arid palate, then let it go. When he had done this a few times, he sank his face into the water, the cold living water, and, letting it drip from his nose, found a spot below on which he could lie without slipping down the slope.

The afternoon passed. No one came. When the sun was going down over a far ridge in the west, drawing a shadow up the rock's face, he filled his tin and turned back to the cave. He went very slowly for his body was stiffening all over. Five yards from the entrance, the tin tipped and emptied. But he did not mind, though he grudged the effort he had made. In the cave, he jerked the blanket free, and then went to bed, tucking the blanket round him, for suddenly he was shivering.

He missed his jacket, would have buttoned it tight round. In a short time fever had him and his teeth were clicking. Perhaps the spot he had lain on had been damp. He was disappointed, very disappointed. This at least could have been avoided.

But when the wild man came and made some hot tea, the chill would burn and pass.

Only the darkness came.

He snuggled deep into the heather, taking out a hand occasionally when a runnel of sweat troubled his eyes. There was no wind and he fancied the night was rather close. But the trick for overcoming the shivers was to snuggle deep and then lie dead still. With every hole choked up, the sweat began to break out and run.

During the night Peter woke suddenly out of a doze, feeling that someone had come into the cave. He listened with every sense alert. Nothing stirred. "Hallo!" he cried. Nothing answered. Then he had the distinct impression that a presence —a man's figure—was standing quite still, as the wild man had stood by the bridge, looking at him and seeing him through the darkness.

"Can't you speak?" he asked.

There was no answer.

A shiver travelled over his skin, but his fear was far from abject.

"I'm here," said Peter. "Here!"

But there was neither movement nor sound.

The latent hope that the presence was that of the real wild man himself, too shy or wary to speak, now left Peter.

But he felt that the ghost, the spirit of the man, was still looking at him . . . he could not rid himself of this feeling. His apprehension of the supernatural became unbearably acute.

In a blind reach for reason he called himself a victim of atavism. But the very sound of thinking left him vulnerable. He could be touched—sprung upon—unless he kept his awareness silent and knife-edged.

It took a time for the tension to ease. Nothing happened, neither movement nor sound, and he began to wonder if it was the cave, the influence of the cave . . . the first men lived in caves, aeons ago . . . the carry-over by the unconscious, starting up images in his sleep? . . . yet he could not remember any dream. . . .

Those early ape-like beings, who could hardly walk upright and hadn't developed a throat box for real speech, the Neanderthals, buried their dead in their cave-mouths, did it in such a way, with such gear, that it was plain they believed in a life after death. They were not even afraid of the spirits of the dead or they would not have buried them beneath the very ground where they dwelt.

Peter's thought about the Neanderthals began to affect him in a peculiar way. Before primitive men as we knew them; before the Cromagnons, those sub-men who painted their bisons on the walls of far interior caves darker than any night; countless thousands of years before them, the half-crouching ape-like Neanderthal had dealings with his dead. Extraordinary that the one thing man believed in from the beginning was the existence of the spirit after death.

Peter knew the endless arguments against, the explanations that explained away, the intricate rebuttals of the intellect. What a clean sweep of all that clutter could be made by the simplification that the spirit did survive the body's death!

This came from him not as an expression of belief but as a peculiar and daring temptation. It was outside him—like the wild man's spirit . . . which might still be standing there . . . watching him.

But he was growing less afraid. Then, on its own, his mind moved away from the invisible figure of the wild man to the ancient traffic in the cave mouth, and, with a feeling of being ignored, he realised that he was not in danger, had not been in danger from the beginning. Evil was not here. Nothing would touch him. And though he knew that he now was reassuring himself, he went through all the motions of being reassured, pulled the blanket past his ear, snuggled down, closed his eyes and went to sleep.

When he awoke a dim grey light was in the cave and as he looked about the floor, around the dark rock, he was surprised into a curious suspension of being that hearkened for some last sound from the departing. But they were all gone. The place was deserted. His eyes roved to make sure of this.

After a little time he wondered if he had dreamt the whole thing, and it was only when he moved and the bruised flesh shot its pains that he came fully to his mortal condition.

The fever that had flared up seemed to have gone. A thick smell of sweat came with an arm from under the blanket. Now, for the first time, he realised his head had been on a pillow of sorts. It was sodden with sweat. He felt light rather than weak and an air of optimism pervaded him. He had better think out his position while the sunlight grew warm enough for him to adventure outside.

But his midnight experience would not leave him. And then the thought came: why should the wild man's *spirit* visit the cave when his body would be dossing comfortably in one of probably many other sleeping places? Unless, of course, he had come and gone in the dark? But if he had entered in the darkness he could not have seen anyone on his bed; he would have moved about, struck a light or sat down on the bed. No, there had been no physical presence. And as there was neither supernatural rhyme nor reason in the spirit leaving the man's living body to come on its own. . . . So it had probably been a dream.

But he knew it hadn't been a dream. He would never be able to demonstrate this; but to him it was as certain as that he had fallen over the cliff and been saved by the lamb.

It was so difficult to demonstrate anything that penetrated the spirit's circle. Why had he come on this journey, for example? What strange inner need had propelled him? And what had happened to him as a result?

Nothing had happened—beyond his present condition, and the possibility that he might die on the long arduous way to the Picts Houses.

But that wasn't quite all. No. From the beginning there had been more than just a pleasant feeling of freedom. In particular, whenever he had got away from himself, life had opened out an extra dimension or two, often in an astonishing and delightful way. This had accompanied him like a brightness in the air. Then there had been the special moments. Jock's face when he was told of the search for the well at the world's end. Alick in his Spanish garden. The shepherd who, looking upon his world, did not want to go home. Cocklebuster's paradisal gleam beyond the wood. Even the stout woman with whom he had danced in Badenscro . . . he saw her fat smooth reddish face, her remarkably clear eyes, the light in them. . . . "I just loved it!" The same matron as went dancing through the glens of ancient Greece, as Euripides knew. The self-same, beyond mortal doubt. . . .

Here and there, amongst all conditions of people, young and old, the tranced moment, the fleeting gleam from some realm of rare delight.

A delusion? In the moment of experience it was not a delusion. In that moment it was the reality, and the delusion was the "explanation" which the man who had not experienced it produced for his own comfort.

But the moment of delight was unpredictable and so fleeting that the sceptic had nearly all the innings. But not quite.

No, not quite. . . .

Peter's thought reached Malcolm, methodically coiling the heaving line and pitching it into the sea. Not much delight there. Courage, a terrible challenge. An ultimate of action, denying authority, authority that would impose, compel . . . that would cripple the spirit's wholeness, its freedom. . . . And yet—let it be seen—with the pride of race, of family, carrying the old man into the blind moment beyond thought, beyond consequences to others, like a vanity, a viking pride doing the blinding . . . yet not altogether, for the unique was not arguable . . . as though in some last realm of pure action decision to act carried in itself a certainty of fulfilment. The old man had done it. Difficult to see everything because of the glisten of splendour. . . .

Peter turned half over and stirred up his nest of aches and pains. The light was getting stronger. He looked for a long time at it. The light coming into the cave. And he suddenly thought of Plato's cave. *The* cave from which European philosophy stemmed! The astonishment was so bright that it winded him even as he smiled and glanced at the walls as though he might see the shadows pass there.

Had he been held here by his aches and pains since childhood, like Plato's imagined prisoners by their chains, seeing no more than the wall, then the shadows cast on the wall from humans and animals passing the cave's mouth against the westering sun would be reality to him. . . . It doesn't need much to start a parable!

But the thought of philosophic systems grew heavy, as always. And at least a man could get out of an enclosed system, as out of a cave, by going into the light. Peter decided to make the effort.

His right foot would not take his weight; he was now sore and stiff all over, so he crawled out. Sweat broke on his forehead. He sneezed and half-collapsed. But he came into the cool morning light under a hazed sky.

The freshness was like cold water in the mouth. He set out for the well.

When he had refreshed himself he lay for a little while. He had not believed he was so weak. By midday it would be two whole days since he had eaten any food. If he waited another day and no one came, he would never make over the mountain and the long miles beyond.

If only he had some food he could lie up and recover. Without food he would die where he was—or die in his tracks. Pain sucks the vital energy like an evil mouth.

It came upon him very clearly that he might be beaten.

To rely on help from the wild man—that illusion which had haunted him—could definitely be fatal.

He would have to start out to-day and leave the rest to chance; the only way in which chance ever did help, he thought with a touch of arid humour. He might have ransacked the cave for food before coming so far. He started back for the cave.

The futile searching of the cave took such a lot out of him that he lay on the heather bed for a while before starting off again. An hour later, his heart thumping, his weakness sweeping him in dizzying flushes, he went flat on the heather by the rucksack and was lost for a long time in a sort of stertorous sleep. He gathered himself and looked in and about the heather. There wasn't even a bit of eggshell visible. He sat up and slowly got the rucksack slung to his back. Then the struggle started: why should he go all the way along the crest for his jacket and all the way back? Because when it came to a night in the open he would need all the clothes he could put on. His hands were hot, his nostrils had a sort of sickly smell, as if the fever was not gone but lying in wait. Yet he rebelled, he rebelled so bitterly that when he found himself using his right knee in the crawl he did not care about the pain. He took his bitterness out on the pain. He grunted and cursed and lay, and got going again. For now he realised how terribly easy it was to give in. Its lure was like a dream, a dream through which he would fall into eternal ease.

When he saw the kicking legs he was hardly astonished. The ewe had fallen on her back and couldn't get up. That was just about the measure of the savage fool! Towards the cliff edge he saw his jacket, a few yards from the ewe. He thought: I am not going to murder myself trying to heave that brute on her legs. She won't trick me a second time. But he went towards her, knowing he would struggle to get her up should he die for it. It was enough to make a man weep. Dear God, hadn't he had enough?

He lay a yard away watching her do her fantastic dance on the air, with wild rollings to this side and then to that. He could see from the fresh condition of the ground and the absence of droppings that she hadn't been long on her back. She lay on flat ground just perceptibly hollowed; she might last a day or so; had her head been a shade up, she might have lasted three or four days.

Then his eyes saw something else and his heart started its tumultuous beating.

When he had her broadside on, he crawled forward and got his hands on her body. These hind hooves could split his face open. When she had momentarily exhausted herself he moved his head towards her udder, speaking soothingly, caressing her.

He had just got his mouth to one of the teats, when it was snatched from him, but amid the welter of kicking legs, heaving head and arching thrusting body, he held on. It was as fantastic a dance as ever he was likely to have with any savage goddess. He was sweating and she smelt strongly, an acrid smell that stimulated his appetite. Her wool got into his mouth. The more she high-kicked the more relentless grew his desire. As she threw him on his right hip, he called her a stupid bitch with a shepherd's fondly savage mastery and got his full face on her udder and searched closely, and sucked, and got nothing. So she was holding back, was she? After another dancing bout he got her canted over, and, with fists knotted in her wool, held her there. This time a soft warmth like a rich creamy spittle bathed his tongue and palate. And she lay. And he sucked. But not for long. Though now he drew back a little from her too active thighs, for he was exhausted and in any case had sense enough to take her rich food slowly. It was a long time since he had drunk from the breast.

Half-an-hour later he sat up and wiped his mouth, his weight on his left hip, for she had savaged his bruises. Didn't the ancient Savage Goddess, when properly roused, eat her own young? He could well believe it. A snapshot of his struggle with her at its height would have interested Cocklebuster. He stretched himself full length to give the milk time to work and allay that curdling in the stomach of which he had known new-born lambs to die.

When he had got the ewe on her feet, he put on his jacket and the rucksack, crossed the dip, and began a slow slant up the mountain side. A knot gathered inside him, a hard lump. Was this it? His belly caved in—and a magnificent belch rocketed along the heathery slope. With a feeling of great comfort, he proceeded, chewing the flavoured aftermath.

It was a grim climb that seemed to grow in extent the farther he went, but he rested, and went on, and rested, and at last he saw the rising ground curve over and, though it took him yet a little while to reach the actual crest, reach it he did.

The latter part of the way he had been haunted by the thought that the country beyond the mountain would be unknown to him, that there would be still another expanse of moor, still more hills, as always in the Highland wilds; and when first he looked into the beyond, so it seemed. There was a stream where he had expected a stream to be, but there was no bridge, and, far as his eyes could travel, no green slopes with grey ruins, no distant prospect of Fand's domain. To think that he could ever travel beyond the reach of his eyes was so fantastic that his head fell between his arms and as the weakness flooded over him he let go.

He awoke with a feeling of bodily lightness, of a strange refreshment. The wind was blowing but not strongly. It was afternoon. He looked at the brightness the sun made in the hazed sky. He did not want to go on. He could not bear the thought of crawling on again. He would rather die lightly on a hill-top than heavily in a dead-end. But already he was moving, and he hadn't gone fifteen yards when he saw the wire bridge far below him.

He smiled then. He would at least complete the circle.

At the back of his mind the bridge had been his objective for it could be help's passing place. There, failing all others, surely the wild man would come at last.

30

He chose places of the right steepness, so that lying over towards his left side, he could let himself slide down feet first, steadying the descent by gripping fistfuls of heather. The progress was wonderful. Twice as he thumped to a stop he grinned. Stiffness in some of his joints was eased by the exercise and to sudden thrusts of pain he had become used. Pain that was too much merely darkened the old brain. When he reached the foot he was trembling all over, but he was down. As he crawled forward, the lie of the ground became familiar to him. Here was the boulder where the wild man had stood for a few moments just before he had disappeared. Peter remembered that long gaze and the fear of the uncanny it had engendered in his own breast. He had thought that the wild man had looked like himself, so that the whole scene for a translated moment had had an ominous magical air.

After resting for a little while he decided he would cross the bridge and lie on the green mound which commanded the approaches better. In particular he would be able to follow the winding way which he himself had taken to old Phemie. Besides, he had a great longing to walk upright, and with hands on the twisted wire rope-supports of the bridge he should at least be able to cross on one foot and properly test the other. With this notion in mind and with the help of the boulder he got upright. Tentatively feeling the ground with his right foot and staring towards the bridge, he became aware of a presence to his right. At once his eyes switched and there was a man— a stalker or local hillman in brown tweeds—staring at him. Peter could hardly draw breath because of the man's expression. Then all at once the fellow was walking towards the bridge and

Peter knew that he was afraid. It was in his walk, the quick upright walk that dared not run. For several seconds Peter was so bewildered that he could neither move nor utter a sound. Then he started forward and went several paces before his right leg gave. As he fell he shouted in a voice so high and shrill that it was hardly his own. The man was crossing the swaying bridge like one wading a high river in frantic haste. Peter shouted again. But the man was now striding up over the knoll. When his head disappeared he was running. He had never looked back.

Carried on by the blind urgency of his need, Peter reached the bridge, pulled himself upright, bore down with either hand on the stout wire ropes and reached the other side. When he gained the green mound he could see nothing of the man.

Despair took him where he lay, for he knew he had missed his chance. He could not hope for a second chance that day. It was too late, too late for everyone, except—perhaps—the wild man. On that thought he let himself sink into the mound.

The old earth never refused you; the more exhausted you were the softer grew its breast.

As his mind stirred it had not to think out what had happened. The hillman had mistaken him, Peter, for the wild man.

A remote humour glimmered in his opened unwinking eyes, then his fingers went to his chin. Not exactly the wild man's whiskers yet, but a third day's growth could create deception at a distance. I'm on the way, he thought. The Tao is beginning to sprout its beard.

Presently he found himself looking around on a familiar country. The path on the off side that wound with the hill slopes above the small river and finally disappeared between the hills on its way to old Phemie's croft seemed peculiarly intimate, as though he had tramped it through many years, and he had the sudden notion that he was now actually seeing it as the wild man saw it, seeing something in it, the untranslatable something within and behind the appearance, that only the spirit knew. He had never got this kind of glimpse but it had lightened and refreshed him. It was as though the urgencies of consciousness, concentrated in the fighting persistent ego,

285

eased off into some ampler air of the whole self where even the ambition to pursue the practical end, even the end of living, was apprehended and given its place.

Another point to plot in the old graph, or just the same point with a different appearance? He felt happy beyond all reason. . . . Though for that matter he had accomplished a lot, had come a long way. The distance and the struggle stretched far back in his mind and the rumbling roar of the water in the ravine carried it still farther away, away and up and far off. His eyes landed on the bridge and he experienced the pure sensation of having crossed the chasm.

His eyes wandered over the green mound and saw two or three balls of crumpled paper, a crushed cigarette carton, a couple of black screw-tops out of beer bottles, a gleaming point of blue that, when he raised himself higher, became the edge of the small discarded cap of a milk bottle, and just beyond it a folded newspaper, and beyond that, where the dip down of the mound began to rise against a peaty bank, the ashes of a fire between two large flat stones.

Usually the sight of such litter annoyed him. But now it did not affect him much. Yet this large-scale intrusion left a certain unease and in a few moments he found himself wondering why the local hillman—he would have called him a shepherd but for the absence of dogs—had been afraid. In a solitary stranger it might have been understandable, as he had reason to know. But not in the case of a hillman, who was bound to know how harmless the wandering gillie was and who must have given him help and even got help from him—as old Phemie had got it—many a time.

The unease robbed his mind of its capacity to think and presently he was back in the cave staring at the figure he couldn't see in the darkness. But his mind refused the toil of thought there, too.

A few minutes ago he had been happy, now he was sickened by despair. Did everything finally depend on the body? Come and go, come and go, until the end? But he was aware, vaguely, that something was watching him, and he realised that the eyes in that calmer, ampler self, which he had experienced a little while ago, were looking back at him. Their glimmer of under-standing was strangely compassionate and profound.

He turned his head away.

On the slopes of the hills, the eastern slopes beyond the bridge, the evening was deepening. Against a great reluctance to gather the newspaper, he moved across the mound. In the cold of the night he might need it to light a fire. He thought of the distance to Fand. All he could do was keep going. If death had to come, let it come to him on the way to Fand. Here, as in the cave, it would be weakness to rely on the wild man.

His eyes landed on the folded newspaper, on the large type of a featured story containing the three words: THE WILD MAN.

He began to read.

"Alexander Mackay, a shepherd on the hill sheep farm of Altanduin, was searching for a stray ewe and lamb on the slopes of Creag Mhor when he discovered the dead body of a man identified as that of Peter Mackay, a former gillie and known locally as 'the wild man'. The local police . . ." The print began to waver before Peter's eyes but he blinked and read on about the medical examination . . . the assumption that he had fallen over a cliff in the neighbourhood of the cave where he usually slept and had dragged himself to the threshold of the cave where the body was found. . . .

In his analysis of this mountain mystery, the correspondent made it clear that he had experienced some difficulty in piercing the native reticence of the inhabitants of this remote sparsely populated area. An aged woman, named Euphemia Bethune, who lived all alone in the mountains and was deeply moved by the tragedy, was the first to repel any suggestion of "wildness" in the character of the deceased and went on to disclose unob-trusive acts of kindness which showed among other attributes of his unusual personality an uncanny knowledge of the ways of wild life. Other interviews confirmed this, and altogether it appeared as though he had been called "the wild man" for no reason other than that he preferred living alone in the wilds. . . .

Peter's eyes slowly lifted from the newspaper and stared in front of him. The wild man was dead.

For a little while a blankness, a numb lack of feeling, inhibited thought and feeling.

Slowly he looked about him; his eyes fell on the litter and each item had a peculiar distinctness. A party of humans had come this way, to investigate. He felt their absence like an invisible thing left behind, left behind from their presence . . . This kind of feeling he had experienced in the cave, and remembering his disturbed night there, he realised that the wild man could not have visited him in the flesh, because the wild man was then dead.

His mind lifted and his lips fell apart as if he were listening. But he wasn't consciously listening. The boulder beyond the bridge came into focus and he recalled the local hill man who had, a little while ago, ran away from him. The hill man, knowing the wild man was dead, would have thought that he, Peter, was the wild man's ghost.

But Peter could not get through the numbness altogether. Far from being moved or excited, he was aware only of the aftermath of fatality, the acceptance of what had happened as in an order of things which had no boundary. Yet it had in some mysterious way a relevance to himself. There had been something which the wild man and himself had had in common, even if they would never now discuss it in this life.

An intuition of the state of death came very close to Peter now. From the wild man a shadow touched him.

Presently he crawled down to the ravine where tree-tops showed above the verge and then along the verge until the ravine grew shallow. From the high edge of a winter flood, he picked up an old hard stick about as long as himself and nearly as thick as his wrist, climbed back to the path, rested, and heaved himself to his feet. But the stick was too long. Wedging it in a rock fissure, he broke off about a foot, and, opening his rucksack, proceeded to pad one end of the stick with a shirt, and then made the pad more resilient by stuffing his silken underwear inside the shirt. All this took a long time, but when at last he got up and tried the crutch he found that he could hobble along dizzily.

After a short while he began to crawl again; but he dragged

the stick with him and it comforted him a little. It was more difficult following the footpath, which went up and down by the river bank, than the open sweep of moor. Sudden declivities he slowly bypassed, but he kept doggedly by the path lest someone come. He was vaguely comforted by a curious bodily knowledge that there was none of those "internal injuries" which had, by the medical report, proved fatal in the case of the wild man. He knew that a stiff neck could last a week; mere lumbago stiffen a man to a sweating "object".

A dry smile touched his features as he rested. I'm an object all right, he thought. But that wasn't what was really worrying him. It was his head, the light-headed feeling, the desperate weakness, the desire to throw everything down and lie.

He began to rest more and more, to move shorter distances. It was getting dark. No one would come by the path now.

Somewhere he had struck this stream when he had crossed the moors from the first ravine. . . . Where should he turn off?

Exhaustion settled the question for him, but his will didn't let him collapse until he had found a hollow.

He awoke in the dark, his teeth chittering uncontrollably. But his head was clear. It was with a grim humour that he slowly pulled his silk pants over his trousers. A shirt went over his jacket and he tied what he could round his waist, and then, when all that was done, he made his final effort with the silken oilskin jacket and legs. Gradually the chittering subsided and he began to sweat. The nightly fever was having another innings. But there was no more he could do so he let go.

He had dreams and half-waking fantasies of crawling under great tongues of land . . . coming on a cave . . . and he saw some Neanderthal figures very clearly. . . . Then he had one remarkably clear dream; he was alone in the cave, which had in some way slewed round, for its entrance was not the entrance he knew; the cave was now long and narrow and dark and its sides were damp, but beyond its entrance was the light, a golden paradisal light, from the country beyond. Suddenly on the threshold of the cave there was a movement and he saw the body of a lion, not crouching but squatting across the threshold. As its head lifted and swung, its mouth opened and a low growl rumbled about the cave's mouth. It was a playful rather than an angry growl, yet there was something terribly ominous in it, as though it were waiting. . . . Now he was in an appalling dilemma; he might be able to hide in the cave . . . die in the cave . . . but he would never get out unless he got past the lion. The black walls sweated their dampness upon him. The decision sweated agony out of him, but he made it; he crawled forward, in a sickness of terror he went on; the lion's head lifted but looked into the country of light and its growl was a hollow roar that ended abruptly as its mouth closed. Its tail switched; the golden skin rippled over the upthrust of the haunches, for its hind paws were gathered underneath. Peter wanted to speak to the lion, to placate the beast, but his mouth clove against all sound. In the end, in the end, he lifted a hand to put it on the lion's back; the lion twitched and roared like a great beast in a game; Peter got up and was stepping over the lion when he awoke.

He saw the golden hide of that beast for a long time, and he saw the light in the country beyond.

31

It was his last day. When this was quite certain he took off the rucksack and lay beside it for a little while. He could not make use of it any more. Without its weight, he might go farther.

Fand had seldom troubled his thought after he had met the lamb and realised that death was the presence that waited, the invisible companion.

To think of her would weaken him, so he left her far back in the cave of his mind. But she had been there, and without looking at her, without speaking to her, he had vowed in silence: I'll do my best.

Doing his best meant being a miser with his resources, calculating many moves ahead and each move as it came. Chance had helped, as it always did help when decision was taken and action followed. But chance, too, was niggardly, its hand spare, its humour grim with the grimness in which there is no smile, like the face of the moor. With an innocence bland as the smooth peat, tough as the yielding heather, the earth put hags in his way. The day was fresh and the wind played over leagues of hag-hollowed moor.

But now on this last lap of his journey, where chance would do no more, where the invisible one, death, would wait until the final mortal burden was shed, he brought Fand from the darkness of the cave to be with him.

And she came and did not weaken him any more; as he felt the strength of her presence he wondered vaguely what instinct had made him reserve her help for this last hour. . . .

A light now was in the lightness round his head, and in this light the tenderness that was the core of her being rose like a spring, like a springing fountain, and was crystal as the well from which a man could drink and be strengthened. . . . Beyond times and accidents and sorrow, graces and vanities, child-death and desolation, beyond the hanging gardens of happiness, he saw in her that which was the immortal fountain, and her face and hair had the brightness of the rainbow.

And at last he knew that this was the ultimate vision, that this was what remained and rose up when time and chance had done their best and worst, through the deceits and faithlessness of the mortal flesh, and withered away. Here, the bravery and the brightness, the light from her eyes, for this step and the step to follow, round this hag and beyond that.

If, beyond all, there was no gleaming country, no immortal well, no place for them and their vision, then—let there be no place; and the challenge of his thought moved within him, and his defiance.

Thus the vision of Fand strengthened him.

But the bright moments grew fewer amid the long spells of brute endurance, the fallings and restings, the flounderings that went but a short distance in a long time.

The sun was falling away from its zenith when he admitted to himself that he was finished. A surge of bitterness was in his mouth, but he was beyond the sob, and his teeth bit on the heather weakly.

Thought stirred in the black cave, suggesting that he leave a note for Fand, a few words. . . . His breath came heavily, hazing his brain, and as if the thought had fulfilled itself he gave way with a boneless feeling of sinking comfortably and deep.

His mind rose up and went wandering.

His mind went over his journey and saw again the people he had met, saw them with the clarity of ordinary life and of the dream. There was no effort in this; it was quite involuntary, full of a light ease.

The wild man and the swinging bridge—the wild man whom he had never found but whom he knew with an intimacy near as his own heart's moment of panic, and yet a man more remote from him than any other, as though in oneself were two quite different men, who were yet the same man . . . old

Phemie on her way into the earth, having business there, observed by her cat, watched by the spiders, dropping her egg in wonder. . . . Alastair the shepherd, looking across the moor into the far dimension, going through the boundary . . . Cocklebuster in the maze of the forest, touched by sin at sight of the paradisal gleam beyond the tree-trunks . . . Alick's face. He saw what was behind Alick's face, knew his journey amid rocks and primordial places, the arid unbelief that dogs and withers; all the incidents of his long story about drowning and the nations came together in the one moment of silence at the window looking out on the Spanish garden . . . that was the moment he would never forget, let him arrive where he would . . . and this Peter saw rather than thought, as if thought at its highest were but a description of vision. . . . His eyes lifted to the sea, the swinging boat . . . and Peggy with her bandaged wrist was dancing before Angus. . . .

The story went round in a circle, round with the sun, from the swinging bridge that spanned the chasm back to the bridge and the chasm.

Now he was looking down upon it from the air, and he saw that its simple wonder was more wonderful than any immortal story that could be imagined, for there it was, there the ordinary folk went about their human business, more incomprehensible in earthly time than in any transcendent timelessness which yet, in some mysterious way, was suggested. . . .

Moving from one to another went that figure of himself which he could see, a small distant figure . . . and then, as in a sudden close-up, he was looking at its thought, the thought that it half hid from itself, as though to hold it in seriousness would, by this very exercise of importance, self-importance, tend to destroy what cannot be held, as the dry hand destroys the iridescent scales of the living fish. . . . From the very beginning the figure had had the slight wit to drop such importance and enjoy the fresh air. That was the right beginning: to wander over the land and look through far vistas; and then in a moment to look very closely at each individual thing, a rock, a flower, a wrinkle, at thought as it was born and faded again in a human face. In the elusive freedom that this engendered consciousness itself was heightened, but the heightening though often vague and delightful could also in an instant focus itself to an eye of insight that could not be deceived, and knew it could not be deceived, yet knew nothing of judgment but only of understanding.

That's the way it went . . . the way.

No one could see the end of the way, but of the way itself, in insight, in understanding, there could be no doubt. For man could experience that, and know its relief, and know its strange extended gladness.

That was the beginning. . . . If the lure of transcendence, of timeless or immortal implication, came around, pay no great attention, but move from one step to the next, and look at this face and stay with that . . . and let what would happen in the place where happenings and boundaries were.

As a last look lingered on the circle of his journey he saw all the figures in a moment of time and there moved in him a feeling of friendliness and of blessing. The leap into the mystery would come, was coming. . . .

His eyes opened and stared between stalks of heather and he thought: I must go on, I must keep going on. For not to go on would be to deny the chance that is part of the action, to deny the companion in life who had chosen him and whom he had chosen, to finish before the natural end, the end that was the end; and that, too, he knew in some place far within him. But his body was heavy. He could feel the weight of it sagging into the earth. His reluctance to move it was greater than he had yet known.

But he drew it up and on hands and knees, with head hanging, he slowly dragged himself over the heather. The effort was too much. He stopped. "I cannot do it, Fand," he said. His haunches collapsed, then his hands.

But that last brutish struggle had been seen.

He heard his name called from what seemed a great distance and slowly, with reluctance, through the darkness, he came back and his eyes opened.

She was there . . . she was coming out of the brightness; her colour, her swift movement . . . her hands.

He could now afford to let go and the peace of darkness came over him . . . he must not lose the far sound of her voice . . . only, he could not respond. She was crying to him, crying to her own love . . . and it was comforting. If only she had the sense to leave him for a while . . . but no. Before his opened eyes she drew back into herself . . . and he saw the silent cry in her face. He smiled and she came to him on her knees and her arm went under his head, her hand was on his face and she kissed him.

"Hunger," he muttered, releasing her.

It was the living Fand now. Supporting his head and shoulders, she brought the cup of milk to his mouth. "I have been searching for you," she said. "I had an awful feeling that something was wrong." She was making word-sounds, lapping him about. She had control. He had the foreknowledge of being with her for a long time and its ease was rare and delectable, like the beauty beyond what was seen of the mortal eye in Fand's face.